IN A
DREAM'S
EYE

BASED ON A TRUE STORY

HOUSTON CROSS
AND
SHARON VALEN

authorHOUSE®

AuthorHouse™
1663 Liberty Drive
Bloomington, IN 47403
www.authorhouse.com
Phone: 1-800-839-8640

Published by AuthorHouse 3/18/2013

ISBN: 978-1-4817-1965-0 (sc)
ISBN: 978-1-4817-1966-7 (hc)
ISBN: 978-1-4817-1967-4 (e)

Library of Congress Control Number: 2013903394

DEDICATION

In loving memory of my mother "Sharon." The perfect mom and best friend, my love for you is everlasting!

ACKNOWLEDGMENTS

Special thanks to Jim and Irma Craft for all of their support throughout this conquest. On behalf of Houston Cross and Sharon Valen, we want to thank everyone that is willing to take that journey "IN A DREAM'S EYE".

TABLE OF CONTENTS

PROLOGUE

AFTER FINDING THE FRONT of the building, she searched for a place to park. Backing-in, she parked the Honda in one of just a few spots in the last row.

Nervously looking through the windshield, she stared at the two-story building. The structure was completely overshadowed by towering pines and a beautiful day. Normally, she paid little attention to her surrounding, but the beauty here was unshakable.

Terrified and excited at the same time, she walked away from the car. Pressing the locking mechanism, two sharp chirps told Diana that the alarm was set. While focused toward the emergency room, she began to ponder the deeper implications of this new commitment. Never in her career, had she worked with this type of patient. It was as if she were about to start her first day of school.

Entering the E.R. dock, she passed by a couple of ambulances on her way to the emergency entrance. Opening her purse, she dropped the keys inside as the automatic glass doors slid open. It only took her two steps before she stopped. The first day on a new job always scared the hell-out-of-her. Anxiety level at its peak, she realized it was time to shake away any apprehensions.

Diana was merely a woman seeking to find a new and more meaningful existence. Several of her resumes had been sent to various cities and towns. But this opportunity caught her attention much more than the others. Beside the hospital being located in the middle of paradise, it offered her a major challenge.

The real test now was if she could rise above her new apprehensions concerning the Coma Ward. "I can do this…I can do this…Get it together, Diana…Make it happen!" Murmuring to herself as the urgent care doors closed behind her.

Checking into a place she knew nearly nothing about was unnerving at best. Keeping a positive optimism was the only thing she saw in her favor. Now, it was all up to her to make it work. Unsure as what to expect, she could only hope that it was the first day toward a fresh start.

After a couple deep breaths, she made her way through the waiting area. Diana hated the emergency room, the air was always thick with the familiar odor of antiseptic and medicine. Just like every hospital she worked at, the admissions lobby was always filled to capacity. There were no empty seats, people were sitting on the floor and standing around the entrance.

Dressed in her green hospital togs, she tried to appear calm and professional as she passed by the sick and those in obvious pain. All emergency waiting rooms made Diana depressed. Especially when she saw parents trying to comfort their ailing or injured infants.

Though still extremely nervous, she walked straight toward the reception desk. Diana could see that all the reception widows were occupied. Walking up to the closest receptionist, she tapped on the Plexiglas to get the clerks attention.

The clerk sitting behind the glass was a short, pudgy woman, with an expression like a hungry bear. Eyes unwavering from the computer monitor, she continued to take information from a patient to be.

"Excuse me! I start work today…Can you tell me where I can find Dr. Stevens?"

The silence was frustrating as she waited for a response. The receptionist continued to sit behind her cheap metal desk and type commands on the keyboard.

Once again, Diana confronted the receptionist. "Excuse me! I really don't want to be late!"

Showing her frustration, the receptionist rolled her eyes and shook her head.

Diana began to feel as if she were being deliberately ignored. It was obvious that the receptionist was busy, but it was getting ridiculous. Nervous enough already, she refused to let this woman wear out what was left of her patience.

"Can you at least tell me where the "Coma Ward" is?" Diana's voice and demeanor teetered on the edge of rudeness.

The question was not that difficult, but it seemed to irritate the squatty clerk. Sliding her glasses to the end of her nose, the woman turned her stare from the monitor toward Diana. Staring over the rims of her reading glasses, the receptionist looked as if she could not believe this lady's persistence.

Now that she finally had her attention, it was time to get the day started. "I was told to check in at the emergency room reception desk. Is there a certain person I should talk to?" Diana noticed her voice sounded like all the others in the emergency room, upset and impatiently pleading for some kind of help.

The chubby woman turned and waved to another receptionist down the aisle. A tall slender woman stood from her desk and began walking toward the clerk.

Counter to her frustration, Diana managed to thank the disinterested woman. "Thank you for your time."

"You're welcome." Lacking all sincerity, her response was filled with an air of boredom.

After swiping her ID card through a scanner, there was a loud buzz and the access door opened. As if just going through the motions, the tall woman stepped out from behind the reception partition. Walking toward the hall, she gestured Diana toward the elevators. Nodding in compliance, she followed the lanky woman.

Reaching the elevators at the same time, it was a pleasant surprise when her escort reached her hand out. "Hi, I'm Janyce."

"It's nice to meet you...I'm Diana O'nell." Feeling a little relief, she smiled and shook Janyce's hand.

There was a brief silence then Janyce restarted the conversation. "So...It's your fist day?"

"Yes...I'm very excited. But at the same time, I'm really nervous too." Just as Diana finished, the elevator doors slid apart.

After stepping inside, Janyce pressed the second floor button. As a bell rang, they both turned and faced the doors as they promptly recoiled shut.

"Well...I'm sure you'll enjoy it here."

As they watched the lights of the elevator panel, Janyce continued with polite chitchat. "Are you from around here?"

As the elevator rose, Diana let out a weary sigh. "No! I just moved here a couple days ago...I'm not even unpacked yet."

Though staring at the steel doors, Janyce gave Diana a reassuring smile. "Just take your time and you'll be settled in soon enough. If you don't mind me asking, what part of ICU are you gonna be working?"

Though extremely nervous, Diana kept on her best poker face. "I've been assigned to the Coma Ward."

"Oh...You'll be taking care of Ziggy. Take good care of him, Ziggy's kinda special around here. He's been here so long, he's become a part of the family."

"I'm not really sure what to expect? I've never worked with coma patients before."

"Don't worry...You'll do just fine. Beside, Ziggy's not gonna give you any trouble."

When the second floor button lit-up, Diana's adrenaline

quickly took hold. While waiting for the elevator to open, her hands instantly became clammy and cold. As the steel doors retracted, she found herself looking at what would be her new home-away-from-home.

Stepping out onto the second floor landing, Janyce lead the way as Diana followed in her wake. While walking through the small waiting area she gave a quick inspection of her new surroundings. The first thing she noticed was that the main hallway was entirely deserted. There was no sign of any human presence, not even a word from a faceless voice. Beside the sound of their shoes against the tile floor, there was only dead silence. They might as well have been walking through the morgue.

Arriving at the nurse's station, Diana looked for anyone on duty. Following the counter further down, she spotted a woman doing paperwork in her office.

"Excuse me!" Her voice gave off a short echo in the barren hallway.

The nurse held up her hand. "I'll be with you in just a minute."

With an apprehensive smile, Diana nodded in agreement. Within a few seconds, a stiff, no-nonsense nurse emerged from the back office. "Would you happen to be the hospitals new addition?"

"Yes…That would be me. I'm Diana O'nell."

The nurse pulled a file from the wall rack. "I'm Sharon Nolen…I'll be your shift supervisor."

Janyce turned and looked in Diana direction. "It's time for me to get downstairs. Good luck…It was nice meeting you."

Shaking her hand once again, Diana returned the compliment. "It was nice meeting you…And thanks so much for your help."

As Janyce made her way back to the elevator, she left Diana with a final request. "Make sure to take good care of Ziggy!"

Nurse Sharon let out a brief chuckle. "It sounds like you've already heard about your patient."

Diana could feel herself beginning to nervously perspire as the nurse examined her personnel file. "All I know is what Janyce told me. She said that he's been here for quite some time." Her voice gained confidence the more she spoke. "And it sounded like the hospital has a special bond with him."

A sympathetic smile pulled at Sharon's lips. "Yes...He's been here for quite some time...And Ziggy's very special."

Diana looked up and down the hall as Nurse Sharon thumbed through her file. "It's so quiet...Where is everyone?"

"Beside yours-truly, it's just you. It's the middle of shift-change. In a few minutes, they'll be nurses and orderlies bustling around everywhere. The night crew always takes a couple extra minutes to get going...You'll understand that soon enough."

The nurse picked up a second file folder and handed it to Diana. "This is some paper work for you to sign. It's all just formalities, take care of it whenever you've got time."

"Thanks...I'll take care of it later. I'm really anxious to get familiar with everything."

"If you need a little pick-me-up, the nurse's coffee station is at the end of the counter. I don't mean to seem rude, but I've got some paperwork I need to finish." Nurse Sharon turned and began to walk away. "By-the-way, your resume is very impressive...Welcome to the night shift!" Reassuring Diana as she walked back into her tiny office.

A smile of relief covered her face as she made her way toward the coffee pot. After filling a paper cup, she took a much needed sip of coffee. Opening the file that Sharon had given her, she browsed through the paperwork.

As the passing minutes ticked by, Diana's curiosity finally got the best of her. Unable to tolerate any further delay, she had to find the Coma Ward and see her special patient.

Anxious but composed, she surveyed her new surroundings. After refilling her coffee, she started down the long corridor. While maneuvering around gurneys and parked beds, Diana took-in the layout of the ICU. As the hallway came to an end, she finally spotted what she was looking for. Above an open doorway, a sign read "COMA WARD."

Though the doorway was open, she suddenly became hesitant. After a couple seconds to collect herself, Diana passed through the threshold of the private room.

The room was cold and impersonal. No flowers, no get well cards, nothing that recognized that there was a person in the room. Lying motionless, in an ill-fitting hospital gown, the lone patient was propped against the pillows. On closer inspection, she realized he was a younger looking man hidden behind a full beard. Though Diana knew he was a coma patient, an eerie feeling consumed her as she noticed something she never expected. The man's eyes were wide open as if looking right at her.

The man was hooked up to an electrocardiograph and several other monitors. Various plastic fluid bags hung from metal racks beside the bed. There were IV's in both arms, intravenously feeding him with fluids and antibiotics.

Once she looked at the identification band on his wrist, there was no doubt she had found her patient. There was no middle name, no last name, only the name Ziggy. It also verified that he had been admitted six months earlier. Ready to get to work, she located the blood-pressure cuff. Diana could not get over his blank stare as she wrapped the cuff around his arm. While busy pumping the bulb of the blood-pressure gauge, a Doctor entered the room undetected.

As the cuff deflated, the Doctor read the gauge and began writing on Ziggy's medical chart. Once the Doctor finished his notes, he cleared his throat to get the nurses attention. Unaware that the Doctor was standing right behind her, Diana quickly turned toward the noise.

Slipping the file back into the rack, the Doctor introduced himself. "Hello, I'm Dr. Stevens"

Diana had heard that the Doctor had an easy-going,

undemanding demeanor. She just hoped he was like that toward her. "Hi...Dr. Stevens...I'm Diana O'nell. It's a real pleasure to be working with you."

A smile pulled at the corner of the Doctor's mouth. "The pleasure's all mine. So how's, Ziggy?"

Unsure what to say, Diana went with what she knew best - the truth. "I'm not sure...I just got here...But I do have one question?" looking back at Ziggy. "Are his eyes always open like that?"

"Pretty crazy, huh?"

While putting away the blood-pressure cuff, Diana responded. "More like creepy."

"It can be a little unsettling. But yes, that's normal for some coma patients. Ziggy just happens to be one of those unfortunate few." Dr. Stevens picked up a dropper prescription next to the bed. "Make sure you give him these eye-drops at least four times during your shift."

Diana sympathetically looked into Ziggy's vacant stare. "I know I just got here, but I can't help but feel so sorry for him."

Slightly concerned, Dr. Stevens turned toward the nurse. "Well, don't get too attached."

Confused, her expression became one of curious concern. "I don't understand,"

"His family is signing him off pretty soon."

"What do you mean, signing him off?"

"The family is signing him off life-support. He's been here for six months with no improvement. The machines are the only thing keeping him alive. The family thinks it's about time to let him expire."

"That's terrible! They can't let him go. What about the possibility of him getting better, showing some improvement."

"If there was any chance of improvement, he would have shown some by now."

"Does he understand anything that's going on around him?"

"No...His brain has no motor function...He has no awareness of anything. He doesn't respond to any outside stimulation. No response to touch or speech. For six straight months, brain activity has been non-existent. Basically, he's been dead since they brought him in."

"It doesn't seem possible that he's physically alive, but mentally dead. You would think he has to be experiencing something."

"For patients like Ziggy that are totally brain-dead, it's impossible for him to experience anything." Explaining Ziggy's hopeless situation.

"If he's totally brain-dead, does his soul still exist? He has to be somewhere?" Looking at Doctor with inquisitive concern.

In a gaze of wonder, Dr. Stevens responded. "That's the million dollar question? Where is he? Wherever he is...I hope he's having a pleasant experience."

PART ONE
"DEAD WEIGHT"

CHAPTER 1

SETTLED BACK INTO HIS seat, Jack tried to get as comfortable as possible. Turning on the trucks stereo, he searched for a little music to keep him company.

The dashboard clock read 2:00 pm as he passed the city limit sign. Considering it was mid- afternoon, traffic was almost non-existent. The temperature was in the mid-sixties and thin white clouds occupied the blue sky.

Looking beyond his image in the rearview mirror, he watched as the cities reflection faded away. Gradually, mile by mile, Sacramento slowly became a part of Jack's past. Getting away from the big city was something he had needed to do for what seemed forever. At that moment, he vowed never to return.

Much more than a road trip, this was a journey eastward toward a new beginning. What he had just left behind was all water under the bridge now.

The humming of tires and the drone of the engine accompanied Jack as he cruised along the highway. Keeping the needle right on the speed limit, his ascent began up the long incline that fed directly into the heart of the Sierra Nevada Mountains.

As the Valley vanished behind, Jack sped through the fringe of the foothills. The hills were ablaze with a kaleidoscope of colors as a variety of trees had turned from Autumn's touch.

In a matter of minutes, the highway entered the intriguing and deep-rooted town of Placerville. Full of history, the same buildings that existed in the "California Gold Rush Days" still stood proudly.

Jack looked on in appreciation as the historic town glided by the passenger side window. Guided by a gentle breeze, red, yellow and brown leaves flipped and fluttered across the road as he drove through the outskirts of town.

Reaching the top of the foothills, Jack drove out of the Autumn covered trees to an elevation where pine trees dominated the terrain. The pine-timbered woods were so serene that he felt compelled to stop and take advantage of the surrounding beauty.

Traffic thinned the further he ascended into the mountains. After climbing steadily for about fifteen minutes, he decided to stop and relax.

Before reaching the top of the grade, he chose to take the next available off-ramp. Just as he rounded a long curve, the divided highway ended. As soon as the two lane highway began, he spotted an almost unnoticeable exit. There were no signs identifying this offshoot of a road. But, before the exit was missed entirely, Jack swerved to the right.

Turning off the highway, Jack followed the road the only way he could. The narrow path of pavement circled back underneath the highway into the woods. Just before the truck entered the first line of trees, a lone road sign read "SCENIC ROAD".

The mountain road continued to narrow the further it angled upward. Jack came to the conclusion that cars probably rarely ventured along this stretch. This was perfect as far as he was concerned. With no chosen destination in mind and no other desire than to casually walk through the woods, he was totally content on being entirely by himself.

While not sure what he hoped to accomplish by coming here, Jack reflected on his current state of affairs. For all intents and purposes, his life seemed to retain no value. Bitterness and doubt choked at his soul as each passing day brought only more disappointment. But, he was hopeful that this road-trip could help salvage himself and regain some sort of control over his life.

Jack was jerked from his thoughts as unidentified birds swooped down out of the trees and across the road, narrowly missing the front grill.

While following the twists and turns, the radio reception became weak. The distant stations were nothing but a mass of static, so he turned the radio off.

Rolling down the driver window, Jack cocked his elbow out the opening. As the wind blew through his hair, his city lungs were filled with the joys of mountain air. Surrounded by the stimulating essence of fresh pine, Jack drove in soothing silence.

There seemed to be a richness and peacefulness that he had never felt within the confines of the city. There was something about being in the forest that seemed to feed his weary spirit.

Maybe I can find a little peace of mind up here? Questioning himself as the truck climbed higher into the mountains.

Various ranks of evergreens towered from both sides of the road. The afternoon sunshine angled through the needled branches of the pines, throwing strobe-like shadows across the windshield.

The tree-lined road became a serpentine course as the truck rose into more mountainous territory. As the terrain became steeper, the pavement narrowed to a point not much wider than a single lane road.

Coming out of a sharp turn, Jack caught sight of a river. Dense trees flanked the left side of the road as the gentle river ran along the right. Jack's eyes followed the flowing waters until it abruptly disappeared behind a wall of towering pines.

Maneuvering through the rising woods, the river quickly reappeared. When the river rejoined the road it was no longer a gentle waterway. It roared as it raced aggressively over rocks and crashed into huge boulders.

The river was now united with the road as he veered sharply back and forth. Absorbing it all in, Jack continued to snake-up the mountain. Without notice, the tiny road came to an abrupt end. This was as far as he could go.

The tires crunched down on the small dirt shoulder as Jack pulled off the pavement. After easing to a stop, Jack shut off the engine and stared through the windshield.

While observing the breathtaking beauty, the truck began to rock slightly in the mountain breeze. Along with the tick of the engine as it cooled, the river and the wind pushing through the trees were the only sounds.

Jack racked his fingers through his hair and lifted his sunglasses to his forehead. Resting his forearms on top of the steering wheel, he gazed over the hood. Squinting his eyes, he stared ahead to where the road ended. At the base of the trees, vented with shotgun holes, stood a battered sign that read "Desolation Wilderness."

Though never here before, he had heard rumors about this-neck-of-the-woods. It was common knowledge that several people had mysteriously vanished in this section of the forest. As the story was told, "Desolation Wilderness" was haunted. And all who visited this part of the woods were never seen again.

Several people that Jack had talked too, said the legends of this area were nothing but rumors. But, even if the rumors were true, he did not plan on being here long enough to find out first hand.

Looking at his watch, Jack noticed that it was closing in on three o'clock. Knowing it would be completely dark in a couple hours, he exhaled a sigh of anticipation and pushed open the door. A gust of cool air swept through the cab of the truck as he climbed out from behind the wheel.

Jack walked to the front of the truck and leaned against

the grill. Standing motionless, arms folded, he looked off the road down toward the river. It was a surreal feeling to breath the impossibly clean air and watch the river race down the mountain.

The banks of the river were shrouded with small boulders. While the white-water rapids consumed most of the river, there were calm pools at the river's edge. The motionless water mirrored the scattered clouds in the blue sky above.

Jack felt as if civilization was a million miles away. Though not exactly the woodsy type, he realized that being alone up here in the forest might be just what he needed.

The huge Ponderosa Pines rose straight and tall as he stared into the timbered horizon. While taking in all the beauty, small clouds drifted across the sun, casting moving shadows over the mountain terrain.

Mesmerized, Jack nurtured the beautiful scenery for a moment. Moving away from the river, he crossed the road toward the edge of the woods.

Entering the tree-line, he left his vehicle and the lonely road behind. Though no longer able to see the river, he could hear the roar of the white-water.

Hooking his thumbs in his front pockets, he ventured further into the woods. It was a welcome relief of sorts to walk through nature. At that point in time, he was grateful for the opportunity to keep a much needed distance between himself and any sign of man's existence.

The pine-scented breeze filled his senses with refreshing sensations of contentment. There was clarity in the air, a sense of space and freedom that made him feel like he had just shed a ton of unwanted baggage. The confinement of the city, the grime, already seemed to be falling away.

The forest stood brilliant beneath the columns of sunlight as the giant pines stirred above. Intermittent up-thrusts of granite rock shared the forest floor as he walked amidst the ancient pines.

Jack stopped in a tiny sunlit spot and sat on a warm granite boulder. His eyes narrowed against the sun as he laid back on the rock. Beside himself and the surrounding forest, it seemed as if nothing else in the world existed.

While gazing through the towering treetops, Jack felt small and insignificant. It was as if the forest was stressing the fact, that there were bigger and more important things than himself.

For the first time, he began to look at his life self- consciously. Serious thoughts began to rise as he focused on the questions concerning his past and future.

There was no fighting it any longer, when it came right down to it, the time for denial was over. Jack was a product of his own making. Personality wise, ordinary behavior was not in his repertoire. Unlike most men, he avoided responsibility like the plague. His greatest fear was being hopelessly grounded into a boring and unfulfilling routine.

Always throwing caution to the wind, Jack was not your typical participant in the John Q. Public world. Worshipping his total independence and freedom, he maneuvered through life just biding time until something better came along.

It went without saying that up until now, his life had little if any meaning. Just a collage of non-productive, insignificant events. Most of which, he never wished to relive again. Life, as far as he was concerned, showed him nothing but a lousy sense of humor.

Honed by years of experience, Jack had finally come to a point in time where he acknowledged one inescapable fact. The undeniable truth was that his life would never quite unfold the way he wished.

It was a miserable time. Eroding from the inside out, his very existence had become one misguided path to nowhere. Making no attempt to hide his unforgiving heart, it had become difficult to feel anything but resentment toward society. Beside becoming a hollow empty shell of a man, Jack disliked everyone - even himself.

Always retreating into his private world of denial, confronting problems was not a high priority. Never wanting to confront the problems that plagued him, the same nonproductive values always landed him in the gutter.

Over the long hall, misguided concepts caused him a lot of bumps and bruises. Jack had reached a point where hitting rock-bottom was just a stone's throw away. The desperate desire to pull out of this regretful funk had led to this very moment.

Deeply inhaling the intoxicating pine-scented air, his mind searched for some kind of enlightenment. In a hidden corner of his mind, a silent resolve began to manifest itself. Despite all of his short-comings, the realization of his deep resentment toward society and everything within it ran counter to what his heart really wished for.

Jack knew something had to be done to save face. It was time to wake up and escape from the garbage and crude instability that branded him. Starting from scratch and a lifestyle adjustment seemed to be the only option. Conquering all short-comings and redefining his destiny, could possibly present a new and meaningful direction.

After thinking it though, everything started to become clear. The real test now was to rise above the issues and find a new niche in life. It was time to rescue himself and save what was left of his withering soul.

Deep inside, there began to be traces of hope. As if truly seeing life's potential for the very first time, Jack had a new perspective on the future. Suddenly fueled by an optimistic anticipation, an overwhelming epiphany revealed a solution.

It was time to deal with and dismiss the setbacks of the past.

It was time for an immediate and drastic change.

Only then, would he finally come into his own.

Suddenly, a glow of commitment began to burn inside. After all these years, the hurtful belief that life was utterly hopeless had momentarily been eliminated.

Now, in a more upbeat disposition, a tranquil smile began to pull at his lips. With a seldom felt sensation of inner peace, he understood it was not the end of the world. While lost in this mind-set of change, Jack shut his eyes letting the warm sunlight glow through his eyelids.

***

When Jack's eyes reopened, the sun had already slipped well behind the treetops. Looking at his watch, he realized that sleep had taken advantage of him for over an hour.

Beneath the limbs of the trees, what daylight remained projected vast slanted shadows across the forest floor. With darkness just around the corner, it was time to get back to the truck.

Now, filled with a new found energy and intensions, Jack stood up and began retracing his steps toward the road. While consuming the last bits of warmth the day had to offer, the simple pleasures in life began to present themselves. The possibility of a new beginning was almost beyond imagination.

Being filled with a new conviction was an awesome feeling. After years of daily struggles, Jack was now convinced, rooted in hope, that his life could take a turn for the better.

Every thought was put on hold as a noise that did not belong to the forest invaded his ears. Unexpectedly, the once calm and silent forest was now filled with the sound of running footfalls.

CHAPTER 2

EYES OPENING WIDE, AN instant uneasiness took hold. *Who else is out here?*

Jack quickly kneeled, becoming as small as possible. While only moving his head from side-to-side, he carefully inspected the woods around him. Looking down into a small ravine, an indistinct movement caught the corner of his eye.

A sense of alarm gripped him as a small figure emerged from the trees down below. Confusion swirled around in his mind as a female frantically ran through the trees repeatedly looking over her shoulder.

Dumbfounded, Jack could not fathom what might be taking place to make her run through the woods so hastily. Not wanting to lose sight of her, he moved parallel along the hillside. While following her every movement, a distracting noise from behind caught his attention.

Quickly, she was out of his field of vision. Jack's focus was now on the obscure movements amidst the tree-line shadows behind him. Too far away to make out any details, it was almost impossible to be sure who or what was loitering within the woods. The situation quickly thickened as a man of immense size slipped clear of the shadows.

While watching the man's movements, Jack's eyes were drawn back to the point in the trees where the big man first appeared. After a few puzzling seconds, another man-shape came into sight. While unable to make out their faces, he could see that the second man was wearing what looked like a Doctor's smock.

Continuing to watch, the enormity of the situation began to sink in. Unless the evening shadows were playing tricks on him, it seemed as if the two men were chasing the girl. Jack was not an easily intimidated person, but just the same, the disturbing scenario in front of him sent a fearful chill through his heart.

Studying the shadows behind the two men, he looked for anyone else who might be lingering within the trees. When no other images emerged, his vision refocused on the two men.

Now, face to face, the smaller man in the white coat seemed to be giving instructions. Though listening intently, the conversation was unintelligible. Unable to make sense of the scenario, Jack looked on intently trying to sort out was going on.

Continuing to assess the situation, a discouraging picture began to assemble in his mind. *Maybe the girl's running for her life?*

The two men seemed to know their way around the woods as they quickly went off in different directions. For a moment, Jack's mind raced, captured in a loop of indecision. More often than not, his actions were derived of self-serving intentions. But, this time, concern was more about the girl than himself.

Jack could not come up with any explanation to justify what was taking place. In spite of his selfish instincts, instead of fleeing the scene, it became a necessity to make sure the girl was not a subject to any foul-play.

Without hesitation, he made his way in the direction the girl was headed. Following a narrow path, he found himself looking over a small Hollow. Trudging higher into the forest, scanning the area, he caught sight of more movement.

At the lowest point of the Hollow, the girl fought her way through a section of thick brush. Upon clearing the dense thicket, she ran back into the woods.

Picking up the pace, Jack followed the girl deeper into the

mountain. In the rapidly fading warmth of the setting sun, the breeze that was once so enjoyable had now succumb to an ever hardening chill. The terrain grew steeper as the final shadows of the day took control. His watchful eyes tried to stay fixated on the girl, but she finally vanished into the darkening woods. Though the girl was out of his line-of-sight, his progress was aimed in the direction she had taken.

Darkness was settling quickly amidst the trees, causing Jack's pace to slow the further he ventured. With the wind increasing, the forest released an eerie whistle and the trees began to wildly swing their limbs.

As minutes passed, the chill of the mountain air closed in and drew goose-bumps. Walking against the blustering wind, Jack pushed and picked his way through the dense underbrush.

While darkness continued its descent, a terrible vision arose. *What if I get lost and I can't find my way out?*

For some strange reason, the thought of turning-tail and leaving quickly disappeared. If only for his own peace of mind, it became essential to find her.

Though darkness was preparing to dominate, he spotted what seemed to be the last line of trees. Night sounds began to rule the pending darkness as the forest quickly thinned. Within a few steps the trees were suddenly gone, giving way to a small grassy meadow. Jack found himself with a vantage point that put him in full view of the clearing and surrounding woods.

While standing in the shadows of twilight, an apprehensive inner voice needled him. Running his fingertips over the beard stubble on his chin, he became undecided whether to proceed any further?"

While facing the grassy meadow, a swarm of gnats buzzed his head. In the silence of his temporary hiding spot, Jack swatted at their relentless attack. There was still a trace of dusk in the sky as he spied across the clearing. While surveying the area, a house came into sight. But then, Jack's city eyes realized that it was not a house, it was a tiny cabin.

Virtually lost in the shadows of the forest, the silent and lonely cabin was submerged in gloom. Seemingly cowering beneath the enormous looming branches that surrounded it.

Inspecting the cabin one last time, he stepped from the last line of trees and stood at the edge of the clearing. While pausing for a moment and taking a deep breath, a perplexed expression covered his face while digesting the idea of confronting the cabin. With no clue what to expect, a bad taste began to develop in his mouth.

Though reluctant to go any further, there was an overwhelming feeling that the girl was inside. Before his nerves abandoned him all together, the venture across the meadow began. Making his way through the knee-high grass, Jack took the precaution of stopping every couple of steps to listen and scan the area. The nearer he drew to the cabin, the more imposing the tiny structure appeared.

With the exception of knowing the girl might be inside, the place appeared to be totally deserted. Not a single light appeared to be on. Nothing repelling the darkness outside and no signs of light penetrated the drawn curtains.

Just prior to reaching the cabin, Jack felt as if someone was taking inventory of his movements. Unexpectedly, the cabin's front curtains moved as if someone inside were peering out.

In a particular way, the idea of being observed seemed strange and threatening. Partly because there was no way of knowing what he was about to get himself into. And partly, because the last place in the world he probably needed to be was here.

Staring at the window with increasing interest, he watched as the curtains quickly fell back into place. Jack cautiously moved past the last tangle of tall grass until he reached his destination.

In the frigid shadows of dusk, he stood at the base of the front steps. Though the cabin seemed in decent shape from a distance, it was actually a run-down shack.

The hovering tree branches swung violently in the gusting wind, casting a frenzy of distorted shadows to dance wildly along the cabin walls. The mammoth, low hanging limbs scratched against the cabin's aluminum roof. Like long hardened fingernails scraping against a classroom chalkboard, the tree branches clawed at the overhead metal.

As the mountain sunset was coming to a conclusion, the sky began to darken into a deep purple. Slowly climbing the wooden steps, the dried and withered boards cried beneath Jack's weight. Cracking and splitting in protest of his every movement.

Upon reaching the front door, he took a couple of tentative deep breaths. A thrill of wary anticipation cursed through his veins as he lightly tapped on the door. For a few anxious moments, Jack awaited a response. When none came, he knocked again.

The lack of response was puzzling, Jack knew someone was inside. But for some reason, they refused to acknowledge his presence. When he pushed against the door, it surprisingly clicked open. There was a sharp squeal as the rusty hinges swung inward. With the entrance now wide open, he stepped through the doorway into the darkened threshold of the cabin.

CHAPTER 3

STANDING JUST INSIDE THE cold entryway, Jack scanned the interior of the cabin. The initial smell that invaded his senses was moldy and dank. A pungent odor, that of an old run-down basement in desperate need of attention.

Though the room was virtually engulfed in darkness, Jack spotted an old kerosene lamp hanging next to the door. Still standing just inside the doorway, he grabbed the hanging lamp from its hook. Retrieving his cigarette liter from his pocket, he lit the antique lamp and pulled down the glass cover. As the flame grew stronger, the cabin began to come to life.

Jack stepped further into the room while pushing the creaking door shut behind him. Looking around, he took in all that he could see in the dim lamplight.

The interior of the cabin appeared neat at first glance. But upon closer scrutiny, nothing could hide its rustic shabbiness. Everything about the place was well dated. The walls and woodwork were discolored and cracked from age and neglect. Beside a grungy couch in the middle of the room, the interior of the cabin was sparsely furnished. Totally exempt of anything modern or contemporary, the highlight of the room was a deteriorating river-rock and mortar fireplace.

The only personal touch that existed within the dismal dwelling, were the various stuffed birds of prey and mounted deer heads that adorned the cabin walls. When the lantern light washed over the animal heads, it sent spooky, vaporous shadows pressing against the pinewood.

The animal heads that adorned the walls instantly gave Jack the creeps. Their unseeing marble eyes glowed in the putrefied light. The hairs on his neck began to stand on end as he became mesmerized by the dead luminous eyes that gawked down upon him. It was as if he could feel their stares radiating an eerie demonic presence.

While standing amidst this private collection of disembodied creatures, Jack had the irrational sensation that the stuffed trophies were watching and following his every move. Roosting overhead, like a committee of bodiless jurors waiting to pass a most prejudice judgment. It was suddenly the most uncomfortable place he had ever been.

While casting the lamplight in front of him, it appeared he was in an empty room - but he knew otherwise. Jack's eyes continued to probe his surroundings, studying every shadowy outline and darkened corner. While standing within the mysterious half-lit cabin, he heard a sound. There was definitely someone in the room with him.

Letting the light penetrate into the deepest corner of the room, he noticed a tiny figure. In complete tunnel-vision, his focus was fixated on the darkness where this half-hidden silhouette lay in wait. Almost untouched by the tainted glow of the lamp, the shadow amidst shadows stood motionless, wedged into the darkened corner.

Arm outstretched, lantern leading the way, Jack took a couple steps towards the image. When the lamplight began to enhance the corner of the room, the once hidden silhouette began to materialize. Though hiding in the shadows as to not reveal herself, Jack knew it was the same girl he had seen running through the forest.

With the lantern extended, Jack widened his eyes at the revolting sight in front of him. The features of the strange personage seemed grossly distorted by the flickering lamplight. But, her distortions were not the result of the pale light that hung throughout the room.

Jack stared spellbound, thoroughly seized by the sight of the terrified woman. His eyes took a discouraging inventory as his stare poured over the full length of her body.

While remaining frozen in the glow of the lamp, the girl looked like a scornful bag of dirty laundry. She wore a pair of torn, grey sweat pants and a filthy, frayed t-shirt. Her hair hung in shapeless, unwashed, uncombed straggles. In the lamplights sour glow, her skin had an unhealthy, decaying tone to it. Her facial features were disturbingly drawn. Framed by hard, dark-rings, her eyes were sunken into their sockets. They were hollow and empty, almost dead eyes, the most implacable eyes he had ever seen.

Jack and the woman stood opposite each other, nothing between them but a tremendous tension. Awkwardly, they watched each other. Anticipating the other to speak, they waited for the silence to be broken and set the tone for the uncomfortable meeting.

Neither one said a word, just standing in contemplation of their own thoughts. Jack's eyes were locked into the woman's frenzied stare. For an instant, he noticed the pre-mature crows-feet extending from the corners of her terrified eyes. Deep crevices that should only inhabit the unfortunate face of a woman four times her age.

Still transfixed by the girl's decrepit outer shell, he curiously moved closer. Upon further advancement, the frightened figure shifted in the shadows. Then, Jack saw something that stopped him dead in his tracks. It was almost more than he could grasp as he gawked at the grotesque sight in front of him. Like the bodiless heads that observed from above, the girl's eyes followed his every move - all six of them.

CHAPTER 4

JACK'S HORROR REFUSED TO let him blink. Instantly, his blood chilled as his eyes were besieged in disbelief. Though showing little emotion on the surface, terror engulfed him from within. While the atrocity in front of him was undeniable, he still had to convince himself it was not a hallucination.

The girl's face framed a nightmarish collage. The right side of her forehead and cheek housed two sets of eyes. Totally misaligned from the bloodshot eyes he had first seen. These sets of eyeballs seemed to be independent from each other. Frenzied with fear, her numerous eyes blinked independently as they took a fearful inventory of Jack. Like the unnatural stares from above, the girl's scared paranoid eyes watched his every move.

Though the random sets of eyes were totally developed and functioning, the side of her neck appeared to house other strange configurations. Surrounded by clumps of bristly, black hair, these undeveloped dysfunctional forms appeared to be additional facial features.

Numerous perplexing thoughts bombarded his mind. But, there was one thought that dominated above all the others. *What happened to this poor girl?*

Unexpectedly, a frightened whisper cut through the silence. "Who are you? Please don't hurt me."

Jack suddenly looked at her with passionate concern. While the woman that stood in front of him seemed somewhat normal, this disgruntled creature was disturbingly different - almost

21

alien. But, there was no doubt that there was a real person trapped beneath those mutinous layers of skin.

Disheartened, Jack could not help but feel sorry for the scared girl. But, at the same time, he could not dismiss the terror of her grotesque image. Pausing for several moments, he searched for the right words before attempting to pursue any further conversation.

Before he could think of anything to say, the girl's frightened voice interrupted his thoughts. "We have to do something! They're out there! They're going to find us! He…They won't stop until they do." There was an undeniable trembling of fear in her voice.

Completely dumbfounded by the girl's hysteric ranting, Jack confronted her. "Who's they? The men that were chasing you?"

She gave no response, but had a crazed desperate look.

"Talk to me. Why are these guys after you?"

After a short period of silence, it became apparent that the girl was not going to give him an explanation - so he demanded one. "What the hell is going on?"

In fearful silence, she continued to press herself into the cabin's darkest shadows. Jack became uneasy and on edge. It was increasingly evident, that something weird was going on and he was right in the middle of it.

An immediate twinge of nervousness consumed him as he tried to gather a rational train of thought. Jack's eyes narrowed as suspicion and mistrust suddenly occupied his thoughts. He wondered if it was just paranoia, but his instincts told him otherwise. With each passing second, he began to feel more and more ill-at-ease.

With their glowing eyes still surveying his every move, the dead menagerie which hung ominously on the surrounding walls made him instantly antsy. Jack could not quite put a finger on why his instincts were taking him in this direction. But, it was as if he sensed an onrushing threat, but not sure where it was coming from.

All of a sudden, feeling ensnared and trapped, an uncanny rush of adrenaline invaded his body. Jack tore his eyes away from the pathetic sight in front of him and quickly walked to the front window.

Standing in front of the drawn curtains, Jack looked back at the girl. A gesture of nervous tension followed as she flung back a strand of matted hair that had fallen across her disfigured face.

Draping the window was a tattered, stained brown curtain. Jack pushed it aside just enough to secretly peer out. Beyond the window darkness now ruled the forest. As he studied the night, his vision scanned the surrounding woods.

Along the darkened tree-line, something caught his attention. Squinting into the murky gloom of the bordering woods, he spotted a faint image and the fire of a cigarette.

Anxiously, he watched as the orange glow of the cigarette casually moved up and down, briefly flaring in front of the figures face. Jack assumed that the same men he had witnessed before were now patiently observing the cabin. After a few seconds, the glow of the cigarette vanished along with the figure.

With his back still toward the girl, Jack continued to study the night. While running his vision back and forth along the outer limits of the clearing, he always returned to the point in which he first saw the glow of the cigarette.

Allowing the frayed curtain to fall back into place, his stare returned to the girl. The strange female began frantically pacing in the corner, impatiently raking her fingers through her matted hair. Constantly holding on to the panicked look of someone who harbored some sort of expectant knowledge.

There was nothing coincidental about what was transpiring. Something was definitely off kilter, and Jack needed to know what it was? "Whose out there? What do they want?" Insistent on an answer as he walked back to the center of the room.

For a second, she stood wide-mouthed as if searching for an answer. But in the end, she remained silent. Either unable or unwilling to give him any insight on what was taking place.

Their eyes momentarily met, but that was long enough for him to realize that something was seriously wrong. Jack came to the conclusion that it was pointless to try to communicate with this ghastly looking creature any longer. At the end of his rope, he was now beyond the limits of his tolerance. The events of the afternoon had finally taken its toll. Getting away from this crazy situation was now top priority.

Jack held his hands up as if signaling surrender. "Fine...If you don't want my help...I'm out-of-here!" Dropping his frustrated hands, he started across the room toward the door.

"Where are you going?" Her multiple pairs of eyes feverishly glowing in the lamplight.

Jack slowly spun around on his heels, drawing his gaze back to the girl. "Where does it look like I'm going? I'm leaving... You're on your own."

"But...They're out there."

Jack's features took on the lines of a determined man. Looking square into those hooded, dark ringed eyes of hers, he threw her a final question. "One last time...Whose they? Who is out there? You need to tell me what's going on...Now!"

Without hesitation she quickly moved across the room. "Don't go out there! Please...Don't leave me!" Pleading as she shouldered her way past Jack and blocked the front door.

Inhaling the girl's scent as she abruptly brushed past, Jack noticed she carried a dingy, musty essence. While most women wore a fresh, clean perfumed scent, this girl harbored an extremely dirty aroma. One of total neglected hygiene that possessed an appalling decadence all its own.

Panic overwhelmed her as she emphatically gestured with her hands as if it would help her find the right words. "They're monsters...They're coming...They're coming for me...They're coming for us." Her voice became intense, even persuasive as ultimate terror cloaked her face.

Jack furrowed his brow at the peculiar response. As the girl's words took flight in his mind, he gawked at the bizarre woman in total disbelief. There was a heavy, silent pause as the word "Monsters" cut deep into the furthest crevices of his imagination.

"What do you mean, monsters?" Jack responded as a throb of concern began to form in his chest.

The girl appeared to be on the brink of hysteria. "You can't go out there! They'll...They'll kill you!" She continued, her story growing along with her tone. "They'll...He'll kill you! Or turn you into something hideous like me! He'll make you wish you were never born!"

There was something in the girl's voice, something urgent, bordering on the worst sort of finality. Her tremendous fear instantly infected Jack. He had no idea what was happening, but every instinct that he possessed told him to leave, get out of the cabin - now!

Jack's features took on the lines of determination, there was no need to think about his next words. "Move away from the door! I've had about all I can stand of this craziness for one night."

Reluctantly, she moved away from the door.

Urgency gripped Jack. Convinced it was time to get out, he took two hungry strides and grabbed the brass doorknob.

"Please...Please don't go out there!"

Declining to respond, he accepted her frantic plea by ignoring it. But, just as he was about to open the door, something caught his attention.

Though the girl was still pleading with him, he no longer heard what she was saying. Jack suddenly became disturbingly aware of another sound. Faint at first, but gradually becoming more distinct, it was the sound of approaching footsteps.

As the steps grew nearer, Jack snatched his hand from the doorknob. Immediately, he backed away while looking over at the girl's terrified face. Her multiple eyes went wild, darting in all directions. Her nervous tongue slid back and forth across her lips as though she knew exactly what resided on the other side of the door. As if death were about to step inside, she fearfully retreated back into the darkest portion of the cabin and was gone.

Turning his attention back to the door, Jack realized he was in a unstable dilemma. All at once, a flash of warning shot through his mind. Every internal instinct he possessed began screaming in alarm. Whoever it was outside, his gut feeling told him that things were about to get out-of-hand.

Acknowledging the fact that things had just gone from bad to disastrous, he let out a deep, agitated sigh. While staring transfixed at the antique doorknob, the awful truth of the crazy scenario began to take shape.

Dull despair instantly struck him like a kick in the face as an incredible feeling of hopelessness mentally crippled him. Jack was swallowed-up in confusion and paralyzed with indecision. A sickening nervousness trembled through his soul with the realization that there was nothing he could do, nowhere to go - he was trapped.

I don't believe this. Jack silently berated himself for not seizing the opportunity to leave the cabin earlier.

Dead silence smothered the small cabin. In terrified anticipation, time seemed to slow down. Jack went rigid, unable to move, not even able to take a breath. Tensing his muscles and gritting his teeth, he wished he could will himself into another place and time.

Blind to everything but the brass doorknob, Jack watched in ominous dread as the knob slowly began to turn.

CHAPTER 5

THE EDGE OF TIME seemed to hang forever as the gravity of the situation took hold. A threatening, clutching sensation gripped Jack's heart as the squealing door swung wildly open. Violently, it crashed into the back wall. As the entryway lay wide open, the brisk chill of the Autumn night instantly engulfed the room.

Stunned by the explosion of the door, Jack remained motionless, glaring mystified at what was taking place. A slow creeping chill crawled up his back as a shadowy figure casually stepped into the threshold of the doorway. The unexpected intruder gave Jack a cynical but expectant smile.

The man's threatening presence was more than enough to cause Jack to retreat a couple steps. Adrenaline blistering and his pulse pounding viciously, Jack's eyes were glued to the man in the doorway. Compelling himself to stay calm, he mentally struggled to assess the crazy twist of events.

Though the man looked at Jack with a glare of false welcome, he seemed to be amused by the encounter. Amused in a cynical way that only he could appreciate. Though he never said a word, there was something in his silence that made Jack exceptionally nervous and wishing for a way to retreat.

As the man stepped further into the cabin, Jack forced down the panic that was rising in his chest. With all that was happening, he stood his ground, making sure not to flinch or let any emotion register on his face. Doing whatever he needed to not show the degree of his actual distress.

Just as he prepared himself to confront the man, another image emerged from the darkness outside. When the second figure came into full view, Jack immediately knew that it was the same man he had first seen chasing the girl. And most likely, the same figure he had just witnessed lurking at the edge of the meadow.

The Neanderthal looking stranger wore an expression of cold indifference as he closed the door and stood guard. The circumstances of the dilemma did not take long to sink in. With the unexpected presence of the two men, Jack realized he was in way over his head.

Right then, he felt totally helpless, stripped of any power or control of the situation. For this was now their turf and he was just an unwelcome trespasser trapped within it.

While looking at both men, Jack mentally debated which of the two might be his most menacing adversary. But deep down inside, he knew without a doubt, that the man in the doctor's coat was the biggest threat.

The air was thick and electric with friction. With everything ill-at-ease and silent, Jack closely watched the two men. Then, all at once, the intensity heightened when the first man's slow, deliberate voice broke the silence. "Well…Well…Well…Look what we have here. Surprised to see me Laura?" Directing his stare toward the mutated girl that hid in the darkness.

Laura never uttered a word as she pressed herself even deeper into the shadows.

There was another long strained silence before he spoke again. "I'm sorry to bust in on you like this. But, I just happened to be in the neighborhood and decided to drop by." Delivering an intentional jab of sarcasm.

Unwilling to let down his guard, a hesitant smirk flickered across Jack's face. Without thinking, an uncontrollable surge of recklessness fell upon his tongue. "Come on…You can do better than that."

The response obviously caught the man off guard. Jack had definitely hit a nerve. The man's previous cool disposition of calm arrogance instantly vanished. Eyes growing narrow, he regarded Jack with renewed contempt.

Quickly regaining his composure, Laura's pursuer began clapping his hands in mocking glee. As the short-lived patter of applause died away, he continued to speak in a dismissive and undermining tone. "You're right...I can do better than that."

The man studied Jack, evaluating, sizing him up like a predator stalking his prey. "I see you've got an obnoxious, sarcastic sense of humor. I despise that." There was a noticeable hint of venom and irritation in his voice.

Jack let the man's words sink in for a second, then responded. "Don't you have somewhere else to be, whoever you are?"

Jack regretted saying the words even as they were leaving his lips. It was instantly apparent that no one talked to this man like that. Responding to Jack's sarcasm, the man's reaction was one of an intimidating and dangerous scowl. It was obvious that Jack's comment had gone too far.

The man countered Jack's remark with a question of his own. "By the way, what the hell are you doing in my cabin?" Inquiring with a controlled viciousness.

Jack did not respond. Remaining silent, he tried to keep his poise. Revealing none of the signs of fear and distress he inwardly felt.

The man quickly picked up where he had left off. "You've been alone with my daughter abusing her, haven't you?"

Jack became very concerned about where the conversation was heading. A furious objection hung on his tongue. But not wanting to inflame the situation, he quickly decided to suppress it.

"You were just about to run away and flee the scene...Weren't you." The man's tone was unassuming, but his words were anything but that.

Jack did not like the ominous sound of his words and as the man continued, he liked them even less. "I'd say I got here just in time. It would have been a damn shame if you'd been able to sneak away before I could rescue my daughter." Voice rising with each word.

Jack was quick to respond. "Just relax, don't turn this into something it's not." Peripherally, Jack could see the girl wedged into the corner frightened to death. "If it's any conciliation, nothing happened and I was just leaving. So if you and your friend will step aside, it's time for me to…"

"That's not good enough," cutting Jack off with a hard retort. "You can save your breath, it's not going to do you any good. Beside, you're in no position whatsoever to negotiate." Making it very apparent that he was in charge.

Though Jack knew better than to take the confrontation to the next level, he did it anyway. "Well that's a comforting thought." As he spoke, his eyes averted to the other stranger standing behind the man.

Noticing Jack's distracted stare, the man's lips quirked into a cynical smile once again. "Please forgive me. This gentleman is an associate of mine, Mr. Jones." Jack was listening, but his eyes were fixed on the big man from the forest. "Mr. Jones, this is…I'm sorry…I didn't catch your name."

"Jack…My name's Jack." Trying to restrain the nervousness from his voice.

"Mr. Jones, this is Jack, our new pain in the ass. In order to complete these pleasantries, I am Doctor Simone."

Jack eyed Mr. Jones thoroughly. It was obvious that this guy had been Dr. Simone's lackey for quite some time - his right-hand man.

Lock-jawed, a wooden toothpick protruded from the corner of his mouth. Jones's very appearance had a vile and threatening repugnance. Greedy-eyed and unshaven, Jones featured a livid purple scare that cut across the left side of his face. The gouged tissue extended from the middle of his ear, down his cheek, ending at the corner of his chin. With a leathery face that was callous and unforgiving, he sported a hardened scowl that appeared to be his life's permanent expression.

Mr. Jones wore a pair of worn, faded blue jeans. A brown leather jacket and a pair of square toed boots that had seen better days. The ensemble was completed with a silver chain that hung from his belt and connected to an oversize wallet that stuck out from his back pocket.

An obvious product of the street, he definitely fit the description of a long-time thug of a degenerate biker gang. The type of character that caused people to cross the road in an effort to avoid confrontation.

Like a bored bouncer, he stood between Jack and the door, blocking any chance of escape. While Jones stood fast at his post, the Doctor strolled slowly across the room. Stopping at the front window, he pulled back a corner of the curtains.

Staring into the darkness, he rubbed his jaw as if pondering his thoughts. The Doctor's mannerisms never changed, his every movement was precise and methodical. Unshakably calm and calculated, he carried an aura of dominance and superiority that was daunting. While at the same time possessing a glint of madness that never left his stare.

"Alright Jack...Let's get to the bottom-line shall we?" The Doctor announced, still looking out into the night. "Let me spell things out to you. Like I told Mr. Jones, you've become an unforeseen problem." Reflecting in a resentful tone.

Turning away from the window, he let the frayed curtain fall back into place. "You're more annoying than you're worth, Jack. You remind me of a nagging toothache that needs to be eliminated." Explaining as he casually walked in the direction where the pale light burned.

A tight knot of panic lodged in Jack's stomach as he followed the Doctor with his eyes. Roaming about the room, the Doctor nodded his head as if still appraising the situation. Eventually, he strolled toward his daughter and sat next to her in a rickety armchair. Crossing his legs, he steepled his fingers in contemplation of his next move. After a couple of stressed packed moments, the Doctor began to set the stage. As if giving a silent command, he nodded his head at Mr. Jones.

Jones reacted immediately, anxious to cooperate. Leaving his post at the door, Jones pushed Jack forward, forcing him into the center of the room.

Over the years, Jack had learned to take the good times with the bad. But this had all the ingredients of something extremely hazardous.

Doctor Simone casually gazed around the room. Peering through the dim lamplight, he reviewed every detail of the cabin. "Quite a cozy little place I've got here...Don't you think.?" Acknowledging his words with a brief, sadistic laugh. "It's very... How should I say this...Gothic...Dark ages...I love it. It's got a certain foreboding, demonic aura to it. It's a perfect venue for something ill-fated and final to happen to some poor soul." The Doctor's comments carried the ripe promise of someone's demise - most likely Jack's.

Overcome by the uncanny sensation that his destiny may hang in the outcome of this unexpected encounter, Jack thought better than to speak his mind. As much as the Doctor's words and arrogance infuriated him, he knew the man would not appreciate his candor.

The Doctor re-crossed his legs and placed his forearms on the arms of the chair before continuing. "If by some chance you don't understand what's about to happen here, you'll definitely understand very shortly." Speaking evenly and to the point.

As for this night, beside the Doctor himself, no one in the room was privy to the grand plan scripted. Nor, could anyone have possibly imagined the sinister agenda that was architected just for Jack.

Slowly uncrossing his legs, the heavy-set man's movements caused the old armchair to creek under stress. Jaw set, the Doctor leaned toward his unexpected guest. With a savage darkness, the vengeful stare that enveloped in his eyes burned right into Jack's soul.

Jack could not find it within him to return the Doctor's stare. An irreversible sigh of despair seeped from his lungs as he grimly faced the disastrous facts of this worsening plight.

Dr. Simone rose to his feet and clasp his hands behind his back. Slowly, he began to pace back and forth in front of Jack. "You know, Jack...By coming here tonight, you really screwed up my previous plans." Though very composed, his words were nothing less than vindictive.

Walking past Jack, the Doctor spun on his heels and slowly retraced his steps. Within arm's reach, Dr. Simone clinched a fist and with one violent motion, drove it into Jack's midsection. The power of the strike exploded the air from his lungs and sent Jack stumbling back into the pinewood wall.

Falling to his knees, doubled over in pain, Jack's stomach knotted in agonizing spasms. For a dazed instant, the thought of passing-out lingered. Mouth hanging open, all his focus and energy was directed on the next breath.

"I hate my schedule being compromised...Especially by the likes of someone like you!" The Doctor's angry voice was filled with vengeful resentment.

After several futile attempts, Jack's lungs finally succeeded to suck in some much welcome air. Every breath was a labored effort as the burning taste of bile pushed up in his throat.

The Doctor's specifics were still somewhat unclear, but not his intent. Jack quickly understood that he was about to be put on the business end of this man's madness.

While slouched against the cabin wall, Jack barely had a chance to allow himself to recover before Mr. Jones got a hold of him. Grabbing his hair, the big man jerked Jack's head back and pulled him to his feet.

The Doctor's quest to show Jack his dominance and power was relentless as he continued his onslaught. "As you're about to find out, I'm a man of many talents and wherewithal, Jack."

Pulling out a pair of handcuffs from his jacket pocket, Dr. Simone then tossed the restraints to Mr. Jones. Still recovering, Jones proceeded to smash Jack's face against the wall and wrench his arms behind his back. Arms twisted behind him, Jack suddenly felt the pinch of cold steel crunch down around his wrists. The tightness of the cuffs bit deep into his flesh.

To this point, the remorseless evils that now lurked within the cabin had not welcomed Jack with open arms. Teetering on the edge of disaster, any hope he once had of getting away unscathed was now non-existent.

Jones grabbed Jack's handcuffed wrists and led him in front of the Doctor. In frustration over the injustice of it all, Jack's eyes were glazed over in stark hatred as the nerve-racking ordeal continued to play itself out.

CHAPTER 6

THE DOCTOR LAUGHED, THE outrageous man seemed genuinely amused with himself. And why not, by nature, violence and intimidation was standard operating procedure. Diabolical types like the Doctor thrived on cruel and unusual tactics. Loving to look you straight in the eye, explain exactly what he was going to do to you, then carry it out. With no fear whatsoever of the repercussions or consequences of his actions.

Dr. Simone's eyes gleamed menacingly, staring at Jack with cold-hearted intolerance. "You're about to witness an inkling of what I'm capable of."

Momentarily absent of any response, Jack's mind weighed the Doctor's threat. Only silent thoughts of desperation raced through his head. The realization of something more sinister began to slither through his mind. Frightfully aware, that his future, if not his life was about to be decided.

Am I going to die tonight? Jack asked himself in silent horror. The unfortunate encounter was almost impossible for him to even comprehend.

Stepping forward, the Doctor stood in front of Jack with a satisfied smirk. "As far as killing you goes…As much as I'd like to…I'm not going to kill you, Jack." His voice had an arrogant, baiting quality to it. "But, I can't speak for my daughter or Mr. Jones. They might have different plans for you?"

Jones jumped in and took a momentary part in the conversation.

"You never know, Jack...You just might have an appointment with the Grim-Reaper himself tonight."

Dr. Simone looked around the cabin as if searching for something in particular. "Before you have your rendezvous with the hereafter, I think my daughter has something special for you?" Explaining as he spotted what he was looking for.

Strolling within a few feet of his daughter, he grabbed a wooden walking cane that rested against the wall.

"Laura, come here!" Ordering more than asking.

The terrified girl cringed in the corner as her father held the cane. Laura hesitated, then did what she was told. Reluctantly, she slowly moved toward her father.

"That's my girl." Presenting a tender, comforting facade as he put his hand to her cheek.

Laura tried to stay calm, breathing erratically as her father placed his hands on her shoulders. Dr. Simone positioned his daughter directly in front of him. Leaning forward, he whispered into her ear, speaking in a voice only meant for her.

Looking at her father in total shock, all six panicked eyes aliened in union as she shook her head as if saying no.

Visibly displeased, the Doctor returned her stare with a glare of cold disapproval. The apparent ruthlessness in his eyes ruled out any chance of negotiation.

Briefly, Laura lost herself in her father's sadistic, crucifying stare. As if her life depended on it and it probably did, she quickly rethought her decision. Now, the girl fearfully nodded in a positive way.

Laura refocused her attention away from her dad's stare. While her two normal eyes looked at Jack, her four independent eyes scanned over the thick walking cane.

As Jack observed the girl, that decadent mask she previously wore began to change. Laura's demeanor now began to hang on the edge of insanity. With a look of pure fanatic determination, she snatched the cane from her father's grasp and turned toward Jack.

All at once, his paranoia turned in a completely different direction. Attention now focused strictly on the girl, Jack silently watched in horror as the true insanities of the situation began to unfold.

Laura fixed her eyes upon Jack with a stare that made his skin crawl. Utterly dispassionate, her hardened stare possessed a haunting, evil quality. Festering like an infected sore, the once timid creature, now expressed total disgust.

"I'm sure you've watched baseball before, Jack. So I know you can appreciate this." The Doctor conveyed, sitting gently back into his chair. "Take a couple practice swings, Laura. Show Jack what you've got."

Laura gripped the heavy oak cane as if it were a baseball bat. Eyes riveted on the girl, Jack watched as she furiously swung the cane in an psychotic rage. Standing statue still, he looked on in bewildered disbelief.

The Doctor held up one hand, telling Laura to stop swinging the cane. "She's got a beautiful swing, don't you think, Jack?"

Not wanting to inflame the situation any further, he refused to respond. Instead, nervous anxiety took control over his body. Feet refusing to move, he could not control his anxious body as it awaited the inevitable. Jack's movements, little of them as there were, were panicky and uncertain.

"Since it appears that our unwelcome guest is at a loss for words, what do you think, Mr. Jones?" Dr. Simone asked, never taking his eyes off of Jack.

"Whatever you decide...Works for me, boss," Jones answered with a lopsided smile.

Dr. Simone looked at his watch then returned his stare to Jack. "Well, the moment of truth has finally arrived, Jack. My daughter is about to show you how much I appreciate this little get-together."

Jack looked on helplessly as the girl slid further into an insane mental state. With the insanity that dwelled in her stare, he instantly knew that things were about to go way beyond the realm of his wildest imagination.

While trying to digest the girl's crazed image in his mind, a far worse image began to form. It took only a couple of seconds before his stunned mind figured out what was about to take place.

Ensnared in the midst of this demented scheme of events, Jack realized that the girl was about to turn that simple walking cane into a weapon of destruction.

Looking at his daughter, the Doctor gave her a nod of reassurance. "Okay Laura, it's time to step up to the plate and make your dad proud."

On that note, Laura's face began to contort into a mask of rage and hate. Right then, Jack knew that the upcoming moments would leave a permanent mark on his life. First-hand, he was about to witness the insanities only to be experienced in a nightmarish scenario. Unbelieving as it was, this was about to become Jack's terrifying reality.

As if she were ready for war, the monstrosities on Laura's face and neck flushed. Jaws tightened and teeth clinched, she stared at Jack with murderous intent.

"You don't think she'll do it, do ya, Jack?" Dr. Simone challenged him with unwavering contempt.

Jack could not believe what he was seeing. In fact, in his disbelieving state of mind, he refused to believe the girl would actually follow through with it. But, then again, with the intimidation factor of her father, the game of life in the Doctor's cabin was played by a prejudice set of rules. And the games played here, where played for keeps.

"Prepare for the same pain I feel every day." Laura screamed in a harsh, raspy voice.

Jack became transfixed in horror as she reared the stout stick behind her head and locked her multiple eyes upon her target. Handcuffed and helpless, there was nothing Jack could do to defend himself. A lump formed in his throat as the terrifying unreality began to play itself out.

With a few quick strides the neurotic girl was within striking distance. The lines in Laura's face deepened, her teeth clinched and her neck muscles tightened like steel rods. With no signs of weakness or doubt, not a notion of shame crossed her face as she prepared to swing the cane.

Jack dropped back a pace as the girl approached. But Jones was right there to grab his handcuffs and hold him in place. At that very moment, his entire body stiffened in defense. Every muscle tensed, even his toes curled in his boots.

Noooo! Jack silently screamed as he squeezed his defenseless eyes shut. Panicked adrenaline cursed through his veins as he anticipated the blow.

Then it came, a crisp, whooshing sound as the thick oak cane cut through the air. Knowing that the wooden weapon was now racing toward his face, Jack's teeth locked in desperation.

CHAPTER 7

WITH UNBELIEVING SPEED AND force, the heavy cane collided alongside Jack's temple and eye. It felt as if the eye had exploded as the concussion ripped through his skull. Like an electric shock, a bolt of white-hot pain shot through his entire body. For a bone-jarring instant, his teeth and every bone seemed to shudder from the strike.

Instantly dazed and disoriented, his eyes rolled back into his head. Falling away from the impact, he awkwardly back-peddled and crumbled to the floor. Landing with a heavy thud on his cuffed hands, searing jolts of pain ripped through his arms and shoulders. Upon hitting the ground, his head abruptly snapped back, smashing against the hardwood floor.

Jack let out an agonizing grunt as once again the air rushed from his lungs. Instinctively, he rolled to the side, freeing his throbbing arms from the weight of his body. Piercing shards of pain continued as the after-shocks of the vicious blow echoed back into the depths of his skull.

Within the fraction of a second that followed, his eyes began to flutter, drifting into a state of limbo. Lost in a dreamscape of bright, pulsating, spinning motes, his senses were overrun with delirium and confusion.

Desperately trying to return from his excursion in uncertainty, he attempted to raise his head. But in an ocean of dizziness, his head clumsily fell back against the wood floor.

Jack was too far out of himself to register what was going

on around him. For a brief moment, he was not sure if he was conscious or not. And for another crazy moment, the thought of death entered his mind. But that thought quickly vanished as the absurd pain strewn throughout his body continued to intensify.

Though in a state of traumatized shock, Jack had not succumb to unconsciousness yet. But he was much more than dazed, floating vainly on the brink of passing out. The mixture of out-and-out fear and panic was the only thing that enabled him to desperately cling to the edge of consciousness.

Jack gritted his teeth, doing all he could to hold back a scream. Instead, a guttural groan of misery escaped from his lips as he struggled to maintain some sort of a grip on reality.

The next few seconds were nothing but a blur. While totally disoriented, a deep, loud ringing, steady and insistent rendered his hearing temporarily useless.

Jack held his breath, attempting to force back some of the excruciating pain that engulfed him. But it failed miserably as his eyes turned into liquid pools of agony.

In the midst of this blind chaos, his vision, what remained of it was nothing more than a haze of unfocused confusion. Jack blinked his eyes furiously in a futile attempt to locate his female assailant.

Though plagued by an indistinguishable world of distortions, Jack could sense movement. Knowing she was near, every nerve in his body was aware of her threatening presence. In anticipation of another blow, he struggled to find his attacker.

While still on the brink of unconsciousness, he was virtually defenseless as another vicious blow cracked against his rib cage. Before he knew what was happening, the next brutal strike smashed against his right shoulder.

In a defensive reflex, Jack curled into a tight ball, trying to protect himself from the next life-threatening assault. So vulnerable to attack, he realized if he were to sustain another severe blow to the head he would lose consciousness and most likely never awaken again.

In his semi-blind state, with everything confusing and clouded around him, Jack was attacked with two more strikes to the ribs. Adrenalin-provoked strength, only born from shock and panic began to shut out the pain. Dissipating as if he were being covered with some sort of defensive, self-protecting numbness.

Though Jack's pulse pounded relentlessly in his ears, distorted fragments of sound slowly evolved into disembodied voices and laughter. The deafening roar that drilled through his skull was now so intense, that the vague, hollow voices seemed distant as if reverberating from another dimension.

Shattered and bemused by the onslaught, he was not clear headed enough to understand anything. The distorted words entered his mind as nonsense. Fighting to regain control of his faculties, Jack tried to concentrate and make sense of what was being said.

All of a sudden, he began to recognize Laura's voice as she viciously shouted. The girl was still consumed in an uncontrollable fury as she violently cursed him. Along with the clarity of voices his vision began to return.

Everything was drifting in and out of focus. Through his delirium, the shapes and images surrounding him seemed to melt into one another. Like circling vultures, the figures hovering above were just shadows, silhouettes without detail.

Jack blinked his eyes against his dizziness, trying to focus on the distorted images that looked upon him. Then, with sickening clarity, the blurred shapes became more distinct, forming into faces.

As his sight began to jell back into focus, the room slowly came back into view. Bringing with it the menacing image of the girl standing above him. Backlit by the shallow lantern light, the girl's silhouette possessed a fiendish maliciousness.

Looking up at her, Jack could not help but notice the dementia that dwelled in her eyes. Her glare did not have the vaguest concern for the pain and agony she had just inflected.

Jack watched with unbelievable intensity as the girl stalked from above. She appeared to be teetering on the edge of some sort of psychological abyss. If the woman was not totally insane before, she had definitely crossed that line tonight.

Without warning, Jones violently yanked Jack from the floor by his restrained wrists. Sharp shafts of pain tore through Jack's arms as the sickening rip of muscles threatened to shred from their sockets.

Just as Jones released his fierce grip, Jack was overwhelmed as a wave of vertigo besieged him. The room began to spin and tilt crazily in a whirlpool of distorted images. Instinctively, he wanted to reach out and grab something for balance. But to his dismay, his cuffed hands were unable to respond. Fighting to maintain balance, his efforts were all for not as the cabin continued to spin violently. As if entering a drunken blackout, he became lost in a nauseous dizziness that sent him collapsing back to the floor.

After crashing to the ground, Jack immediately tried to struggle his way onto his knees. It seemed to take a Herculean effort, but he got to his knees, then to his feet. Once standing upright, he weaved for a moment as another wave of vertigo hit him. Holding his breath, Jack stared straight ahead as he gradually began to regain his bearings.

With a throbbing in his head that matched the beating of his heart, the muscles in Jack's face tightened against his agony. Physically debilitated, he sensed his pain much more now than he did a moment ago.

Jack's left eye had swollen shut so fast, that it felt as if it were ready to implode inside the socket. A lump of rage lodged in Jack's throat as drops of blood dripped from his face and splattered on the floor.

Not sure if it was blood or the inner fluid of a ruptured eye, the prospect of blindness enthralled him. Jack quivered with revulsion as the crimson liquid oozed from his eye. In pure anger he turned his hazy stare toward the man in the white coat. It was Dr. Simone's ruthless glare that sent all of Jack's worst apprehensions into perspective.

Looking deep within the man's dark, intimidating eyes he caught sight of an evil that was terrifying. Jack now realized that Dr. Simone had no respect for human life. It was obvious, that he would kill someone, or give the order to kill with no second thoughts.

Just then, he felt the cold hand of death clutching and squeezing at his soul. Jack's hopes of surviving the night were rapidly fading. For he was fairly positive, that there was a high probability of never seeing the light of day again.

"I don't want to be here all night, so let's get on with it." The Doctor's demeanor had an essence of urgency and malice.

As Jack absorbed the Doctor's comment, he glanced at Jones who leered back with menacing intent. Like a mercenary awaiting his marching orders, Jones stood patiently, arms crossed casually over his chest. Jack studied the big thug and noticed a curious bulge in his leather jacket. In that stomach-turning moment, he knew it was a gun, most likely a weapon to be used on him.

As if responsive to Jacks thoughts, Jones unzipped his jacket and revealed the blue-steel revolver tucked in his pants. Pulling the high caliber pistol out, Mr. Jones eased it up in Jack's direction.

Eyes fixed upon the gun, Jack took a tentative step backward. The gun gave him a glimpse of what his adversaries actually intended. The truth of the matter could not be avoided, Jack's vision of doom had just escalated. Without a doubt in his mind, he fully expecting to be shot and cut down right where he stood.

Jones gave him a sneer of anticipation as the Doctor moved in behind him. With the twist of a small key and the soft click from the cuffs, he was released from his temporary bondage.

Once the handcuffs were removed, Jack immediately raised

his hand to the battered side of his face. Slightly grimacing, his shaking fingers roamed across the open gash that extended from the corner of his eye.

Puffed up with self-inflicted egotism, the Doctor crossed back in front of Jack. "Like I said before, you've been a royal pain in the ass. It's time to settle things once and for all."

Without warning, he backhanded Jack across the face with his closed fist. The blow sent Jack's head twisting violently to the side. Instantaneously, the Doctor followed with another blow to the midsection.

Robbed of breath, Jack gasped and fell to his hands and knees. Vision blurred with tears, Jack's reality began to blur with it. Once again on the verge of unconsciousness, he struggled for some air that would not soon come.

Jack's face went numb as blood gushed from his nose and eye. With his lips in a direct path of the running blood, the coppery taste of crimson now swam throughout his mouth.

"I think you've worn out your welcome." The Doctor's voice was sharp like a knife as it sliced through Jack's pain.

In spite of his dilemma, a short-lived chuckle escaped from his lips. "This is some kind of welcome, Doc." Jack continued, knowing his words just might lead to more pain - if not death. "Your idea of hospitality really sucks asshole."

Instead of responding, the Doctor gave Jones a nod of his head. Mr. Jones viciously grabbed Jack by the hair and pulled him to his feet. Jack was barely able to stand upright as the muscles in his stomach were knotted and strained.

The Doctor gestured with his head toward the door. "Get him the hell out of here!"

Jones nodded in agreement. "Let's go." Motioning with his gun, he directed Jack toward the door. "You belong to me now, Jack."

Barely able to keep his legs under him, Jack proceeded with what little strength he had left.

"Jack," Dr. Simone's voice catching him halfway to the door.

Jack stopped, slowly turned and directed his attention toward the Doctor.

The Doctor's ruthless eyes seemed to glow like the eyes mounted on the walls. "Welcome to my world, Jack." Then, in an almost sincere if not disarming tone, the Doctor finished the conversation. "I hope our little get-together was as much fun for you as it was for me."

With a death grip latched to his arm, Jones led the blurry-eyed, punch-drunk Jack out the front door.

CHAPTER 8

ONCE THE CABIN DOOR closed behind Jack and Mr. Jones, Dr. Simone turned toward his daughter. A sharp, deep line appeared between his brows. Although his displaced anger was taken out on Jack, the Doctor's initial fury lie with his daughter. Unbeknownst to Laura, her father was about to act upon his displeasure cold-bloodedly and decisively.

"You've pushed my patients for the last time, Girl!" There was nothing pleasant or loving in the Doctor's tone.

Laura let out a snort of rebellion. It was a dismissive, retched noise that emerged from the depths of her soured throat.

"Did you really think you could escape?" His point was clear there was no need to elaborate.

Laura turned her head, ignoring him.

Insofar as his daughter was concerned, Dr. Simone knew that she was unreliable. A contingency he could easily do without. She could put his whole operation in jeopardy and that could not be allowed.

Noticeably irritated, her father exhaled impatiently. "Don't turn your head away from me! When I ask you a question…You damn well better answer me!"

Laura remained defiant and silent.

It annoyed the Doctor to no end that she refused to respond. "Answer me, damn-it!"

Still filled with aggression and adrenaline from her assault on Jack, she lashed back. "Don't threaten me! I know what you are! I know what you can do!" But even Laura could not predict what was about to happen.

The girl's caustic tone quickly broke the Doctor's patience. Despising the rebellious behavior, the resentment on his face became plainly clear. Dr. Simone's demeanor turned ice-cold and his eyes darkened as he crossed the room toward her.

Then and there, Laura instantly knew she had overstepped her bounds. She could clearly see the danger that now existed in her father's stare. Immediately concerned, her expression of defiance now took on an expectant wariness of what was about to happen.

Without the smallest shred of human decency, the Doctor slapped his daughter across the face with the flat of his hand. Laura let out a penetrating scream that cut through the night's silence. All six eyes widened in anger, her nostrils flared as a fine trickle of blood ran down from her nose.

Laura responded with a fierce dose of hatred and spite. "You bastard! One day I'll get mine. I'll kill you if it's the last thing I ever do!"

Without warning, Dr. Simone struck again. With the back of a closed fist, he landed squarely along-side his daughter's cheek and jaw.

Head snapping sideway, she let out another blood-curdling scream. Laura began to say something, but her father's threatening stare rendered her silent. Though wanting to unleash the extent of her rage, she dared not to utter a word. But the truth was in her eyes.

"I don't want to hear another word." Her father's hard voice indicating there was not to be any further discussion. "I've tolerated all I can handle out of you. As far as I'm concerned, I no longer have any use for you."

Void of all compassion or concern, Dr. Simone's features began to take on cruel angles. Eyes cold and dark, he looked at his daughter as a lower than life form.

Grabbing his daughter by the collar of her t-shirt, he yanked his mutated offspring toward him. Incensed, the Doctor's wrath escalated as he slammed her against the wall.

Laura quickly realized that her feet were not touching the ground. With little effort at all, her father had lifted her off the floor. With a clinch-fisted stranglehold on her shirt collar, their faces were now just an inch apart. As Laura's enormous sets of eyes pleaded in genuine fear, her previous anger turned into instant terror.

"Please don't hurt me, Daddy." It was a frightful plea.

The Doctor's eyes radiated pure anger. Though he tried to control himself, he quickly lost it. "Pain is the only thing you seem to understand! You refuse to respond to anything else." While his daughter's feet flailed about searching for the floor, the Doctor proceeded to slam her into the wall.

As Laura's head bounced off the cabin wall, an expression of inescapable torment shadowed her face. Clinching a handful of her hair Dr. Simone jerked Laura's head back, pinning her between himself and the wall. "I treat you far better than the others...And you thank me by trying to escape?" Voice hard, intensity on high, he continued. "You disrespect me, mock me... I've got news for you little girl. I'm going to hurt a lot more than your feelings this time. Your chance to kill me just came and went."

The Doctor watched the horror grow in her eyes as he reared back his fist. There was a kind of macabre satisfaction in his face as he struck her again. The force of the blow caused Laura to fall to the ground. Cowering on the floor, her arms covered her face in self-defense.

Dr. Simone took tremendous pleasure in his ruthless acts. The feeling that flowed through his veins was one of pure pleasure and dominance. The sight of his daughter in agony only heightened his desire to inflict more pain. Holding back nothing, he kicked the helpless girl in the ribcage.

Clutching her side, Laura screamed pitifully in response to the excruciating pain. The cry she let loose was much more than a plea, it was a prayer. But her pleas of mercy seemed to fall upon deaf ears. The girl's hurtful cries meant nothing to the man standing over her.

Possessing only an untamed, ruthless violence within, the Doctor's brutality knew no bounds. Dr. Simone was far too immersed in his abuse to care about the pain he was inflicting.

There was no love or understanding in the Doctor's make-up. He was not a caring father by any stretch of the imagination. There was no paternal instinct that tugged at his heart while listening to his daughter's frantic cries. There was no guilt or resentment for what he had just done or was about to do. Dr. Simone knew exactly what he was and he embraced that fact.

With a discouraging sigh, the Doctor looked at his daughter and shook his head in disgust. There was no display of compassion toward the girl on the floor. Only regret and anger at the knowledge that she was of his own flesh and blood.

Allowing only the look of indulgence to register on his face, the beating of his only child continued. The effects of the Doctor's viciousness were quickly apparent as Laura's screams turned to ragged gasps. Ribs broken, face swollen and bruised, she was almost unrecognizable as blood streamed from her nose and mouth.

In an attempt to avoid another attack, she slid across the floor retreating into the corner of the room. Terrified and trembling, back pressed against the wall, Laura squeezed into the corner like a trapped animal. Tears flowing steadily, she looked up into her father's merciless eyes. Quivering violently, she pressed her knees against her chest and wrapped her arms around her drawn legs. Fingernails digging into her forearms, she rocked back and forth like a traumatized child.

Arms folded, Dr. Simone glared down at his distraught daughter. Revulsion consumed his thoughts as he watched the pitiful creature sobbing and cringing on the floor. It unnerved him to be in the presence of such a neurotic display of emotions. The Doctor had no time or patience for this kind of nonsense.

With her face stained with tears and blood, Laura's liquid eyes were locked on her father. "Please don't!" Voice trembling as she frantically attempted to plead her distress. "Please don't hurt me anymore!"

More than scared, her terror was a fixity in her stare as her father crouched down in front of her. Bringing his gaze level with hers, he peered angrily into her horrified stare.

Sobbing uncontrollably, Laura tried to shrink deeper into the corner, wrapping herself into a fetal knot. As she fought to speak, her words just trembled over one another. Producing only chocking noises as she frantically begged for mercy.

Dr. Simone put up a hand in a gesture for her to stop her feverish babbling. "Shut up! Put it to rest!"

Laura was incapacitated in fear at the sight of her enraged father. Terrified gooseflesh ravaged her skin as her father's stare burned into her. Incoherently mumbling, Laura pressed a clinched fist against her mouth. Except for her murmurs of distress, the room fell virtually silent.

"Are you through with this pathetic display of weakness?" Asking in a matter-a-fact tone. "You're weak, girl! You're just like your mother...You always have been...You always will be."

Laura's bottom lip twitched nervously. When she tried to repress a sob, it involuntarily burst from her lips with wretched force. In instant panic, she feverishly shuttered in an attempt to strangle her sobs down in her throat. Gradually, her sobs diminished into a throaty, spasmodic quake.

The immediate danger in the Doctor's eyes gradually dissipated. Though his eyes were hard, they did not display the coldness they had before. It was as if he was showing a small amount of sympathy toward the battered girl.

Laura remained huddled within herself, whimpering, rocking

back and forth in a jerky motion. Averting her eyes from his, she tried to hide her intensely wounded look.

Dr. Simone extended his hand toward his daughter's trembling body. Frenzied with panic, Laura threw up her hands protectively. Without hesitation, the Doctor attempted to grab his daughter's arm and pull her from the floor.

Cringing from his touch, the girl's multiple eyes went wild. In fear for her life, she shoved at his hand and tried to jerk away. Refusing to be touched, she twisted and struggled to escape his grasp. Breaking free from his stronghold, she cowered back into the corner curling up into a ball.

Frustrated, Dr. Simone ignored her feeble gesture and reached for her again. Glaring at his daughter with a vacant, unpredictable stare, he took hold of her upper arm and yanked her from the corner. Exhausted of all patience, Dr. Simone dragged the girl's kicking and screaming body across the cabin floor. Latching his right hand around her throat, he pulled Laura to her feet, then viciously pushed her down into the chair.

Letting out a startled cry, Laura crashed backwards into the old, wooden chair. Eyes riveted upon her father, she gathered up her legs and pressed her stunned body into the seat.

"Don't move! Keep your worthless butt in the chair!"

Drawing in a labored breath that came in jerks, she answered in a hushed, lifeless voice, "Yes, Daddy."

The glowing flicker from the lantern played off Laura's frightened eyes. She could never escape from her father's inhuman and tyrannical abuse - and she knew it. T-shirt ripped and wet with blood, Laura fought the need to cry.

Dr. Simone's attitude suddenly changed, now appearing exceedingly calm. Leaning forward, he put his cold, clammy hand to his daughter's cheek.

Although knowing that this moment of physical affection was all a façade, Laura forced herself not to pull away from her father's nauseating touch.

After a vain attempt at compassion toward his mutated daughter, the Doctor took a step back.

"That's my girl," his voice now tender and apologetic.

It was all Laura could do to meet her father's stare. Breathing deeply and erratically, she tried to compose herself. Upon calming somewhat, she brought forth a reluctant smile.

The mind-set of the Doctor had always made him a very dangerous man. As far as reality was concerned, it was just a fanciful game in which he manipulated all the pieces. Control meant everything, it was his lifeblood. And any resistance toward his quest for control and dominance was to be eliminated - no questions asked.

From within the Doctor, resonated a diabolical ruthlessness that went beyond the borders of madness. But, in his twisted mind, he was not a madman at all. Just a man that was willing to commit any crime. A ruthless shot-caller that would do whatever it took to protect his deplorable agenda.

Dark, cold and numb, nothing but ice flowed through this man's sadistic veins. Unlike a majority of psychopaths, he created and pursued his objectives with such disregard that it put all other lunatics to shame. The Doctor possessed no conscious, his very survival was based on his ruthlessness. At his best, he was the essence of evil, and in that lay the Doctor's power.

The more Dr. Simone considered what he had to do, the more impassioned he became. Reaching into his side coat pocket, he pulled out a gun. A pitiless, cynical smile teased the corners of his mouth as he directed the revolver at his daughter.

"Goodbye, Laura." It was a simple, irreversible message.

Dr. Simone had no reservations whatsoever as his index finger pulled the trigger.

CHAPTER 9

WITH THE BLUE-STEELED PISTOL in his right hand, Mr. Jones pushed Jack out the cabin into the threshold of the night. The temperature had dropped several degrees as it approached the freezing mark. The chilled mountain air slapped Jack in the face, driving away some of the lingering grogginess. As the freezing night took hold, his breath quickened and short puffs of frozen breath dispelled from his lips.

Weak-kneed and still partially disoriented, Jack struggled to shake-off his previous encounter with the Doctor. Nerves pushed to their limit, he crossed the meadow. The once tall grass, now wrapped around his ankles as the force of the mounting wind pushed it against the ground.

Swallowing hard, Jack began to tense up in panic as they continued to follow a path toward the woods. Momentarily, he felt light-headed as a sensation of morbid helplessness flooded through him. A feeling he had never known before and one he had no power over. It was as if death was so near he could almost taste it.

Haunted with fearful anticipation a frightening tremor of dread cursed through his soul. Silently, he prayed that somehow fate would swing his way. But deep inside, he knew that it would take some quirk of twisted luck to get out of this morbid ending. For, he had some bleak obstacles to overcome - mainly Jones's gun.

As they drew closer to the forest tree-line, Jack thought he heard Laura scream. For a long, uneasy moment, he mentally shook himself. While trying to convince himself he was hearing things, another blood-curdling scream pierced the night.

The girl's unexpected, merciful protest was unnerving. The screams of terror caused Jack to stop dead in his tracks and look back toward the cabin.

In that brief instant, his own dilemma was forgotten. While focused on the desperate screams that resided within the cabin, an instant image arose in his mind's eye. An image of the deranged Doctor viciously beating down his only daughter.

Impervious to the tortured screams, Jones continued to press the business end of the gun into the small of Jack's back. "Let's go!" Jones demanded, pushing Jack forward. "What's happening to Laura is nothing compared to what I have in store for you."

Jack found himself mesmerized in despair as they reached the end of the clearing. There was no light at the end of this tunnel, only the darkness beyond the tree-line.

The urge to escape was overwhelming. But, he was trapped in a scenario where his slightest move could result in the gravest of repercussions. Jack knew he could not out-run Jones's bullets, but the desperate urge to flee was there just the same.

As if reading his mind, Jones broke the stressful silence. "Don't try anything stupid, Jack. I've killed before and I'll blow ya away and not lose a second sleep over it."

Though completely unprepared for what might lay ahead, the frantic impulse to run was not an option. Jack grimly accepted the fact that there was no plan of escape even remotely tempting. The reality was, even if there was a plan, there was no strength left in his body for such an attempt.

Suddenly, out of nowhere, two gun shots rang out, followed by an eerie silence. The shock of the gunfire was numbing, sending a frozen rope of alarm rushing through Jack's veins. With sickening certainty, he knew that something tragic and final had just taken place back at the cabin.

Jack had to remind himself to breath as Jones pushed him into the dark tree-line. Just as their intermittent footsteps passed the first line of trees, the moon revealed itself from behind a veil of clouds.

As the moon slipped between clouds, the sky began to glow, shedding some clarity throughout the darkened woods. With the forest partially illuminated, thousands of eerie outlines and ghostly shadows filled Jack's vision.

As shafts of moonlight filtered past the swaying branches overhead, the woods all of a sudden came to life. Like phantom shapes looming in a bad dream, the medley of shadows flickered, then, vanished. Just a barrage of disjointed images passing through one another, then, abruptly withdrawing back into the black voids from which they came.

Jones's pace and posture was uncompromising as he continued to push Jack forward. They weaved around tree-trunks as the woods gradually began to descend toward a small ravine. The denseness of the forest quickly closed in around them as they maneuvered down the hillside. Not a word was spoken as the two drudged deeper into the woods. Nothing broke the tormenting silence but the wind and the crunch of dead twigs snapping beneath their feet.

As the wind pushed its way through the forest, the surrounding trees seemed to bring forth voices of their own. From the bowels of the woodland, the rustling of overhead branches and underbrush seemed to mimic the drone and murmuring whispers of archaic voices.

All at once, the woods seemed to shrink as a huge passing cloud drifted across the face of the moon. With a blockade of clouds now sheathing the moon, the shadows that once streaked across the forest floor disappeared. With no light to penetrate the trees, the woods surrendered itself to an inky blackness. Without the benefit of moonlight and only half his vision to guide him, the dense forest suddenly became a disorienting obstacle course.

Impatiently, Jones shoved his hostage forward, leading him deeper into the black abyss. Though keeping a chock-hold on his panic, Jack knew what the near future had in store for him. Escorted by a gun, he found himself on an uncertain path that would ultimately lead him to his final destination.

Drifting into a state of disgruntled helplessness, the events that were transpiring took on a vague, unreal quality. Jack's mind went into overdrive as he began to visualize what would soon take place. An image of his dead body lying in a pool of blood on the cold, dark forest floor was imprinted in his mind.

The further they ventured into the woods, the darker his chances of living seemed to become. Though the longing for escape still burned within, Jack's face was completely drained of hope. Conceding to the fact that the end was almost upon him. While devoured in visions of death, the next sightless step he took proved to be unforgiving.

Jack's foot became entangled in a fallen tree branch, sending him sprawling to the ground. Rolling to his side, his body unexpectedly began to slide. Jack had rolled over the edge of a steep drop-off. The decline of the hillside was almost straight down as he began sliding and tumbling uncontrollably. After several spine-crunching barrel-rolls through the brush and thicket, he slammed into a huge granite boulder.

Jack's features were pain-ridden as he laid there next to the massive rock. With a muffled grunt, he sat up next to the boulder. While allowing himself a moment to regroup, he took a painful inventory of the new injuries.

In the seconds that followed, the fear of impending doom disappeared. Jack realized, he had just pushed the fringes of death and survived. The promise of his imminent demise had been postponed. Now, the idea of escape was a possibility.

There was one thing for certain, if he did not seize this opportunity to escape, there would be no other. There was no time to waste, he had just obtained the few seconds he needed to get away.

Somehow, I've got to get out of here? Silently evaluating his new circumstances.

Knowing that Jones was somewhere right behind him, Jack experienced a brief twinge of uncertainty. Like an animal on the run, he was a target being hunted. Jack was now elusive prey, trying to avoid an untimely and undeserving departure from this world.

If he wanted to survive, he could not afford to sit still any longer. With Jones on the prowl, it did not take long to figure out his next move. Uphill from the road, his only chance was to head downhill and locate the truck.

Aware of only the need to escape, Jack's features took on the lines of a determined man. With his intent and destination now clear, he pushed himself to his feet. Moving to the edge of the granite boulder, he craned his neck around the outcropping of granite.

Jack studied the darkness for signs, anything that might show the whereabouts of his pursuer. With no one in sight, he took a tentative step forward. Senses alert, Jack slowly and carefully picked his way down the ravine. With no sense of direction, there was no way of telling if he was headed toward danger or safety. Without even a hint of a moon, he continued to creep through the woods on pure instinct.

Jack took the precaution of stopping every few seconds so he could examine his surroundings. Concentrating and listening to the darkness, making himself aware of every sound no matter how slight. Head on a constant swivel, Jack searched the shadows for something he could not see - at least not yet.

"So far, so good," he quietly reassured himself.

For what seemed an eternity, Jack took one uncertain step after another. While hunkering down to avoid some low-hanging branches, the night sounds of chirping crickets unexpectedly stopped. Instantly, the fear of death that he had temporary pushed away rushed through him once again.

Kneeling down in the underbrush, Jack's eye refused to blink as he assessed his surroundings. While his breath dispelled visibly, his vision swept the landscape and his ears listened for any threatening noise.

Knowing something was out there, Jack slowly retreated in a crouch. Straining to be silent, he eased back further into the heavy brush. Squatting down on his haunches, he watched and waited from the confines of his new hiding place.

For several moments, the forest night seemed dark and still. Then, Jack's head jerked toward a sudden sound. Holding his breath, all attention was focused on any movement in the underbrush.

Probing the night, all that could be seen was darkness receding into absurd blackness. While scanning the darkest of shadows, the scar-faced Jones appeared amidst the trees.

Sudden panic told him to make a run for it, but instead, he remained still and silent. Jack's stare was constant on the dark silhouette prowling amongst the trees. While watching his pursuers every movement, the big-man finally disappeared into the darker realms of the forest.

Jack knew, his one hope was to find the river. It was the only landmark that would lead him directly to his truck.

Holding his position a moment longer, his anxious stare scoured the area once again. After taking a good look around in every direction, Jack slipped quickly into the shadows of darkness.

Spurred on by the fact that Jones and the Doctor were somewhere close behind, Jack declared war against the underbrush. Branches snapping in his wake, he moved as fast as he could through the thicket.

Scrambling through the trees, Jack frantically pushed past the out-thrusting limbs. Mindless of the new scrapes and lacerations from the back-lashing branches, he relentlessly pressed on.

Seemingly running lost, weaving in and out of trees, Jack tried to ignore the exhaustion that was sweeping through his legs. Momentarily stumbling, he felt his body quickly weakening. It became painfully apparent, that he could not keep this pace up much longer.

Blinking back tears of exhaustion, he continued to grope recklessly ahead. Jack's harsh, labored breaths roared in his ears as he advanced further down the mountain-side.

While hastily making his way down an unstable section of hillside, the ground gave-way. Losing his footing, Jack fell heavily to the ground. A short-lived scream of pain slipped past his lips as his knee crashed against a sharp protruding rock.

Even before he had a chance to recover from the fall, Jack painfully crawled to the base of a tree. Knowing to stay out of sight, the tree-trunk was used as a shield. Tree-bark hard-pressed against his back, Jack winced in pain. Clutching the throbbing leg, he sat beneath the branches of the giant pine.

Too exhausted to move, he felt he had nothing left. In that moment of defeated emotions, Jack began to think of how easy it would be just to sit there and surrender himself.

Instantly, an inner voice cursed him for thinking of giving up. *Move, damn you! You want to die! You've gotten this far, you can't stop now!*

Jack understood that every moment that passed was one moment closer toward his ruination. Letting the Doctor win was not an option. There was still a shot at freedom and his will was not about to go down without a fight. Getting the hell away from these lunatics was the only priority.

Knowing that Jones was somewhere close, his attention was focused back up the hill. Peering around the tree, Jack looked at everything from all possible angles, then, grudgingly and painfully pushed his ravaged body upright.

Attention now downhill, Jack studied the dark terrain, trying to figure out where to go next. After making a decision, there was no hesitation, he was on the move again.

Jack hitched along clutching his leg. Progression came in spurts as he searched for the path of least resistance. From tree to tree, his only movements were revealed within the darkest of shadows.

Before long, Jack was well down the mountainside. Though the dark forest still stretched out before him, there was the faint hope that anytime there would be some kind of clearing. But, before any type of clearing appeared, the sound of fast-flowing water presented itself.

Filled with a desperate surge of hope, a peculiar kind of excitement fluttered in his stomach. Fending off the insistent darkness, Jack picked up the pace and steered himself toward the sound of the river.

CHAPTER 10

THE FOREST BEGAN TOO thin as the roar of the river became more distinct. All at once, Jack was passing through the last line of trees. After a few eager strides, dirt and gravel crunched beneath his feet, the paved road was close. Instant relief consumed him once he spotted the truck about fifty yards up the road.

Though needing to take advantage of the opportunity, Jack had to be smart. Leaving nothing to chance, it was time to execute every move on the side of caution.

Just a short distance was all that was needed to reach the awaiting truck. But, Jack chose to be safe and retreat back into the tree-line. Ducking down out of view, it became time to listen and watch the forest for any threat of danger.

Not seeing any immediate threat, Jack could not entertain the idea of staying-put. Before his nerves abandoned him altogether, he was up and running. Jack limply ran down the shoulder of the road, fanatically digging for the keys in his pocket.

Once the keys were in hand, it was a race for the driver's door. Watching over his shoulder, he tried to key the lock. Once the lock-latch clicked, Jack jerked open the door. After jumping in, the frigid wind all but slammed the door behind him.

Scrambling to find the ignition, the key-ring slipped and dropped onto the dark floorboard. Reaching down between his legs, Jack frantically searched for the lost keys.

After a feudal attempt to find anything, there was no choice but to turn on the cab light. Upon locating the key-ring, the ignition was engaged and the starter was triggered. As usual, the starter refused to turn-over. Jack tried several more times, pounding on the steering wheel begging the engine to start.

As always, before giving it another try, it was time to let the starter rest for a few seconds. As the starter cooled, he raised his stare to the rearview mirror.

Jack grimaced at the devastation to his face. Staring at his reflection, it was almost impossible to recognize the grotesque image that stared back. Unbelievably, he looked even worse than he felt.

The walking cane had missed his eye by a fraction of an inch. The gash next to his eyebrow lay wide open, revealing the bone. The swelling from the blow had closed his eye into a tiny slit. His forehead and the whole side of his face had already turned dark purple, almost black.

Raising his hand to his face, Jack traced his battered reflection with his fingertips. Leaning closer to the mirror, the severity of the injury became painfully clear.

Using his thumb and forefinger, Jack grit his teeth and pushed apart his swollen eyelids. The image that proceeded revealed a bloody redness that now encased the white of his eye. But, to his great relief, the eye still retained some blurred vision.

Pulling his fingers away from his face, Jack allowed the swollen eyelids to slide back into a slit. Still examining himself, it became very apparent of the beating he received while running through the forest. Cuts and bloodied lacerations covered his face and hands.

Dropping his gaze to the ignition, it was time to try the starter. Turning the key, the starter refused to cooperate once again.

"Come on, Baby...You can do it." Reassuring himself more than the truck.

While relentlessly working the ignition, Jack returned his

attention back to the mirror. Not regarding himself this time, but looking past his reflection into the darkness behind.

Because of the cab light, it was difficult to see anything through the back window. After extinguishing the light, the cab of the truck went dark. Now, vision through all the windows was clear.

Instant horror encased Jack's eye as he looked out the back window. Panicked adrenaline ran rapid as he watched his scar-faced nemeses running up behind him. Instinctively slamming down the door-locks, he immediately turned his attention back to the steering column.

Almost breaking the key, Jack triggered the ignition. The starter continued to fail him. With every attempt to start the truck, the instrument panel illuminated. Adding to Jack's on the spot panic, he noticed the alternator charge was getting low. The battery would be dead very soon.

In an incensed outburst, he began to shout at the uncooperative truck. "Come on! Come on! Come-oooon!"

Clinging to his last frantic hope, Jack keyed the ignition one more time. From the last bit of energy the battery held, the engine finally turned over. Without a second to spare the truck roared to life.

"Thank you, Jesus!" Uttering a quick prayer of thanks as he shifted into drive.

Just as Jones grabbed the driver's door, Jack stomped on the accelerator. Gunning the engine, dirt and debris flew everywhere as the rear wheels spun and skidded wildly through the gravel.

Jones continued to hold on as Jack accelerated from the shoulder of the road. Sharply cutting the wheel, the truck swung toward the road. Hitting the pavement with the gas-peddle floored, the transition between the dirt shoulder and the pavement jerked Jack back in the seat. As traction from the rear tires dug into the asphalt, Jack leaned into the desperate turn.

Rubber screeched as the tires stuttered sideways across the

pavement. The force of the sharp turn sent Jones flying off the opposite side of the road. The truck spun end-to-end until it faced downhill.

Foot crushed against the accelerator, the truck lurched forward. Not caring what was in his way, Jack plowed straight ahead, leaving Jones and a billowing trail of dust in his wake. Looking in the mirror, he could see no sign of Jones, only a cloud of dust drifting into the forest tree-line.

While turning on the high-beam lights, an unnerving and overwhelming frustration attacked him. It was not only deeply disturbing that he was running for his life, but more infuriating was not knowing the reason why.

Jack checked the mirrors again and saw nothing. But, that did not mean a thing. From what he had just experienced, Jack knew these guys were relentless. In fact, at that very moment, they could be fast on his heels.

As the dark terrain unrolled before him, all attention was glued to the roads vanishing point just beyond the headlights. Focused on getting away, the truck raced down the winding road.

After some hard driving and numerous turns, Jack let out a quick sigh of relief. After calming somewhat, sudden elation set in, enough jubilation to make him laugh. Feeling lucky to be alive, Jack's brutalized face began to shine. Praising his previous efforts, the exhilaration of escaping gave him a sense of triumph all its own.

"I did it! I made it!" Rejoicing as more distanced was put between himself and his pursuers.

While celebrating in his mind, something appeared in the driver-side mirror. Once again, his worst fear came to life. Behind him, a light shimmered against the black moonless sky. With a quick look over his shoulder, all fears where verified. There was definitely another pair of headlights coming down the hill.

Jack sped up as his vision darted from mirror to mirror.

Pushing the truck as fast as possible, he watched the pursuing headlights fade in and out around the twisting turns.

With unnerving certainty, the realization that he was being chased took hold. Instantly, the thought of not making it out of the forest alive reentered his mind. As Jack sped forward, his mind fought through a dozen scenarios. Each one, more terrifying and sickening than the other.

Racing through a long curve, it was apparent that the van had rapidly closed the gap between them. As the vehicle grew larger in the mirror, Jack noticed that it was a white van.

Quickly closing in, the pair of headlights now had Jack fixed in its sights. With no other route for escape, there was no other option than to follow the snaking road straight down to the freeway.

To Jack's dismay, all aspects of what was about to take place on this deserted road would go unnoticed to the rest of the world. Now, he was just a desperate man that had no choice but to take desperate measures. Just like that, it was all a matter of getting away. Driven by fear and the overwhelming desire to survive, it became time to do something evasive - and fast.

No longer concerned with any aspect of safe driving, Jack drove with reckless abandoned. Hastily accelerating, he descended the steepest portion of the hill. Like a bat out-of-hell, the truck rocketed down the decline gaining speed as it entered into a sharp curve. The tires screamed and smoked as the truck rounded the corner. In a high-speed slide, the headlights seem to bounce through the turn.

Jack began talking to the truck as if it would help keep it under control. "Stay with me, Baby! Hang in there!" Barely missing the trees that lined the side of the road.

Tapping the brakes while wrestling the steering-wheel, the truck finally straightened out. Regaining control, Jack proceeded to streak down the abandoned two-lane road.

The speedometer continued to climb as Jack frantically stared through the bug-splattered windshield. Weaving lane to lane, he fought without success to shake his pursuers.

Quickly filling the rearview mirror, the white van was right on his tail. It was a hell-of-a-lot faster than Jack anticipated. It was gaining precious yards. Yards he could not afford to give away.

The van's grill was now just a few feet from the truck's bumper. Its headlights burned straight through the rear window. The light beams blasted into the cab of the truck, imposing a blinding reflection in the mirrors.

Squinting into the rearview mirror, Jack watched the lights lunge ahead and hit the back of the truck. It was a minor collision, but effective just the same.

The van fell back about ten feet, then, sped forward. Once again, the van was on him, slamming into the truck. Jack's head whip lashed back and his stomach rushed up into his throat as the truck lunged forward. Almost out-of control, the rear tires began to side-slip and fishtail.

Brakes were unacceptable now it was time to take his escape tactics to the extreme. Just as the van attempted to smash the rear bumper for a third time, he stomped the gas pedal. The truck jumped forward, just in time to pull away from the van's grill.

Driving only by instinct, Jack jetted hell-bent down the deserted road. Barreling through the dead of night so fast, the headlights made little difference. Though barely able to see ten feet ahead, the truck continued to increase in speed. As the two cars shot down the hill, the curves became sharper and steeper. Jack careened around the hairpin turns at three times the posted speed.

The tires spun and screeched violently as the truck side-slipped dangerously through the turns. The protesting tires screamed for traction, but letting up on the accelerator was not an option.

Repeatedly checking the mirrors, Jack watched as the van screeched around the corners right behind him. With the raging waters of the river on his left and the thick forest hugging the road to his right, Jack raced insanely down the mountain.

With the truck's speedometer reading sixty, Jack flew into a twenty mile-per-hour turn. Realizing the vehicle would not make the curve at that speed, he hit the brakes. But it was too late. The truck began to skid, seemingly gaining speed as it slid across the pavement. Jack released the brake and tried to steer his way out of trouble.

Sliding through the turn out-of-control, the truck spun three-hundred-sixty degrees. No longer in control, Jack held his breath in anticipation of sure disaster.

CHAPTER 11

BRACED FOR THE WORST, Jack waited for some sort of impact. With a death grip on the steering wheel, locked arms pushed him back against the seat.

Trapped in a moment of unreality, the cab of the truck began to tip. Jack felt everything lifting as gravity took over and tilted the truck vertically upon the driver-side wheels.

As the truck began to tip over, Jack's body was forced against the driver door. In that split-second, the ground outside his window came up in a rush.

In a grinding crunch, the truck fell to its side on the pavement. As it half-skidded on its side, the incredible bone-scratching sound of grinding metal shuddered through the body of the truck. Jack pushed against the door panel and held on for dear life. Then, just like that, it happened.

Shockingly, the road disappeared and the truck went airborne. There was an immediate and bleak silence as Jack's world began to spin crazily. Instant horror shifted all perception into slow motion as everything that was not fastened down flew wildly throughout the cab. Jack's face was a petrified mask of terror as the truck flipped violently through the air.

Clutching the door-panel with one hand, the other pressed against the headliner. All vision had been reduced to a spinning unreality. Preparing for impact, Jack was about to pay the price for his reckless driving.

There was an ear-splitting rip of steel as the truck came

crashing back to the ground. Upon impact, Jack's head and shoulder slammed into the side window. Every muscle and bone absorbed punishment as his body pin-balled crazily inside the cab.

The horrendous sound of tortured metal accompanied the vehicle as it rocketed off the side of the road. In a high-speed roll, the truck's momentum hurled itself down the embankment toward the river.

Pieces of metal and plastic flew in every direction as the truck hit the surface of the river's black waters. Landing on the rear corner-panel, it crashed down onto the driver door. The hair-raising chase had come to a hard pounding halt. With a final metallic groan, the truck came to rest on its side.

Jack had no idea how many times the truck had rolled, it was relief enough that the bone-jarring ride was over. With the truck lying on its side, Jack hung precariously sideways in space. Partially wedged between the door and the steering wheel he found himself suspended by the safety belt.

After a couple of disoriented seconds, Jack came far enough out of his daze to understand where he was. Though surrounded in darkness, the intense roaring that invaded his ears was not from the impact of the crash. But rather, the rushing waters that pounded against the truck. Jack was trapped in a distorted and sideways world beneath the surface of the river.

Though severely damaged, the truck's windshield had somehow remained intact. Barely penetrating the black rushing waters, the headlights faced against the thunderous current. Jack looked on in amazement as half the windshield was submerged a few feet beneath the surface, while the other half was being bombarded by a crushing wall of surface water.

Endless waves of raging water slammed savagely into the passenger side windshield. Jack was jolted out of his shock-like state by the sudden sound of creaking and scrapping metal. The ghastly noise was continuous as the submerged side of the truck began to shift against the river bottom.

The incredible force of the merciless current pushed the truck further and further toward its roof. Still strapped into the safety belt, Jack fell forward as the cab rolled entirely upside down.

Caught in the fast moving current, the truck began to move again. With a nonstop metallic grinding, the roof slowly slid over the rocks and debris on the bottom of the river.

Finding a deeper portion of the dark waters, the truck was quickly swallowed by the remorseless river. While hanging from his restraint, Jack could feel himself sinking as the truck drifted further down into the dark depths. Completely submerged, several feet below the surface, the truck finally came to rest - up-side-down. No longer moving along the rocky bottom, Jack realized he was now a prisoner beneath the freezing waters.

Though the headlights no longer burned, the dashboard lights were still illuminated. In the dim light that radiated from the instrument panel, the sight that ensued filled him with pure terror.

It could have only been a couple of seconds, but to Jack, the moment seemed to linger forever as the black water began ascending from beneath.

The icy river quickly found its way through the nooks and crannies of the dashboard and door panels. Without delay, the freezing water began to fill the cab. Now that the truck was totally submerged, it would be only a matter of seconds before the cab would be completely flooded.

While hanging there struggling to free himself, the water level rapidly rose up toward Jack's face. Under the deluge of freezing water, he frantically fought the safety harness. At that instant, nothing mattered beyond the need to escape.

When the frigid water touched his head, a freezing sting began biting at his scalp. Pain cut into his face as the water rushed up to his chin. The muscles in Jack's face began to knot and his scalp burned with cold agony as he desperately tried to keep his head above water.

As the seatbelt cut into his waist, he took a desperate breath just before the water climbed above his chin. Jack ducked his head into the inky water, frantic to release himself.

Knowing the water level was rising fast, he raised his mouth to steal one more breath. After gulping some air, it was time to go back down beneath the bitter-cold water.

Head and shoulders totally immersed, Jack continued to attack the safety belt. While underwater, the windshield began to pop against the force of the river's powerful current. A long horizontal crack now split the center of the window. Then, came a series of pops as fractured lines embedded the glass.

Mesmerized by the sight, he watched as the windshield splintered into a spider web of cracks. With clinched teeth, Jack unleashed a scream of terror as the splintered windshield blew out in front of him..

The implosion of glass was immediately followed by a crushing wall of water. Jack's breath was sucked from his lungs as the freezing-cold river encased the cab of the truck. After that, there was only a frozen blackness that momentarily paralyzed him.

The cold shock was much worse than even his imagination could comprehend. Every inch of his body was instantly saturated with several degrees of searing pain. Skin screaming with unrelenting agony, the freezing water reached through his clothes and pierced the flesh. Like a million burning needles stabbing all at once, the continuous ice-cold pounding ravaged his body.

In total sensory deprivation, Jack could not move, every part of his body was physically rebelling against the obscene cold. Though his frozen body screamed in protest, Jack knew if he were to survive, it was time to find some air.

Lungs aching for its next breath, the fear of death and

panicked adrenaline worked like a narcotic throughout his body. The strange numbness enabled Jack to summon enough strength to fight through the extreme cold.

From the force and volume of water entering the cab, Jack's body became weightless and began to lift. With all tension now freed from the safety belt, it was possible to locate and release the latch mechanism. Scrambling and feeling his way around, Jack struggled blindly, desperately searching for a place to take another breath.

Totally disoriented beneath the blackest of water, finding the water's surface was all guess-work. In a frantic attempt to reorient himself, Jack pressed his hand in front of his mouth and blew out. What air was left in his lungs, bubbled and ran up his forearm - he was facing the bottom of the river.

Using the locked steering wheel to maneuver, Jack spun around and pushed himself upward. In a frenzied effort to locate some air, his head smashed against the floorboard.

In an attempt to keep his face against the floor of the truck, Jack reached behind the dashboard. After grabbing a handhold of wiring for leverage, an air-pocket was finally found.

The smell of hot oil and gas filled the small pocket of air. Overriding the sound of the rushing river, were his own desperate gasps for air. Stinging gooseflesh covered his entire body as the near frozen water continued to burn into his flesh. With every frantic gasp of air, Jack screamed and cursed the numbing cold.

Every second the arctic water hammered against his body, the faster hypothermia set in. Jack would never again imagine Hell as being a hot, flaming furnace. It quickly became obvious, that Hell was actually freezing cold, little by little, sucking the life right out of you.

Unwilling to surrender to the frozen monster that was about to devour him, Jack understood there was no time for weakness. There was only time for one last shot at life.

Jack's breath quickened into short, sharp gasps as he prepared for one last breath. A second later, the water level rushed passed his face. Just before his face went under, he filled his lungs with what might be the last breath he would ever take.

The cab of the truck was now completely encased with water. There was no more air. All that could be done was hold his breath and find a way out.

The only escape route was through the shattered windshield. Jack pulled himself back down toward the roof. Even in the faint glow from the dash-lights, everything was dark and distorted. Virtually blind, he blinked back the icy waters and reached for freedom.

Intact shards of glass cut into his fingers and palms as he reached around the dashboard and gripped the rim of the windshield. Jack pulled and maneuvered to a position in which there would be a chance at escape. .

Torturously pressing against the unyielding current, Jack tried to pull himself through the opening where the windshield once had been. But, as if in an effort to deny his freedom, the mammoth power of the river relentlessly forced him back inside his soon-to-be coffin.

Hands embedded with glass, Jack pulled himself into a position where his knee was on the back of the steering wheel. In a war against the resistance, every bit of leverage was pushed against the current. Almost depleted of strength, he finally worked his way out.

Upon abandoning the cab, Jack grabbed the fender-well with one hand and reached for the undercarriage with the other. But, before reaching the next handhold, the monster current snatched him up and launched him downstream.

CHAPTER 12

LOST IN THE BLACKNESS of the rushing waters, Jack was at the mercy of the rivers current. As if incensed at the successful escape, the river's fury seemed to intensify.

What air remained in his lungs, burst from his body upon an unexpected impact with a huge boulder.

Jack's features became angst-ridden as searing pain ran through his arm and ribs. The river increased its attack as the deluge of bottom feeding current held him beneath the surface. Crazily, Jack tumbled and spun along the floor of the river, repeatedly bouncing off and slamming into submerged boulders.

In terrified anticipation of his next certain collision with another of the river's obstacles, Jack screamed a mental prayer. *Please let me breath! Please let me get to the surface!*

Just as the plea was finished, he was caught in a massive flow of water that angled upward. Following the course of least resistance, the rushing current raced up the side of another giant rock toward the river's surface. Like a giant hand reaching down from above, the vicious current jetted his body upward.

As if shot out of a cannon, his body exploded through the water's surface. Jack briefly flew wildly through the air, then, came splashing back into the freezing rapids.

The river threw the two-hundred pound man around like a rag doll. Water shot up his nostrils and into his lungs while gasping for breath. Coughing and chocking, Jack thrashed his arms about in a feeble attempt to keep his head above the surface.

Caught-up in an uncontrollable swim, the vindictive river consistently forced him back underwater. Each time he broke back through the surface, Jack gagged-up river water while battling for another breath.

Summoning what strength was left, he braved the raging waters. Though in near shock from the frozen beating heaved upon him, Jack continued to fight for control of his body.

After a few more misery-filled moments, the supremacy of the river began to recede. Now, as the current slowed, he gradually obtained the ability to control his movements. Finally able to ride the current, Jack inched closer to the river's edge.

All of a sudden, he could hear the threatening roar of another section of rough water. Despite a body that was stiff and basically useless, he urgently amplified all efforts to reach the riverbank.

Upon reaching the calmer waters, Jack was finally able to get a foot-hold on the river-bottom. With each step nearer toward dry land, more of his body emerged from the freezing water.

In just a foot of water, Jack fell to his hands and knees in total exhaustion. Jack's fight against the monster river was over. Breathing fast and shallow, he crawled out of the frozen river.

The all-consuming rush of adrenaline that had just enabled him to defeat the raging waters was now dispersing from his system. Only to be replaced by an escalating piercing agony.

As hypothermia bit deeper into his flesh, excruciating flashes of pain ruptured throughout his body. Wet and shaking uncontrollably, Jack collapsed face first into the embankment.

Legs still in the water, Jack's frozen breath spewed heavily from his mouth while coughing-up the last of the river from his lungs. Shivering miserably, Jack realized he needed to retrieve the remainder of his body out of the bone freezing water. Ignoring the protest of screaming, cramping muscles, he lifted his head from the cold, wet sandbar. Fingers digging through the sand and moss covered rocks, only deep claw-marks were left while dragging himself further onto dry land.

No longer able to move, his head lowered down onto the frozen riverbank. Jack had no clue how far downstream he had traveled and he did not care. All that mattered was that he had somehow survived.

***

Jack moaned in agony as he awoke from a short stint of unconsciousness. Shaking violently, total numbness ravaged his face and hands, As if missing both legs, there was no feeling from the waist down.

An internal alarm within Jack's body went off while regaining his faculties. In a disoriented daze, his eye attempted to focus into the freezing darkness. Barely lifting his head, Jack attempted to survey what immediately surrounded him.

Accompanied by a small sliver of moonlight, an excruciating memory returned as the riverbank became recognizable. The surface of the rocky sandbar was covered with a glistening sheath of frost and ice.

Unaware of how long he had been out, all thoughts were hard-pressed with a sense of urgency. It became imperative to find a place to hide and wait for daylight.

Laying on the riverbank, Jack's body trembled visibly as tremors of frozen misery quaked and shuddered through every inch of flesh. With his muscles rigor-mortis stiff and knotted, it seemed impossible to relax any part of his body.

Against the raw, freezing agony, he tried to push himself up. Watching his hands and fingers shake and twitch uncontrollably, Jack painfully pulled his forearms under him.

A questioning look passed over his face as a sharp, cracking sound accompanied every movement. To Jack's amazement, during unconsciousness, a layer of ice had formed around him. Like the rocks and sandbar, his body and wet clothes were cover in a blanket of ice. Even his hair had frozen into a solid state of disarray. If there was ever such a thing as a human ice-cube, it was him.

While shakily getting to his knees, the sheet of ice that encased him continued to bust loose and fall to the ground. Barely able to produce any physical movement, Jack painfully rubbed his hands together.

Like useless blocks of ice, he was unable to get his fingers to move. Batting his hands together, it was all about removing the numbness from his fingers. After several seconds, his fingers began to tingle with a prickly pain.

The pain assured him that his circulation was coming back. After some feeling returned in his hands, Jack began to concentrate on his lower extremities. While flexing his hands, he slapped and rubbed his stiff and senseless legs.

Though batting his thawing hands against his thighs, there was still no feeling - it was a bad sign. Jack frightfully began to envision that maybe frost-bite had set in. Instant panic assaulted his thoughts as he became strangely afraid that his circulation was gone forever.

Fearful about his legs, Jack slapped and kneaded the muscles in his thighs and calves. For several minutes it was all about a brutal attack on his lower extremities. While still trembling uncontrollably, a tiny fragment of life returned to his unfeeling legs. The tingling sensation started in the thighs, then, spread to his calves.

Within a couple minutes, it was as if a thousand needle-sharp spears were piercing the skin. As the thawing process took hold deeper into the meat of his flesh, the pins-and-needles feeling progressed into an intensified throbbing burn. The pain that was now digging down to the bone was impossible to ignore.

As circulation returned, he began to gasp for air. Not so much gasping for breath, but gasping in a battle not to cry-out against the penetrating torment. Grinding his teeth, he inwardly screamed against the excruciating surge of agony. Finally, after what seemed a lifetime, the stinging burn began to subside.

Though still obsessed with a need to run and hide, his legs required more attention. Jack surveyed the area while trying to jump-start his circulation. After catching sight of a possible hiding-spot, it became time to stand and test his legs.

Like a crippled old man, it was all he could do to partially straighten-up. Hot bursts of shooting pain ran from joint-to-joint as he forced himself into an upright position.

Struggling to stay balanced, Jack shifted from one throbbing leg to the other. After brushing the remainder of ice from his clothes, Jack knew it was time to start moving. Not only to find a place to hide, but to regain the rest of his circulation.

It took every bit of strength to compel his legs to function. Jack's legs felt like rubber, almost out of control as he tried to take a step. Barely able to lift a knee, he pushed forward the first tiny stride. Jack's boots crunched against the icy riverbank as he fought to keep his still thawing legs from collapsing.

While concentrating on the next step, something crashed into the back of his knee. Jack's unthawed legs collapsed, sending him crashing back down to the ground. In unison with an agonizing cry, every frozen joint and bone in his body exploded in pain.

For a heart stopping instant, an alarm of warning and finality went off deep within his wary soul. Unable to be completely sure who was behind him, it had to be one of two people - or both.

The dreadful severity of the moment instantly took flight in his mind. Jack felt for certain that this would be his spot of execution - his final resting place.

Jones grabbed him by his frozen hair and pulled him upright onto his knees. "This is as good a place as any," he informed Jack.

Without warning, Jones crushed his knee into Jack's kidney. The blow was paralyzing as more raw pain ripped through his torso. Jones released his hair and simultaneously kicked him between the shoulder blades. The force of the kick sent Jack face first into the rocky embankment.

Hovering above, Jones quickly smashed the soul of his boot against the back of Jack's neck, grinding his swollen and battered face into the rocky sand. Overcome with misery, he laid there helpless and completely at Jones's mercy.

Jack's mind flinched as Jones flipped-open the revolver's cylinder. After making sure that it was fully loaded, Jones slammed the cylinder shut and lowered the pistol to point blank range. During this key-grip of terror, Jack was sure that this was it - he was about to die.

Jones began toying with Jack as he pressed the barrel of the gun against his skull. "Do ya think you'll be standing in front of the gates of Heaven or the gates of Hell after I waste ya?"

Head crushed against the frozen, rocky ground, Jack didn't bother to utter a response. It was over, all hope was gone.

"As for me...I know where I'm goin'." Continuing his little game of torment. "I've got my feet so firmly planted in Hell's fiery pit, I can feel the heat. That's why I'm not worried about finishin' ya off."

Jack heard the click of the safety being released on the heavy caliber weapon. "Do ya have anythin' to say before I blow your brains out?" Jones heartlessly inquired, pulling back the double action hammer of the gun.

Painfully awaiting death, Jack knew that Jones wanted the pleasure of watching him beg and plead for mercy. But, there was no way he was going to show any last acts of desperation. The one thought that resonated in his mind was wanting to tell Jones to go screw himself. But, the intense pain kept the words from reaching his lips. Jones gave Jack a final shove with his boot, then, lifted his size twelve's from his neck.

There was something about being so close to death that was absolutely maddening. Any moment, a single bullet would shatter his dreams of starting a new life.

Any moment, a single bullet would come smashing through his skull and it would all be over.

Any moment, a single bullet would terminate his existence and the cold river would be his death bed.

Jack's whole world was about to come to an abrupt holt and there was nothing he could do about it. In anticipation to the explosion of the gun, he pulled in a final breath into his lungs.

While Jack waited for Jones to pull the trigger, nothing seemed to matter anymore. His beaten body had been driven to the point in which he did not care whether he lived or died.

Peripherally, through the darkness, he took one last look at those callous, menacing eyes, framed by that grotesquely scared face. Though Jones continued to talk, Jack no longer heard what spewed from his pathetic lips. Jones's words penetrated his ears clearly enough, but his brain seemed to completely ignore them.

The only thing he could hear was the roar of rushing water. Unbelievably, he began to experience a sort of morbid, sick relief at the thought of dying. Feeling almost surreal, a surprising calm flowed through him as he began to welcome the prospect of death.

Jack thought that he might see a high-light reel of his life flash through his mind. But, no such thing occurred. The only thing he could see was the cold darkness that surrounded him.

Then it happened, something came smashing into the back of his skull. His head seemed to split open with a dull roar, instantly driving him into a cloudy oblivion.

In that split second, Jack realized his life was now over as he raced towards unconsciousness. Irreversible inner darkness took hold as he fell into a deepening delirium. It was a merciful relief as the river and woods around him vanished, giving way to ultimate darkness and silence.

CHAPTER 13

THERE WAS A VELVETY calmness as if floating through some sort of unknown consciousness. Encircled by an aura of ghostly silence, Jack was blind to what plain of existence his soul actually resided. As if in a dream state, he was now just a disembodied spirit lost between worlds, drifting in a vast empty void within himself.

Nothing seemed to make any sense during these unearthly moments. While wandering in this dimension of unreality, Jack could not be sure if he was among the realm of the living or that of the dead.

The level of uncertainty consumed him with curious thoughts of death. In the dim bleakness of this bizarre consciousness, he dismayingly entertained the notion that he might be the newest member of the after-life.

If in fact, he were caught-up in some spectral darkness at the edge of the hereafter, it was hard to believe that this was all there was to the aftermath of death.

Is this death?

Am I dead?

Or is this just a temporary time-out from what's really going to happen?

While drifting in this vacuum of nonexistence, the cone of silence began to fade. Gradually, a connection with reality began to slowly creep back.

All at once, a thundering pulse of agony took the place of

silence. Temple to temple, an intense and violent pain pulsated and hammered through his skull.

Though Jack's left eye remained swollen shut, his right eye flickered open. Teetering on the rim of consciousness, he found himself staring into a lightless world. Anxiously needing to find a moment of clarity within the darkness, Jack wanted to push himself up. But, with his head so heavy and laden with pain, his body seemed to rebel and refused to obey. Still in a mental fog, he just laid there half-conscious, painfully trying to will his body to respond.

All of a sudden, Jack became aware of the extreme cold that encased his body. As if afflicted with arthritis, every joint throbbed against the chill that embedded his bones. Muscles twitching spasmodically, he fought back against the uncontrollable shivering that dominated his flesh.

In a haze of misery, Jack laid face-down on the cold, hard surface. The dark world around was silent as he continued to trembled violently. It took a minute before Jack relaxed enough to move. But finally, enough energy was summoned to lift his head.

Holding his breath, Jack moaned against the unyielding pain while pushing himself up. Feeling the full force of the throbbing between his temples, nausea and dizziness instantly attacked. Reclaimed by delirium, his head fell back to the floor. Losing sight of consciousness once again, Jack's body remained a part of the darkness.

***

Finally, perception began to resurface. Once again, his right eye flickered open only to close again. Eventually, he was able to open his eye long enough to try to focus on the perpetual blackness.

Belly to the hard floor, he swallowed against a harsh dry throat. Pushing upward, Jack screamed inwardly while managing to get to his hands and knees. Dizzy and weak, he awkwardly twisted his body into a sitting position.

Jack raised a shaky hand to the back of his head where the most pain resided. Though the touch was gentle, the response was one of white-hot agony. Hair wet to the touch, he tentatively rubbed the knot that had risen from his skull. Wincing in pain, he withdrew his hand from the wet-matted hair. Jack's fingers came back warm and tacky with blood.

Mind jumbled and confused, there was no recollection of what had happened or where he could possibly be. Attempting to adjust to the absence of light, Jack tried to kick-start a memory that might reconstruct the events that took place earlier.

Setting in the heavy stillness of the strange room, disjointed flash-backs began to present themselves. One thing was for sure, this was not the place of his last memory. It was not the spot where he had accepted an undeserving and untimely death. But to Jack's amazement, there was one inescapable fact - he was not dead.

As Jack's blurry mind began to balance out, all reflection was directed toward the last frantic moments on the riverbed. All at once, the events on the river came racing back!

As the cobwebs continued to clear, Jack recalled the very last moments when Jones pressed the gun against his head. The double action click of the hammer pulling back and that anticipation of uncontrollable death. Jack now understood that Jones had not shot the gun, but rather struck him in the back of the head. Pistol-whipped and rendered unconscious - not dead.

Deeply troubled, there was no way to fathom why he was left among the living. *Why am I still alive? Why didn't Jones finish me off?* None of it made any sense.

Not knowing why or what was going on Jack was forced into a reality check. For some reason, Jones's bullet had been avoided. Somehow, he had hard-pressed the borders of Death and survived.

It scarcely seemed possible that the end had been avoided and that he held on to any glimmer of life at all. But, the extreme pain from his previous injuries was insurance enough of his worldly existence.

While attempting to contemplate what it all meant, Jack was filled with a desperate sense of unease. The idea that he was not sent to an early grave gnawed at him. Without a doubt, something unforeseen was playing out beyond his knowledge.

Jack's mind began to question the Doctor's motives. *There's a reason I'm still alive - but for what possible purpose? Could the Doctor have something more demented and diabolical in store for me than death?*

Whether it was luck or fate that spared his life was not important now. Far more pressing matters occupied his mind. Still alive and with a little strength left, there was still a chance at escape. With that thought, a sense of urgency took hold.

Sitting on the cold floor, Jack rubbed the nap of his neck. Fingertips still sticky with blood all effort was put toward the knots of tension that throttled his muscles. Trying to understand where he was, he stared blankly into the absurd blackness. Unable to make sense of his surroundings, Jack sat in silence - listening to the darkness.

The only sound to be heard was the faint trickling of water as if flowing down a sewer or drain. Listening more intently, the nearby sound of swarming flies was recognizable. Wherever he was, the flies seemed to be thriving.

Jack continued to examine the lightless area until he began to feel a strong sensation of dread. Despite the trauma to his head, his sense of smell was still very acute.

Rank and harsh, a troubling odor assaulted his senses. One conclusion came fairly quickly; it was a stench that could only be derived from rotting, decomposing flesh. The paralyzing darkness that dominated the room was suddenly thick with the morbid and rancid odor of death.

Desperate for any hint of light, Jack remembered the cigarette lighter. Rubbing his front pockets, instant relief proceeded with the awareness that he still possessed the lighter.

After retrieving the only source of light, he quickly began trying to produce a flame. After numerous attempts, the lighter finally flickered to life.

Holding the lighter just above eye level, his crimson covered fingers appeared black beneath the flame. The tiny light was a spotlight as far as Jack was concerned. The lighter presented a small possibility of hope within the absurd darkness.

Knowing the lighter would not last forever, Jack quickly tried to orient himself. Though his eye was intent, at first there was nothing. Blinking at the darkness, his vision refocused into a misty blur.

What little could be seen was featurelessly dark. Unmoving and indistinct, the figures were just murky shapes against the blackness of the strange room. But one thing was for sure, whatever was strewn across the floor was definitely the source of the noxious cloud of stench.

The back of his neck prickled as his eye slowly scanned back and forth. Suddenly, he felt nauseated and strangely afraid. In this mounting anxiety, Jack twisted and attempted to stretch his aching legs. But, there was something in the way.

After lowering the flame down toward where contact was made, Jack's heartbeat spiked in terror. There was no way to swallow against the horrified knot that had formed in his throat.

It was a body! And judging by the decomposition, it had been there for quite some time.

Jack instantly went pale as a wave of revulsion hit. Staring in horrified silence, he let out a chocking cough trying not to throw up. Too shaken to react immediately, a disbelieving sort of shock instantly set-in. A plea inside his mind told his body to get away, but he was too stunned to move.

Eye wide open, the urge to panic was overwhelming. Jack tried to impose a control on the horror, but it was too much to handle. Instinctively, he shoved the body aside with his leg. Letting his stare rise from the body, Jack took a longer look at the other images within the room. Still fighting the urge to be sick, the enormity of the situation evolved.

Jack's unbelieving heart hammered with the sickening idea of what he might be looking at. The mysterious images quickly became clear enough to make him shudder. The dark silhouettes that surrounded him were all corpses, an entanglement of dead, decaying bodies.

While fixated on the grotesque sight before him, the lighter began to flicker and the flame went out. Jack frantically began working the lighter. After several futile attempts, what was left of his rational mind finally convinced him that his temporary light was lost forever. Jack had no choice but to challenge the darkness.

Even in the painful and horrified persistence of his present state, Jack could no longer sit still. Clothes wet and clinging to his body, he pushed himself up from the floor. Attempting to stand, the first thing that grabbed his attention was the pain and stiffness that was strewn throughout his body. Though every muscle and joint screamed in agony, there was no time to dwell on anything but getting away from the bodies.

Shakily maneuvering upright, Jack stood unsteady, swaying on his feet. Legs unstable and ice-cold, he struggled to maintain balance. After a brief moment to gather himself, the journey through the lake of bodies began.

Hands out-in-front to steady himself, Jack inched forward with ghost-like caution. Placing each advancing step in a sure-footed position, he uncertainly sidestepped the body that lay at his feet.

Limitless blackness confronted Jack as he continually tried to adapt to the lightless room. While thinking his eye was wide-open, he could not be sure. It was so dark he could not even see his hands in front of his face.

With unsteady burdened clumsiness, Jack crept blindly through the dreary darkness. Sidestepping the next decomposing body, the souls of his shoes began to stick to the blood-soaked concrete. Cold, hungry and disoriented, he proceeded through the carnage.

Jack possessed no sense of direction. Each movement was guided by touch and feel. Reaching through the dense blackness, he grouped blindly, constantly stumbling over the bodies on the floor.

Each awkward and misplaced step brought on rivers of agony, magnifying the pain strewn throughout every body part. Unstable and bent at the knees, Jack pressed on through the corpse laden obstacle course. Without warning, the next blind step proved remorseless.

Falling forward with outstretched arms he tried to break his fall. Jack landed with a sickening crunch on his forearms. But, the crunch did not come from his body hitting the concrete floor. The bizarre sound came from his arms crushing and splintering through the ribcage of a body.

After seeing the first body, he could only imagine what now lay beneath him. At that moment, Jack was just one more body lying amidst all the carnage.

Frantically trying to get to his feet, Jack attempted to stand only to fall again. Letting out a terrifying scream, he landed with a slimy squish on what was left of the same body. Hysterically wanting away from the gore, he tried to push off the human remains.

As the corpse shifted beneath, Jack could feel rotten flesh and muscles shred away from its bone. With horrified certainty, he knew that he was now completely soiled with blood and body fluids that were not his own.

Kicking and whipping his body, Jack rolled off the corpse,

only to end up on another body. Scrambling on all fours, he crazily pawed the area around him. Desperately searching for a small piece of floor, anywhere he was safe from contact with another unburied remnant.

Unable to find a vacant portion of concrete, Jack finally gave up. Too terrified to move, Jack sat up on his knees, trying to calm down from the experience.

The sound of flies was now everywhere. In his frenzied state of panic, he had disrupted the carnage of death. The stirring of the lifeless remains had made the stench in the room more intense. Unable to ignore the odor, Jack pulled his shirt over his nose and mouth.

While lost within the surrounding darkness, his mind held on to one panic-stricken plea. It was crucial that he get out of this sickening collage of death before he mentally lost it altogether. Jack understood that trying to walk in this darkness was impossible. With so many bodies to contend with, there was no other alternative but to crawl out.

Knowing full-well he was about to crawl through every excretion a body could submit, he slowly pressed forward. Grotesquely pawing the area around him, Jack searched for the path with the less body mass. But, with so many post-mortem obstacles, there was no way to keep the decadence at arm-length.

Left with no other choice, Jack put all panicked anxiety in check and challenged the depravities. With outstretched hands, he picked up the pace and blindly kneed his way through and over the rotting flesh.

Ravenous waves of horror raced from within as worms and maggots crawled beneath the weight of his hands and forearms. Whatever progress that was being made, if any, was accompanied by the stench of death. The putrid odor seemed to grow stronger the deeper he ventured into the bodies. Doing his best to bare through it, there was nothing to be done about the horrid smell.

Jack had never experienced sickening terror on such a constant level as now.

Breathing only through his mouth, he inched through the decimation. Jack had no idea where he was in the room. As far as he knew, the possibility of crawling in circles was not far-fetched.

With each passing second, the distressing urge to give up and join this mountain of death grew stronger. Just as his last fragment of hope was about to vanish, something caught his eye. There was finally something in which to orient himself. If he was not mistaken, the obscene blackness was revealing a tiny sliver of light.

CHAPTER 14

THE VAGUE GLOW FILTERED into the room from about thirty feet away. With the hope of a miracle in mind, the possibility of freedom made his movements became more aggressive. There was no time to dwell on the mounds of lifelessness that lay between him and the new destination.

The further Jack advanced, the stronger the small fragment of light grew. Though his knees and hands constantly slipped in the bloody excretions, more than half the distance to the light was quickly covered.

While Jack's vision was riveted on the objective, the corner of his eye could not help but notice the horrors that were being navigated through. The nearer to the light, the more he could make out the decomposed features of the long since dead.

With only a few feet to go, the bodies on the concrete floor began to thin. Frantically crawling over the last of the bodies, the prospect of escape became real. With no more obstacles in the way, Jack pushed himself up from the blood soaked floor and focused all attention on the source of the light.

Reaching the far end of the huge room, it quickly became apparent that he was standing in front of a door. Though the source of the light resided on the opposite side, it penetrated the room from the bottom of the door and the floor.

The door was made of metal and had no doorknob or latch. Jack had been praying for a way out, but there was no way to open the door from his side. Feeling the wall next to the door-jam, his fingers slid across a light-switch.

After turning on the switch, Jack mentally braced himself as light was about to fill the room. While expecting an instant flood of light, all that appeared was a weak flicker from overhead.

All around the room, there was a scuffle of squealing rats as the dying fluorescent bulbs attempted to illuminate. Jack watched in disturbed anticipation as the darkness that once dominated the room began to dissipate. Even though the bulb was weak, his prolonged absence of light forced him to squint.

There was just enough light to vaguely make out the details of the room and that was enough. The first thing that Jack noticed was his blood covered arms and hands. Then, the bloody footprints that lead to where he was standing.

Focusing beyond the footprints, unbelievable horror shot up his spine. Taking in the atrocity, Jack stared around the room in excessive revulsion. Mouth open in total shock, his stomach once again began to sicken. One hand against the wall, it was all he could do to steady himself.

It was a gruesome and nauseating scene, overwhelming him with mind-numbing realities he never dreamed existed. The room was littered with lifeless remains. Jack wanted so badly to squeeze his eye shut and see nothing. But, for some perverted reason his stare could not avert from the horrific sight.

Most of the bodies lie entangled, lying eerily in pools of their own body fluids. Water ran from a wound hose on the wall to a drain in the center of the floor. The tiny stream of water was pink with crimson as it flowed through the congealed blood beneath the twisted bodies.

Even the dim flicker from the fluorescent bulb seemed to burn into their decomposing features. The carnage that loomed before him, had long since surrendered to the decrepit deterioration of lifeless time.

Most likely, a majority of them were dead when they were

delivered here. But a few, sat with their backs against the paint-chipped walls. Looking as if they were desperately holding on to life awaiting a rescuer.

But, all the faces revealed the same expression, a death-mask of terrified hopelessness. A frozen in time expression that revealed their last moment of life.

In the dreary flicker of the overhead light, his disbelief turned to cold fury as he spotted Laura's naked body. Jack pushed himself away from the wall and approached her. Kneeling down in front of her, he saw the results of the gunshots heard in the forest.

One bullet had entered dead-center in her forehead, while the other had exploded into her chest. A fine trickle of dried blood extended from the bullet wound to the forehead down the middle of her face. Upon closer scrutiny, he could not help but noticed the absolute terror that was etched into the lines of her battered face.

Jack turned away from Laura's corpse and returned to the door. In the presence of this bloodbath, Jack suddenly realized what was in front of him. The rumors about these mountains were more than rumors. The carcasses of these unknown, tortured souls were the people missing from the forest.

Far removed from everything they once knew, they were now just decomposing fragments of their former self. Those whose hopes and dreams had all but been forgotten. As far as anyone knew, they had just vanished from the face of the earth.

The thought itself was nearly paralyzing. The little hope he possessed a moment ago, seemed to die just then. Jack's body went limp as his back slid down against the door to the floor.

Turning his stare back to Laura's lifeless remains, the memory of what she had said at the cabin re-entered his thoughts. She was right, behind her father's arrogant façade, hid a monster. There was no doubt that the Doctor was the mastermind behind this atrocity, a maverick predator, a diabolical parasite with his own agenda.

Operating under the radar of anyone's knowledge, the Doctor possessed powers that made him an extremely treacherous man. Placing no value on life, he was capable of countless acts of barbarity. The man's evil knew no bounds and Jack's blood ran cold with the understanding that the Doctor's evil would soon show itself again - on him.

In an effort to momentarily escape the horrors around him, Jack closed his eye. Even with his eye tightly shut, the images of the travesty that surrounded him flashed through his mind. While in the isolation of his own thoughts, Jack heard sounds from beyond the door.

Quickly standing up, he turned out the light and pressed his ear to the door. Rattling keys and heavy shoes pounded somewhere outside. Not sure from what direction the sound was coming, Jack listened more closely.

Suddenly, there was no longer any movement. Though the sound of boot heels had ceased, there were voices. A conversation was taking place between two men. One voice belonged to Jones, the other was unfamiliar. If the Doctor was out there, he was not taking a part in the conversation.

Though completely focused on the voices, there was no way of telling what was being said. But, somehow, Jack knew he was the subject of their discussion. While trying to absorb what was being said, the sound of footfalls and dangling keys returned. As the sounds became more distinct, it became obvious that they were headed in his direction. Something inevitable was about to happen and Jack had a very short time in which to plan a move.

At the point of no return, an instant twinge of apprehension enveloped him. Charged with anxiety, he quickly worked himself into a panicky state. Painfully aware of the enormity of the dilemma, his mind raced relentlessly. One way or the other, it was time to do something - and fast.

Jack's anxiety continued to swell as the heavy footsteps drew closer. For an instant, he was driven beyond the realm of rational thought. With the awareness of what was about to happen, his thoughts began to overlap one another. Feverishly, he weighed his options.

Like the Doctor, Jack knew even with no motivation, Jones could be a fearsome engine of destruction. The whole scenario had the makings for disaster. The more Jack desperately explored his possibilities, the more extreme the situation became. While every idea seemed to prove fatal, there was no getting around it. If escape was to be possible, it would take one more confrontation with Jones.

Stumbling over his options, one fact finally became obvious. The need to get away from this unrelenting nightmare far outweighed anything else. While the results could be messy, his only chance to survive was to be ruthless.

A moment ago, Jack was ready to give up, but now, he possessed a glimmer of optimism. This was no time or place to call it quits, there still might be a chance. While not sure exactly how to do it, Jack was determined to take whatever measures necessary. Now, his only priority was survival - whatever the cost.

Body pumped with adrenaline, he positioned himself next to the door. Jack's awareness of their movements was his only advantage. At exactly the right moment, he had to attack. Otherwise, Jones would take control in a heart-beat.

All at once, the sound of jingling keys was right outside the door. Harsh reality set in as bolts shifted and locks began to turn. Far beyond caring about the insidious pain throughout his body, he waited in the darkness for the door to open.

Jack no longer felt like a real person, but rather a desperate, trapped animal. His intent quickly hardened into certainty as he anticipated the inevitable. The thin line separating right from wrong had totally been erased. For the first time in his life, Jack was filled with the necessity to kill.

CHAPTER 15

THE MEN ABOUT TO enter the room held all the cards, but Jack had other plans. The element of surprise was the only advantage he had going for him, the only strategy that might remotely grant him the upper-hand.

Jack's flesh and bones were still painfully chilled, but that was the least of his worries. Staring at the door, eye enlarged in readiness, he listened closely to what was happening on the other side. Gearing-up for what was about to take place, all focus was on nothing but escape.

Jack's mind flinched as the locking mechanism disengaged. As the door swung inward, the first man began to pass through the threshold. Jones entered the room leaving his counterpart stationed outside. There was no time to think, Jack just acted. As soon as the all-too-familiar scar was spotted, the tone for the battle was set.

Before Jones found the light switch, Jack's raised hands were ready to attack. In that split second, anger, fear and determination all came together. In desperation and rage, the first blow came before Jones could react.

In one violent motion, fingers interlocked, his fists came down like a savage sledge hammer to the back of Jones's neck. Under-estimating his own strength, Jack was amazed as the scared faced nemesis went crumbling to the floor.

As the door stood open, Jack's second threat came at him in a bum-rush. Not showing any signs of weakness or doubt, Jack struck out with his right fist. Right on target, the punch landed squarely on the man's jaw. Blood spurt from his mouth as his head whipped to the side. But, his hopeful attempt for a knockout blow was short-lived. Before Jack could get by the man, his adversary had already recovered from the strike.

The conflict of the battle intensified when the wet fabric of Jack's shirt ripped. Yanked from the doorway, the big man was obviously quicker and more powerful than first thought. Before Jack knew it, he was thrown across the hallway, hurtling through the air backward. Just before impact, every muscle reflexively tensed-up. Unable to protect himself, his spine collided against the cinder-block wall. Jack slammed the wall so hard his teeth seemed to loosen.

Exploding forward, the enormous man went straight for a stranglehold. An instant entanglement of arms ensued as the two combatants battled for leverage.

For an instant, their eyes were fixed on each other. Jack was up against a Neanderthal looking man, whose size and girth was much looser and more ambling than Jones. But Jack could tell, this ruffian's power was capable of inflicting a massive amount of damage.

Pinned against the wall, there was nowhere to go. The attacker's hands were suddenly around his face, forcing his head back against the brickwork. As they fought at close range, Jack twisted his head back and forth, attempting to evade the powerful grasp.

As his aggressor's palms smashed against Jack's face, the man's giant thumbs were working toward his eyes. Desperately avoiding his fingers, it was all he could do to keep the threatening claws away from his eye sockets.

Arms still intertwined, Jack's actions became fearfully instinctive. Pushing his extended hand into the attacker's face, some much needed leverage was provided. Unable to get an effective hold, the combatants grip loosened. Searching for another stronghold, the goon's fingers slid down until his hand locked around Jack's neck.

As the grip tightened, the crushing pressure against his larynx and jugular quickly became suffocating. Trying to break free, Jack grabbed the strangler's wrists. Jack could feel his face beginning to flush from the lack of oxygen.

Chocking against the wall, he released one of the man's wrists and fanatically pawed the area next to him, blindly searching for anything that could be used as a weapon. Unable to locate anything that might help, the situation became increasingly desperate.

Arms once again intertwined, Jack squeezed his eye shut, violently resisting the stranglehold. The muscles in his neck were ripped like steel bars against the mounting pressure around his throat.

Determined to break free, Jack viciously fought against the choke-hold. Bowing his back, he twisted and contorted his body and shoulders. Even with all the resistance put forth, the assailant's vise-like grip would not budge.

Jack's efforts to break free were rapidly proving to be useless. With every unsuccessful attempt to loosen the death-hold, the grip grew even stronger. All that was left of his adrenaline was dwindling. The pressure that was crushing his throat was becoming overwhelming. Unable to breath, legs weakening, his body began to slide toward the floor.

With the realization that the battle was nearly lost, Jack knew that something drastic had to be done. Brought about from what he had already experienced, Jack brought forth the last surviving surge of vigor to his muscles. Summoning every bit of strength that was left, Jack exploded with a final, frantic effort to break free.

Crazily embracing the will to live, Jack launched himself upward. In a fiery, uncontrolled anger, his hands shot out catching the attacker just beneath the chin. Lunging forward into the man, Jack managed to knock him backward.

The sudden shift of weight through them both off balance. Stumbling sideways, the man's immense girth toppled over. Arms still entangled, the big man's downward momentum carried Jack with him. Falling side by side, there was no way to cushion their fall. The two heavy bodies crashed down and hit the floor with a hard thud.

Though the man's hands still clutched Jack's throat, the death-grip seemed to weaken. In one final twisting motion, Jack broke away from the iron grip.

In a frantic need to fill his lungs, Jack gasp for breath. Breathing explosively, his nearly crushed throat painfully sucked down air. The battle was far from over as his adversary gave him no time to recover.

Energized by pure fury, Jack's wrath went on the offensive. In a diving lunge, position was gained on the top of the assailant. Without losing the slightest bit of momentum, Jack re-engaged the battle with renewed vitality.

Against tremendous resistance and after several failed attempts, he finally got control of the man's arm. Despite the man's mammoth size, he finally managed to roll the three-hundred pound monster on his stomach. As if making an arrest, Jack wrenched the wrist and forearm behind the brutes back.

Ferociously fighting to free himself, the man fiercely whipped his legs in an attempt to get off his stomach. Trying to gain control of the fight, Jack pressed his inner thighs into the sides of the wild-man's ribcage. But, like riding a Brahma bull, the oversized man thrashed and threw Jack around like a child.

"I'm goin' to kill you!" Emphatically cursing and screaming for Jack's ruination.

Disregarding the constant bombardment of threats and verbal abuse, Jack searched for a way to gain more control. After shifting his weight, it became possible to put a heavy knee in the center of the man's back. Even with the brunt of his weight pressing down, Jack was stupefied by the man's unrelenting exhibition of awesome power.

Though in a position advantage, the big man's superior size was becoming too much to handle. Even with an enormous arm wrenched behind and a knee between the shoulder blades, Jack began to struggle. It took everything to keep the man's titanic girth facing the floor.

Jack's weight and what strength remained, was not enough to keep the gargantuan pinned down much longer. Realizing this would probably be his only chance to incapacitate this massive mound of flesh, it instantly became imperative to finish the conflict.

More than ready to seize the opportunity, Jack raised his fisted hand into position. Just when it was time to deliver a devastating strike, Jones intervened.

Before the final blow could be unleashed, what felt like a bolt of lightning hit him from behind. An all-consuming pain pierced the flesh as his whole body was jolted with total numbness. Lying on the floor in a dazed stupor, Jack's time for fighting was over.

The frenzy of the battle had come to an abrupt end as Jones stood above, holding a stun-gun. Shocked to the point of being incapacitated, his body lay heavy and unresponsive.

Arms limp and useless, Jack watched as the implications concerning his future took another turn for the worse. Though totally immobilized, Jones was not taking any chances. Bending over, Jones pressed the end of the Taser against Jack's chest.

Everything was beyond his control as Jones prepared to juice him up once again. Terrified anticipation was fixated in Jack's stare as he prepared for the inevitable.

As the conquering rival pulled the trigger, another jolt of debilitating electricity exploded throughout his torso. Jack's jaw locked shut and his face went instantly pale. Beneath the skin, every muscle jerked and contorted in uncontrollable spasms.

Immediately after the spasms subsided, Jones activated the Taser and hit Jack with a final dose of electricity. This time, the tremendous shock nearly sent Jack into complete electrified unconsciousness.

Jack just lay there, not quite unconscious, but much more than dazed. Face white and drawn, Jack was not merely stunned, he was paralyzed. All hope for escape had been sent plummeting into despair.

The massive girth that Jack had tried to subdue now joined Jones. "Now what?" Jones's side-kick asked.

"Just grab an arm and let's get him to the Doctor." Jones responded, while locking the padlock to the death-room.

Once Jack heard the order, there was a mental cringe at the thought of another encounter with the Doctor. Looking weakly through his last bit of consciousness, he helplessly watched as each man grabbed an arm.

Shoulders slightly off the floor, they began dragging Jack's body. Keys dangling from Jones's belt, the two men said nothing as they made their way down the first of a maze of corridors.

Jack could not fight delirium much longer. In a way, the idea of losing consciousness was comforting. At least he could temporarily escape from the wretchedness that enshrouded him.

Though his mind was running with thoughts of what could possibly come next. Jack could have never guessed the horrors that awaited him.

CHAPTER 16

FEARFUL UNAWARENESS CAUSED JACK'S eye to snap open. The first thing that came into view was the ghastly fluorescent lights that hung from above. Throat dry and raw, tongue swollen from thirst, he realized that he was lying in a bed.

While trying to understand where he was, Jack attempted to move his legs off the bed. But, something held them down to the mattress. Jack's arms were restrained as well. Thick leather straps connected to heavy chains held his wrists and ankles bound to the bed-frame. The restraints made it impossible to get up from the mattress.

Considering everything that had already happened, waking up tied to a bed should not have been too surprising. But, at that moment, it was more than could be handle.

With all extremities restrained, instant rage took hold. Determined to break free, he began jerking against the restraints. The more the struggle turned unsuccessful the more his frustration level grew.

With a spasmodic thrusting torso, Jack lashed out against the bindings. In an unwavering crusade to break loose, the fight against the restraints was relentless. While violently bucking and thrashing atop the mattress, the bed frame began to bounce and inch its way across the floor. Jack struggled with such ferocity, that his state of rage developed into a psychotic frenzy.

With every muscle knotted with tension, the struggle now was for any source of leverage. Jack could feel his eyes beginning to bulge as his face twisted in a fit of strain and fury. Vigorously trying to break free, Jack's back began to arch off the mattress. The bindings were pulled to such an extreme that only the back of his head and heels touched the bed.

Jack fought against his bindings until physical exhaustion began to take its toll. The efforts to regain freedom had finally proved pointless. In a fit of frustrated hopelessness his thrashing torso grew still. One second, Jack was ripping at the restraints with wild recklessness. The next, he lay on the bed in absolute and total defeat.

Heart hammering and breathing erratically, Jack closed his eye and tried to calm. While lying beneath the harsh lights, the distant sound of floor-fans could be heard. Except for the heat radiating from above, the room itself was exceedingly cold. After a short recovery from the losing battle with the restraints, his eye reopened.

Taking in what was visible, Jack listlessly rolled his head from side to side. Beneath the high ceiling, it quickly became clear that he was lying in the middle of a huge room. While examining the room, Jack flexed his wrists and ankles against the pain acquired while fighting the bindings. In sudden surprise, the ability to slide his wrist-chains along the bed frame was noticed. Though all extremities were bound, there was the possibility of sitting up.

After sliding the wrist-binds down the frame, a little relief was felt with the ability to sit up. With the ability to somewhat move, Jack began to survey his surroundings. Deeply unnerved at the odd sight, a perplexed expression devoured his stare.

Not even the wildest of imaginations could have prepared him for anything like this. Forehead wrinkled in bemusement, he looked upon seemingly endless rows of beds. The huge room was dominated with small, metal framed beds. And every bed had an occupant.

It was around a fifty bed facility, where dozens of individuals lay naked and motionless. Their unblanketed bodies lie on dirty, make-shift mattresses.

"What the hell is this place?" Jack questioned himself.

Jack put his own dilemma aside as the instantly sobering images grew to a crescendo in his mind. Out of the blue, the answer hit like a lead weight. Like the decomposed bodies he had crawled through, these people were all victims of the Doctor.

To Jack's unbelieving dismay, things got even stranger. The room full of people were not awake, but they were not asleep either. Spittle dripped from the corners of their mouths as they all appeared to be under some kind of heavy sedation. Like zombies, they stared with vacant eyes, disconnected from any sort of reality. Just quivering forms in coma-like trances.

The air was thick with the smell of fever and gangrene. Jack searched the area for the source, but it seemed to be coming from everywhere. Shaking and sweat-drenched, most of the inhabitants showed noticeable signs of unrelenting fever.

On closer observation, probing from bed to bed, face to face, the unbelievable scene got even more unthinkable. As Jack differentiated between the bodies, a ripple of sheer shock ran through his heart. Beside their lost, disillusioned faces, the bedridden people were showing various stages of mutation.

CHAPTER 17

BESIDE THE LOW HUM from floor fans, the depraved room was dominated by a dispiriting silence. Struggling to endure the unbelievable scene, it felt as if he had been plunged into another man's body.

It was impossible to describe the countless atrocities that were occurring. It was so all-consuming that Jack was quickly becoming overwhelmed with mind numbing realities that he never knew existed. If not seeing it for himself, it would have been a reality that was too absurd to believe.

Staring up and down the aisles of mutated humanity, Jack received another unpredictable taste of the Doctor's insanities. The concept of all these imprisoned, comatose people filled him with an intensified loathing for the Doctor. With each unnerving second that passed, the weight of mounting questions grew heavy in his mind.

Though the scene playing-out was way beyond his comprehension, there was one thing that was dismayingly certain. Jack had fallen under the heavy hand of a fiendish tormenter and now had a front row seat in the travesty that was the Doctor's handiwork.

As the new reality digested, he swallowed hard against the decadence that surrounded him. Jack's expression lingered between confusion and anger. Confused as to why this atrocity was taking place. But at the same time, anger, knowing for a fact, that the Doctor took total pleasure in the misery he was inflicting.

Though sickening to observe, Jack continued to witness the horrors of one man's obsessions. There was no justifying the cruelty that was taking place here. It was a dissolute breeding ground where mayhem and unthinkable suffering resided.

The depravities and misery that thrived in this Godforsaken entrapment were limitless. It was here, in this pit of cold isolation, where a man's soul so rapidly became lost and forgotten. A last stop perverted boarding house for those whose luck had long since run out.

In this demoralizing institution of treachery, still warm bodies were being held in tormenting purgatory. It was a macabre, man-made hellhole, a place where men, women and children were being treated like a species other than human. A degenerate refuge, where the Doctor dealt with his victims as human genie-pigs for his own inconceivable experiments.

Jack now understood, like these poor souls, Laura's face was not a mishap of nature. But rather a deliberate, contorted creation of her father's madness.

Everyone in the room held one thing in common. At some point in time, these poor individuals had unsuspectingly crossed the Doctor's sadistic path, only to be abducted and become the Doctor's personal property.

Outwardly, no one would have ever guessed these were once just normal, everyday people. But thanks to the Doctor, they were no longer real people, just imprisoned lab rats in horrific stages of genetic evolvement. A group of innocent victims who were having their very soul's slowly siphoned away.

All of the mutating captives harbored IV lines, being injected with whatever debilitating cocktail the Doctor concocted. Whatever the madman was pumping into everyone, it was clearly designed to minimize the awareness of what was actually happening.

Dark circles accompanied their blood-filled eyes. The trapped images before him acknowledged nothing, not even the roaches and flies that seemed to ravage their flesh at will. Under heavy sedation, the unresponsive group of people lie in silence, their only expression was that of hopeless denial.

As Jack gawked at the countless acts of barbarity, it quickly became obvious that these people had been here for quite some time. Blue and red veins covered their flesh as their skin appeared almost transparent. Locked away from the sun, the dazed people whimpered and moaned as their flesh shivered with convulsions. Several fever-ridden captives also showed advanced signs of gangrene.

Although their extra body parts were obviously underdeveloped and dysfunctional, others appeared fully functioning. Like Laura, some displayed multiple sets of eyes and other facial abnormalities. Large distorted heads with tilted mouths and grossly misaligned teeth. Nightmarish faces with several additional features in different stages of development. All of which, were accompanied with clumps of thick, bristly black hair.

A couple of people, while their cheeks housed multiple eyes, appeared to have massive protruding bone formations growing from their flesh. As if another complete skull were developing from their neck and collarbone.

Some lay in fetal positions, just dormant, comatose souls that outwardly resembled hideous beasts. Totally nude on their tiny beds, tormenting pain and suffering was imprinted deep within their pale faces. Many had hands and feet producing eight or more fingers and toes. It appeared that these parts were growing randomly, manifesting with no rhyme or reason.

Mesmerized in horror, Jack was forced to shake himself and pull his attention away from the Doctor's ghastly creations. Teetering on the rim of sanity, he found himself intently peering above the dehumanized bodies and focusing on the grim and menacing confines.

The disrepair of the room itself was more than appalling. The interior was nothing less than dreary, an almost alien environment. The dungeonous atmosphere consisted entirely of concrete and cinder-blocks.

It was an imposing confinement in which they all lay imprisoned. The entire facility resembled a huge fortress. The only difference was that this fortress was not to keep people from getting in, but rather getting away. There was no doubt, that every detail of these confines was designed with debilitating discomfort in mind.

There was nothing sanitary about the grim and foreboding structure. The building, with its years of accumulated filth, housed not one window. Aged peeling paint covered every inch of the ceiling and walls. Old, moldy tile covered the entire floor. No matter what his vision surveyed, everything looked the same.

The wretched conditions were saturated with an aura of dread and depression. Creeping decay seemed to seep from the filth that clung to the deteriorating walls. The essence of utter hopelessness that ran unrestrained throughout this decadent habitat was enough to gag on. The last place in the world anyone would want to be.

Outside these walls, the rest of the world went on as usual. As one day ends, another one begins. But, inside this windowless purgatory, there was no night or day. Days never ended or began, time remained stagnant.

In its wildest dreams, society at large could never imagine the evil that resided within this arcane existence. Any regard for human dignity was nonexistent. Logic and natural laws of the world did not apply here, it had laws unto itself. A private, ruthless world where heartless cruelties and brutal acts of savagery were played out routinely. It was simply an assembly-line of broken spirits and mutated parts.

The evil-doers that ruled this insidious habitat played a never-ending game of damnation. It was nothing less than a sadistic stronghold that irrefutably fortified the frightening truth that Hell really existed.

At its core, this fluorescent lit fortress was nothing more than a demented zoo. Until an individual had been yanked from society and locked away like a useless, diseased animal, one cannot comprehend the physical and psychological torture that must constantly be endured.

Inside this concrete cage dwelt a society in which its unwilling residents were looked upon as worthless residue. And once their usefulness had ended, they were discarded as human debris.

Jack looked at all the tragedy once again. Nothing remotely made any sense while staring at all the cataclysmic deformities. The occupants came in all shapes and sizes; old, young, every creed and color. The Doctor was indifferent to his victims; the evil man experimented and mutilated them all with equal diligence. They had all been dehumanized and transformed into complete abominations in which there was no recovering from.

The seemingly endless rows of beds had become the final destination for so many undeserving souls. The very idea of this mass mutilation of humanity was mind-boggling. Overrun by a queasy sense of despair, the unsettling images around him began to fade into a disgruntled haze.

Without warning, Jack realized that someone had just entered the room. While dreadfully anticipating the first glimpse of the madman, Jack watched with lowered eyes. When the Doctor finally came into view, a surge of loathing and helpless fury seized him. Instant anger began to feed off the seething resentment toward the man.

The instant rage of emotion caused his eye to open to its widest point. Jack wanted nothing less than to clutch the Doctor's throat and squeeze every bit of life out of him.

CHAPTER 18

As the Doctor strolled through the aisles of beds, the hired hands followed close behind. Jones and the side-kick were nothing more than Dr. Simone's personal patsy's. Trailed by a totally disinterested crew, the Doctor appeared to be making his periodic rounds.

Wearing a holy-than-thou look, the Doctor was in standard operating mode. The underlying contempt for everything and everyone in the room was obvious in the man's nonchalant demeanor. Even in his more casual moments, the Doctor's movements and gestures were precise and methodical.

Among all the man's disturbing qualities, one stood out by itself. So sure of himself, so arrogant and confident, he carried a self-righteous air of impartial superiority that demanded respect. Without compassion or concern, the Doctor's heartless aura conveyed the very force of fate.

Jack watched every movement as the Doctor made his way through his deviant creation. With an unmistakable ring of authority, he looked down at his abductions as lower than life forms. Looking alternately at the beds on both sides of the aisle, he steadily passed by the unfortunate soul's that lie incapacitated. Suddenly, the Doctor stopped at one of the beds and began examining a young woman.

After a brief exam, the Doctor dispassionately shrugged his shoulders. "This one's dead, get her out of here." Explaining and terminating the situation with an indifference that was absolutely chilling.

The two goons responded without haste. Jones wasted no time in yanking out the young women's I.V. lines. Both grabbed an ankle and began pulling the woman off the bed. They were already moving down the aisle while the woman's torso still lay on the mattress. Dragging the rest of the body to the floor, the corpse's skull cracked against the tile. Though the men and the body quickly disappeared from Jack's view, there was no doubt where they were going - the Death room.

Just like that, she was no longer a real person. Now, the dead woman was merely a piece of trash that was to be immediately discarded. For what would be considered abominable and inhuman in the outside world, was obviously viewed as insignificant in here - and the unthinkable was acceptable.

Jack was now an eye-witness to the terrors of the man's true madness. It was impossible to come up with anything that could justify Dr. Simone's motives for such cruel and immoral acts.

There was an underhandedness about the man that was utterly disturbing. Proving to Jack, that the Doctor was quite capable of saying or doing anything at any given time. Through the years, Jack had thought he had seen every ugly and evil characteristic of a man. But, this vile and malign act by the Doctor was one like he had never witnessed before.

Staring across the room in total disbelief, a dismal sense of grief ravaged his heart. The morbid and sickening finality of the young woman's existence was more than appalling. Completely repulsed by the sight, a full-blown disgust swept through him.

Manned by a cynical stare that seemed standard issue, the Doctor turned and gazed at Jack with undisguised indifference. The coldness in his eyes made his cynical grin even more disturbing. Whatever the Doctor was thinking, Jack knew for a fact, that soon he would be at the top of Dr. Simone's agenda.

With the sudden unnerving recognition, Jack quickly averted

his stare from the Doctor. In transfixed silence, it was all about trying not to appear too startled by the revolting occurrence.

In no hurry, Dr. Simone began walking between the beds, weaving his way in Jack's direction. The man was unshakably calm, seemingly self-possessed, flaunting a core of power that was daunting. All the while embracing a constant look of madness that never left his eyes.

The lunatic's coming to see me, Jack mentally warned himself.

After crossing through the aisles, the Doctor was standing within inches. It was all Jack could do to meet the Doctor's eyes directly.

"Their bodies are still functioning, Jack. Well...Except one. I knew she was a long-shot, but I had to try...You understand?"

Jack did not give him the satisfaction of acknowledging his assumption.

"Just so we understand each other, callous as it might seem, what you see here is just the nature of the beast." Explaining as to emphasize that his cruel and ruthless work was a necessity.

Though the Doctor's tone was light, there was no mistaking the threat behind the words. Making himself precise and clear, Dr. Simone's underlying meaning was very apparent. It was either his way or the dead way. Whatever the man's motives were, he was very sincere when regarding his madness.

Trying not to be obviously unnerved by Dr. Simone's sudden presence, Jack spoke not a word. At this point, the slightest sign of outrage or weakness would only make the crazed maniac feel stronger and more powerful.

"As a general rule, I usually would've just killed you at the cabin. But since I had an open bed, welcome to your new home. But, if you continue to refuse to cooperate, you're just going to make things a lot harder on yourself. Jack...I'd remember... There's nowhere to go."

Though Jack did not want to push the confrontation into

something even more threatening, there was no controlling himself. "Spare me the psychotic psycho-babble. You can't threaten someone and expect any gratitude or loyalty in return."

Circling the bed, Dr. Simone's eyes bored into him with an intensity that was impossible to ignore. Jack was scared to guess what had just entered the Doctor's mind.

"It's apparent that you possess a descent amount of intelligence, Jack. But, I suggest you keep your thoughts to yourself." It was not a lightly veiled threat, for Dr. Simone's requests and demands were one and the same.

With menacing intent, Jack looked at the brutal puppet-master and continued. "It doesn't take a lot of intelligence to realize you're a charter-member of the lunatic fringe. How can you just destroy people's lives and desecrate them on a whim?" But Jack could not leave it there. "Is it just one of your sadistic abilities that flows at will? This place is nothing more than a death chamber. Why don't you just kill me now?"

"Maybe you're right? It looks to me, that maybe I should've killed you last night? If you interrupt me again, you'll definitely find out first-hand what I'm capable of!"

Behind the Doctor's arrogant façade hid a sadistic thug capable of anything. Considering himself above the law, there was no fear of ramification from the outside world. Getting exactly what he wanted or needed was just a matter of bending, twisting or eliminating any obstacle in the way. For the Doctor adhered to only one set of rules - his own.

Dr. Simone's expression did not change, but there was a rougher edge in his voice. "Your shallow-minded conclusions are your prerogative. As you have obviously noticed...I have another open bed. But, if you continue to test me...I'll have two openings. And believe me, it won't take me long to fill your vacancy."

After putting forth the ripe promise of his demise, Jack now knew, when properly motivated, the Doctor could implement and orchestrate sorted brutal acts of savagery.

The very thought of what the Doctor might do was too appalling to entertain. Uncertain how to continue, Jack knew in the end, nothing that he said was going to matter.

"Do you have the slightest idea what is taking place here?" The Doctor's tone had its familiar, arrogant, baiting quality to it.

Desperate for enlightenment, Jack's eye opened wide at the boldness of his thoughts. Though failing to respond, deep within he demanded some sort of comprehensive explanation for the atrocities that were being committed.

"Are you ready to have all your questions answered?"

Jack carefully chose his moment to speak. "Do you really think you can explain what you've done here," asking nervously.

Dr. Simone's voice continued in an irritating calm. "Look at it this way, Jack. What's taking place here is not a matter of right or wrong. It's far more simplistic than that."

Failing to make sense of the remark, Jack looked at the Doctor with total contempt. "Do you actually expect me to even try to understand what you've done here?"

"Ultimately, my motives don't really matter, only the outcome. In due course, my research will enhance life as the world's never seen."

"Are you trying to tell me that you've enhanced these people's lives?" Jack was not scoring high marks with the Doctor.

Arms crossed, the Doctor's face became etched with impatience. "Let me spell it out for you, Jack. Sacrifices have to be made to expand the world's horizons. Mankind will advance by leaps-and-bounds from my achievements. The few lives that are lost here will ultimately help millions of others."

Talking in terms totally unbecoming a normal doctor, another morbid dimension of the man's personality was being unveiled. As if knowing the inflection of torture and the domination over life and death belonged to him. Gambling shamelessly with people's lives, the Doctor created a world in which he was God and the Creator.

"For years I've been involved in DNA and stem-cell research. My ideas and breakthroughs were looked upon by a few narrow-minded heavyweights as far-fetched and unachievable. Thus, they had my funding cancelled and forced the hands of the medical board to revoke my research license. After that, even my colleagues who portrayed me as brilliant were pressured by the medical world to regard my work as too obscene to entertain."

A satisfied grin began to spread across the Doctor's face. "But, looking back on it now, that's the most fortunate thing that could of happened." The Doctor continued as if reprinting the memories in his mind. "After a short stint of being blackballed in the job market, I decided to take matters into my own hands."

Though refusing to respond, Jack's fuming posture expressed his feelings.

With little delay, Dr. Simone continued. "Even though I've been able to tap into the DNA strand and isolate certain things, there are still side effects. As you can see, there are multiple appendages developing from each patient. Fingers, toes, facial features, and in some cases complete arms and legs - even heads.

But, what you see outwardly is not my objective. Beside the eyes, these external growths are useless to me...There's no market. The money exists in eternal life." Trying to paint a picture of the torture chamber in a more sympathetic light. "You have no idea what people are willing to pay in order to extend their miserable lives. The real payday resides with internal organs.

As you can see, they all appear to be quite bloated. It's not swelling due to sickness or infection. But rather, the multiple organs that are in development.

Hearts, livers and kidneys are the most sought after organs. People are on organ waiting lists that may never see the opportunity for a transplant. But, with the right amount of money, I can put anyone to the front of the list.

Even with the ability to isolate the DNA sequence for these various organs, I've been unable to control the side-effects. Every time I stimulate the specific development of an additional organ, it usually cultivates another part of the body into development. Thus, we have what you see before you…Including that primal, coarse, black hair.

Unfortunately, the independent cloning of these organs is still in the baby-step stage. Until my research is furthered, the organs I'm producing must have a host. Out of all the mammals on the planet the human body is the most adaptable and resilient - the perfect host. It's the only way the organs can fully develop. Ultimately, my motives don't really matter, only the outcome." The callous indifference in his voice was chilling.

Jack could not control the ripples of pure distain that boiled in his blood. "Is that why you murdered your daughter?"

With a cold-blooded ruthlessness that dwelt in few individuals, Dr. Simone responded. "She's was a loose end… A very loose end! But…That's not the point, Jack. No one will put my achievements in jeopardy. None of this will ever get beyond my control!" To show compassion toward the world, or those within it, would be the same as surrendering his entire demented reality.

For a moment words eluded Jack, then, the fear of expressing himself became nonexistent. "You can shove your twisted world up your ass."

"I'll bare that in mind," raising his voice slightly.

Dr. Simone's evil knew no bounds, and Jack knew the man's evil was about to expose itself - on him. The mind-set of the Doctor made him a very dangerous man. To him, people were merely lab rats, tools-of-the trade, implements to be experimented on and discarded. In his mind, he wasn't a madman at all. The Doctor considered himself just an opportunist, willing to do anything to further his quest.

Jack was relieved when the Doctor finally turned and started to walk away. Jack suddenly realized, the Doctor was not going to kill him, most likely because he probably filled the qualifications of a perfect specimen. But all relief was put on hold as the Doctor's footsteps stopped a few beds away. The only sound in the room was that of Dr. Simone's squeaky-heels as he turned back around.

What Jack was bearing witness to was terrifying enough, but when the Doctor's lynch-men approached, everything escalated. The anticipation of the Doctor's voice chilled his flesh as the evil-man drew-up from behind.

With nowhere to go, Jack watched helplessly as the two men grabbed his shoulders and pinned him against the mattress. Beside the Doctor's goons, the wrist and ankle bindings made it impossible to resist.

Then, the climax of the moment presented itself. Jack began to struggle and squirm at the sight of what the Doctor held. While one hand held a syringe, the other possessed a vile of something Jack wanted nothing to do with.

After half-filling the syringe, the Doctor's eyes became bright with the intensity of torturous anticipation. Without even rechecking the dosage, Dr. Simone stuck the needle into Jack's neck. Once the drug was completely dispersed, the needle was removed.

As the injection began radiating throughout his body, a burning sensation spread down his neck and spine. Jack's muscles began to twitch and jerk in small spasms. There was no way to stop it, as the drug ravaged his system, the depravities that surrounded him began to fade out of focus. As a deeper drowsiness took hold, his body suddenly went limp.

The Doctor leaned over Jack just before his eye rolled back in his head. "Welcome home." It was a simple message, but one that hit the nail on the head.

CHAPTER 19

WHILE LYING IN THE small bed, Jack's eye snapped open. Beneath the glare of the fluorescent lights, the paint-chipped ceiling began to come into focus. Throat dry and raw, his swollen tongue was stuck to the roof of his mouth. In nauseous awe of his imprisonment, Jack realized his existence had been reduced to a caged animal.

It was maddening to be wrongly imprisoned and unable to do anything about it. In an effort to test the restraints, he flexed both arms. Unexpectedly, there was no resistance. Jack's lost spirit silently looked around the room. Noticing that the Doctor and his hooligans were nowhere in sight, Jack quickly sat up. The chains and handcuffs had been removed, there was nothing holding him to the bed.

Shifting his legs off the bed, Jack sat up in the middle of the giant room. As soon as his feet touched the floor, a glimmer of hope materialized. Harboring no windows, everything in the disgusting building looked the same. Far removed from everything he once knew, Jack wondered if it were daylight outside.

With each passing moment, Jack's blood ran colder with the anticipation of what might come next. But, he had no desire to stick around long enough to become another sacrificial lamb in the Doctor's devious scheme. If this opportunity was not seized, there would never be another. In the seconds that followed, nothing else mattered but escape. Though unsure how to do it, he was more than willing to run the risk.

With no sense of direction, it was all about getting to the closest door. Hoping to locate an exit, Jack finally noticed a steel door on the far side of the room. Ready to take whatever he could get, the door appeared to be the best option.

Desperately clinging to what might be the last illusion of hope, Jack staggered away from the bed. With each advancing step, the air seemed to feel heavier and more ruthless. Weak-kneed, he stared at the atrocities as each bed was passed.

The quivering forms were all victims, trapped and in need of rescue. These people had just vanished from the face of the earth and Jack wanted no part of it. Stomach churning with revulsion, he maneuvered through the aisles of beds. Trying not to react to the horrors pressing in, Jack concentrated on the escape route.

Heart pumping wildly, he just stared at the door. Envisioning an escape, Jack crazily calculating how much time might be needed to get outside the building. Within a few feet of possibly reaching freedom, an unwanted voice made his mind grimace.

"You're full of surprises." The voice was instantly recognizable.

After hearing the Doctor, all hope for an escape was sent plummeting into despair. Jack did not dare move as the Doctor's lynch-men came into view and took up positions. What little hope he had, died just then.

The Doctor approached from behind. "There you go, Jack... Your only chance. I'm giving you one last shot to regain your freedom."

Directly in front of the door, unwilling to move, he refused to turn and face the Doctor. Jack cringed as Jones and company quickly closed in. The time for escape had come and gone.

As if expecting resistance, the thugs grabbed both of Jack's arms. But there was not going to be any protest. There was no need to give them an excuse to inflict any additional pain. While looking alternately at each man, they turned him around to face Dr. Simone.

It took all of his psychological strength to meet those evil eyes once again. The nervous terror that stare aroused in Jack was infuriating. Seething with a surge of helpless anger, he looked past the man toward his creation. With the Doctor as the center-piece, the background just focused on the magnitude of dementia that was imprisoned here.

At the Doctor's initiation, the two men released Jack and slowly backed off. Just a few yards away they stopped and stood by. "Okay Jack, I enjoy a challenge just like the next man. So I'm going to give you one final chance to get away."

Dr. Simone pointed toward the steel door. "That door is the only way out," explaining in an irritating calm. "If you plan on getting away...That's your only chance."

Jack slowly retreated until his back pressed against the cold brick wall. Never taking his eye off the three antagonists, Jack slid his hand along the door-jam until the doorknob was found.

Gripping the doorknob, a surge of onrushing anxiety ravaged him. Something was not right, for some crazed reason Jack felt safer on this side of the door.

"What kind of a sick game are you playing!" Pulling his hand away from the door.

"It's not a game...It's your life were talking about. If you don't leave now...I can assure you...There will not be another opportunity."

Jack was dealing with a psychopath that could never be trusted. But, for some bizarre reason, he also knew he wanted nothing to do with what was on the other side of that door. They would have to kill him before he would cross that threshold. The finale had arrived and there was no way out.

Jack's life was mercilessly being played with. "What do you want with me!" Screaming as his body weakened and began to slide down the wall.

"Take him…If worse comes to worse…Kill him."

"My pleasure," Jones cracked his knuckles in amusing anticipation.

Jack heard the order and instantly cringed. Wanted nothing to do with the Doctor's henchmen he looked on in helpless terror. In complete tunnel vision, Jack watched as Jones's cold-blooded glare closed in. Jack sat slumped over, his head now lowered in helpless submission.

Even though he did nothing to resist, the callousness of the two adversaries ruled out any chance of negotiation. Yanked to his feet, Jones secured one arm while the other goon wrenched the opposite arm around Jack's back. The roughing-up process continued as Jones twisted the other wrist behind him. Now both arms were rendered useless.

Hands pulled-up from behind, they lead Jack back toward his bed. Weak and out of hope, Jack's legs quickly lost their strength and collapsed. Accompanied on each side by the Doctor's thugs, they carried Jack by his arms.

They drug Jack's limp body back to his small bed and threw him on the musty mattress. Lying beneath the harsh lights, there was no resistance as the two men began securing his wrists. Once his arms were securely bound to the bed-frame, they quickly followed suit with his ankles.

With Jack now immobilized, it was time to continue business as usual. Dr. Simone pulled up a chair next to the bed and straddled it backwards. Resting his forearms on the chair-back, the Doctor shook his head in disapproval.

"I can see you're not going to be easy to deal with." The Doctor's expression did not change. But, there was a much more threatening tone in his voice. "I definitely should've killed you last night."

Aware that the Doctor was also his judge and jury, Jack said nothing. "Don't get me wrong, Jack…I can appreciate a man's quest for freedom. But that's not the issue here."

"And what might that issue be?" Jack's voice was horse with fatigue.

"The issue is...You don't follow the rules." The Doctor responded with eyes as cold as his voice. "You need to understand that any chance at escape is unattainable. Sorry, Jack...But there is no way out...Only in."

Born of anger and frustration in a no-win situation, Jack's despair took control. "Kill me...Just get it over with." Heatedly flexing his arms and legs against the bindings.

"I'm sorry to inform you, Jack...Killing you would be too simple. I haven't quite decided what to do with you? But until I do, you might as well get use to the place." The Doctor proposed tauntingly.

"What about all these people? What about their lives?"

"Like yourself, Jack...Their fate was set into motion the minute they ventured in these woods. And now, their destiny is to provide me with the resources I need to help mankind." The Doctor's eyes seemed to slightly misalign as he continued. "The course of their destiny has been decided...Just as yours shall be."

Jack was looking at a man that reeked with insanity. "How in the world could you mutilate all these people and at the same time convince yourself you're a realest."

"You have no idea what this endeavor entails." There was a definite irritation in Dr. Simone's voice.

"You're sick!" Shouting in disgust.

"Think what you want, Jack. But if I were you, I'd remember your fate belongs to me."

The comment struck Jack as ludicrous. "Give up the ego trip, Doc...For your information...You're not God!"

"Oh, but I beg to differ. For all intent and purposes...To a lot of people...I am God." As if preaching from the pulpit, the Doctor continued to praise himself. "I'm the only one they can come to in order to stay alive. And that waiting list for an extended life gets longer every day."

"You're nothing but a sadistic murderer."

"Alright, Jack. Let's get down to brass tacks, shall we?" The Doctor announced standing from the chair.

As if he were ten feet tall, Dr. Simone stood above the bed. "Let me make one thing perfectly clear. You're going to help me help the world, Jack." Making his intentions very clear.

To this man, reality was just a fanciful game in which he manipulated all the pieces. Control meant everything, it was his lifeblood - it's what he lived for. A methodical machine with nothing but ice flowing through his sadistic veins.

Dr. Simone once again pulled a syringe from his white hospital coat. After pulling the plastic needle-cover off with his teeth, the Doctor briefly held the syringe to the light. Once the dosage was checked, he lowered the dripping needle to Jack's neck.

Jack had no choice in the matter as the syringe came toward him. But, at this point in time, Jack more than embraced the sight of the syringe. Anything that helped release him from this horror-filled reality was welcome.

As the needle stabbed into Jack's neck, the Doctor discharged whatever was housed in the huge syringe. Immediately after the injection, his entire body began to tingle. Within seconds, there was a severe inner-burn. The drug that flowed through his veins rendered his insides on fire.

Rapidly becoming incapacitated, his stare turned toward Jones. Jack could not but notice that pale, grotesque scar. Watching Jones with dope-heavy eyes, it appeared that the scar had formed into a question-mark from his giant smile.

Like the others, he had done nothing to deserve this, but there he was just the same. "What are you going to do to me?" Jack's words were slurred and barely audible.

"You'll find out soon enough." The Doctor proposed with

a cynical sneer. "But, no matter what I decide…I think we can both agree…You have no choice in the matter."

Terrifying revelations revealed themselves as Dr. Simone continued. "You know, Jack…By being here…You've given up any trace of your existence."

With an overpowering finality the drug took-its-toll. Body heavy and useless, Jack lay paralyzed against the mattress. Spittle dripped from the corner of his mouth as his head lazily rolled to the side.

"You must now admit, Jack…Your destiny belongs to me. I can assure you, that when you wake up you'll immediately know what I decided for you."

The self-proclaimed maverick was just a master predator in a world of pure madness. Jack understood that all sense of reality as he knew it was about to be altered. Preoccupied by his own demise, he was no longer aware of the other lost souls around him. Jack looked through a hazy stare as the room once again began to fade.

The Doctor spoke one last time before Jack lost consciousness. "Soon it will be show-time…And you'll wish you were never born."

There was no escaping the realm of his current reality. Jack had become one of the numerous, unwilling guests of Dr. Simone. In this arcane world, logic and natural laws did not apply. Unprepared for the misery about to be inflicted upon him, Jack's eye flickered shut.

CHAPTER 20

As the sedative wore off, Jack struggled back from delirium. A perplexed expression devoured his face as he began to recover. Against the painful insistence of his new reality, Jack opened his eye. Shaking and sweat-drenched, he stared weakly through the fog of semi-consciousness.

Lying on his side, he could see that there were no bindings holding him down. Unsure why he was not bound to the bed, Jack tried to sit up. But, his body was so heavy and laden with pain it made it nearly impossible to move.

Jack tried to roll over, but something behind him preventing it. Simultaneously, the rancid stench of corrupted flesh invaded his senses. The same smell as encountered in the Death room.

When Jack rolled back onto his side, an arm feel limply across his chest - and it was not his own. After frantically grabbing the arm to push it away, things got even stranger. The flesh on the arm was grey and stiff. An instant alarm went off, a terrifying warning that the arm was not amongst the living. Irrationality took-off, horrific thoughts sped away like a runaway train. In an involuntary reflex, Jack shoved the decomposing limb behind him.

The sound of protesting rigor mortis echoed throughout the room. The snapping and cracking of bone and dehydrated tendon was mind chilling. Unwilling to cooperate, the stiffened arm sprung back across Jack's chest.

While hysterically pushing at the dead arm, a head limply

rolled over his shoulder. The decaying skull now rested against Jack's cheek. Panicked shock shuddered within as his vision turned toward the head.

Eye enlarged in horror, mouth gawking in sickening disgust, what he saw pushed him to the point of passing out. Along with the stench of death, the withered face housed a single bullet hole and six blank stares - it was Laura.

Tightly shutting his eye, it was everything he could do to subdue the uncontrollable horror. As Jack's shock began to evaporate, it became all about getting away from the hideous corpse. In an effort to distance himself from Laura, he reached behind and crazily pushed at the rotting body.

Each time the dead body was shoved, unbearable stabbing pains pierced at his back. Moving his hand to where the worst pain resided, Jack's mind finally snapped with the realization that Laura's decomposing corpse was attached to his back. Their backs and shoulders were sown together by some kind of wire.

Unable to breath, the shock of the event caused every inch of his flesh to go stiff. Unable to speak, swallow or move, petrified horror was strewn throughout his entire being.

Past the breaking-point, Jack screamed in a surge of unforgiving fury. "What'd I ever do to deserve this?" Shrieking in an infuriating roar meant for the Heavens.

Upon regrouping somewhat, Jack scanned his vision around the huge room. At that moment, it did not appear he was carefully guarded. Grabbing the bed-frame, Jack pulled himself and his deceased companion off the mattress.

When the two bodies hit the floor, Jack's back and spine ruptured in pain as the stitches threatened to tear from the flesh. The tremendous agony and the weight of the decomposing Laura made it impossible to walk.

With fear and determination all bound together, he began dragging himself and the heavy corpse across the floor. Jack had no idea that such a small person could weigh so much.

Accompanied by the snapping and cracking of decomposition, they slide side-by-side. Laura's rotting skin tried to stick to the old tile as he relentlessly pulled them forward. Sight directed on a lone mirror, Jack was unaware that pieces of dead flesh and a trail of maggots had been left in their wake.

Once in front of the mirror, Jack turned his back to the reflection. What filled his eye drove him beyond the realm of rational thought. As the image grew into a crescendo in his mind, ravenous waves of horror raced through him. Unable to do anything, he just stared at the horrifying truth.

Jack's vision was consumed with unbelieving terror as the stitches in his back stretched against Laura's weight. Focused on the stitches, it became obvious that his flesh and that of the nude, mutated woman had been surgically sown together. Jack was in critical shock with the realization of what had been done to him. The girl's decomposing corpse was now a part of him. Jack was not merely an abomination, he was two abominations.

The swarms of maggots that infested her rotten flesh where on the move to his body. Within no time, the tiny creepy-crawlies were covering Jacks skin. Completely traumatized, paralyzed in dread, his thoughts were instantly twisted into madness.

Stare directed toward the ceiling, Jack raised his hands and screamed once again. "Why is this happening?"

Just as Jack's cries of anger subsided, the Doctor's arrogant, self-serving voice smothered the air. "Look what we have here."

At that instant, pure distain surfaced. Jack's breathing quickened in disgust at the sight of Dr. Simone. "You bastard... Get this thing off of me." If looks could kill, Jack would have been wanted for murder.

The Doctor smiled at his handy-work. "What do you think, Mr. Jones?" Folding his arms in front of his chest

"I'm not sure...He's kinda hard to look at." Jones responded as the two men approached Jack.

For some reason, the Doctor found Jack's sudden misery

somewhat amusing. "You're right. It's not my best work...But you got to appreciate the effort. How about you, Jack...What do you think?"

Jack's eye was filled with burning tears. "What the hell have you done to me?"

Staring with a satisfied smirk, the Doctor did not bother to answer.

When Jack tried to speak, his voice was choked. "I'll kill you...If it's the last thing I do...I'm gonna kill you!"

In the end, nothing he said was going to matter. Without compassion or concern, Dr. Simone began to circle him. Not having the slightest idea of what to do, Jack awkwardly laid in front of the Doctor. While stalking from overhead, the coldness in the man's eyes made his smile even more sinister.

"Laura's just a little extra ballast to help you behave." Allowing himself a brief chuckle before continuing. "You're a perfect specimen, Jack...You're going nowhere." Enjoying every bit of his torment.

Jack continued to stare at the Doctor with murderous intent. "I'll get out of here somehow." His voice was deep and torn with grief.

"I'll keep that in mind. But until then, you know what they say. There's nothing like a little DEAD-WEIGHT to help Jack be a good boy." Dr. Simone turned and left the room as Jones followed.

The inflection of torture and the overpowering dominance of life and death belonged to him. An overwhelming sense of finality filled his heart. The Doctor had robbed Jack of his life, at least the life he once knew. Difficult as it was, Jack looked back into the mirror. Despondently, he stared at the outstretched limbs of Laura's decaying body.

Looking through a blurry, tear-filled eye, Jack continued to look at what the Doctor had done. Haunted by his thoughts, the mirrors reflection also presented Jack with a glimpse of his new home.

Jack now resided within the sadistic grip of Dr. Simone's insanities. Now, everything was beyond his control. Thoroughly defeated, he became numb with one final fact. The inescapable truth that the course of his destiny had just been made.

All sense of what reality had once been was gone forever. There was nothing left as he made sounds of inconsolable grief. With all that had been taken from him, there was neither the willpower or the desire to resist the inevitable.

Hurled into a void of existence that few ever experience, Jack's body grew still. His world was now confined to the cinder block melting pot of misery in which there was no breaking free.

It was here, within these imposing corridors that the unseen horrors of the Doctor's obsessions dwelt.

It was here, in this asylum of treachery and human misfortune, where a single monster preyed on the weak.

It was here, Jack had become one of many unwilling and unfortunate guests of Dr. Simone.

A man acquires a certain look when all humanity and dignity has been mercilessly stripped away - now Jack had that look. There was no denying the torturing knowledge that he would spend the rest of his days in this asylum of death. In this new twist in the tale of his life, all his dreams, half-assed or otherwise were gone forever.

The cards of fate had dealt Jack an unfair and defenseless hand. A dead-man's hand, in which there was no escape. The once free Jack was now a prisoner of fate. Now, the only way out was to die.

PART TWO

"FACE TO FACE WITH THE ENEMY"

CHAPTER 1

FOR NATHAN, IT SHOULD have been just another lonely day at the trailer park. But somehow, this day felt different from any other. Not sure whether that was good or bad, Nathan realized he would just have to wait and see. But there was one thing that was definite, he was about to do something that had been avoided for over a month.

For the most part, he enjoyed the other people in the park, especially old Mrs. Ellis. In spite of his apprehensions, Nathan told the old woman he would take on the task. In any event, it was time to follow through with his promise. After putting it off all morning and most of the afternoon, it became time to get it over with.

Gaining sight of the objective, Nathan's heart began to race. A chill of uncertain fear shivered through his flesh as he approached the small shed. The storage-shed was a lot less inviting than the others in the RV Park. It was an old, run-down structure that backed up against the woods.

After unlocking the padlock, he pulled open the rickety door. Standing in the threshold of the doorway, Nathan was instantly consumed by a life-long terror. A quivering anxiety took control as he prepared to enter into enemy territory.

Nathan knew, that within this ten by ten space of shadows and darkness existed a dominion of eight-legged terrorists. A decadent breeding ground where the most terrifying of God's creatures resided.

Everyone harbors their own special fear, their own special phobia, a private horror that festers in the furthest depths of their being. Nathan's personal phobia was spiders, an irrational fear that he hid from his entire life.

In Nathan's eyes, the likes of snakes, rats, insects and other creatures of the wild were not worth a second glance. But, the sight of the smallest insignificant spider could turn him into a squirming, cowering mouse. Though the foolish fear of spiders made him feel like a child, he went out-of-his-way to avoid any and all eight-legged adversaries.

Nathan could not help but close his eyes in terrified expectancy. It took a moment to prepare for what he was about to engage in. After a few deep breaths, he reopened his eyes and began surveying the shadows. Brow sweat-beaded, he anxiously searched for the nearest nemesis.

After turning on the flashlight, he immediately took a step back. Unlike most storage units, surrendering themselves to a few scattered webs, Nathan was staring at what had to be hundreds of webs. A network of independent silk spun structures, but at the same time, they also appeared to have a connecting relationship.

Seemingly undisturbed for an eternity, dust and cobwebs covered everything. Though the entire shed was festooned with these bizarre webs, he could see no sign of the enemy. Though it appeared safe enough, his senses told him differently. Nathan was positive the little blood-suckers were in there somewhere, waiting and watching within the shadows.

"I can't believe I promised old women Ellis I'd clean this mess." Quietly chastising himself as he stepped through the doorway.

Nathan was now standing within the one place on earth that could turn him into a spineless coward. As it had always been, when he entered the realm of the spider world, he felt as if he were no longer the hunter - but rather the prey.

As his eyes sought out the details of the small enclosure, he noticed that the boxes were marked with a word he did not recognize. After looking closer, Nathan realized it had to be the name of a town, because it was followed by the word "Africa".

Once before, Old Mrs. Ellis had told him that she had lived in Africa. This had to be the belongings she brought with her when she returned to the United States.

Moving one of the marked boxes, he noticed a large hole at the base of the back wall. With the forest underbrush on the other side, it became obvious that the shed backed up against the woods. Looking around the edges of the hole, it was apparent that a descent sized animal had clawed and chewed its way through. Nathan became a little tentative about moving another box, fearing that the animal might be in there at that moment.

Sometimes, his imagination could get the best of him, especially when it came to the creepy-crawlies. Just the thought of a threatening spider would cause him to begin scratching his skin as if something had bitten him. Nathan suddenly felt vulnerable and alone, it was time to get out of the web infested shed. But as he turned to leave, Nathan discovered that he was not alone after all. Throat dry as dust, he took a deep, panicked breath. Nathan was now face to face with the enemy.

Head shaking in denial, his mind began to give in to a crawling arachnophobic terror. The unnerving recognition of paranoia and fear was now surging unrestrained throughout his body. Hanging down in the middle of the doorway was the biggest spider he had ever seen. As if confronting a trespasser, its giant green body and yellow eyes followed Nathan's every movement.

Dangling from its self-made strand of thread, the huge, green monster now hung between him and freedom. Without warning, it seemed the putrefied room and its residents were closing in to suck the life out of him. Nathan began to feel as if he were suffocating. Paralyzed in horror, his phobia had taken control over his body and mentally crippled him.

After a few seconds of frozen terror, the spider began to move. As if giving Nathan a reprieve, his menacing opposition began to ascend toward the ceiling. Once his rival had reached the top of the doorframe, Nathan had the clearance he needed to make an escape. But there was only one problem, could he block out his phobia long enough to convince his body to move.

Though his mind was in panic-mode, he forced his body to react to the opportunity. Staying as low as possible, he took a desperate step forward and lunged toward daylight. Diving through the doorway, he landed on his forearms and knees. Skidding to a stop, Nathan jumped to his feet and slammed the shed door.

Arms outstretched along the shed, his backside pressed against the door. In an effort to keep the monster from getting out, Nathan pushed against the door with all his leverage. Even with the shed door closed and the enemy sealed inside, the phobia continued to ravage his very being. Just the short time in the shed had taken more out of him than a full day of hard labor. Pale-skinned from fear, Nathan was mentally and physically exhausted.

With the shed's inhabitants once again hidden away from the rest of the world, he took a series of long anxious breaths. While the shed supported his shaking body, Nathan noticed someone knocking on his trailer door.

While his arachnophobia was still in partial control, he tried to regain composure the best he could. Standing and brushing himself off, he tried to separate his thoughts from that frozen moment in the shed. But Nathan knew that helpless, incapacitating confrontation would be embedded in his mind for eternity.

CHAPTER 2

JUST A HALF-MILE FROM Stateline, the RV Park was on the Nevada side of Lake Tahoe. Hidden in a section of town that most tourists would never see - or want to. Invisible from the frontage street, Nathan's trailer resided in the very back of the park.

Something was up, only a few people knew where he lived. There was definitely a reason for this person to be there. Starting toward the trailer, Nathan noticed that the man was dressed in an expensive suit. It was highly unusual to see someone of that stature in this section of town. Nathan became a little apprehensive as he approached the man. Sensing that something was not right, a smile was forced on his face, but his eyes were not smiling.

"Can I help you?" Stopping a few feet from the man.

"Are you Nathan?"

"Yes."

"You've been served."

After handing Nathan the paperwork, the man turned and began walking away.

"What's this all about?" Responding as kindly as he could.

"It's a restraining order."

"From who?"

"How should I know...Read it...I just deliver 'em...I don't issue 'em." Sarcastically replying as he continued to walk away.

Nathan knew exactly who it was from. Beyond bitterness, he was mad enough to begin screaming in rage. Inside himself, Nathan cursed everything about her. For some reason, he knew that she would somehow ruin the day. The thought of the legal paper burned in his mind as the man disappeared from view.

Fury and anger colored his eyes. Consumed with so much resentment, Nathan could not help but acknowledge the smoldering pit where the feelings for his ex-wife dwelt. Sucking in a deep, infuriated breath, he walked inside the trailer and slammed the door.

She had done things like this before, but nothing this final. The restraining order was the straw that broke the camel's back. Nathan never imagined she had the nerve to go this far. The divorce papers were like a slap-in-the-face, but this was way over the top.

With anyone but Julie, it would have been thought impossible for someone to be so deceitful. The reality was, his toleration for her was only because of his daughter. Julie did everything she could to make his life miserable, always tightening the noose. The restraining order was just another reminder that she was in complete control.

Nathan could only imagine what was written on the piece of paper. Without even reading a word, Julie's newest bit of spitefulness was dropped on the floor.

Why do you have to be so deceptive about everything, Julie? You tease me with a small sense of hope concerning Sarah...Then you pull this. Mentally chastising her as if she were right there.

Though fuming with rage and resentment, his present anger ran counter to what he really hoped for. Nathan had always and would continue to cling to the desperate possibility that they might come to some kind of reconciliation concerning Sarah.

Drawing open the front curtains, the trailer instantly became flooded with mountain sunshine. Needing to sit down and think things through, Nathan settled himself in the padded armchair next to the window.

An instant shiver of anxiety cursed through him as he stared at the cobwebs that dwelt on the opposite side of the glass.

Though there was a richness and peacefulness in the mountain air, he never opened the window.

Nathan had always been afraid to disrupt the tiny webs, fearful that the spiders might decide to explore the inside of the trailer. Instead of disturbing them, he was content on leaving them be, not giving them a vendetta against him.

Looking past the webs, Nathan watched as the nearby Ponderosa pines swayed in the gentle breeze. Looking out at the trees and the mountains seemed to feed his weary spirit.

A couple weeks earlier, the weather began to hint toward winter. According to the radio, there was a strong storm warning for the evening hours. The forecast was calling for the cold-front to bring heavy rain and high winds to the Tahoe basin.

Staring across the lake into the northwestern sky, the contours of the mountains had not yet revealed Fall's first major cold-front. While the approaching storm had not begun to materialize, Nathan knew it would come in quick. In the Sierra Nevada's, the weather could change in the blink of an eye.

For several minutes, Nathan lounged in the armchair staring at the velvet blue sky that back-dropped the green treetops. In an effort to alleviate some lingering hostility, he began to think of his daughter.

Searching for a pleasant moment, Nathan rested his elbows on the arms of the chair and stippled his fingers. Looking at Sarah's picture on the wall, he sank further into the chair. Just the precious sight of her momentarily unburdened him from his painful train of thought.

Nathan had been separated from his daughter for several months, but she was never far from his thoughts. Thinking of his energetic little girl was the only thing that gave him a sense of focus and strength. Transfixed on the photograph, he wondered what she was doing right then.

For a moment, Nathan drifted back in remembrance, to a time in his life when he would play with his daughter at the park. Missing Sarah terribly, he cringed at the thought of life without her. She was the cornerstone of his heart. Without her, an essential piece of himself had gone astray. It was a painful reality, but one he had to deal with nonetheless.

All at once, one thing consumed his thoughts. Nathan knew without a doubt, that as far as Julie was concerned, that well was dry. But Sarah was another matter altogether. Somehow he had to recover that part of his life. No matter what, he would never relinquish himself to the possibility of his daughter fading out of his life forever.

When it came right down to it, thoughts of taking his daughter and leaving town crossed his mind. But, for her sake, it was not worth taking that chance. When all the craziness was said and done, Nathan would move on - with his daughter.

Turning on the computer, he decided to search the internet and find out what type of spider was occupying the shed. As he searched through the pictures on spider web-sites, the loathing toward his ex-wife began to resurface. Resentments found only in those hidden depths inside someone where the worst of memories are stored.

Nathan saw Julie more clearly than the rest of the world. Over the years, she had taught herself to be incapable of compassion, shame, guilt, and most of all love. Her character did not contain sympathy or kindheartedness in its repertoire of limited emotions.

She had burned away any decent emotion she had ever possessed, becoming disconnected and desensitized from all unselfish feelings. Julie's disturbed mind looked upon all virtuous qualities as appalling handicaps and mental weaknesses.

Guided by a spiteful, charlatan heart, Julie navigated through life with narcissistic motivations. Her remorseless demeanor was at its most lethal point when her claws were deep-rooted in a self-serving endeavor.

Relentless in her efforts to manipulate any and all gratuitous situations, she greedily took advantage of anyone she could. Julie was far worse than obsessive; she was a vindictive fiend in an unending search for self-fulfillment.

Since her conspiring mind was incapable of passing any moral judgment upon herself, she had a difficult time functioning in the real world. Therefore, she created her own little self-serving reality, influencing and defrauding people as she saw fit. With self-preservation and self-gratification being her highest priority, she thrived on misleading and victimizing unsuspecting targets.

While hiding behind a charismatic alter-ego, she was calculating and convincing in her deceitful schemes. A conniving, systematic woman who was quite capable of saying or doing anything at any given time. Julie's mind was so demented; her diabolical thought process stimulated her own consciousness into believing all the lies and illusions she created. A deceptive and treacherous creature in which guilt or remorse did not exist.

Beneath her alluring, good-natured façade lurked a fiendish creature possessed with a single-minded ruthlessness. Julie was a pathological liar by trade; therefore her entire misguided existence was based on deceit and falsehoods. But, her perverted characteristics did not bother her in the least. It was who she was. It was what she excelled at.

Julie's greatest talent was in her ability to manipulate and betray ones trust. She could spontaneously produce any human emotion or improvise in any given situation with absolute conviction and credibility.

Throughout the years, she had consistently improved and refined her gifts of deception - for her survival depended on it. It was her biggest and most powerful weapon in her endless arsenal of vindictive qualities. She was an ungrateful subversive who took everything she could, but under no circumstances gave anything back.

Julie's neurotic intellect was constantly concocting some sort of enticing, devious game plan. Though her motives were incorrigible, they were simple just the same. While a societal underachiever, Julie was a street-wise mastermind. She was a specialist in hiding and disguising her true ulterior motives.

The way her scheming mind operated was far beyond the realm of normal rationalization. Few people in the world could so cunningly manipulate their environment with such disregard and callousness as she. Deviously manipulating gullible patsies and misleading them so that she could prosper from their good-hearted spirits. She abused and victimized people with as much eagerness as a small child opening presents on Christmas morning.

To Julie, society and the people there within, were merely implements she could use at any time to obtain her objectives. Using her victims as flavor in her poisonous brew, a recipe consisting of misguided emotions and wicked intensions.

Julie looked upon all other human existence with amusement and contempt. To show compassion toward the world, or those within it, would be the same as surrendering control over her reality - it would never happen.

As with most predators, she mercilessly pursued and devoured her unsuspecting prey. Her victims of choice mainly consisted of vulnerable, over-trusting men. This charlatan is what some people refer to as a parasite or "Black-Widow".

A diabolical femme fatale with her own shrewd agenda.

A sexually self-assertive seductress - a menace to all men.

A relentless bloodsucker, masterfully seducing and destroying any man with extreme prejudice.

Ultimately, she exploited and skillfully misused a man's emotions for her own self gain. She was man's mortal enemy, bleeding away everything he had to offer. Working her scheme until he was materially and emotionally drained of everything he possessed. Then, without hesitation or second thought, she would discard his empty shell like foul smelling garbage.

But, like a vampire needing blood, she would soon need to

find another victim. Always in an endless struggle to fill that agonizing bottomless void that dwelt deep inside.

All at once, the depressing thoughts of Julie vanished. Nathan's mind began to race with anxiety as a new and just as terrifying image took its place. Fast-forwarding his mind out of the past to the present, he found himself staring at the same creature that had cornered him in the shed.

Nathan could not believe what he was reading. The monster in Mrs. Ellis's shed was an African flesh-eating spider. It had a technical name he could not pronounce, but that did not matter. "Flesh-eating" was enough information for him.

According to the website, the spider's bite contained a poison that would paralyze its victim. The spider would gain entry through one of the animals orifices - usually its mouth. Then, the intruder would lay its eggs and exit the host. When the victim regained its motor functions, it would go on as usual. Unknowingly, the host's warmth would incubate the eggs until they hatched. Once hatched, the newborn spiders would eat the host's inner-flesh until the animal died. When the animal's corpse lost its body temperature, the spiders would exit the cadaver. After the spiders had reached adulthood, they would seek out their own host and start the process over.

Now, with the knowledge that a green, yellow-eyed cannibal resided in the old shed, he vowed never to enter it again. The terrifying phobia of spiders seemed to be the only thing he had left in life. And he had the worst of the eight-legged monsters living right next door.

After shutting off the computer, Nathan stared back out the front window. Following the sky to the north-west, he noticed the storm-front taking shape over the far-end of the lake. As sunset came to a conclusion, the sun now appeared as a red glow off the upper edges of the distant clouds.

Once the sun dropped behind the Sierra Nevada's, darkness came quickly to the Tahoe basin. Continuing to stare at the western sky, he watched as the evening shadows began to converge over the mountains.

Nathan slapped his hands down on the arms of the chair and heaved himself up to his feet. Letting out a dispirited sigh, he closed the curtains. Kicking off his shoes, he turned on the television and laid down on the couch.

After a couple deep breaths, he rested his hands on his chest. It was time to unwind and relax the best he could. While staring at the ceiling, he listened to the local news. Once again, the weather report was predicting thunder storms to hit the Tahoe area in the late evening. Temperatures were going to drop just above freezing.

As he lay in the darkening trailer, his mind became preoccupied by disgruntled thoughts concerning the restraining order. There seemed to be no remedy or way to resolve his current situation, but he had to try. It was time to call Julie and get a better idea where he stood.

Knowing that Julie usually slept through the morning into the late afternoon, it was still too early to make the call. Beside, Nathan was not quite ready to confront her just yet.

Just the thought of his ex-wife sent a quiver of misery cutting through his heart. Like a knife stabbing deep within, twisting and turning at his very being. He felt so empty, self-betrayed, he had let a woman ruin his life. Everything was going so good until he met her.

Nathan's dreams of a happy life on the lake had been consumed in violent, irreversible flames. As his mind drifted back into the recent past, he could remember only too well the frustrations of their time together. There was no love, no joy, only the procrastination of the inevitable. Their whole marriage had been a charade. Nathan was no more than a man that had been trapped into marriage by an unforeseen pregnancy.

Julie never had any respect for him and she never tried to hide the fact. Beside his daughter, Julie had turned their marriage into the most regretful experience of his life. It had become impossible for him to even coexist with the woman.

Suddenly, Nathan began to harbor tremendous amounts of nervous anxiety concerning the future actions of his ex-wife. With her latest back-stabbing stunt still fresh in his mind, he could not help but wonder what the hell was next.

Nathan's world seemed to be quickly caving in around him. As of late, life seemed to hand him nothing but painful extremes. If his life could be screwed up to any greater degree, he was at a loss to as how. Nearing dyer straights, he felt trapped in a poignant existence in which there was no breaking free. It was almost more than he could bare as his emotional barometer plummeted toward rock-bottom. Everything that mattered the most was now gone.

It was extremely hard for him to accept the thought of Julie and her boyfriend Steve raising his little girl. The two of them were a dangerous nuisance and a threatening influence over his daughter.

Steve had a long rap-sheet with a violent history and was always ready to step out of line. The potential for Steve's hot temper to become borderline murderous was commonplace for him. If there was anything he enjoyed, it was venting his anger and rage on those around him.

Nathan despised their lifestyle and knew neither one of them would ever change. They would always be addicted to their destructive, self-indulgent tendencies. He knew perfectly well, that if Sarah spent the remainder of her adultolescent years with the likes of those two, she would not stand a chance. She would end up amounting to nothing more than her mother reincarnated.

Beside the quest for compromise concerning his daughter, his self-reliant destiny was one of total uncertainty. Nathan felt a cold desolation inside himself, wondering if there was any point of even trying anymore.

But, at the same time, in an effort to maintain his sanity, anything about his life becoming normal was worth a shot. It was clear that what he did today would be a pivotal moment in his life. Maybe he was grasping at straws, but Nathan had to question what the future held if he did not challenge Julie.

Before that confrontation took place, it was time to get a little sleep. A temporarily escape from the added pressure she had just heaved upon him.

For another half-hour his mind raced, captured in a loop of unpleasant scenarios. Eventually, Nathan gradually began to relax. As he drifted off into a uneasy slumber, an unexpected, compelling sensation came over him.

Somehow, he felt that fate had just been laid out for him. As if he were about to be sent down some unforeseen path. A path that would force on him shocking misfortunes, regretful realities and unwished-for destinies.

Compelling himself to force away these anxious thoughts, he made a conscious effort to go to sleep. It was time to get some rest before the dreaded phone-call. For in a couple hours, Nathan would be throwing himself to the wolves. Leaping into a disturbing confrontation that he was not looking forward to.

CHAPTER 3

AFTER A RESTLESS NAP, Nathan shoved himself up from the couch. Reaching toward the ceiling, he groaned in an effort to stretch. Though somewhat relaxed and rested, the thought of the restraining order was still embedded in his mind. As if Julie were standing right in front of him, a seething anger began to burn once again.

The thought of calling his ex-wife nagged at him. Nathan knew exactly what kind of situation he was about to get himself into. Though there was no reason for Julie to give him a bad time, he could not help but expect one.

Nathan had always maintained a very timid spirit toward aggression, especially where Julie was concerned. As in the past, he could never gather enough backbone to challenge the nasty woman. While not easily provoked, Julie was capable of pushing all the buttons needed to send him into total frustration.

The woman's torturous words always put Nathan in a defensive mode. Testing him to the point where total self-control was required. But nowadays, she had forced him to see beyond his timid mannerisms. As it stood, though uneasy with the fact, she gave him no choice but to be as confrontational as herself.

Although Nathan felt justified in hating the woman, he could not help but feel sorry for her at the same time. Julie and women like her had the morals of an alley-cat, prowling amongst society with a true hatred toward the world.

She was poised with the fact, that giving off bad vibes was

one of her strongest traits. It was standard practice for her to be as obnoxious as possible. Never sorry for anything, she was insensitive and unrealistic in ways that few could tolerate. People that really knew Julie felt it wise to have as little to do with her as possible.

While angry and resentful toward everything and everyone, Julie's true bitterness was fueled by her own denials. Her main grievance was based on her total contempt toward Nathan. Despising the fact, that the connection between him and their daughter was stronger than her own.

While uneasy about talking to Julie, Nathan realized that failing to make the phone-call was something he could ill-afford. It was time to take a stand. Time to confront his ex-wife before things got beyond his control.

By all normal probabilities, thinking she might greet the phone-call with a positive response was ridiculous. For he knew, it would be incredibly naïve to trust Julie on anything. But for the time being, he had to maintain a positive line of thought.

While filled with hostility toward the way Julie had dealt with their situation, he was determined to try. Nathan wanted to discuss matters as objectively as possible and remain indifferent to her and everything she had done. Only wishing to avoid a confrontation and possibly talk to his daughter.

Nathan could only surmise that a small miracle was in order for Julie to change her attitude. Perhaps the best that could be hoped for would be that she did not immediately hang-up. Intense with the notion of what he was about to do, he dialed her number.

**

Julie wore the half-dead, strung-out mask of a lost soul slowly committing suicide. With a cigarette smoldering in an overflowing ashtray, another dangled from her disenchanted lips. Smoke trailed from her mouth and nostrils, slowly ascending past her squinting, red-rimmed eyes.

In a semi-catatonic daze, she sat in a high-backed armchair. Next to the chair resided a battered end table where she diligently guarded identical bottles of cheap, rock-gut vodka. One fifth nearly empty, while the other remained untapped.

Happy hour for Julie conveniently began as soon as she had risen from her previous drug-induced blackout. Today she was in classic form, picking up from where she had left off just a few hours ago.

Beside her addiction to drugs, Julie personified the roll of a high achiever in the alcoholic realm. Straight, warm vodka had always been her preference. She had no need or desire for mixers, water or ice. Not even a glass to pour it in. For this was not a bar designated to entertain guests. It was her own private shrine and worship place.

Alcohol and drugs were the essential essence of her being - her only solace. She prayed and gave sacrament to an eighty-proof God, a sacred communion in which no one else was invited. An altered reality she created for herself, totally apart from the rest of world.

For in Julie's lonely existence, she was a woman who had only one objective in life. Making sure her aging body was constantly enhanced with pills, assorted drugs and mass quantities of hard alcohol.

Reaching to the end-table, Julie grabbed the nearly empty vodka bottle and sluggishly raised it to her awaiting lips. Without hesitation, she drank the intoxicating spirits, swallowing hungrily until the clear bottle refused to surrender another drop.

With no further need for her once sacred bottle, she impulsively discarded its empty shell behind the chair. With the back of her hand, she wiped away the excess inebriating dribble from her mouth and quickly returned to her cigarette.

Inhaling greedily as she always did, Julie exhaled a long stream of smoke above her head. In the dimly lit room, the smoke gave the appearance of cloud of toxic gas lingering about the ceiling.

After crushing her expired cigarette into the overflowing ashtray she leaned forward, her lips compressed in irritation. As a cloud of suspended smoke hovered around her scowling face, Julie squinted her venomous, bloodshot eyes at the ringing phone. Conveying an expression that if she answered the call, she had every intension of starting trouble.

Holding her tattered doll, seven year old Sarah silently stared at her mother as the phone continued to ring.

"What the hell are you staring at? Get back in your room and stay there!" Screaming at her daughter in an undeserving outburst.

Sarah's tiny world suddenly froze. Wondering what she had done wrong, she held her doll tightly against her chest. Before her mother could scream at her again, little Sarah turned and ran to her bedroom.

Positive it was Nathan calling about the restraining order, Julie answered the phone. "What the hell do you want?" In typical drunken fashion, her first words of the day were harsh and slurred.

The spontaneous friction she initiated instantly set the tone for the conversation. Lately, Julie sought any excuse to force a confrontation and vent some sort of repressed anger. As in the past, she was in the process of fueling the fire for an argument and setting the stage for an immediate war. At this point in time, Julie's only objective was to feed his anxieties and prolong his frustrations.

A flush of heat crept into Nathan's face when he heard that hateful, thick, cigarette soured voice. It was all he could do to keep a civil tongue. But he knew that the resentment issued by this embittered woman was just an initial step toward a free-for-all. It was nothing that he had not experienced many times before.

160

Though her voice was a little raspier than usual, it was just as irritating as always. As he expected, he immediately recognized the drunken mannerisms in her voice. Like always, she had probably had enough booze in her to give half of Lake Tahoe a hangover. Right then, it would have been easy for him to hang-up. But that would all but kill any further chances of trying to talk to Sarah.

Reminding himself to keep things simple and in perspective, Nathan refused to let her lead him into an unwinnable skirmish. Not answering immediately, he tried to gather a rational train of thought.

Releasing an exasperated sigh, Nathan countered her initial assault with forced empathy. "There's no need to bite my heads off." Basically pleading with her to give it a break. "I didn't call to fight with you...I was just wondering how you and Sarah were doin'." While unintentional, it came out almost as an apology.

Already on the defensive, the vicious and malicious side of her was on the attack. "Why are you calling me? What the hell do you want?" Inquiring in a bitterly mocking tone.

Immediately, Nathan became completely annoyed by the obnoxious woman. It was all he could do to keep a leash on the anger erupting inside him.

It had always astonished him, how Julie's wrath remained so close at hand. With a vengeance, she wore her bitterness on her sleeve, ready to lash out at anyone at any time. As Nathan took another moment to gather his thoughts there was nothing said, just an uncomfortable silence.

While waiting for a response, Julie switched the call over to speaker phone. Now, with her hands free from the phone, she dug out another cigarette from the crumpled Marboro pack. Impatiently, she stuck the cancer-stick between her lips, thumbed her lighter and sparked a flame. After a long greedy drag, she yanked it from her mouth and blew out a cloud of smoke. As she exhaled, she studied the smoke as if she were pondering her next malicious outburst.

Taking another deep, frustrated drag from her cigarette, Julie tried to negatively jump-start the conversation. "Answer me," she commanded. "What do you want?" Smoke rushed from her mouth and nostrils as she spoke.

"You know exactly why I'm calling. I want to know what this restraining order is all about?"

"It means exactly what it says. You're not to call or try to see me or Sarah. And you're not to come within two-hundred feet of us or the house. Does that clear things up?" Taunting him with a confident maliciousness.

"Why'd you do this? Why do you want to take Sarah away from me?"

As much as Nathan ached for answers, he knew this spiteful woman was not about to be forthcoming. Much less give him any straight-forward answers. She had never extended him the courtesy of being truthful about anything before, why would she now?

As predicted, Julie retreated into her world of denial once again, responding with a weak attempt at defending her latest undertaking. "I had my reasons...I don't need to answer to you. I don't need to explain anything to you." Void of any sentiment or concern, her voice retained that familiar mask of defiance. "If it's sympathy you're looking for, you're talking to the wrong person." Her lips peeled back into a fiendish grin as she let out a mocking laugh.

It was obvious she felt no remorse. It never seized to amaze Nathan how the woman could so effortlessly unleash such hatefulness and pain upon others. But, in this, lay Julie's power. She preyed on the vulnerabilities of others, attacking their weaknesses. And Nathan's biggest Achilles-heel was his daughter.

Nathan tried to ignore her comments, but the tension on his

end of the phone instantly grew to a higher level. What composure he had left was slowly slipping away. In that instant, his hatred toward his ex-wife fully blossomed.

Trying to disguise his true feelings, Nathan held his frustration in check. Once again, he forced himself to be as tactful as possible. "I'm not looking for sympathy... Julie...I just want my daughter back in my life."

Always maintaining that devious edge she was so masterful at, Julie went straight for the throat. "Spare me the daddy dearest routine. For some reason, it just doesn't fit you." Her voice no more than a raspy, sarcastic whisper. "She's not your daughter anymore, she belongs to me. As far as Sarah is concerned, that subject isn't open for discussion."

The muscles in Nathan's face and neck tightened as his resentment mounted. "Did it ever occur to you that Sarah's my daughter too?" Madder than a wet cat, he continued. "You have another thing coming if you think I'm just going walk out of Sarah's life." His voice heated and decisive.

Julie continued to bait him with domineering reprimands. It was obvious she had rehearsed her little speech, the words just rolled out too smoothly. "Only on the birth certificate, Nathan, that's as close as you'll ever come to being her dad." Her response attacked every nerve in his body.

Julie's remarks bit deep, cutting him to a quick. Nathan's eyes fixed into a pained, anxious stare as he felt the genuine coldness in her threatening words. But as far as he was concerned, it was an empty threat, but effective just the same.

Releasing another exasperated sigh, he rubbed his forehead and began to read what was written on the restraining order. "It says here, that you said I abused you and Sarah." Feeling an instant pulse of irritation, he responded critically. "What are you talking about? You know that's a lie... I never raised my voice or laid a finger on either of you. That's the job of your new psychopath boyfriend... Isn't it?"

Julie's eyes narrowed spitefully as she prepared to challenge the accusation, but she remained silent. With a scowl of anger, she snatched up the unopened vodka bottle, cracked it open and twisted off the cap. Raising the eighty-proof spirits to her lips, she guzzled from her bottle of courage as if it were no more than tap water. With a vice grip around the neck of the bottle, she proceeded to slam it down next to the overflowing ashtray.

"You and Sarah are a dead issue. You'll never see her again... So live with it." Her voice changing pitch as she became more defiant.

The thought of losing Sarah enraged him. Nathan resented the necessity to raise his voice, but he could not help himself. "Well, that's a comforting thought isn't it?" He had no intensions on accepting this. As his face flushed with anger, his tone became bolder. "What is your problem, Julie?"

In her typical, drug induced, inebriated dignity, Julie shot back. "You're the problem! Every time Sarah's with you...She doesn't want to come home. She's my property and I won't let her choose you over me. Beside, she's got a new daddy now."

Nathan cringed at the thought of his daughter in the same house as that out-of-control nut-case. Pushed passed the limit of self-control, he exploded. "You call that drunk, abusive psychopath a father figure? He's not a dad, he's a predator. Even on his best behavior, I wouldn't leave my worst enemy with the guy! Everything written on this restraining order refers to him, not me."

Not about to let her off the hook, Nathan became more critical. "When's the last time he beat-on you or Sarah? Don't think I don't know about him abusing my daughter. If you let that crazed psychopath beat you down on a regular basis, that's on you. But he better never lay another hand on Sarah or he'll deal with me!" Not wanting to pursue the subject any further, he left it at that.

After his last comment, Julie seemed to ignore him, not

saying a word. Unable to help himself, he continued. "Hello...No comment...Is the truth hitting home?" Drawing her attention to the fact that she was putting Sarah's well-being in jeopardy.

Impulsively, Julie wrapped her lips around her eighty-proof friend. After pulling down a couple deep swallows, she tried to light another cigarette. Unable to get a flame, she became furious and threw the lighter across the room.

In total rage, she jumped up from the chair. Shoulders reared back, chest puffed out, she stood like a drunken drill sergeant barking commands. As if Nathan were standing right there, she began screaming and pointing a demanding finger at the speaker phone. "First of all, what happens over here is none of your business. Second of all, you'll never...I repeat never...Get any custody of Sarah. Do you understand me? It's just the way things are going to be."

Nathan opened his mouth, but found he could not respond. Her words seemed irretrievable. Like a knife stabbing deep within, the word "never" penetrated his very being, sending a cutting blade of misery twisting and turning through his heart.

Before he could deliver a response, the good-for-nothing female continued. "Deal with it, Nathan...You're out of the picture." In a vixen, intoxicated infliction, she concluded her verbal tirade. "You don't have a daughter anymore...So live with it! You're not going to see Sarah again!"

Nathan could not believe her vile attitude about such an issue. It was typical for her to draw a small amount of blood, but this time she was trying to bleed him out.

An intense loathing beyond anything he had ever imagined enthralled him. Helpless frustration enhanced his anger as he realized her threat could turn out to be true. Though he was not about to give into her threats, nothing could remove the vicious sting she had just inflicted.

Eyes raised to the ceiling, he shook his head in incensed

resentment. "Fine, we'll play it your way. I must have been out of my mind to think you could be civil about this."

Sinking back into her chair, Julie left Nathan's last words hanging in the air. Her face assumed a frozen expression of indifference as she reached to the end-table and grabbed her aspirin bottle. It was a container that held not aspirin, but rather various un-prescribed prescription drugs.

Julie dumped the assorted narcotics into the palm of her hand. With multiple pills to choose from, she became undecided of what kind of high she wished to achieve. Not caring what she was about to devour, she tilted her head back and popped the pills in her mouth. Accompanied by a couple swigs of warm vodka, she swallowed them all down. It was just business as usual. It would not be long before she was in another drug-induced delirium.

Awaiting Julie's next attack, his forehead creased in provoked anger. The tension that now saturated the phone line was thick and getting thicker with each passing moment. Though he hated to admit it, he knew there would be no reaching some sort of middle ground or compromise. No matter how hard he tried, all his efforts to negotiate would be for not.

Nathan's amazement regarding her relentless abuse deepened as she spat out more conditions. "It's a dead issue, Nathan. If you don't leave me alone…I'll call the police." With not a hint of hostility in her voice, she concluded her vindictiveness. "And you know I'll do it."

It was almost incomprehensible of what she was threatening to do. In fact, in his mind, he protested and refused to believe she would actually do it. But then again, with mentally unstable drug addicts like Julie, the game called life was played by a totally different set of rules.

After hearing Julie's ultimatums, his blood began to boil. Her nonchalant maliciousness was unnerving. It was not so much what she said; it was how she said it. Nathan had all he could stand of her spiteful games. Without hesitation, his mind put up a wall. Her atrocious threats and deeds had no power over him any longer.

Nathan's frustrations made way all at once. "Go ahead, play your games. If you feel you've got to take this sadistic game to another level, bring it on." Challenging her in a furious outburst.

Knowing that her ex-husband's frustrations had hit its peak, Julie's lips curved into a malicious smile. It was exactly the ambush she wished to ensnare. "It's as simple as this, Nathan. I'll do whatever...Whenever I please...And there's nothing you can do about it." With a Master's Degree in torturing him in very creative ways, she summarized their situation. "You want to test me? Give it your best shot. We'll see who the cops believe...And who goes to jail."

Nathan's grip tightened around the phone until the joints in his fingers popped. "If you want to call the police...Then call 'em. I don't care...I've done nothing wrong."

The whole disheartening conversation had quickly mushroomed into much more than he could handle. Completely fed-up, Nathan had enough of her craziness to last a lifetime. There was nothing left to say or hear. There was no way he could listen to her drunken animosity any longer.

Not ready to end the call, he gave her one last piece of his mind. "You're unbelievable lady...In fact you're sick. And you're living in a dream world if you think I won't come after Sarah."

Before Julie could take to the airwaves once again, something happened. Listening intently, he pressed the phone against his ear. Nathan could hear Steve in the background screaming in rage.

"Get the hell off the phone!" Steve ordered, sounding as if he were right next to the receiver.

"What are you doing?" There was a sense of fear and urgency in Julie's voice.

"Julie, are you okay? What's going on?" Nathan inquired in a stern, concerned voice.

Though Steve was a product of Julie's own stupidity, she could usually keep him somewhat in check. But something was disturbingly different this time. Even Julie could not predict what was about to happen to her and Sarah.

CHAPTER 4

NATHAN FELT HIS BREATH sucked from his lungs as a desperate feeling of disaster gripped him. With a shutter of concern, he knew good and well that something was seriously wrong.

Heart in his throat, he listened to Julie's frightened voice on the other end of the line. "Let her go, Steve...Don't hurt her... She's done nothing wrong!" Ordering Steve with a rare burst of motherly instinct.

The truth of the matter could not be avoided. Something terrible was taking place. Somehow, in that split-second, Julie's past crimes did not seem important. Trying to listen closer to the unruly situation, Nathan pressed the receiver harder against his ear.

As if he had been grievously wronged, Steve seemed to be in some out-of-control rage. Though unable to make out what the psycho was yelling about, one thing was for sure, there was no mercy in his voice.

Awash in the emotional effect of what was taking place, Nathan pleaded with his ex-wife to talk to him. "Talk to me... Julie...What's goin' on? Is Sarah okay?" Instantly, his voice became filled with panicked emotion. "Don't you touch my daughter you son-of-a-bitch!"

All at once, bloodcurdling screams from both Julie and Sarah pierced through the phone. As if the world had come to a holt, Nathan's heart froze while listening to the anguish in Sarah's frantic cries for help.

While yelling his daughter's name, Nathan continued to listen to the attack. Abruptly, he found himself listening in disbelief as their screams trailed off into painful whimpers.

Breathing erratically and deep, he mentally wrestled what to do next. Instinctively, Nathan pulled his cell phone from his shirt pocket and dialed the three digit number. Putting the cellphone to his other ear, he found himself listening intently to both phones.

The call was answered before the first ring had finished. "911 emergency response, what's your emergency?"

Nathan cringed as the call was answered. Not sure what to say, the first words off the top of his head were shouted. "My daughter's been hurt...Send somebody quick!"

"Sir...What's going on?"

"I don't know. But I know their hurt." His sense of urgency heightened at the thought of what that maniac might have done. "Send someone to 565 Dogwood Road...Now!"

While trying to plead his case to the dispatcher, there was a sharp click. Julie's phone experienced a short period of dead space, followed by a dial tone. The call had been terminated from the other end.

"What's your name, sir?" Nathan did not respond, staring at the receiver from which Sarah's screams had resounded.

"Are you at this address right now, sir?"

For some reason, Nathan's thought-process would not let her question register. "Just send someone. I've got to get to Sarah!" Nathan abruptly ended communications with the 911 dispatcher.

Heart pounding against his ribcage, he tried to calm down, But infectious concern was not going to let that happen. If Nathan was going to maintain a hint of sanity, he had to find out if Sarah was okay.

Consumed with an unshakable determination to get to his daughter, Nathan understood there was only one thing left to do.

While it might turn out to be the final nail in his coffin, he had to defy the restraining order and hightail-it to Julie's house.

Truck crippled with a dead battery, there was no choice but to find another way across town - and quick. Nathan knew, it would take much too long to find someone to give him a ride. With no time to waste, the best option was to get to Stateline. It was time to make his way down to the casinos and get a cab.

Concerned with nothing else but getting to Sarah, he grabbed a jacket and exited the trailer. Knowing that the quickest way to Stateline was down the mountainside through the forest, Nathan raced toward the rear of the trailer park.

Within a couple seconds, he approached old Mrs. Ellis's shed. While more than twenty feet away from the structure, a shiver of anxiety cursed through his body. With the knowledge of what hid inside the wooden structure, every hair on his body stood on end. After getting past the shed, Nathan entered the forest and began the descent down the hill.

In less than five minutes, the lights of Stateline became bright and clear through the trees. Since darkness had fallen, the casinos were preparing for another wild night at the lake.

As soon as Nathan exited the woods, he was within a few feet of the highway. Just a short distance from casinos, he began running alongside the four-lane road. Reaching the first casino, it was all about locating a cab. With no taxies in sight, Nathan continued down to the next gambling establishment.

Concentrating on the quest at hand, Nathan proceeded to race down the street. Pedestrian traffic along the sidewalk became more cluttered as he gained ground on the next destination.

No matter what time of day or night, Stateline was always full of people out and about. While some raced to their next gambling sight, the rest just stood around gazing at the glimmering skyline.

Eyes fixed in the direction of the next objective, Nathan hastily dodged the clusters of slow moving sightseers. Incensed with urgency, he weaved and veered through the stagnant crowd.

Once under the casino's promenade, he immediately made his way to where the taxies were stationed. Standing at the entrance to the taxi run, Nathan began frantically waving and whistling. Numerous cabs were lined up as he raised his hand, without delay, the first cab in line raced up to meet him. Opening the rear passenger door, Nathan quickly jumped into the back seat.

"Where to?"

"Just head down So. Tahoe Boulevard…I'll tell you when to stop."

The taxi pulled away from the hotel and joined Stateline's steady flow of traffic. Nathan sank into the back seat, trying to stay as composed as possible. Lost in anxious thought, he watched as the casino lights quickly glided by.

Inside the cab there was no conversation, only the groan of the engine. As the taxi driver steered through a long, gradual turn, Stateline faded out of sight.

Nathan felt anxious and alone as the cab cruised along the lakefront. Looking out the side window, his vision eased up toward the sky. With only a few days until a full moon, its huge presence loomed ominously in the middle of the sky.

As the cold face of the moon stared down, the lake provided a picture perfect reflection. With the dark outline of the shore barely visible, it was almost as if looking at two skies. But Nathan knew that beautiful reflection was to be short-lived.

As the heaters stuffy warmth blew from the dashboard vents, his concentration focused on the northern mountains. The Fall storm was definitely taking shape as its clouds formed a threatening line over the far end of the lake. The mountain peaks had already been devoured by the looming storm-front.

With the promise of rain in the horizon, Nathan watched as a distant flash of lightning lit up the north sky. The momentary flash of brilliant light, revealed the extensive, black thunder clouds that were engulfing the Tahoe basin. The storm would soon be knocking on South Shore's door.

While the Taxi continued down the boulevard, the lake and the approaching storm abruptly vanished. Giving way to the business distract, Nathan watched as the small town unrolled before him.

Three hours had passed since darkness had fallen over the forest, and all the lights around the lakefront were aglow. The intermittent street-lights created brief explosions of light and darkness inside the cab. Looking intently through the backseat window, he sat in silence amidst the racing shadows.

Nathan's face was usually carefree and friendly, but not today. This night, it was tainted with an expression of discontent and doubt. Absorbed in thought, the uncertainty concerning his daughter caused his anxiety to escalate.

Sarah's screams kept echoing over and over in his mind. Worried to death, he had never felt such a heart-wrenching concern. Though his calm was self-imposed, Nathan maintained a gnawing sense of unease.

If not for his own peace of mind, it was time to make it his business and take matters into his own hands. There was no way he could stand by and let his little girl slip beyond his reach. Somehow, Nathan had to rescue Sarah and save her from the same destiny her mother had fallen into.

For any parent, the absolute separation from their child is a painful reality and a devastating ordeal to say the least. But, in Nathan's case, it was even worse. Sarah had been virtually stolen from him. Dishonestly kidnapped by a drunken, drug-addicted pathological liar who claimed to be a loving mother.

Not having the slightest clue as what to expect, Julie and her psycho boyfriend were lock-set in Nathan's mind. As the cab drew closer to the destination, Nathan mentally prepared himself for what might lay ahead. The big question was how they might react when he showed up unexpectedly. Knowing his ex-wife and the boyfriend, nervous anticipation consumed his thoughts. Julie and Steve were anything but predictable.

Nathan's thoughts were put on hold as the Nickel-Night motel came into view. It was a second-rate, single story structure that cornered the street that lead toward his old house.

Nearing the turn-off, the taxi approached a bridge that passed over a small stream. "Let me off here...This is good enough." Deciding to make the rest of the journey on foot.

After pulling over in front of the bridge, the driver turned toward Nathan. "Do you want me to wait?"

"No...I'm good...Thanks for the ride." Reaching over the seat and paying the driver.

After climbing out of the cab, Nathan returned his attention toward the stars. While the moon still remained high in the night sky, it was beginning to be obscured by scattered clouds.

As the taxi pulled from the curb, he started across the bridge. While walking over the bridge, Nathan glared down into the bleak, empty darkness that swallowed the creek. Though the tiny stream was merely fifteen feet below, it might as well have been fifteen miles - a bottomless gorge.

Nathan had visited the creek numerous times during the daylight hours. But he was never able to summon up enough courage to venture down there after dark. While his eyes ran along the base of the dark forbidding bridge, his imagination suddenly seemed to have a will all its own. In his mind's eye, the same bizarre vision that always captured his thoughts arose once again.

Nathan crazily imagined what sort of hidden, nocturnal creatures lurked in those shallow depths where darkness prevailed. Conjuring up mental images of a myriad of wild predators hiding amongst the flourishing shadows. A lair of marauding beasts patiently stalking their next kill. Unknown creatures that hid away in the midst of that black abyss where no human eyes could penetrate.

Nathan quickly shook himself and continued the traverse across the bridge. Wanting to stay out-of-sight, he decided to take a short-cut through the woods.

Approaching the forest tree-line, out-of-the-blue something caught his eye. Focused on the deeper realms of the woods, there was definite movement in the darkness beneath the trees. Nathan was not quite sure, but he could swear someone was running down toward the creek.

Soon after entering the woods, the light from the street-lamp dissipated to nothing. Though sure he was on the right path, nothing looked familiar in the sudden darkness. Advancing further into the murky landscape, he looked for any landmark that might aid his journey.

Nathan's movements were awkward and tentative as he ventured through the obscurity of the darkened woods. The trees groaned and the branches hissed against the rising wind.

Maneuvering through the woods, he repeatedly turned his eyes toward the storm threatened sky. Looking past the top-most limbs of the giant pines, special attention was paid to the narrow slivers of sky. It quickly becoming obvious that the storm-front was rapidly moving in.

As the night sky appeared between racing clouds, moonlight briefly revealed itself. But, each time a set of clouds would shield the moon, the woods were quickly devoured in complete darkness. With the moon's glow being continually interrupted, he constantly fought to adjust to the reoccurring blackness.

Focusing on the obstacles in front of him, he weaved between the huge trunks of the Ponderosa pines. After a hike of about a hundred yards, Nathan came upon a piece of woods that he knew very well. This was the landmark he was looking for. Knowing he was where he needed to be, Nathan directed his sights up the hillside.

While avoiding the tree branches that were head high, the

climb up the hill began. It was a miserable hike, but one that he had made before.

Out of nowhere, something that did not belong to the forest caught his undivided attention. Looking up the hill, he watched as the once lightless woods was now being invaded. Totally mystified to what was taking place ahead, a confused Nathan continued up the hill.

CHAPTER 5

IN A HEAVILY WOODED area, Julie's house was sided by intermittent houses and cabins. It had always been a dark, poorly lit neighborhood. The only light on the street was a lone street-lamp a half-block away. But tonight, while in the isolation of the darkened forest, Nathan watched as pulses of colored lights strobe through the woods.

Embraced by the queer lights, adrenaline began to kick-in. Upon further advancement, the source of the lights was finally revealed.

A barrage of flashing lights engulfed the front of Julie's house. Nathan found himself witnessing a congregation of the most disturbing kind. The once dark street was now clogged with emergency vehicles. Time seemed to stop as he stared in stunned amazement.

As the red and blue light show continued, he moved forward trying not to present an unmistakable silhouette. Nathan's progress was accompanied by the penetrating sound of twigs cracking under each step. The high-pitched snapping of underbrush was disturbingly crisp and loud in the tranquil forest.

Not wanting to give away his whereabouts, Nathan became fearfully hesitant of going any further. But as the complexities of the situation grew in his mind, it became imperative to get closer.

In an attempt to muffle his progress, each advancing step was carefully placed in a non-compromising foothold. With all the stealth possible, Nathan moved discretely from one bit of cover to the next. Creeping up as close as dared, he used the last line of trees as cover.

Masked by shadows, the background of the forest provided perfect camouflage. Positioned behind a huge pine-tree, Nathan had a vantage point that put him in full view of the scene. As if part of the night's darkness, he knelt down and spied across the street.

Captured by the drama of the extraordinary picture, all emotions jumped to a higher intensity. Lungs swollen with anxiety, the insanities unfolding were watched closely. With one part of him shocked and confused, the other part had a good idea of what might be taking place. If his earlier suspicions were correct, something terrible had happened.

Nathan became unnervingly distracted by the number of cops policing the property. As far as he was able to tell, there was at least a half-dozen police cars in various locations. A fire-truck was parked in the street, while another sat in the driveway.

A frigid, steady wind continued to mount as he followed the movements of the police. Though impossible to understand, Nathan could hear the hum of several garbled conversations from the not-so-distant officers. The conversations entered his eyes and ears as a series of serious faces and distorted voices. The only distinctive sound was the annoying squawking that resided from the police-band radios.

The collection of police and emergency vehicles had attracted a lot of attention. Despite the hour, a number of motel overnighters and residents from the neighboring houses had gathered on the street-side.

The crowd of onlookers stamped their feet and hugged themselves in the cold, open wind. The curious gathering was alive with conversation, but Nathan was unable to understand anything being said. While their prying eyes took in the scene, their unintelligible murmurs dispersed from their lips on clouds of frozen breath.

In front of the house, a group of police officers were gathered together. As further details of the scene came into his line-of-sight, he noticed that the patrolmen were congregated around a man in a suit. Obviously a detective, he appeared to be taking charge of the situation. As Nathan watched the detective direct traffic, he could not help but wonder what the officers were being told. Whatever the Detective was saying, it had every man's undivided attention.

Shifting his eyes away from the huddle of men, Nathan spotted another suit standing next to an unmarked police car. This Detective appeared to be interviewing one of Julie's female neighbors.

The woman appeared to be giving a detailed statement. Upon each question asked, she responded with a variety of animated gestures. Watching the detective take notes, Nathan's heart suddenly began to pound wildly as the woman began pointing toward the woods.

Nathan continued to study the commotion around the house. "Where's Julie? Where's Sarah?" Whispering to himself.

"They must still be inside the house," answering his own question. "Julie's probably too drunk to stand up."

Just as he finished that thought, an ambulance pulled in front of the house. The sight of the EMT's instantly filled him with a fearful queasiness. After backing into the driveway, a pair of paramedics quickly jumped out. Pulling a gurney from the back of the ambulance, they hurriedly made their way into the house.

For several minutes Nathan stared at the house, wondering what the hell was going on inside. All at once, the police made way for the paramedics as they pushed the gurney out the front door. After emerging from the house, he recognized that it was

Julie being escorted on the wheeled stretcher. Head wrapped in a mass of blood-soaked bandages, she lay motionless.

With sympathetic concern, he watched the dramatic scene progress. As Julie was being loaded into the ambulance, the police once again backed away from the front door. Within a few seconds, a second gurney appeared only to stop partially exposed in the doorway.

Where's the other ambulance? Silently questioning himself.

Quickly surveying the front of the house, it was spotted. Nathan could not believe he had not noticed it before - it was the Coroner's van.

Right away, the weight of the world seemed to crash down on him. In that instant, all his fears seemed to come true. Slowly and dejectedly, he sank into a sitting position beneath the ancient pine. His body went weak as a sickening sensation seized him. Nathan knew his precious daughter was dead.

Many of the bystanders gasp as the second gurney finally emerged from the house. Unlike Julie, there was no urgency concerning this person. Nathan's heart instantly withered and his throat knotted in mournful pain at the sight of his little girl completely covered in a sheet.

As they rolled Sarah across the driveway, he sat in a catatonic state of disgruntled despair. Nathan's skin began to sting with sheer horror as her tiny body was lifted into Coroner's van.

With the slamming of the van's rear doors, all emotions broke down. Half-paralyzed, helpless tears or remorse began to roll down his face. Face in his hands, he waited for the tears to stop. But that moment was not soon to come.

As Julie's ambulance rolled quietly out of the driveway, Nathan raised his tear-stricken stare. An immediate, powerful internal anger gripped him. For he knew all too well who had done this – who murdered his little girl.

A few moments later, the cluster of spectators looked on as the coroner's van pulled out on the street. Nathan's stare followed the van refusing to believe his Sarah was actually inside. As the Coroner disappeared into the night, another police cruiser pulled up to the house - a K-9 unit.

Nathan was beside himself as he surveyed the movements of the police. The officers continued to mill around the house, speaking in grave tone's while keeping anxious eyes on the surrounding woods.

With an overbearing bravado, the lead Detective began giving orders to the other officers. Trying to absorb what was being said, he strained to hear anything.

Suddenly, in the vagueness of the conversation, the Detective started pointing in Nathan's direction. Simultaneously, every policeman turned their head toward the section of woods where he hid.

With the K-9 straining at his leash, it was obvious that they were quickly gearing up to expand the investigation. Weapons now drawn, the police were preparing to make a sweep through the woods.

Despite the cold weather, beads of nervous sweat began to coat Nathan's face. Staring at the police and their pistols, Nathan stood in disbelief. The scenario playing out before him was way beyond his comprehension. It looked as if the police wanted more from the fugitive than just conversation.

Anticipating a pursuit, Nathan realized he was in an very unstable dilemma. It was not in his best interest to stick around any longer. It became vital that he vanish from this area as soon as possible. Nathan was not about to be stuck holding the bag on this one.

Maintaining surveillance on the cops, he waited for just the right moment to make his move. Prepared to retreat into the darker realms of the forest, he was interrupted by the slamming of a car door.

A jolt of alarm seized him as he turned toward the noise. With the sound of an engine starting, he watched anxiously as a police

Blazer headed up the street. Unexpectedly, the Blazer's brake lights flashed and the cruiser swung wide and made a U-turn.

Nathan shivered with a chill of panic as the vehicle approached. Looking on in terror, the officer switched on the cruiser's high-intensity spotlight.

Nathan pressed his back against the pine-tree as the cop aimed the light into the darkness of the woods. Despite the urge to flee, Nathan knew it was too late to escape - he would be spotted for sure. The only chance was to become a silent and unmoving part of the dark forest.

Drawing ever so close, the penetrating light flickered as it moved along the tree-line. Only a few yards away, the once darkened forest now gave way to brilliant light. Shining through the gaps in the trees, the extreme light caused the towering pines to cast off long, infinite shadows across the forest floor.

Slowly but surely, the searchlight found its way in his direction. The forest seemed to instantly shrink around him. The intense beacon of light tediously crept amidst the trees until its radiance lit the woods all around him.

Virtually glued to the backside of the pine-tree, Nathan became a shadow amidst shadows. With his silhouette concealed within the sharply defined shadow of the tree, he was able to remain out of sight.

Surprisingly, the spotlight stopped moving. Now, his once dark world was brilliantly lit. Nathan's heart seemed to stop beating as he closed his eyes and pressed the back of his head against the tree. A queasy and devastating sense of finality enveloped his soul with the certainty of being caught.

He couldn't have seen me. How could he see me without getting out of the patrol car?

Fearful of his breath being seen, Nathan took in as much air as possible and held it. Sweat ran down his forehead as he stood motionless, listening for the slightest movement.

After several seconds, his lungs began to burn. Nathan

realized he was still holding his breath. Attempting to keep any frozen breath from fogging the air, he slowly and silently exhaled through his nose.

After what seemed forever, Nathan finally heard the much welcome sound of tires rolling along the shoulder of the road. Remaining perfectly still, only his eyes moved in the direction of the sound. The searchlight continued to probe the woods as the departing cruiser slowly eased down the tree-line.

There was an immediate quiver of elation as the spotlight slowly moved away. Nathan inhaled, then, blew it out in a rush of relief. But the moment was short-lived as his name was broadcast over the police radios.

There was a quick moment of static, then, the woman's voice returned on the radio. Listening closely, he heard his name again. According to dispatcher, everyone was being advised that Julie's ex-husband had made the 911 call. As Nathan saw it, the cops must definitely think he was responsible for the travesty.

Swallowing hard against a racing pulse, a voice inside told him not to dwell on the squawking radios. For if he was the prime suspect in this sickening mess, he could not be found here. Whatever had happened in the house, he would have to figure it out and deal with it later. With little time left, Nathan had to get as far away from this neighborhood as possible.

Once the police Blazer disappeared from view, it became time to begin withdrawing into the forest. After backtracking deeper into the woods, he stopped and looked back toward the house. Nathan could see what appeared to be the entire So. Lake Tahoe Police Department taking their positions along the tree-line.

Needing to move quickly, his stare turned back down the dark hillside. The creek and bridge were at the bottom of the ravine. Somehow he had to get there.

Aware of only the need to escape, he aggressively retraced his steps down the hillside. Breath puffing in the chilled air,

Nathan suddenly found himself descending the hill faster than he believed possible.

No longer aided by the lights of the emergency vehicles, the forest quickly gave way to severe darkness. Arms extended, Nathan pin-balled from tree to tree, recklessly fighting his way downhill. Momentum out-of control, a tree was grabbed in a last ditch effort to regain control of his body.

Skin tore away from his forearms and hands as the force of his momentum instantly ripped his grip away from the tree. Unable to keep his balance, Nathan hit the ground with a twig-crunching thud.

The flesh wounds were small, but painful just the same. Hurt and disoriented, Nathan quickly sat up trying to regain his bearings. After a few uncertain moments to collect himself, he got back to his feet. Heart frantically pounding away, he stared intently up the hillside.

Looking back up in the direction of the police, multiple perplexing thoughts raced through his mind. The idea of so many police caused his panic level to sky-rocket. Realizing the chaotic seriousness of the situation, it was obvious that he had become the focal-point of the manhunt.

Nathan was not looking forward to a confrontation with the police. And he was determined not to give them an easy opportunity to arrest him. With no time left to think, Nathan pushed deeper down into the woods. If ever the darkness of night were a friend, he hoped it were now!

CHAPTER 6

WITH THE HOUSE WELL behind, Nathan knew the stream had to be close. Continuing down the hillside, the sound of his crunching footsteps faded into the gentle sound of rippling water. Just as he determined the creek to be about twenty yards ahead, his vision adjusted enough to barely see the last line of trees.

Raising his stare to the treetops, Nathan looked up at the dark, ominous sky. "Just one small crack of moonlight in this crazy darkness is all I ask." Quietly pleading to the clouds.

As if a magic genie were granting his final wish, the moon suddenly appeared between sets of racing clouds. Just as the moon revealed itself, a strange noise caught his attention. Nathan snapped his head around tracking the sound. All at once, the strange noise seemed to be coming from everywhere.

What the hell? Is the wind playing tricks on me? Thinking to himself as he stood perfectly still.

Realizing the noise was not imaginary all attention was on the shadowy bushes just ahead. Something was lurking within the underbrush between him and the creek. Staring into the thicket, Nathan tried to catch a brief glimpse of whatever occupied the shadows.

Though unable to see the animal, Nathan could hear it. It was a low threatening growl. Judging from its predatory warning, there was no misinterpreting the danger or intent of this unseen adversary. Realizing the dark woods around him had just come alive, Nathan's foot took a nervous step back.

Under the temporary moonlight, something was spotted deep within the dark underbrush. Eyes fixed in the direction of movement, Nathan watched as the creature began to materialize. The giant silhouette of a dog crept slowly out of the shadows. First its snarling muzzle, then its head. Ears up and hair on end, the mongrel readily revealed its enormous physique.

Standing transfixed, his instant panic caused every muscle in his body to go rigid. If it were true that animals could smell fear, this animal knew that Nathan was scared to death.

A second later, his anxiety deepened as another outline slowly began to take shape. An even larger dog crept through a patch of moonlight, then, vanished behind a growth of brush. Wide-eyed, Nathan gawked in frozen terror.

As the larger dog emerged from the shadows, the other stood its ground snarling. A shuddering fear ripped through him as both beasts fixed him in their sights.

The hostile, threatening growls chilled Nathan's blood as these dogs of incalculable breed now stood side by side. They were not just any dog's, they were huge, salivating monsters. As he fixed his gaze into their eyes, it was as if looking into the eyes of Satin himself.

Taking another tentative step backward, the animals matched his retreat. Then, the wild canines hesitated as if waiting for Nathan to make a desperate attempt at escape. Wary of making any sudden move, he stood his ground not flinching a muscle.

As moonlight fought its way through the swaying branches, it threw wavering shadows over the dogs snarling snouts. Growing more aggressive, the beast's lips slowly pulled away from their fangs. As their lips peeled back, Nathan could see the pink and black of their quivering gums. With every tooth exposed and their hair bristled, the dogs began to stalk toward him.

All that was needed was a little time and luck to get away. Feverishly considering his limited options, the two animals waited for Nathan's next move.

"It's okay guys. It's alright." Speaking with every ounce of kindness he could put together. "Just relax and I'll be on my way."

The beasts were not responsive to the gentleness in his tone. Alarmingly, the dogs became even more agitated and began to advance. At any instant, he expected to be mauled by the vicious razor sharp claws and fangs that approached.

Nathan's chest tightened as the vicious animals drew closer. Feet feeling the way, he slowly backed up. Twigs snapping under each desperate step, he continued to retreat until the forest resisted him.

Backed up against a tree, Nathan now had nowhere to go. The moon and stars suddenly became completely overrun by a barrier of menacing clouds. With the absence of moonlight, a deeper darkness poured over the forest.

With the huge tree hard against his back, the dogs pursued him slowly, bidding their time for just the right moment. Afraid to move even a fraction of an inch, Nathan looked on in terrified anticipation.

Within striking distance, the dogs continued to stalk straight toward him. Now, just a few feet away, they began to crouch down as if getting ready to attack. Teeth bared, the salivating beasts braced and prepared to launch themselves.

***

With his men in position and ready to go, the lead Detective issued his orders.

"It looks like we have a fugitive on our hands, men. Use whatever means necessary and find this murderer!" The Detective's eyes began to shine with the thought of his final marching orders.

On the release of the K-9, the police swung into action. Angling down toward the creek, the German Shepherd immediately disappeared into the darkened woods. Following the eager barking of their canine partner, the officers began their pursuit.

***

The term "being thrown to the dogs" just took on a whole new meaning. Nathan stood petrified, unable to do anything but look into the crazed eyes of the canine monsters.

While instinct told him to run, logic told him not to move. Even if he turned and ran, there would be no escaping these hostile creatures. For he knew, that the slightest movement would trigger the wild dogs to attack.

With the inevitability of his death fixed within their stare, Nathan stood utterly still. Shivers of complete helplessness cursed through him as the volume of their growls grew more aggressive.

Just as they were ready to tear him to pieces, the dogs fell silent. The growling stopped and their ears pricked up. As their quivering lips slid down over their fangs, the dogs unexpectedly lost all interest in their newest victim.

It did not take long for Nathan to realize what distracted the dogs. From the top of the hill there was the echo of anxious barking, the police had cut their dog loose. As the barking became more pronounced, it was obvious that the K-9 shepherd was coming fast through the trees.

Unbelievable relief flooded through every cell of his body as the two beasts turned their attention toward the approaching canine. Still watching the dogs, Nathan realized he had the few seconds he needed to escape deeper into the woods.

Within a fraction of a second, the animals bolted toward the new, oncoming threat. Heedless of the darkness, the dogs raced up the hillside.

Nathan was consumed with a mixture of relief and anxiety.

Massive relief because the eminent attack had been avoided, but at the same time, anxiety, because the police would soon be hot on his trail.

***

Instantaneously, at full speed, the lead beast and the K-9 launched themselves at each other. The impact of the collision sent both dogs reeling to the ground. In a vicious frenzy, they lunged back to their feet and continued the attack.

The dogs collided once again, ripping at the others neck. Razor sharp teeth snapped viciously as each animal attempted to maim the other. Reared on their back legs, the entangled animals became momentarily inseparable. The two combatants twisted and thrashed violently in an effort to gain an advantage.

Fangs snapping at each-others throat, the dogs jaws strained to reach their mark. In a sudden gang effort, the first dog's companion exploded into the blind-side of the police shepherd.

The dog's teeth clinched and tore into the K-9's hind leg. Now fully engaged in the mêlée, the second beast violently shook and ripped at the K-9's leg. Yelping in pain, the wounded police dog let out an agonizing shriek as it fell backward and rolled to the ground. Now, the wild dogs had easy access to the shepherd.

As the vicious fight ensued, the beasts continued to rip their fangs into the K-9. With a flesh tearing bite, the second dog continued to try and rip the shepherd's leg from its torso, while the other targeted its throat.

The savage cries of the three dogs resounded through the woods. There was an eruption of shouts as the police scrambled through the trees in response to the hurtful cries of their fellow officer.

Like army ants, the police swarmed down the hillside. With their partner's cries swelling in intensity, the patrolman raced toward the canine.

Teeth snapping and ripping, the wild dogs relentlessly sank their fangs into the virtually defenseless shepherd. One ripped at the helpless dog's throat while the other mauled its legs. As the two sets of jaws tore at the shepherd's flesh, a gunshot exploded followed by a yelp.

Upon reaching the scene, several panicked patrolman began firing their weapons. In an effort to save their fallen partner, the police shot the wild dogs repeatedly. Instantly, the battle cries stopped and the mêlée between the dogs was over.

***

Now was the chance he needed to distance himself. There was no time to devise a plan; it was time to fly by the seat of his pants. It was imperative that he get to the creek, then to the bridge. With no time to think, he accepted the task.

As soon as he turned to flee, all hell broke loose. The once silent forest was now filled with the sounds of a canine free-for-all. Taking quick advantage of the chaos with the dogs, he was on the move.

Nathan was close to the creek, he could hear the sound of rippling water. Breaking through the final line of trees, he suddenly stood on the sandbar that ran along the stream. Just as his eyes adjusted enough to see the water's edge, the hysterical shouts of confused police officers dominated the background.

Returning attention to where the dogs were fighting, he listened to the sounds of the distraught police. While wondering what could possibly happen next, the piercing sound of a gunshot split the night.

Everything in the forest seemed to freeze as gunshots swept through the woods. Nathan held his position a little longer as the gunfire continued to explode within the darkness.

All at once, the shooting abruptly stopped and everything went silent. The shock of the rapid-fire was numbing, but the eerie silence afterward was almost more unnerving than the gunfire.

While standing in the narrow clearing next to the creek, Nathan realized he had to put all of these distractions behind and get to the bridge. Concentrating on the task-at-hand, he started toward the bridge.

Following along the water's edge, the soft sandbar gave way to his steps. Impossible to avoid, Nathan knew he was leaving an undeniable trail of his movements. But, at this point, there was little he could do about it.

After about two-hundred feet, the base of the overpass came into view. In a quick flashback, he reflected on the images conjure-up while crossing the bridge. As Nathan envisioned himself hiding beneath the bridge, he came to a disturbing conclusion. He was on the brink of being transformed into one of those unseen, nocturnal predators he was fearful of. Just another creature of the night, struggling to survive.

Pausing at the foot of the bridge, fevered thoughts buzzed through his head. Nathan could not help but wonder what he had done to lead him to this absurd situation. Swallowing hard, he looked back into the woods from which he had come.

It was a situation that under different circumstances he might of acted differently. But, with the knowledge that he was a wanted man and that unseen threats were underfoot, it was time to go.

The area beneath the bridge was completely void of light. The darkness seemed impenetrable, but there was no choice but to challenge it. Desperate to stay ahead of the pursuit, Nathan disappeared into the pool of blackness.

CHAPTER 7

EYES RIVETED INTO THE blackness ahead, Nathan followed the stream under the bridge. It was discouraging as his eyes attempted to adjust to the absence of light. It only took him a couple of steps to realize his eyes were not going to adjust to the darkness.

Lost within the flawless blackness, Nathan could no longer see anything. There were no shadows or traces of light to give any definition to the intimidating darkness that engulfed him. The creek and ground on which he walked was a sightless black void.

Though it did not seem possible, the blackness seemed to expand in intensity the further he preceded. While staring helplessly into this wall of blackness, Nathan told himself to ignore the darkness and press on.

Arms outstretched, he sensed his way along the sandbar. Carefully attempting to navigate his steps, Nathan was virtually just a blind man stumbling through unknown territory.

Nathan's only companion within the absurd darkness was the soothing sound of water rippling over the river-rock. Guided by the gentle gurgling of the water, he crept alongside the creek. Hands still blindly stretched out in front of him, he moved forward in baby steps. There was no way to tell just where he was. But Nathan knew, he had to be at least halfway.

Silently maneuvering along the narrow sandbar, his boots sank and slipped in the wet shifting sand. As the gentle rippling water continued to guide him, a faint silhouette came into view.

The once relentless gloom was now showing Nathan some light at the end of this tunnel.

As the outline of the bridge began to present itself, he picked up his pace. Momentarily stumbling, he continued to walk parallel to the sounds of the creek. Upon reaching the far end of the bridge, Nathan stood between the stream and the base of the overpass.

Even in the uncertain light, he could see several rocks penetrating the surface of the water. Like tiny icebergs, Nathan spotted a section that formed into a semi-straight path to the other side. Thinking that this might be the best place to cross, he began using the murky rocks as stepping stones.

The stream level was low, which made him think it would be an easy crossing. But, the creek stones were wet and slippery. Footing shaky at best, Nathan followed the path of shadowy rocks the best he could. Like a cat afraid of touching the water, he picked his steps carefully, tip-toeing across the slick river rock.

After rock-hopping to the opposite side, he followed the sandbar between the creek and the forest. Knowing the police would soon be closing-in, Nathan's gaze kept sliding back toward the dark bridge. Without a second to spare, it was crucial that he quickly distance himself from the pursuit.

Following the water's edge toward the lake, Nathan came across a small clearing. Climbing the creek embankment, he found himself standing in knee-high grass. Nathan's mind raced in a million different directions. While desperately searching for an escape route, the main concern was to find a place to hide and regroup.

Looking out over the tall grass, he tried to visualize the best place to conceal himself. Studying the dark terrain, a large area of heavy brush was spotted across the clearing. At that desperate moment, that section of thicket was probably the best he could hope for.

Walking away from the creek, Nathan quickly made his way

through the meadow. Looking past the clearing toward the heavy brush, Nathan's pace picked-up as he began running deeper into the tall grass.

The cold night dampness had already settled in. As the nearly waist-high grass slapped at his knees, the moisture soaked his boots and lower pant-legs. While closing in on the thick patch of tundra, he began surveying the bushy landscape for a possible hiding spot.

After fighting his way through the meadow, Nathan finally reached the first patch of thicket. With the creek now well behind, he desperately scanned the area. His only thought was locating a descent spot to hide.

The night's darkness gave his vision only a few feet in each direction in which to make a decision. Upon quick inspection, Nathan located a tiny gap within the brush. With no other choice, he penetrated the first layer of thicket.

Just inside the waist-high brush, Nathan turned to locate his pursuers. It did not take long for the pursuit to come into view. The initial sign of the police came in the form of a flashlight beam. First one, then two, then all at once, the woods in which he had just exited became saturated with advancing lights.

The beams of light bobbed and weaved as they searched the woods, stabbing away at the darkness in a joint effort to cover every inch of ground. Drawing closer to the creek, the police flashlights continued to descend the hill. Nathan could not believe what he was witnessing. While the travesty was not his fault, the police obviously thought differently - the search-party was coming.

Though not sure of the actual number of police, Nathan counted at least nine flashlights. The concept of so many pursuers was mind-boggling. Like in an old black and white movie, it appeared as if he were being chased by a hungry lynch-mob. As his anxiety level peaked, he found himself becoming sickened by the sight.

One by one the powerful beams partially disappeared as they descended onto the creek-bed. Nathan knew they were following his tracks along the sandbar. At that point, all he could do was watch as the distant beams-of-light worked their way toward the bridge.

Unable to see the back side of the overpass, he moved to a different spot in the brush. With the new vantage point, there was an open view of the bridge and meadow. Nathan fixed his eyes upon the area in which the police would eventually venture out.

Anxiously watching for the first policeman to appear, signs of light began seeping from the darkness from which he came. Within just a few seconds, the faint light turned into bright sweeping arcs.

With a clear picture of the entire area, the first flashlight exited from beneath the bridge. Nathan looked on in awe as one powerful beam after another emerged from the base of the overpass. As the situation unfolded, it became obvious what was in store for him. Despite his panicky thoughts, he held his position as the police crossed the creek and moved into the meadow.

Flashlight beams leading the way, the police trudged through the tall grass. The threatening line of advancing officers caused Nathan to finally drop out of sight. If he was not going to be seen, it was time to become part of the night shadows. With little time left, he had to melt into the brush and find a final place to hide.

Staying low and out of sight, Nathan cautiously snaked deeper into the heavy brush. Needing to know the progress of the police, he stopped and looked for his pursuers. For the moment, there was still a view of the meadow.

As they gained ground, their silhouettes became more distinct. Nathan's attention was glued to the wall of uniformed deputies as their flashlights swept through the wild grass directly toward him. As if they were suspecting him to resist arrest, their guns were drawn ready to lay the hammer down.

In an attempt to flush him out of the brush, the approaching task force began to spread out in different directions. Unseen by their eyes, Nathan silently watched the situation like a scared animal sensing danger.

Their dominating presence was now uncomfortably close. Heart viciously pounding, he looked on as one by one his aggressors disappeared into different sections of the brush. Then, there was nothing, Nathan's pursuers had vanished into the first line of thicket.

Staying as low as possible, he quickly stepped deeper into the brush. The fear of not making any distracting noises proved impossible as he pushed harder into the thicket. With the wind on the rise, he could only hope that his desperate movements would go unnoticed.

The thicket became so dense a machete was needed to help carve the way. Nathan had no choice but to get on his hands and knees and burrow along the ground. Squeezing through the base of the snarled brush, his clothes were continually getting hung-up on unseen branches.

Mindless of the branches slapping against his hands and face, he fought forward. Frantically, Nathan searched for that one spot that would camouflage him in all directions. Eyes closed, he pushed and lunged into the base of the entangled tundra.

Nathan had burrowed so far into the heavy thicket, that the swarm of branches that hung just above forced him closer to the ground. The dense brush refused to grant him any further access on his hands and knees. Like a soldier crawling through a war-zone, Nathan found himself slithering beneath the jungle of shadowy vegetation.

Belly to the ground, he maneuvered forward until a mound of thicket denied him any further advancement. Realizing this would be the last opportunity for cover, Nathan flattened himself against the cold ground.

Wrapped in darkness, with a canopy of branches hanging just above, Nathan was temporarily hidden from the police. There was a hollow silence in the air, only broken by his own breathing and the wind rustling through the high foliage. Eyes straining to see, he peered through the mesh of branches.

Nathan's vantage point from the brush was extremely limited. While spying through the lowest of limbs, he continually held his breath and listened for sounds only a man could make.

Knowing they were somewhere close, he intently waited for something to come into view. For uncounted seconds, Nathan laid statue still, hugging the ground in perfect silence.

The cold forest floor was quickly stealing the heat from his body. Trying to combat the sudden chill, Nathan began blowing his heated breath into his cupped hands.

While trying to warm himself, the dreaded moment finally came to life. There was a crisp cracking noise, the snapping sound of twigs breaking. The gusty wind that whistled through the brush was now accompanied by unguarded footsteps - they were not far away.

Motionless, transfixed in fear, his eyes locked in the direction of the sound. Holding his breath, Nathan stared from the depths of the thicket. Concealed by the brush, he spied from ground level and waited for more movement.

It was not long before another out-of-place sound was heard. Within seconds the darkness was quickly invaded with numerous aggressive footfalls. Twigs and branches cracked all around as the cops searched the area. With the threatening sound of approaching footsteps, the nearby brush announced that the police were now present.

While concealed deep within the heavy thicket, he was completely blind to any view outside a couple feet. Too terrified to breath, all attention was on the approaching threat.

Nathan began to hear the squawking sounds from walkie-talkies as they drew nearer. As the officers communicated back and forth, Nathan estimated the men were about ten feet away.

Without warning, along with the approaching voices came two beams of light. A moment later, the two beams split up and entered the brush on either side.

While using their flashlights to probe the area, the two policemen suddenly stopped. The static of their walkie-talkies blared as an updated dispatch came over the air-waves. What Nathan heard pushed him to the abyss of sanity.

The lead Detective took to the airwaves. "The man you're pursuing is now wanted for two murders. The woman died on the way to the hospital...Get the bastard...Whatever it takes!"

The police instantly resumed their search. Nathan cringed with the crackling of each impending step. The men belonging to these footfalls were now just a few feet away. Panic rising, heart viciously pounding, the anticipation of being caught made him nauseous.

Once the nerve-racking footsteps were nearly on top of him, Nathan heard another sound. The brush suddenly rustled out of rhythm to the gusts of wind and the approaching police. The noise was so close it was almost as if he caused it. Yet, his entire body had remained motionless. Something was right there with him. One thing was for sure, whatever it was, it was not human.

Nathan's stomach got a wrenching sensation with the knowledge that he was not alone. The faint sound of some unseen creature was prowling amidst the underbrush not far away.

Like the police, the strange noise was drawing ever closer. Nathan was not sure what kind of animal it was, but he knew exactly where it was. It was some kind of large rodent working its way along his leg.

The urge to move and distance himself from the unknown creature was tremendous. But, he would be a sitting duck if he made the slightest sound. Any movement at all would undoubtedly alert the police. With the cops close enough to step on him, Nathan had to try and ignore the unexpected visitor.

Overwhelmed with the realization that his capture was near, he looked on in terrified expectation. Suddenly, the patrolmen shinned their lights directly into the thicket where he hid.

Shivers of complete hopelessness cursed through him as the flashlight beams washed over the brush. Perfectly still, Nathan lay on his stomach becoming a part of the brush. Pressing as low to the ground as possible, his eyes followed the movements of the flashlights.

Almost as an afterthought, he remembered there was some kind of creature working its way up his body. Nathan had no choice, but to let the unknown predator have its way.

CHAPTER 8

WHATEVER WAS SLITHERING AGAINST his leg was now on top of him. As it crawled up the small of his back, Nathan had no idea what kind of creature it was. What he was sure of, was the animal weighed several pounds.

Branches and twigs snapped all around, there were patrolmen on either side. Nathan's breath stopped in his throat as a pair of feet crunched down right in front of his head, stopping just inches away. Beneath the darkness of the thicket, his vision was fixated on the man's boots. Without blinking or moving a muscle, Nathan remained frozen in place.

As if on cue, the wind died off, everything became very quiet, even the creature on Nathan's back drew still. The fear of being caught was nearly more than tolerable. Eyes pressed shut, he waited for the panicked moment to pass.

After several nerve-racking seconds, the sound of unguarded steps began again. There was a kind of a grim excitement inside him as the police walked passed. Though the squawk of the radios and the crunching of footfalls were beginning to move away, Nathan stayed statue-still.

Spying along the ground, his eyes watched the area the police had last appeared. Within a couple seconds, the police were in another section of thicket. At the same time, to Nathan's relief, the creature on his back seemed to lose interest. While still unsure what sort of animal it was, he was more than ecstatic as the predator crawled off and ventured back into the brush.

The rustling and snapping of branches began to fade as the officers moved off into the darkness. Nathan continued to lay motionless, giving his pursuers every chance to distance themselves.

Gradually raising his head, Nathan listened until the sound of footsteps disappeared. At least for the time-being, the fear of capture had momentarily subsided.

Though the night grew still and quiet, he knew they were out there somewhere. While the silence brought some comfort, there were no intensions of moving until the area was clear.

With the wind on the rise once again, beside the rustling brush, there were no other noises. It slowly became obvious that the pursuers had moved on.

Nathan began to crawl back through the wall of entangled branches. Staring into the darkness ahead, he fought through the thick brush. After worming through the thicket, it finally became possible to get back on his hands and knees.

Crawling a few more feet, the ability to stand upright was regained. Pushing through the last section of brush, he once again found himself looking out over the meadow.

Nathan knew that the police were still somewhere close. It was time to sneak-off before they began back-tracking. Opportunity at hand, Nathan inched his way out of the bush and crouched down in the tall grass. Mind and senses alert, the dark meadow was carefully studied. Determining the coast was clear, the moment of truth had arrived.

The cops were probably already doubling-back. To stay where he was, would be like giving himself up. It was vital that his presence vanish from the area - and quick. Though rejoicing in relief, Nathan dared not enjoy it for long or the chance at escape might disappear.

Head on a swivel, he assessed the area. Seeing nothing, Nathan cautiously rose to his feet. Taking a couple deep breaths, he steadied his nerves and got prepared to run.

Well, it's now or never. With that fact in mind, he was on his way.

Instantly, Nathan felt dangerously exposed while running through the open meadow. Even as the knee high grass wrapped around his legs, Nathan never looked back. In a one man race, it was all about getting to the creek.

It was deeply disturbing that he was running like this. Up until a few hours ago, he believed that the worst of his luck was the restraining order. But now, it was all about running from the authorities. Trying to escape from a situation he had nothing to do with.

Breathing fast and heavily, Nathan finally reached the creek embankment. Shaky and nervous, he deeply inhaled while watching the stream ripple by.

With no one in sight, Nathan searched for the shallowest portion of the creek. Easing sideways on trembling legs, a possible place to cross the stream was spotted. Seizing the moment, the rock-hopping began once again. Within a few giant strides, he was standing on the opposite sandbar.

Frozen in a moment of indecision, Nathan pondered his unsettling options. *"You've really stepped in it this time!"* Silently chastising himself.

Desperately scouring his mind for an idea, Nathan searched himself for what might be the safest course of action - mistakes were not an option.

While his mind struggled for answers, there was one thing he was sure of. It was imperative to get out of the reach of the So. Lake Tahoe Police Dept. Nathan could not stay in the forest all night, especially if they brought in another K-9 unit.

The only conclusion that seemed plausible was to high-tail-it to Stateline - the Nevada side. The casinos would be a perfect place to hide out and mull things over. Plus, he would be sheltered from the approaching storm.

From this side of town, there was quite a grueling hike ahead.

Under normal circumstances, the journey could be made without anyone noticing. But, with the police on alert, the chances on completing the distance were slim. Clearly out-matched, Nathan had no intensions of being an easy catch. With a little luck, the journey to Stateline might be doable.

Now, it was all a test of willpower. Walking away from the tiny creek, Nathan began the journey to vanish from this side of the lake. Once the woods were reentered, he instantly knew where to go next.

With the knowledge that this section of woods would lead him directly toward a lakefront, residential area, he picked up the pace. To be on the safe side, every so often, he doubled back on himself, looking for any kind of threat that might have been missed.

After about a half-mile jaunt, the trees began to thin. Looking ahead, Nathan noticed the soft glow of a streetlight penetrating through the pine trees. Continuing to the edge of the woods, the dark trail that was being followed turned to pavement. The first stage of the journey was over.

Nathan paused another moment to take one last cautious look. A welcome feeling of relief filled him as the fear of capture somewhat subsided. Now out in the open, he understood that a new set of tactics were needed.

Stuffing his hands deep into his coat pockets, he began walking toward the first section of houses. Looking to the sky, black clouds were quickly pressing down over the lake. With the stiff, storm-driven wind on the rise, it was obvious that it would not be long before Tahoe's first winter storm showed its ugly face.

Nathan took a deep breath while acknowledging one undeniable fact. The proceeding venture was all about will. Nathan's will versus the Tahoe police force and the elements of nature. But, little did he know, what kind of elements this journey would entail.

CHAPTER 9

STAYING WITHIN THE BOUNDARIES of the lake shore residence, Nathan traveled in a round-about route through the backstreets and wooded lots. Though trying to avoid any road that would merge with Tahoe Boulevard, he knew sooner or later, there would be no choice but to traverse through the middle of town. Until then, the ability to be just another neighborhood shadow was fine with him.

After an hour of maneuvering through the lakefront neighborhoods, it became time to rest. Beneath a tall hedge that divided two properties, Nathan's sat in anguish. The area was extremely dark and most of the homes had little or no lights to illuminate their yards or porches. But to Nathan, the darkness was somehow comforting.

Nathan sat in contemplation, listening to the lawn sprinklers hissing and splashing in a nearby yard. Understanding that the time to regroup would be short-lived, thoughts concerning the events of the night entered his mind.

With the mounting wind, a cloud of mist from the sprinklers blew into the street. Shaking his head in grief, he became immersed in the remembrance of Sarah's dead body. Nathan began to sob uncontrollably. The greatest thing that ever happened to him was gone and there was no way to get her back.

Get up! It's time to go! Ordering himself as he wiped away his tears.

Temporarily putting a stranglehold on his distress, he pushed himself up. After another half-hour of wondering aimlessly, Nathan realized that the neighborhood was just a maze of cul-de-sacs and dead-end streets. There was no time to be subtle any longer, it was pointless to waste any more time. There was no choice but to take his chances on the main boulevard.

Nathan proceeded up the last residential street until it intersected Tahoe Blvd. Hiding in the shadows of the intersection, traffic was observed in both directions. The fact of the situation was, if he were going to be caught, it would be on this dreaded stretch of pavement.

Unable to spot any movement or activity, Nathan ventured out onto the Blvd. Head shrunk low into his jacket the walk down the exposed street began. Quickly making his way down the sidewalk, Nathan set his sights on the next destination. Just a few blocks away, Regan Beach would divert him off the main drag.

Glancing at his watch, Nathan could not believe that it was almost eleven o'clock. The police man-hunt was already two hours old. The one thing going for him was that movement on the Boulevard was nearly non-existent.

Looking for oncoming headlights, his vision scanned in both directions. For at this time of night, the chances of headlights belonging to a police cruiser were extremely high. Any sign of a vehicle was reason enough for immediate action.

Nathan's pace was accelerated while scrambling through the pools of light that flooded down from the intermittent streetlamps. Avoiding the lit areas like the plague, all efforts were put toward staying in the darkest realms of the street. Deviating from one patch of shadows to the next, Nathan briefly materialized, then all at once, melted away into the darkness.

With unrelenting commitment, he covered the three block distance that lead him to the security of Regan Park. With the objective complete, Nathan quickly disappeared into the darkness of the park.

After weaving around trees and picnic tables, he reached the concrete staircase that descended to the lake. Focused on the stairs, Nathan quickly scaled the cement steps down to the beach.

Standing in the sand at the base of the staircase, he cast his eyes over the frigid, dark waters of the lake. The section of lake that could be seen was blanketed by tiny white-caps. As lightning flashed against the black horizon, his eyes jerked upward. The lightning was far enough away that not even the faintest sound of thunder could be heard.

While watching the approaching storm, another small flash lit up the clouds over the far edge of the lake. As the horizon lit up, it became obvious that the threatening line of black clouds had already dropped down into the Tahoe basin. It was not the picturesque night in paradise Nathan was use to.

As a cold dampness enveloped the wind, his bones began to chill. In the ominous sky above, thick billowing clouds raced past the moon at an incredible rate of speed. Lightning flashed again in the distant clouds, several seconds later he heard the faint growl of thunder. Mother Nature was giving a warning of her arrival.

Though the storm was no more than a distant rumble, he knew it would not be long before its wrath hit the South Shore area. The inevitable storm was a perfect complement to his dilemma.

As jagged streaks of lightning began flashing across the lake, it became apparent it was time to switch gears. Nathan jogged through the sand along the water's edge until the end of the beach-front was reached. After ascending another concrete stairway he found himself standing in the thick grass of the park.

There was not a second to waste as the clouds rapidly descended on the lake. On the run again, he made his way through the park eluding from light to shadow, shadow to light. Upon reaching the park's frontage, Nathan was again faced with the unwanted idea of being totally exposed.

Departure from the park instantly delivered him to a serpentine bike path. During daylight hours, the recreational trail supported heavy foot traffic. But tonight, with the cold winter storm on the rise, not a single soul traveled upon the narrow path.

With the utmost caution, Nathan carefully followed the snaky path that paralleled Tahoe Blvd. Within seconds, much closer than the last, another blaze of lightening lit the sky and a crack of thunder consumed the lake. As the storm continued to roll in from the north, the time between lightning and thunder narrowed. As the growls of thunder edged ever closer, the air suddenly became moist and thick. Nathan's senses became aware of the unmistakable promise of rain.

As the occasional vehicle came into view, he would drift off the bike-path and retreat into the landscaping that ran alongside. The closer he drew to Stateline, the more commercialized the area became, providing him with fewer places to hide.

Both sides of the street were now lined with small buildings, business complexes and shopping centers. This last stretch of Blvd. would prove to be the most unforgiving. If the last mile could be made unscathed, he would be home free.

The bike-path abruptly ended as it merged with a shopping center parking lot. Tall mercury lamps were dispersed throughout the lot, turning the entire area into a huge spotlight.

Contemplating his options, Nathan paused at the threshold of the parking lot. This time of night, the stores and other businesses were all vacated. While the park and bike-path had provided several points of cover, he was about to put himself into a position where anyone could spot him. However, if he could make it to the storefront unseen, it would be easy to escape off the other side of the property.

As the mounting wind grew more intense, the more Nathan could smell the approaching weather. The moon and stars no longer existed, now only a barrier of dark, menacing clouds ruled the sky. As the threatening sky collided with the So. Shore

Mountain Range, the clusters of fat-bellied clouds churned just above the tree-tops. With the storm hanging so low, the air had no choice but became alive with ozone.

With no other options, the only alternative was to challenge the brilliantly lit, wide-open pavement. Feeling totally vulnerable, Nathan prepared to immerse himself into the sea of light.

While standing in the shadows, a few raindrops began to splash against his skin. Looking across the parking lot, Nathan watched as millions of tiny raindrops illuminated as they passed through the glow of the mercury lamps. In mere seconds, the clouds opened up and the parking lot was deluged with a sheet of solid water.

There was no time to waste; this might be the break he needed. If there was anyone around to see him, they were now running for cover. The mad-dash for the store-front was set into motion as Nathan sprinted through the downpour. Immediately his clothes were soaked. With every panicked stride, the soles of his boots splashed against the blacktop. Hoping there were no witnesses, Nathan continued to race through the lashing downpour.

The fiercely gusting wind caused the heavy rain to violently slice sideways through the frigid air. Arms raised to shield his face, he fought against the wind and horizontal rain. As the watery demons cut against his skin, all effort and attention was focused on the store-front.

Upon finding cover beneath the store's awning, Nathan leaned against the wall to catch his breath. The icy rain water drooled from his hair, running down his face and neck. The dripping rain seeped down behind his jacket collar, causing a stream of freezing water to snake down his spine.

Beneath the temporary refuge, Nathan continually wiped away the monotonous water that dripped into his eyes. Satisfied that the race across the parking lot went undetected, Nathan watched as the storm grew in intensity. The huge raindrops seemed to explode as they collided into the asphalt. Every low spot in the pavement was now flooded.

Beneath the eves of a store-front, he looked on as the cloudburst worsened. Though it did not seem possible, the rain intensified, pummeling the awning overhead. Endless steams of water gushed from the buildings rain-gutters. Churning rivers from the chilling downpour began running along the curb, bubbling and gurgling as it channeled its way toward the storm drains.

Becoming more persistent, lightening and rolling drums of thunder echoed through the mountains. The storm was reaching its peak. The next blaze of lightening lit the night sky and an instantaneous crack of thunder shook the building. The blast completely drowned-out the loud drumming of rain that pounded against the awning.

After the roar of thunder had dissipated, there was the distinct sound of water splashing beneath approaching car tires. Nathan turned just in time to spot a police SUV pulling into the shopping center. As the vehicle sent a curtain of spray spattering in its wake, a sigh of helplessness escaped his lips. Panic took the place of surprise as the patrol car headed directly toward him.

Though desperately wanting to run, he became completely paralyzed in a fleeting moment of indecision. There was nowhere to go; Nathan was trapped between the cruiser and the storefront.

CHAPTER 10

Nathan desperately confronted himself. *I've got to get out of here! I've got to hide someplace - fast!*

As the rain peppered the awning, he scrambled to the left and ducked back into the darkness of the store entranceway. The patrol car's headlights reflected off the building windows as it swung through the lot. Like a giant black and white magnet, the cruiser headed straight toward the store-front.

Nathan tried to swallow, but his throat had gone dry. A quiver of terror consumed him as the vehicle approached. Shrinking deeper into the buildings promenade, his eyes did a quick-study of everything around him.

With the patrol car relentlessly approaching, Nathan stuffed himself into a tiny space between a soda machine and a purified water dispenser. Lightning flashed and another crack of thunder exploded overhead. Everything seemed to vibrate as his body was forced as far as possible into the narrow space.

Just before his shoulder pressed up against the building, he went face-first into a huge, sticky spider web. Nathan's face and neck were now enveloped in the massive, tacky structure that was linked together by the two machines.

Pinned motionless, instant horror sunk in at the thought of invading the confines of a black-widow nest. Nathan frantically wanted to tear the nasty web from his face. But so tightly pressed between the machines, his arms were pinned to his sides.

The headlights of the oncoming cruiser grew brighter as it

pulled directly alongside the storefront. The building's entrance was suddenly framed in the patrol cars spotlight. Nathan knew he would be spotted if an effort to remove the nasty web was made.

All at once, there was another flash of lightning, the store-front lit-up brighter than the police spotlight from the forest. Eyes widened in terror, everything around became as clear as day. The lightening revealed the horror that now enveloped his face. Nathan's instantaneous expression reflected everything he felt at that moment - sheer horror.

Seemingly suspended in mid-air, the vast web was no simple structure. It was a complex network of mesh patterns that held bloodless, insect remains dangling eerily. Like the other carcasses, Nathan was imprisoned within its grasp. Now just another unwilling hostage, he fearfully awaited the webs blood-sucking host.

Just as quickly as the brilliant light appeared, it vanished. But, the image of the horrifying sight was embedded in his mind. Leaving Nathan entangled and traumatized in the middle of his greatest fear - with nowhere to go. With the police cruiser just a few feet away, the need to free himself from the clutches of the hideous web was overwhelming.

Nathan's imagination quickly got the best of him as the curse of arachnophobia instantly consumed him. With the police only an arms-reach away, face ensnared within this web of horrors, his mind commenced to fabricate terrifying images.

I know this is a black-widow nest! Black-widows love to build their webs in cool, shadowy places like this.

With no further mental deductions, his scalp began to prickle. Trespassing in dangerous territory, Nathan had no doubt that retribution was about to be taken upon him.

The gruesome web began to conjure up unwanted images. Just as the worst of thoughts were firmly planted, there was the feeling of something crawling on his skin. Beneath his jaw, something was navigating down his neck. The crawling sensation caused his heart to stop and forced his blood to run cold.

Sure that a black-widow was sizing him up, Nathan went into panic-mode. Uncontrollably, an unnerving pressure began swelling in his chest. Nathan's anxiety caused his mouth and throat to begin making wheezing sounds.

What's on my neck? Frantically asking himself. *A short-tempered black-widow has come out to see what has invaded its privacy. Please God, just let it be a drip of rain water making its way down my neck.*

Unable to breath, Nathan closed his eyes and listened for the other problem lurking just a few feet away. Even though the rain still pounded overhead, he could hear the cruisers windshield-wipers thumping back and forth. Nathan listened as the tires of the SUV slowly sloshed across the drenched asphalt.

Forcing himself to open his eyes, he peered from the web. Watching intently from behind the machine, not a movement was made until the patrol car slowly passed.

Once the cruisers taillights disappeared, Nathan waited until the tires were silent. As soon as there was no further threat from the police, he finally took a real breath. With every hair on his body incensed and on end, Nathan pried himself out from between the machines.

As trailing remnants of the sticky spider-web and blood-sucked carcasses clung to his head, his hands swatting across his face and neck as if he had run into a nest of killer bees.

Once convinced there were no more creepy-crawlies on his person, Nathan scanned his eyes around the parking lot. Letting out a sigh of relief, everything became relaxed with the knowledge there was no immediate danger.

The cold rain continued to run down Nathan's face and neck. Blowing away the unwanted drips from his lips, he noticed that the storm had lost some of its fury. After stepping out from the eve of the building, there was no hesitation as he ran across the pavement.

Once across the parking lot, Nathan cautiously worked once again up Tahoe Blvd. The cold rain had penetrated his jacket and now his clothes were completely soaked. Shoulders hunched and hands deep within the pockets, he walked through the drizzling rain. The cold freezing wind caused his eyes to turn to liquid, sending tears of winter down his cheeks. Totally exposed to the elements, Nathan understood that the dark night and the storm were his only allies.

The night was becoming extremely cold, barely above freezing. Soaked and shivering, he repeatedly relived the haunting images at the store-front. While walking along the drenched stretch of road, Nathan became lost in thought. In his wildest imagination, he could not grasp why the police were so hell-bent on finding him. Once again disaster had been narrowly averted.

What else could possibly go wrong? Why me? Why not that baby-killing boyfriend?

Many times during the last couple hours, the thought of giving up loomed heavily in his mind. But, what chance would he have if the authorities had already proven him guilty. Nathan needed to avoid all recognition, anything to keep attention off himself.

Walking through the obscurity of night, the first side-street was taken. The street turned out to be no more than an alley behind a rundown motel. Determined to get to Stateline, his route was diverted into a dark, empty alleyway - or so he thought.

CHAPTER 11

NERVOUSLY, NATHAN CREPT ALONG the discrete alleyway. It was an unfamiliar, threatening excursion in which he would normally never go. Eyes shifting from side to side, he cautiously scrutinized the shadowy dumpsters and dark voids in the night-cloaked alley.

Though the gutters were still filled with rushing water headed toward the storm drains, Mother Nature had temporarily subsided. While pushing a tired hand through his wet hair, the rain-puddled alley splashed beneath his feet.

Leering ahead past the saturated cityscape, the high-rise, hotel casinos came into view. Stateline, Nevada was not far away. At that moment, the not-so-distant casino lights was the most beautiful thing he had ever seen.

With only a few blocks to go, the nerve-racking trip appeared to be complete. Moving from shadow to shadow, Nathan began to relax a bit. Detecting no movement, he watchfully continued through the storm-shrouded night.

The moon's glow was still hidden by the threatening clouds. Easing down the alleyway, all senses went on alert as a misplaced noise interrupted the darkness. Staying in the center of the tiny road, Nathan slowed his pace dramatically.

Nerves on alert, the hair on his neck prickled while studying the blacked-out crevices of the alley. There were eyes on him; something had him in its sights. Standing in a nervous expectancy, Nathan's eyes narrowed as he searched for what lurked within the blackness. Though trying to tell himself it was nothing, he knew better.

Nathan began slowly walking past the dark voids that loomed on both sides. The deeper he ventured into the alleyway the darker it became. The trash cans and dumpsters provided numerous hiding spots for four-legged or two-legged creatures of the night.

Cautiously, he proceeded down the center of the night-cloaked back-street. Like a scared animal, all instincts and senses were at alarm. Something or someone was lurking in the murkiness.

While maneuvering around the rain-filled potholes and standing water puddles, there was another noise. Stopping in his tracks, Nathan jerked his stare toward the crevice of darkness from which the sound originated. A chill of warning ran up his spine as he searched for something or someone that could not yet be seen. Something was about to happen - and it was not good.

Peering deeper into the blackness, Nathan waited for the source of the noise to materialize. At that moment, the silence and stillness in the alley seemed almost unnatural. But something was lying and waiting in the black recesses that surrounded him. Seized with uncertainty, he wrestled with the issue of whether or not to go any further.

Only moving of his eyes, Nathan scanned the alley. While frozen in that moment of indecision, the dark alleyway began to show its hidden secrets. At first, the figure was just a black silhouette against the murkiness of the alley. As the image emerged from the shadows, it became obvious that danger approached. The fear of confrontation that had been temporarily pushed away, rushed through his body once again. Nathan could not believe it, there was only a couple-hundred yards to complete the remaining distance - now this.

Suddenly, other hidden sounds from the depths of the darkness began to present themselves. Frantically looking around, he watched as more threatening forms began to materialize. As they emerged from the darkness, he shifted his gaze from silhouette to silhouette. Before Nathan knew it, he was seriously out-numbered - eight to one.

Fear and nervous energy consumed him as a lone figure separated itself from the others. As the shadowy personage drew closer, Nathan quickly caught sight of something long and slender in his hand. With the immediate threat now in full view, the others silhouettes began to close in.

Resisting the urge to look behind him, he slowly retreated. Within a couple steps, they had him backed-up against a dumpster.

Run, get the hell out of here, Nathan warned himself.

Wanting nothing to do with this, he searched for the slightest opening that might provide a way out. But it was too late; the dangerous threats had sealed off all quick exits, any avenue of escape proved non-existent.

The lead person was definitely packing a knife, while another held a chain that hung down to his ankles. Standing motionless, mounting fear kept him from taking a much needed breath. As the crowded alley closed in, Nathan realized that the gang of antagonists was no older than seventeen.

The one that sported the knife was the first to speak. "Give up your wallet!" Demanding as he raised the six-inch blade into clear view.

Nathan refused to respond. Then, a much smaller figure appeared from the shadows. It was a girl that could not have been more than thirteen. The young girl sluggishly raised a bottle of beer to her lips, guzzling until it was empty. Then, impulsively, she threw the bottle down, shattering it against the pavement.

The girl was not the Shot-Caller of the group, but she was definitely the main instigator. "What ya doin' in 'r' alley? You heard what he said...Give us your money...Asshole!" Shouting maliciously as she took another brave step forward.

Giving the outspoken girl an additional once over, Nathan

concluded that unless she had a gun she was not a threat. The riff-raff that assembled in front had now become nine to one.

At certain times during his life, decisions had been forced upon him, and this was rapidly developing into one of those times. There was no backing down, he was lucky to have made it this far. Though surrounded, there was no backing down.

After what he had already been through, there was no way in hell that he was about to be run-over by a bunch of teenage gangsters.

Total frustration and rage began erupting inside him. Though one man against many, he was no longer afraid. Nathan was in no frame of mind to deal with this nonsense. If push came to shove and things got out of hand, he was more than ready to get ugly. Suddenly, welcoming the challenge, the decision was made to not give these punks the slightest break. It was time to throw down the gauntlet.

Unknown to them, they had just chosen a victim who had a fugitives desperation. No longer needing to assess the situation, it was time to get mean - dig in and fight. These kids had no idea who they were dealing with. No one was going to get in his way, especially a bunch of clueless kids. These hoodlums had just bought themselves a nasty ass-whopping.

The female irritant began barking ultimatums once again. "Give us your money, bastard! Or my boyfriend will take that knife and bleed you out!" Looking quite sure that her drunken request would be followed.

Nathan yielded his vision away from the girl and back to the knife. Realizing the pandemonium that was about to ensue, a desperate strategy was conceived. Looking inside the dumpster, a quick search was made for anything that might help. However primitive, he needed a weapon.

It only took a second until he spotted what was needed. Nathan pulled out a broken tree branch, the perfect length and size for what it was needed for.

All fear and hesitation vacated his body. Nathan's face flushed as his blood-pressure spiked. Though his body was drained, a rush of dangerous adrenaline made him feel invincible. With a twinge of welcomed anticipation, his mental state suddenly matched the weather - cold and unforgiving.

Backed against the dumpster, clutching the broken limb with both hands, Nathan's jaw flexed gearing-up for attack. As the black bellies of the thunderheads watched from above, he prepared to get mid-evil on these adolescent thugs.

Staring directly into the punks eyes, the knife in his hand became just a faint glimmer. It was time to go to battle and Nathan's fury was more than ready to confront anyone that stood in his way. There was no more looking for the path of least resistance, it was time to create his own path.

For a split second, they stood in deadlock. Getting into a fighting stance, he displayed the large limb in front of him. Now Nathan viewed the alley as a combat zone. It was time to kick some quick ass and be on his way.

Like an athlete anxiously waiting to compete, he began bouncing on the balls of his feet. Nathan gestured with his head as if telling the one with the knife to bring it on. Almost devilishly, he tauntingly grinned awaiting the first threatening movement.

All at once, the time for strategy was over as everything seemed to explode into action. Nathan should have been afraid, but his intense rage had sent him over the edge. A desperate wildness entered his eyes as pure animal instinct took over. Quickly maneuvering from a defensive to an offensive position, it became all about the one with the knife.

Zeroed-in on the target, Nathan let out a howling battle cry and went to work. Before the punk could even react, the branch hit its mark. After the thudding impact, there was the sharp sound of bones cracking. Simultaneously, the attacker grabbed his forearm and let out a pain-chilling scream. Though Nathan knew he had just broken the kids arm, he was far from done.

The punk's arrogance was quickly replaced by fear and desperation. Barbarically raising the tree-limb, Nathan moved in for the kill. As if wielding an ax, the wooden weapon raced downward. Nathan could feel and hear the crunch of another bone as the tree branch smashed into the attackers shoulder.

Dropping in a heap to the pavement, the young punk let out the ultimate scream. The bone-crunching blow incapacitated the first target, but there was still eight to go.

Nathan whirled around ready for the next attacker. With a grimace of pure fury, every muscle in his body tightened in rage. Somehow the victory in defending himself made him want some more.

"Bring it on!" Nathan screamed, begging for the battle to continue.

Like a sword, Nathan held the branch with both hands. Even though surrounded, every nerve in his body was aware of each assailant. As the others angled toward him, his eyes grew even harder as he prepared to confront the next target.

In a gang-rush the others closed in quick. As soon as the next aggressor got within striking distance, Nathan cut loose. Though his rain-drenched clothes pulled heavily against his body, the big branch was flailed violently as if weighing nothing. The tree-limb caught the next aggressor flush in the ribs. The attacker's breath heaved from his lungs as the devastating blow lifted him off the pavement.

The kid dropped hard into a storm-drenched puddle and lay motionless. Nathan was so beside himself, that if another attacker had not been coming at him, he would have continued to hit the guy's motionless body.

Nathan ducked just in time as something solid grazed his face - it was the chain. Just short of a devastating hit, the weapon's momentum caused it to wrap around Nathan's defensive forearm. Gripping the chain, he yanked the aggressor toward him. With a quick, sharp swing, the branch crunched into the side of his aggressors face. The sound of another smashing bone just fed his rage.

As soon as the screaming punk hit the ground, the others made a charge. Desperate, like a wounded dog backed into a corner, pure animal aggression surged. Like a man possessed, Nathan swung blindly in all directions. Anything that came close enough was an instant target. Swinging in a frenzy, he struck one advancing assailant after another. Screams echoed throughout the dark alley as he proceeded to pummel the combatants with repeated swings.

Refusing to take a chance on serious injury, the remaining thugs tumbled over one another in retreat. They scattered down the alley, leaving their wounded comrades in their wake.

Within a split-second, there was no one else to fight. With most of the assailants at bay, Nathan noticed one punk attempting to get back to his feet. Once again, aggressive fury overcame his actions. Walking slowly toward the recuperating attacker, he lifted the limb and thrust it downward one last time. The kid let out a cry that scorched the night as the branch smashed into his knee.

Heart hammering with exertion, adrenaline-provoked excitement filled his being. Unable to walk away, Nathan gawked at his work for several seconds. A strange sense of triumph and satisfaction filled his gut. It was not the attack that made him feel awe-struck; it was the fact that he had done it so easily.

Nathan finally turned away from the remnants of the brawl. Eyes sweeping the alley, the drunken girl that instigated the whole ordeal was spotted. Shrinking down to the ground, she crawled on all fours around the dumpster.

"Please don't hurt me!" The obnoxious girl cried.

Nathan did not respond. The insane rage he was experiencing would not permit it. Following the female antagonist around the back of the dumpster, the tree-limb was raised above her head. Terror radiated from her eyes as she lay crumpled-up in the shadows of the dumpster.

Trembling violently, her arms protectively covered her face as she whimpered incoherently. Nathan could see her lips moving, but none of the girl's mumblings made any sense - nor did he care. Madder than hell, he wanted nothing more than to put her out of her misery.

In a brief moment of sanity, Nathan stopped his arms from smashing the weapon across her skull. In spite of what they had just put him through, he could not help but feel sorry for her. Although one side of him was tempted to carry-out the atrocity, the rational side embraced the notion that hurting her would not help the current dilemma.

With the reality of what he was about to do, the limb was dropped to the ground. Back toward the others, Nathan's casualties lay on the pavement dazed, whimpering and moaning. Considering what had taken place, the wounded punks got off amazingly light. Nathan could have done a lot more damage to this band of misfits.

Nerves shot to hell, overdosed with adrenaline, his hands refused to stop shaking. Standing in front of the dumpster where it all started, he desperately tried to steady himself.

Leering ahead through the rain-soaked night, Nathan walked past the unavoidable carnage that he was accountable for. With only a couple blocks to go, the escape from So. Lake Tahoe was almost complete.

Nathan could not believe he survived the assault with no injuries. After somewhat regaining control of himself, his sights were once again set on the lights of the casinos.

After pushing a trembling hand through his hair, it was time to make a quick exit out of the alley. Feet moving faster than ever, he splashed through the puddle-filled asphalt without reservation. With the high-rise, hotel-casinos in site, he could only hope that the remainder of the night would unfold with a little less intensity.

CHAPTER 12

WITHOUT BREAKING STRIDE, NATHAN ran from the alley. Upon reaching the next street, he took the first sidewalk that lead toward the lights of Stateline. Continuing to be just a shadow within the darkness, Nathan rapidly maneuvered toward the destination.

The next set of low threatening clouds were now colliding and stacking up against the mountains. Within seconds, the sky hung so low, the clusters of black-bellied clouds churned just above the tree-tops.

I'll be in the casino in less than five minutes. Silently reassuring himself.

Desperately picking up the pace, it was all about finding cover before the second phase of the storm unleashed its fury. As Nathan's long strides drew closer to the casinos, a saw-toothed flash of lightning scorched the black sky. Then, like a dynamite blast, an explosion of thunder instantly followed.

Intermittent raindrops began to splash in the standing water-puddles. Only lacking about fifty yards to the casino entrance, there was another blaze of absolute light accompanied by a crack of thunder loud enough to wake the dead. Then, all hell broke loose.

The heavens opened up and hurled down a merciless battery of torrential rain. The unforgiving weather instantly covered Stateline in a sheath of water. The wind-driven, needle sharp rain slashed against Nathan's face as he rounded the final corner.

Within a couple seconds, the barrage of freezing water had penetrated his clothes once again.

Sprinting through the wall of water, he finally reached the casino. Bursting through the glass entrance, Nathan held the door open for several other storm-drenched pedestrians running for cover.

Once the streets and sidewalks had emptied, he stood in amazement, watching the vicious storm through the glass doors. The entire area outside was instantly flooded as the storm bombarded the cityscape. As if Mother Nature herself were demanding to come inside, great flashes of lightning transformed the hotel entrance into a grotto of leaping shadows. She increased her power and threw down thunder that crashed over the huge building in long, rolling repercussions. The cracks of thunder seemed to rumble and crawl up the buildings walls, vibrating the foundation and windows as if an earthquake were taking place.

As the light-show continued, impatient blasts of thunder powerfully shook the building. Nathan turned from the windows and began weaving through the crowd of onlookers who stood stagnant, gawking at the magnificent sight.

Now on the Nevada side, there was a small feeling of relief. Entering the gaming area, his ears were instantly greeted by the rhythmic chatter of hundreds of gaming machines.

Casinos were nothing but an adult fantasy land, a pleasure-ridden atmosphere that constantly surged with an ecstatic addictive energy. A place were one could split away from reality and vault themselves into an electrifying fantasy world.

An artificial utopia made to tantalize and stimulate one's senses and desires. A place where no clocks, no closing time and no last calls were permitted. Twenty-four hours a day, under the artificial lights, there existed a wild sleepless energy. An energy that enhanced ones judgment, making the patron more intense. Enabling one to gamble harder, drink heavier, while in a constant chaotic quest for fun and fortune.

Nathan had usually loved the sensation he received after entering a lively casino. But under the present circumstances, the thrill of being here took on a whole different meaning.

As the storm continued to bombard the city, it shook the windows and everything within. Trying to draw as little attention to himself as possible, Nathan wandered through the gambling crowd.

While gazing at the flashing lights and exotic décor, he understood his time here was limited. In the midst of the multitude of people, everything and everyone suddenly became a threat. Nathan's paranoia was getting the best of him as it became a necessity to get away from everyone and regroup.

Walking through a large isle of slot machines, he looked on as the patrons held that familiar expression of concentration and anticipation. The gamblers were so involved they gave Nathan little if any acknowledgment.

Anxious, but trying to stay composed, he did not want to give the appearance of just hanging around. It was time to rest, at least until he could dry out a little and get his anxiety under control.

Maneuvering through the Keno lounge, Nathan headed to a bar he had visited several times. It was time to get a stiff drink and try to blend in. At that point in time, resting and sorting things out was all that mattered. If nothing else, it was a time to sit and mournfully reflect.

Surveying the lounge, a couple people sat at the bar, while others relaxed at tables. Entering the temporary safe-haven, he headed directly to the bar.

Nathan chose a seat at the bar that provided an unobstructed view of the casino floor. Taking a seat, Nathan took off his rain-soaked jacket and laid it on the barstool next to him. Sitting in front of a poker machine, he looked at the losing cards the last player had bet on. Nathan could only wish that his bad luck was due to a hand of losing cards dealt by a machine.

Leaning forward, elbows on the bar, Nathan stared at the

liquor display. Though the display housed everything imaginable, he knew exactly what he needed to warm up.

While preparing an order for the cocktail waitress, the bartender briefly glanced in Nathan's direction and nodded. A nod that indicated he would be there as soon as possible. Waiting to be served, he cast a brief look around.

About a half-dozen patrons were perched on bar-stools. In their various stages of drunkenness, the storm seemed to be the main topic of conversation.

With the elevated view, Nathan could see most of the casino. There were hundreds of fortune seekers making their way through isles of machines and rows of gaming tables. In the main isle, dealers, roulette croupier's and crap table crews tended to business as usual.

The countless multi-colored, musical gaming machines roared to a pitch that utterly devoured the crowd. The only sound that overshadowed the machines was the shouts and cheers that emerged from a high-spirited craps game. Jubilantly, the participants shouted and whooped-it-up as the crap dice rolled to a stop on another winning number.

The atmosphere of the busy casino surged with an ecstatic, addictive energy. Like junkies after a fix, people become lost in the midst of a gambling euphoria.

With a descent view of the perimeter, he wondered from which direction his next attack might come. As he had all night, his eyes searched for any kind of threat. Nathan was not going to be caught flat-footed or be blind-sided. If the police were in the casino, he would immediately be warned. The last thing he wanted was a major confrontation in public.

Returning his attention back to the bar, Nathan looked into the mirror behind the liquor display. The reflection that looked back was pale and waxy. Unfortunately, he looked exactly as he felt. Emotionally numb, a profound sadness existed in his stare. With a mixture of weariness and doubt strewn across his haggard face, Nathan's eyes were pain-ridden and haunted with despair. Turning from the troubled image in the mirror, he began to study the lacerations to his hands and arms.

While finalizing the tray of drinks for the waitress, the bartender glanced back at Nathan. "What can I get for ya?" casually inquiring.

"Could I get a shot of Brandy, please?"

When the waitress picked up her tray of drinks, the barkeep headed directly toward Nathan. The tall, broad shouldered man sported a clean shaven head with a diamond stud earring.

The bartender grabbed a shot glass and placed it in front of him. "Just a shot of Brandy for starters."

"Brandy's always a good jump-start."

As the drink was poured, Nathan dug into his rain-soaked pants and pulled out a soggy twenty dollar bill. Placing the wet bill on the counter, all anticipation was on that first sip of Brandy.

The generous bartender poured him two-fingers worth of Brandy and sat the bottle on the counter.

"Thanks," responding gratefully. Nathan picked up the shot glass and downed it with one long swallow. A relaxing sensation surged through him as the Brandy began to melt away some of his fatigue and built up tension.

"Another one please," placing the shot glass back on the bar-top.

The bartender started a conversation as he filled the glass for a second time. "It looks like you were outside when all hell broke loose?"

"What makes you think that?"

"Well...For one thing...It looks like you just swam across the lake." Chuckling from his sarcastic observation.

Nathan gave him a weary stare. "Ya...I was out there...It's pretty nasty." Admitting as he spun the shot glass between his fingers.

"I'm sorry." Snickering as he put the Brandy bottle back in its place. "I'm not laughing at you. I'm laughing because I should look just like you. I got to work about twenty minutes ago, right before the storm unloaded." Still smiling as he snatched-up the twenty.

As the barkeep stepped to the cash register, Nathan picked up the glass and took a soothing sip. The warmth of the brandy was a welcomed friend.

After returning with Nathan's change, the bartender gave him a word of encouragement. "If it makes you feel any better, you're not the only one I've seen looking like a drown rat." Behind the bar, he grabbed a wash towel and commenced to wipe down the counter.

Nathan took another sip of brandy before responding. "That's reassuring…But not as reassuring as this Brandy." The eighty-proof drink seemed to kick on his inner furnace.

After taking another drink, he slowly lowered the glass to the counter. As Nathan stared at the Brandy in the shot-glass, the night began to play back in his mind.

Paying little attention to the other patrons, his mind became completely engaged in his own dilemma. Drifting into serious deliberation, Nathan wondered what he could have done to make things turn out differently.

How could someone have so much bad luck in the same day? In the same lifetime for what that matters. But no amount of second-guessing was going to change the situation.

Unfortunately, as of late, life seemed to hand Nathan nothing but extremes. The more he thought about it, the more none of it seemed real. In a matter of a few hours, his whole world had disintegrated before his very eyes.

Nathan's disconnected thoughts took him back to the house. Painfully reliving the events that would forever leave a permanent scar on his life.

While his memory jumped from event to event, deep within

he knew he was fighting a losing battle. Becoming restless, it became too apparent that the situation was not going to get any better. Right then, he felt a powerful need to get back to the trailer.

Nathan's attention slowly drew back to the matter at hand. It was time to leave the solitude of the bar and return back to the unknown reality that existed outside.

After finishing the drink, Nathan thanked the bartender with what remained of the twenty. Though reluctant to venture out from the casino, it was time to make a move. Sliding off the barstool, he exited the lounge and focused on the next destination.

Once again, the gaming machines devoured the atmosphere. The whimsical sounds of slot machines rang; coins clanked into metal trays and energized gamblers cheered in excitement.

Nathan cast an unsuspecting glance around the casino floor, then, tried to melt into the crowd. Untrustingly watching everyone around him, he made his way through clusters of people.

In order to avoid the slow moving crowd, Nathan headed directly toward the escalator that led down to the lobby. The musical chatter of the gaming machines faded as he descended from the casino level. Approaching the lower floor, the odor of chlorinated water filled the air. After disembarking the escalator, Nathan guided his path past the tropical ponds and waterfalls. Nathan paid little attention to the lavish lobby as his mind was occupied on more serious matters.

The huge lobby was basically deserted as he walked past the registration desk. It was time to take the battle back into the night. After pressing the push-bar on the exit door, he emerged outside. Within a couple steps, Nathan found himself walking along the same taxi-run where it all started.

CHAPTER 13

THOUGH THE STORM HAD subsided, the taxi-cab windows were still streaked with rain. Reaching the front sidewalk, Nathan came to a halt beneath the bright lights of Stateline. Looking up past the high-rise hotels, the casino's lit the Tahoe night revealing a terrestrial glow off the low-flying clouds.

A misty drizzle filled the air as the lakefront temperature dropped toward freezing. Finally, unencumbered from the weight of the storm, Nathan began walking down the rain-swept sidewalk. The scrutiny in his eyes was dead serious as he kept a watchful eye around him.

Clouds-of-mist hissed and fanned out behind each passing car. The liquid glimmer of the wet street, reflected a weird, distorted afterglow from the flashing multi-colored lights.

Moving against a tide of people, Nathan walked beneath the brilliantly lit marquees. The sidewalks were filled with fast-paced pedestrians in eager anticipation of their next gambling experience.

While walking through the drizzly night, the smell of pinewood smoke filled the air from nearby chimneys. Flipping up his jacket collar, Nathan carefully glanced around, trying to call as little attention to himself as possible.

Just beyond the bright marquee lights, he moved silently within the shadows of the street. Contemplating what to do next, a light rain began to fall. While searching for an escape from the storm, something caught his attention.

Nathan's eyes widened in alarm as a police cruiser headed straight toward him. As the patrol-car passed, he was no longer concerned about what was ahead - but what was behind him.

Nathan's anxiety was well founded as the cruiser brake-lights came on. With an upbeat tempo, he continued to walk down the wet sidewalk. Rubber squealed against the pavement as the patrol car spun a U-turn. In no time, the cruiser had reversed direction and was headed his way.

As far as arrest was concerned, one thing was for sure, it was not going to take place here. Disregarding the other pedestrians, Nathan swiftly made a break for it. Running along the storm battered street, his choices of escape were few.

Determined to run as far as his out-of-shape body would carry him, he maintained a rigorously fast pace. Looking for the police, Nathan shot a desperate glance over his shoulder.

After another thirty yards, his breaths began turning to gasps. Boots pounding against the sidewalk, his legs began to feel like lead weights. Nathan's cold, drenched body was a lot more worn-out than he thought. Despite the fatigue, there was no choice but to keep moving.

For the time being, he knew the police would be looking for him on this side of the street, leaving him no choice but to change his route. It was clearly evident that the shortest course was across the street and through the casino parking lot. Suddenly, it became a necessity to get to the other side of Tahoe Boulevard.

Traffic was racing steadily in both directions. Casting an evaluating glance, Nathan searched for a break between cars. Just the smallest gap in traffic was all that was needed to escape to the other side. When the first opening showed itself, the opportunity was seized.

By the time Nathan stepped off the sidewalk, he was in a dead run. Steering himself through four lanes of speeding vehicles, he zig-zagged from lane to lane. Taking advantage of the last opening, his long legs quickly devoured the remaining distance.

Finally, his struggling body reached the opposite sidewalk. Nathan felt somewhat relieved, but at the same time, his body was used up - ready to collapse. Nathan directed his exhausted stare toward the rows of cars just a couple hundred feet away.

Before his breathing calmed, the police cruiser slowly passed on the far side of the street. As soon as the patrol-car spotted him, the flashing lights lit-up and the chase was on. With the cruiser trying to cut across traffic, Nathan realized he might have the time needed to get away. Without hesitation, Nathan bolted toward the parking-lot.

Within a few running strides, the muscles in his legs began to cramp. Nathan's chest heaved with the effort to get enough air. Pain cut into his sides as his lungs burned with cold exertion. Fighting against total exhaustion, he ran the length of the building.

Pushed to the limits of endurance, he realized total collapse was imminent. Just in front of the parking entrance, Nathan's legs finally betrayed him. Dropping like the proverbial rock, he hit the pavement. Sprawling full-length, his knees and hands took the brunt of the punishment.

A faint dizzy spell shot through his head as dark motes began flying before his eyes. The palms of his hands and knees were scraped raw from the fall. Harsh labored breathing filled his ears as excruciating pain stabbed into his sides.

"Get up!" Abruptly demanding himself.

Nathan could barely force himself to his feet. Mouth hanging open, harsh exhausted breaths tore at his throat. Groaning in exhaustion, hands grabbing his sides, he attempted to regain his breath.

Steam bellowed from his mouth as stinging sweat ran down into his eyes. Wobbly and weak kneed, he had little energy left. But he was in too deep to stop now. Temporarily unnoticed, Nathan half-walked half-jogged into the parking lot.

Despite the cold, he was sweating profusely. Wiping away the stinging sweat from his eyes, he lumbered through the parking lot. Isle by isle, he maneuvered through the rows of parked cars.

Legs like jelly, Nathan allowed himself a brief chance to rest. Concealing himself between parked cars, he began taking a series of gasping breaths. Slouched over, hands braced on his knees, he felt as if he were going to pass-out. After a few strenuous moments of light-headedness his mind began to straighten out.

Still dripping with sweat, he forced himself to straighten up. Nathan focused on the portion of the forest that resided just beyond the rear of the property. For not far away, resided the cover he needed to lead the way home. The chance to elude the cops was near.

While concentrating on the next move, something caught his attention. A quick backward glance confirmed what he needed to know. In anticipation of a patrol car, his fears were answered. The cruiser was pulling into the entrance of the parking area.

Slumping down between cars, Nathan stayed out-of-sight. Compelling himself to keep his thoughts straight, he carefully peered through the windows of a parked car. Watching the vehicles every move, the cruiser began searching the parking isles.

As the car weaved through the parking lot, it began to edge ever closer. Staying where he was, would be the same as giving up. The fear of being caught was now his only source of energy. Moving once again, Nathan stayed as low as possible.

Eyes and body burning from sweat and fatigue, he crept on bent legs. Indecisively, he hiked between cars, navigating a path toward the forest. Pressing on, there was no way to tell whether he was heading toward disaster or safety. The fact of the matter was they were lurking out there somewhere.

One second the police were nowhere to be seen, the next, they were headed down the aisle next door. Ducking down, he surveyed its movements until it passed by. Nathan was not sure how long he could survive this cat and mouse game. The tail-lights were barely out of sight when he commenced to race toward the forest.

In a half-crouch, on exhausted legs, he made his way through the maze of vehicles. Eyes fixed on the destination; he fought to ignore the exhaustion that was once again sweeping through his legs. Nathan's body would not put up with much more abuse.

As air pumped into his lungs, he continued to bee-line-it toward the forest. Wheezing, legs straining, Nathan did not care, he was a fugitive and had to get away. Lungs heaving, he took a final glance over his shoulder before entering the forest. With the police still nowhere in sight, Nathan penetrated the closest line of trees and was as good-as-gone.

CHAPTER 14

PANTING AND DRIPPING WITH perspiration, Nathan's lungs burned malignantly. Laboring for breath, he felt as if he had just run a marathon. There was no telling how much more he could take.

Clothes drenched and heavy against his skin, Nathan wiped the sweat from his face. Steam dispersed from his overheated body as he stopped to rest beneath the shelter of a tree. Even though it was not raining, water dripped heavily from the overhead branches.

Looking up through the treetops, he watched as the glowing radiance of the moon tried to break through the low-hanging clouds. Nathan felt lucky to be in one piece, even luckier to still be alive.

As his body cooled, his wet clothes just magnified the chill in the air. The heavy toll of the night had driven him to the limits of his endurance.

Nathan undoubtedly knew that this day was going to be a pivotal turning point in his life. Squeezing his eyes shut, he wished for a way to go back in time, retreating just long enough to start the day over. Taking every obstacle of the day, and doing the exact opposite of what he had done earlier.

But come hell or high water, he was somehow going to make it. Burrowing into his jacket, Nathan walked into the murky, sodden forest. As the sounds of Stateline died away, he was left only with the gusting wind through the trees. Shoulders hunched, hands deep within his pockets, it was now all about mind over matter.

Nathan's weakened condition made it difficult to start up the hill. Searching for some inner strength, he demanded himself to finish the remaining distance. Now, his only concern was putting one foot in front of the other.

As if still raining, remnants of the storm dripped heavily from the trees. With each step, his feet sank into the soggy forest floor. Amidst the dripping trees, Nathan ascended the hill fighting through the spongy, sodden ground. Though the storm had subsided, the wind had returned with a vengeance, bringing a razor-sharp chill that cut through the trees like a knife.

Wetness was everywhere, and his drenched clothes were becoming a burden. Moving further into the wet forest, the soggy, tacky mud attempted to suck the shoes from his feet. The brutal and miserable conditions of this rural wilderness was taking a final toll on his body.

Joints popping, muscles knotted with cramps, Nathan used the forest for balance. Tired and unsteady, he stayed close to the trees for support. Barely able to carry his weight any longer, he carefully moved from tree-trunk to tree-trunk.

As Nathan pushed through the icy wind, he began to withdraw into himself. Dwelling on the aches and pains, weighed down by despair and fatigue, he walked listlessly. After wary consideration, he decided it was time to rest. Leaning against a tree, he watched as the moon emerged from behind a dark cloud.

It was a cold and hostile environment. Everything was dark and soaking wet. Rain continued to drip from the trees, pelting Nathan and the already saturated ground.

Despite the cold, he continued to sweat. Face pale from exhaustion, his only source of energy was coming from his determination to survive. Nathan's body protested the exertions it took to climb the hillside. The short stop was far from the rest he needed, but it was time to finish the journey.

Drudging forward in determined silence, he took a path that would lead him to the back of the trailer park. Still soaked from the night's rain, the sodden forest continued to suck at his feet. Clods of mud clung to the soles of his boots as he fought forward.

As the terrain became steeper, the wind was now a constant pounding in his ears. It was not the cold night that he dreaded most, but rather the freezing wind that intensified everything. Nathan felt like a cold demon spirit was occupying his body.

As the night's cold darkness pushed toward freezing, he walked deeper into the forest. Willing his muscles to continue, Nathan strained to keep his feet under him. Legs numb and trembling with fatigue, the cold surroundings suddenly began to fade in and out.

The weight of the whole ordeal was taking its final toll. Lungs burning, his chest felt as if it were being crushed in a vise. For an instant, Nathan thought that he was about to give in to a heart attack. As exhaustion pulled at him, he experienced a short period of disorientation.

Breathing heavily, a deep exhaustion bit in. Nathan's last bits of strength vanished as he was ravaged by a severe dizzy spell. The tedium of the march had brought him to the brink of total exhaustion.

Summoning all his resources, Nathan forced himself to walk. Almost incapable of moving, he progressed in shaky spurts. Just as Nathan had nearly exhausted the remainder of his energy, the trailer park came into view. Circling back to the rear of the property, he focused his attention in the direction of his trailer. Gaining sight of his spot, he watched from the wooded darkness.

The police were inside Nathan's trailer and all around the RV Park. Moving closer, he hid behind a tree about fifty yards from the property line. Studying the area around Mrs. Ellis's shed, he noticed a few policemen patrolling around the perimeter of the property. Nathan's home-field advantage had just gone out the window.

For a long moment, he watched the movements of the police. Nathan's immediate future had narrowed down to the obvious; there was no place to hide other than the shed. But, the other side of the coin entailed, coming face to face with the enemy - once again.

Nathan was not wild about the idea of going into the shed, in fact, the intense horror that filled his thoughts were almost overwhelming. But there were no other alternatives, it was either hide in the shed or be caught.

The moment of truth churned in his stomach as he thought of what he was about to do. After a couple of deep breaths, he pushed all distracting thoughts aside and focused on the obstacle ahead.

Nathan stared at the shed for several seconds before he made his move. Strength depleting rapidly, he began sneaking toward the backside of the shed. In the cover of shadows, no one was the wiser as he prowled the edge of the property line.

Nathan's presence brought a sudden silence to the chirping of crickets. Mind blurred from fatigue, his body was being driven by what little adrenaline was left in his system. With the police busy talking to each other, he took the opportunity to climb over the park's chain-link fence. To the best of his knowledge, the police were unaware of his presence.

Nathan knew this day was somehow going to be different, he just did not know how different. Crawling into the spider-infested shed was probably the craziest idea he had ever had. But at this point, it was the only option. Filled with anxiety, he could not believe he was about to enter the place he feared most.

Disappearing into the depths of the tall foliage, Nathan made his own path through the wet underbrush. Moving secretly along the ground, he found the hole in the back wall. Anxiety level off the charts, he began crawling into the shed.

Getting through the hole proved more difficult than anticipated, the wetness of his clothes was becoming an added hindrance as he struggled forward. With unyielding persistence, he finally pushed himself through the small opening.

Nathan's sudden existence within the shed was a traumatizing ordeal of the most insidious kind. With the police right outside, he sat on the dirty floor and leaned against the back wall.

Nervously rubbing his bloodshot eyes, Nathan took a long subdued breath, then, reluctantly withdrew his hands. Eyes wide open, he found himself sitting in the one place he swore he would never go into again.

Patrol-car spotlights lit up everything, including the old woman's shed. Normally, the shed would have been a complete void of blackness. But with the aid of all the police lights, the gaps in the wooden slats made his confines somewhat visible. In the seclusion of the temporary refuge, he watched through tiny slits. Nathan felt bizarrely elated as he sat hidden watching the police look for him. At least for the moment, he was safe within the mildewed, musty smelling darkness.

The chill of the storm remained in the air. Burrowing deeper into the jacket, he tried to escape from the night's cold bite. All at once, his legs began to knot and cramp and momentarily refused to straighten out.

Rubbing the protesting muscles, he tried to silently expel the attacking cramps. Nathan wanted nothing more than to scream in pain. But he knew that if any sound was made, the police would certainly find him. After a couple agonizing minutes, he was able to flatten his legs to the floor.

Wet and cold, Nathan's thoughts turned to his warm bed inside the trailer. It was amazing how accustom he had become to basic luxuries. A warm bed, running water, television and a refrigerator filled with more food than he needed. These things were usually thoughtless aspects to his life - until now. The cold, spider infested shed was now his home.

The night's ill-fated events had thrown his life in an unforeseeable direction. Nathan was consumed with just a lonely memory of his previous existence, a past life and reality that had been mercilessly stripped away.

The fatigue and stress of the night was beginning to become more than he could withstand. Ensnared in a nest of spiders with nowhere to go, Nathan considered submitting to his inevitable and traumatic capture.

All I have to do is walk out the shed door and surrender. Silently challenging himself.

The police were milling around everywhere, chomping at-the-bit to find him. Though his nerves were shot, his mind refused to rest. Nathan could only envision what might happen if they got their claws in him - it would not be pretty.

Knowing the Tahoe police and their bias, if caught, he would be aggressively arrested and tormented to no end. Nathan was not about to end this tragic day by going to jail.

Despite the horror of spiders, one thing was sure, there was no way in hell he was leaving the shed. Even in the terror of his present reality, he felt safer in the shed than what might lie on the other side of the door.

Body so exhausted, he could not even bring himself to keep an eye on the police. Nathan knew what was going on outside, there was no need to see the details. The only thing he was interested in was staying out of the grasp of the man-hunt.

While trying to dismiss the surrounding images from his mind, he caught himself intently peering around the shed. Nathan's vision explored every inch of the filthy structure. The most threatening thought was the horrifying knowledge that he was in the midst of hundreds of flesh-eating spiders.

Nathan now resided in a world where he was the low man on the food chain. At that moment, he felt as if he were being sized-up by the predators that he shared the shed with. For he knew, that sooner or later, he would be greeted by his eight-legged nemesis.

The nightmare of a night seemed to go on relentlessly, getting worse and worse with each passing second. Surrounded by madness, Nathan trembled uncontrollably as the dreary chill tore at his bones. Sitting silently in the darkness, Nathan became lost in his own private torment.

As the wind whistled around the shed, the images at the house played back in his mind. Sick in his heart, he realized he would never see Sarah again. Surrendering to tears, Nathan grieved for the loss of his daughter

An accusing voice needled at him. *Why didn't I do something sooner?*"

Squeezing his eyes shut, he pressed his face into his shaking hands. Stubbornly, he embraced the possibility that none of this was actually happening. Then, without warning, the worst thing that could happen - happened. As desperate as his situation was, it just got worse - something had bit him.

Before Nathan could react, he was bitten again. The horrifying world in which he hid, had just come alive with a vendetta. Fear knotted his gut as he searched the darkness for the next attacker. From the darkest of the sheds shadows, the eight-legged monsters began to show themselves.

Nathan did not have an option, the spiders were all over him. Scrambling under Nathan's jacket and pant-legs, the spiders sank their fangs into their target. The venomous injections raced through his veins, spreading throughout his body. Just as fast as they attacked, they retreated. The soldier spiders hastily vanished back into the privacy of their unseen webs.

Once the spiders poison began to take control, the commotion outside the shed became meaningless. Nathan's hands and feet became overrun by a tingling sensation. Then, while beginning to slip into a relaxed, almost medicated state, a strange numbness began to radiate throughout his body. The odd numbness rapidly rendered his extremities virtually useless.

As the poison ran its course, his breathing began to thicken. Then, his heart-rate slowed to an almost critical point. It was not long before he began to shiver. Sitting on the freezing floor, uncontrollable tremors began to quake and shudder through his muscles. Feeling desperately dehydrated, it became nearly impossible to swallow. Nathan's body was slowly crashing.

As the numerous doses of poison reached its peak, his flesh became numb to the outside elements. Nathan tried to sit up, but his body refused to respond. All extremities were numb and senseless. It was as if his entire being had been shot with Novocain.

Nathan laid paralyzed in a physically sedated coma. Though his body was not physically conscious, his mind raced in horrified anticipation. Slowly drifting toward a trance-like state, he stared into the darkness, searching for the next attacker. Nathan watched the darkest part of the ceiling where light failed to reach. Finally, he was no longer able to hold his head up. Mouth wide open, his head limply fell backward. With all his strength, he tried to raise his head, but nothing happened.

Then he saw it, an all too familiar shape loomed in the corner of the ceiling. Eyes now on the ultimate threat, Nathan watched in horror as the huge predator made its way across the ceiling. Stopping directly above his head, he stared in horror as the blood-sucking cannibal sized him up.

Nathan's only movement was the faint rise and fall of his chest. Unable to move, he watched as the eight-legged silhouette began to descend toward his immobilized body.

All fear instantly magnified as the spider seemed to be getting bigger. But it was not getting bigger, it was getting closer. Nathan wanted so badly to close his mouth and squeeze his eyes shut. But, even the muscles in his face were paralyzed in place.

Helpless terror consumed his stare as the giant spider dropped nearer. Nathan became blind to all rational thought when the creature stopped an inch from his chin. Once again, Nathan was face to face with the enemy. The monster's oversized yellow eyes seemed possessed as it glared into Nathan's frightened stare.

As his imagination took hold of his present reality, he could swear the spider smiled as it landed on his chin. Nathan was sure that what was left of his sad life was about to be cut short.

As the remaining remnants of Nathan's day came to a conclusion, his final terrifying thoughts were focused on the spider that had entered his mouth and was now crawling down his throat.

PART THREE
"THE SWAP MEET"

CHAPTER 1

IN A FITFUL SLEEP, squirming beneath the sheets and blanket, Bennett awoke with a start. Sweat drenched and disoriented, he jolted up in bed. Filled with an anxiety that was off the charts, his pulse raced at a furious pace. Unable to draw enough air, he desperately gasped, searching for the smallest fragment of breath.

Still somewhat embraced by sleep, Bennett sat motionless, just a jittery bundle of nerves. Enwrapped in darkness, he frantically swept his eyes throughout the lightless room. Anxious to understand his confusion, he tried to focus on a moment of clarity. A fragment of anything he might recognize.

Blinking at the darkness, his vision began to adapt to the dim outlines of his immediate surroundings. Bennett's agitated state gradually subsided as the shadowy contours of the room began to take shape. In the hazy murkiness of his mind, the familiarities of his temporary living space slowly took form.

After a few tension filled seconds, Bennett realized he had just awakened from some sort of horrid dream. Desperately trying to resurrect his memory, he became feverishly obsessed with recalling what he had just dreamt. But the fuzzy details seemed to evade his grasp.

The only recollection he held on to was the image of a beautiful woman in a white dress. The basis for the dream was unclear, but one thing stood out - the woman. The same beautiful woman that entered his dreams every night since that fateful day.

Bennett was powerless to prevent these unconscious experiences from reoccurring. The nightmares were driving him crazy. It was as if he were being stalked and tormented every time he went to sleep. But, at the same time, he was unable to rid himself of the captivating vision of the mysterious woman.

While his dreams were vague and confusing, he always recalled her in vivid detail. Though he could not escape from these horrid nightmares, his anxiety was always quickly quenched as his mind became mesmerized with the very thought of the unknown female.

While stricken by a deep sense of wonder, he slid from beneath the tangle of sheets. Sleepily, he stood and scuffled away from the bed. With outstretched arms leading the way, he found his way to the wall. Like a blind man, he slid his left hand along the wall, while the other led the way through the darkness. Within a few disoriented steps, he staggered into the bathroom.

After snapping on the light, he went to the sink and began running hot water. Forearms resting on the edges of the sink, he let the warming water fill his trembling cupped hands. Bennett's lips were so dry they felt ready to split. After repeatedly dousing his lips and face, he let the steamy vapors give his body a sense of revitalization.

Shutting off the facet, he lifted his rheumy eyes to the medicine cabinet mirror. The mirror was dripping with condensation. Bennett wiped away just enough of the steamy residue to see his face.

The unsettling picture in the mirror did nothing to heighten his withered spirit. The reflected image that stared back was the wary likeness of a man who was marked by doubt.

Unshaven and still puffy-eyed from sleep, he glared at his desperate and pale reflection. As the hot water continued to run, he stood in a mesmeric state.

Eyes locked and immersed in the replicate eyes in the mirror, Bennett glared at his troubled reflection. Lurking deep within the reflected stare, resided a creeping expectancy he was unable to identify. An unrelenting, private agony that continued to swell from within.

Bennett's already diminished spirits were pushing him to an all-time low. He could not help but ponder what could be lingering in his unforeseeable future to put him at such unease. How his destiny could seem so unbearably bleak.

Helplessly obsessed by the presence of these unnatural tensions, he felt imprisoned in his own self-contained hell. Drowning in an emotional whirlpool of despair and conflicting emotions. Unable to purge and free himself from the persistent anguish that seemed embedded in his very soul.

Inhale. Exhale.

Inhale. Exhale. Bennett silently reminded himself.

With each new breath, small torrents of irrational tension began to fade. Bennett blinked and gave himself a mental shake. Lethargically, he averted his angst-ridden gaze from the troubled image that occupied the mirror.

Stepping away from his reflection, Bennett listlessly left the confines of the tiny bathroom. Crossing the room, he headed toward the thick drapes that covered the front window. Passing the digital clock, he noticed it read 5:46am.

Pushing aside a corner of the drawn curtains, he stared out from the second story window. It would not be long before the sun showed itself over the eastern mountains. But, until then, darkness still reigned and dawn was no more than a promise in the sky.

Reaching out toward the night, he pressed the palm of his hand against the window. In return, the cold darkness pressed back against the other side of the glass.

Bennett raised his stare toward the stars, but he did not notice the starry sky. As with the beginning to every day, his vision was filled with an agonizing, distant gaze, the same familiar haunting presence that shadowed his every thought and emotion. Like a primal terror, icily rippling through his veins, it was time to face another unwished-for day.

CHAPTER 2

AFTER DRYING OFF FROM a much needed shower, Bennett draped the towel around his neck and exited the steamy bathroom. While getting dressed, he watched as a border of grey morning light fought to penetrate the edges of the drawn curtains. It was almost time to test himself against the horrid realm of the outside world.

As of late, each disheartened day began like the previous one. At first light, the daily routine started off with a walk to Regan Beach. But his early morning strolls were not to get a fresh start for the day. Rather, a conscious effort to avoid as much social intervention as possible.

Though others might see the world as a wonderful place, he was convinced that society itself had a lot to answer for. A part of Bennett had died and he no longer wanted to fit-in or advance in the public sector. For the most part, he had cut himself away from the outside world and everyone in it. Just a lost soul running from reality, he did whatever necessary to stay away from societies grasp.

Bennett was going through a tremendous amount of pain. Not physical, but mental. Emotional scaring that could not be remedied by bandages or medicine.

Day after day, all day long, he found himself being drained of his will to endure. In the smashed landscape of his mind, he constantly fought a war with uncertainty. A never-ending battle against personal demons that seemed to be in control of his very being. Psychologically vulnerable, Bennett realized if he were not careful his very existence was about to push him over the razors edge.

Terminally depressed, he was a revolting shell of his former self. Bennett no longer knew who he was, his life seemed pointless. In his tiny little world of depression and self-pity, he had become nothing more than an emotional pile of mush. Refusing to let up, his anxiety was wearing him down to nothing. One miserable day after another, the bitterness and denial he kept locked-up inside swelled. While not a bitter person at heart, he now detested everything in general.

Though he brought it on himself, the isolation he desired had become his greatest enemy. The loneliness he felt seemed to descend on him like a smothering cloud. Lost and alone, he found that lately, even the simplest of things had become difficult. It was just one of the many depressing symptoms he had to come to grips with. Now-days, the smallest glimmer of hope was the only antidote for his despair. It was the only thing that life had not already taken from him.

* * *

After dressing for the chill of the morning, Bennett was ready to proceed with the usual excursion. When he grabbed his watch off the dresser, he noticed that it was blinking 5:46am. The exact time he had viewed when he had first awakened.

Though not sure of the actual time, Bennett knew he had been up for at least an hour. Looking at the alarm clock, he watched as the digital display still flashed 5:46am. When he tried to randomly reset his watch, it was unresponsive to any touch command he gave it.

Frustrated, he went to the alarm clock to set it to any time to keep it from blinking. But to his exasperation, after pressing every necessary button, the clock refused to cooperate. It was as if time had stopped at 5:46am.

Giving up on the clock, Bennett grabbed his jacket and headed toward the door. Stepping outside into the early morning light, he was promptly greeted by a blast of icy wind. The frigid grip of dawn buffeted his face and instantly drew goose-bumps. The October morning was consumed with the unmistakable bite of winter. A bitter chill that whispered the promise of Autumn's demise. Shivering against the cold wind, he quickly put on his coat.

After locking the door, he walked out into another cheerless morning. Bennett thought he was starting out this day like any other, but something was definitely different. Not different in an unusual way, different in an extremely bizarre way. As he crossed the terrace toward the stairs, he found himself looking over an empty parking lot. It was still hours before the motels check-out. Though he knew better, it was as if there were no other tenants in the motel.

Confused as to what he was witnessing, Bennett leaned his forearms on the second story railing. Just a short time ago, when he looked out his room window, the parking lot was filled. Curiously, he stared out over the vacant section of pavement that usually housed numerous vehicles. But this morning, not one car occupied a parking spot.

After descending the stairs, Bennett started across the deserted lot. On every other morning, he would have to maneuver through several cars to get off the property. That was not a problem today, because there was not a four-wheeled obstacle anywhere to be seen.

In total amazement, he made his way toward the main boulevard. With each step, his thoughts drifted into a state of remembrance. One after another, daunting images began to swim back into his memory. In this reminiscent mind frame, the past and the present suddenly began to intermingle until the past took control.

As the memories effortlessly came to life, Bennett became consumed with images of what had been. Back to another place and time not so long ago. To a simpler time when his life was so uncomplicated and all his own.

A time before his world had been so grotesquely turned upside down. Anymore, even his most cherished memories were not a source of escape. Rather, an all-consuming reminder of what he no longer had.

As Bennett allowed his mind to reflect, he abruptly reverted to the unbelievable recollections of the past six months. Not-so-distant yesterdays that were filled with the unpredictable events that forced him down that unforeseen path. Mercilessly leading him to that one despairingly desperate moment.

From the darkest crevices of his consciousness, an appalling scrap of memory clawed at his very being. The same inexcusable mental souvenir that always tugged at his soul. Like a crushing weight stalking from above, it was as if it were just waiting for the perfect moment to crush and destroy him.

As he approached the boulevard, vivid and disturbing images ingrained themselves upon him. The last thing he wanted to do was to be stuck in a memory he consciously detested. But no matter how hard he fought it, he could not seem to defeat his most ruthless enemy - himself.

As if it were yesterday, with crystalline clarity, he found himself reliving that day when the insanities started. Haunted in never-ending torment, that painful moment was now imprinted in his soul once again.

The day his world would began to end and slip through his fingers.

The day that turned out to be the beginning of the most unpredictable and dramatic turning-point of his life.

The day he took his first unforeseen steps towards the gates of Hell.

Absorbed with anxiety, Bennett became transfixed in remembrance of the moment he tried to take his life. From that day forward, his sins haunted him. Life as he once knew it was over, dead and buried, never to be resurrected. Bennett now resided in a guilt-ridden purgatory of his own making.

While doing nothing to enhance the high-light reel of that hideous decision, reliving his attempt at death was beyond his control. Bennett's failed escape from his dreaded existence now ruled every second of his life.

It was almost impossible to think of the future when he could not come to grips with the past. Just the slightest recollection of that day sent a quiver of misery cutting through his heart. The constant rerun of his weakest moment was almost more than he could endure.

Silently, he mentally cursed, accusing himself of cowardice and self-betrayal. Bennett was now and would forever be, cloaked with guilt for what he attempted to do. Every time that moment presented itself, he wished he had succeeded in the efforts to put himself out of misery.

Reaching Tahoe Boulevard, he continued his short journey toward the park. As he stepped onto the sidewalk to begin his walk, his eyes suddenly widened as he froze in mid-stride. As if being plunged into another world, his gut knotted with a terrified sense of the unknown.

At that moment, his growing anxiety toward this day was becoming out of proportion to everything else he felt. It was clear; no explanation whatsoever could justify or penetrate the unseen realm of reality he was experiencing.

CHAPTER 3

STANDING MESMERIZED, A SHIVER of instant fear shot through him. Little else concerned him as he stared at the bizarre sight in front of him.

"I'm losing my mind?" Glancing up and down the street. "None of this can be real...Can it?" Nervously asking himself.

Bennett's amazement deepened as he continued to stare. While appearances could be deceiving, there was nothing deceiving about this morning. Lake Tahoe was a rather quiet town this time of year, but what he was witnessing was impossible. There were none of the familiar sounds of civilization. It was anything but business as usual, the entire town was quiet and still. Bennett was looking at nothing but a long, empty street. There were no signs of everyday life, no movement anywhere. It was as if the outside world did not exist anymore.

Since first arriving to the lake, Tahoe mornings always brought out a steady flow of people. Even during the off season, the streets were busy with tourists and locals. But today, the normally traveled sidewalks were eerily vacant.

Bennett never paid any attention to the strangers that shared the sidewalk with him. Usually, he just lowered his head in order not to make eye contact. But today, there was no one to ignore.

Standing alone, Bennett found himself on a street that should have been active with people. The usual stream of morning pedestrians had somehow vanished. No one on their way to work, none of the usual breakfast crowds filling the restaurants.

No mom's pushing their baby strollers or children skipping passed him on their way to school. Not a soul waiting patiently at the bus stops. The joggers, bikers and power-walkers that always festooned the sidewalks and bike-path were nowhere to be seen. No wandering tourist's window shopping along the store-fronts. Not even a dog, cat, bird or even a bug was visible. The only movement in the entire town was that of his own.

Troubled and agitated, Bennett's disgruntled brain refused to relax, searching for answers that were just not there. Too paranoid to move, his unbelieving eyes continued to scan the empty street. Beside the absence of pedestrians, there were no parked cars and traffic was non-existent. Not a single early morning commuter racing to work. No squealing brakes from the lumbering transit buses.

With no traces of life whatsoever, Bennett started making his way down the street. Walking backwards, he studied the deserted area from which he just came, looking for any signs of life or movement that he may have missed.

Unbelievingly preoccupied by the surroundings, he crept down the sidewalk as if waiting for someone to jump out and yell "April fools!" After a short distance, he decided to sit down on the bus-stops wooden bench. But Bennett disturbingly knew there would be no buses stopping here on this day.

For several minutes, he sat and focused his attention on the buildings and businesses on both sides of the street. It was as if the structures had been abandoned for a hundred years. The grass and shrubs were overgrown and dying. The paint was cracked and chipping, accompanied by windows that were filthy and weather-beaten.

The town was immersed with an unnatural, self-possessed atmosphere. All the stores and businesses were shut down and the streets and sidewalks were uninhabited as far as he could see. Imagination pumping, the only conclusion he could come up with was that civilization had been wiped off the face of the earth. Bennett was not sure what disturbed him more, the fact that his wish for society to vanish from his life had come true. Or, that it was time to come to grips with the fact that he was the only one left.

Searching for some sort of alternative enlightenment, he searched for anything that might explain what was happening. As Bennett continued down the street, he noticed that all the traffic lights were working. But they never changed, they just blinked yellow.

Though the temperature was no more than 40 degrees, he was now looking through what appeared to be vapors, heat-waves ascending from the pavement and sidewalks. Raising his stare to the sky, he could not believe what he saw. While impossible, the sun looked at him from straight overhead. Though he knew it was no later than 7:00am, the sun appeared to be at high noon.

Strange as everything was, nothing that he had already witnessed compared to what he experienced next. All at once, the wind began to gust, but to his amazement, the trees remained motionless. Even the leaves and paper on the ground failed to move. While Bennett could hear the wind howling and whistling through the trees, everything remained still. Everything appeared and seemed impossibly unreal.

Then, as fast as the wind arrived, it vanished. While the air was perfectly still, the tree-limbs and tall grass began flailing as if fighting against a gale-force wind. At the same instant, the street became littered with flying leaves and debris. Just as fast as the bizarre occurrence began, it stopped. Everything in town became quiet and still once again. It only took a split second before he began struggling with what was reality and what was not.

"Am I losing my mind?" Pressing the palms of his hands against his temples as if trying to suppress a migraine.

With no traffic to worry about, he slowly crossed the street. As Bennett drew nearer to the park, he was overcome by the notion that someone's eyes were upon him. As if some faceless stalker were taking inventory of his every movement. Bennett could not begin to conceive where this intrusive sense was coming from. Any other day, he would contribute it to his imagination, but this was not just any other day. In an unnerving, strange way, the idea of being under observation in a lifeless world became more than threatening.

Convinced he was being melodramatic, he tried to shrug off his suspicions. Yet, though trying not to give it a second thought, Bennett was gripped by the unsettling certainty that he was being watched by an unseen observer - unseen but not unfelt.

When the destination came into view, he saw the same thing he had witnessed in the rest of the town - nothing. Everything was so quiet, even the ever-present morning songs of unseen birds were nowhere to be heard. The silence was so intense, that if a pin dropped it would have sounded like a sonic-boom.

As soon as Bennett entered the park, the temperature seemed to jump about thirty degrees. The drastic change in temperature caused him to instantaneously overheat. Perspiration immediately covered his brow. Bennett's shirt instantly stuck to his body as beads of perspiration spewed from his skin.

Needing to cool down, he stripped off the jacket. While wiping the sweat from his forehead, a strange smell invaded his nostrils. Though he was use to inhaling the delicious fragrance of fresh pine, the mountain air was suddenly filled with the disgusting smell of rotten, burning garbage.

Looking for the source of the odor, something in the sky stirred his interest. Bennett's inquisitive stare became locked on the curious scene overhead. Though the lake shoreline was around 6000 feet above sea level, seagulls usually dominated the area. Crying their plaintive wails while swooping and gliding into the wind.

Watching mesmerized, it was visually apparent that prehistoric looking birds had taken the place of seagulls. With a wingspan of at least ten feet, the birds circled above like vultures, Bennett looked on in bemusement, never in his life had he seen birds that even resembled these flying creatures.

"I've had good days and I've had weird days. But this is a day to beat all." Shaking his head as he continued to study the bizarre sight.

Completely engaged at the sight overhead, Bennett never noticed the dust-devil that swirled through the air. Without warning, the tiny twister was on top of him. The swirling wind grew more intense as it encircled him. Blowing dust and debris attacked him from every angle. Unable to react in time, dirt and grit hit him directly in the face and embedded into his eyes. Bennett's eyes stung and teared-up from the invasion of debris. Once the tiny twister dissipated and his vision cleared, he realized he was no longer alone.

Confused, he mentally challenged what he saw. *A second ago there was no one in sight. Where'd she come from? How could she just appear out of nowhere?*

CHAPTER 4

EVEN IF IT WAS a hallucination, Bennett was just grateful to see another person. Seated atop a picnic bench overlooking the beach was a young woman. Never letting his eyes leave her presence, his hands brushed away the twister-dirt from his clothes.

Realizing it was not simply a figment of his imagination, Bennett's mind was now filled with nothing but heightened curiosity. The longer he looked at her, the more his spirit became incensed with a feeling of eerie familiarity.

The entire scene had an instant déjà vu quality. Bennett had been here and done this before - he could swear to it. It was as if he had regressed into a hidden place deep within his psyche and was reliving a previous experience.

Even from a distance, there was something mysterious and tantalizing about her. In an attempt to quench his all-consuming curiosity, he decided to confront the mystery woman. Though still sensing that he was being watched and nursing the sensation of déjà vu, Bennett headed straight toward the park bench where she sat.

Drawing closer, he could see that she was a younger blond woman wearing a loose-fitting, white summer dress. Reaching into his memories, he thought of his reoccurring dreams and nightmares. The only thing that any of these nightmarish events had in common was the women. As if someone had jolted him with a live wire, Bennett quickly realized he was about to confront the mysterious woman from his dreams.

In a long studying gaze, his pulse quickened as he drank in the sight of her. Not knowing whether to be excited or devastated by her presence, Bennett proceeded toward the park bench. Barely able to contain himself, his body became immersed with nervous anticipation. For months, while never knowing why, his soul had somehow been consumed with the expectancy of this very moment.

Once within a certain distance of her, she seemed to sense his presence. Revealing a captivating smile, her lovely face seemed to light-up in acknowledgment of his presence. Mesmerized by the enchanting vision that enveloped his eyes, Bennett returned her smile. With the enthusiasm of someone who had just found a long lost friend, excitement scorched through his veins as they held each-others stare.

Though there was not a hint of wind, her dress began to swish between her legs. At the same time, the non-existent breeze softly lifted her blond hair off her bare shoulders. She was perfect, owning all the attractive qualities that would attract any man

When Bennett had finally reached her, he instantly became intoxicated by her demeanor and beauty. Even with all of her physical magnificence, she possessed something far more alluring. Unable to recognize what the mystifying enticement was, her mere presence was impossible to ignore. It was as if he were gradually being cast under some kind of indefensible hypnotic spell.

Awe-struck by her stunning grey eyes, he momentarily fell speechless. The woman's overwhelming beauty temporarily robbed him of all train of thought and ability to communicate. The fleeting moment of silence had him completely unnerved and on the verge of incoherent panic. Trying to recover from his sudden lapse of rational thought, Bennett searched his brain for something to jump-start the conversation. But with no effort of his own, she remedied his tongue-tied silence.

"Hello Bennett...It is Bennett...Isn't it?" Asking with a curious grin.

"Yes...It's Bennett. But...How...Never mind."

On any other day, Bennett would have inquired on how she knew his name. But this was not any other day; it was the strangest morning of his life. The fact that she knew his name was at the bottom of his list of questions. Besides, he was standing in front of the most captivating woman he had ever seen and he did not want to do anything that might tarnish this unbelievable encounter.

Once again, Bennett searched himself for the right words. Clearing his throat, he prepared to ask her a somewhat embarrassing question. "I'm sorry...And I don't mean to sound stupid...But I can't remember your name." As soon as the words were said, his smile faded into an apologetic grin.

Though Bennett could not recall her name, he knew exactly where he had seen her before. Every time he awoke from one of his panic-ridden dreams, her radiant image was the only thing he could remember.

"I'm Destiny." Responding while giving him a comforting smile. Without hesitation, she picked-up the conversation once again. "Weird weather were having, isn't it?"

"Weird is a mild way of putting it. There's a lot of weird stuff going on today."

"That's funny, beside how hot it is...I haven't noticed anything unusual. Then again...What's strange to some is quite normal to others...You know what I mean?"

Bennett was not sure what she meant. But, how anyone could consider this as a normal day was way beyond his comprehension. Not wanting to challenge her remark, he let her comment slide by the way-side.

Desperate to keep their dialogue alive, Bennett pointed toward the sky behind her. "Have you ever seen birds like that around here before?"

Destiny stood up from the bench and turned her stare toward where he was pointing. As if meant to be, their shoulders lightly touched as they both looked out over the beach. Excitement filled his spirit when she gently leaned her exquisite body into his. An unfamiliar expression of happiness crossed Bennett's face as she let the intimate moment linger.

The woman had Bennett's undivided attention as she studied the giant birds. "I don't think so…They're acting like vultures…It's almost as if their waiting for something to die."

"Beside me, have you seen anyone else this morning?"

"As far as I know, everyone's at the swap meet." Turning her gaze to the far side of the park.

"I've never seen that before…How long's it been here?" Looking intently into her stunning eyes.

"It just opened today…That's where I work." The sound of her voice was tender and entrancing.

At that very moment, nothing else seemed to matter. There was something almost mystical about her. While her grey eyes seemed to exude with mystery, everything else about her seemed so pure. Bennett could not help but inhale her clean enticing scent. There appeared to be nothing fake about her, she was purely natural. Everything about her was so refreshing, it was impossible not to instantly fall in love with the woman.

Trying to hide his nervousness, he continued the best he could. "I know it sounds corny…But you look so familiar." Bennett could barely contain himself. "I really feel like I know you from somewhere." It seemed to be the only words he could come up with.

She responded in a calm soothing tone. "We've never met personally…But I knew you would find me." Awarding him with an amazingly exquisite smile.

Eyes warm and glowing, Destiny placed her soft, delicate hand on his forearm. All unpleasant aspects of his own reality seemed to melt away. The suspense of what was taking place was almost overwhelming. Suddenly, nothing else mattered but that moment.

Just as the encounter was becoming spine-tingling, Destiny looked at Bennett apologetically. "I've got to go…I'm sorry."

"That's okay." Taking refuge in the fact that he might see her again.

"Maybe I'll see you at the swap meet?" She asked with a hint of certainty in her smile.

Listening with enhanced spirits, her words seemed to have some special meaning. Eyes never leaving hers, he nodded his head yes. "I hope so." With that being said, she went gracefully on her way.

Bennett felt totally relaxed, thoroughly enjoying the fact that he was just standing with her. As Destiny walked away, she glanced over her shoulder. There seemed to be hidden promises in her consoling smile. As if saying "until next time."

Bennett found it hard to believe that she was actually real. There were so many things he wished he had asked. But it was too late, she was already gone.

As in his dreams, she was an incredibly captivating woman, tall and lean with a flawless statuesque figure. The way Destiny carried herself, drew his attention like a magnet. With a model-like quality, she seemed to effortlessly glide through the park. Bennett's eyes followed her with sheer delight; he had never seen a woman so beautiful. Maybe this vision of loveliness was just a tantalizing glimpse of what awaited him.

As if suspended in time, Bennett felt as if he were under some kind of hypnotic spell. While not a word between them was spoken, it was as if he could hear her sweat voice continuously inviting him to come see her.

Just before she entered the swap-meet, she turned and waved. Not waving as if saying goodbye, but as if gesturing for him to follow. Absorbed in his own thoughts, he smiled and sighed in astonishment as she disappeared.

Once out of his line-of-sight, a wave of exhilaration rushed throughout his body. Bennett was suddenly crazed with a passion he could not begin to describe. There was an intense, curious feeling toward her. As if his instincts were telling him that this was fate.

CHAPTER 5

FEELING REJUVENATED, BENNETT'S DEPLETED ego had just received some much needed fresh air. As if he were on a drug-induced high, a feeling of exhilaration began to entice his spirit. The same excitement he had experienced during the happier times of his life. Finally, his life had appeared to have taken a fleeting, new direction for the better.

Though it had just occurred, he immediately began to relive their brief encounter. Excited and invigorated, Bennett found himself unable to shake off the strange fascination toward Destiny. She had somehow made him feel alive again, something that as of late had completely eluded him.

After delighting in a few moments of recently obtained bliss, he began walking toward the beach. Once through the park, Bennett stood at the top of the cement stairs. Leaning against the guard-railing, he reached toward the sky in an effort to stretch. Barely able to contain himself, Bennett released a growl of exhilaration as his arms fell lazily to his sides.

Up until now, his existence in the world did not seem to matter. With his psyche in such dire straits, he took solace in the possibility that the worst might be behind him. Maybe the days of being a self-destructive rogue were over. Perhaps Destiny was just what was needed to fill that gaping hole that resided within his soul.

The emptiness that sadly dwelt in his heart could not be filled until some serious changes were made. But was he strong enough to face up to his psychological short-comings.

Following the steps down to the beach, his eyes swept across the pristine beauty of the Tahoe basin. The unbridled grandeur appeared limitless as the green forest ran down to the lakes deep blue waters.

Kicking off his shoes, Bennett decided to do something he had not thought about for months. While the brilliant sunshine glistened off the lakes surface, he strolled through the soft sands along the deserted shoreline. Within a few steps, the temptation to put his feet in the water became overwhelming.

To Bennett's shock as soon as his feet touched the water everything changed. While standing ankle-deep in the water's edge, the air suddenly became still and heavy. As if all laws of nature shifted into overdrive, scattered clouds began streaking across the sky at an unthinkable rate of speed. Clouds raced in front of the sun, causing frantic shadows to jet across the lake and mountain terrain.

At the same time, the indescribable birds that stalked from above formed a tight circle. In unison, the huge creatures began to screech and squawk. Almost audible, it was though they were chanting some sort of demonic verse.

In the remoteness of this out-of-control reality, Bennett retreated from the lake. After withdrawing from the shallow waters, the whistling sound of high winds immersed from the nearby forest. But as before, the trees never moved. Though there was not the slightest hint of wind, the lake became blanketed in white-caps. What should have been gentle waters was now a bombardment of violent miniature waves crashing against the shoreline.

Strangely enough, just as fast as the raging waters appeared, the white-caps disappeared and the water was like glass. Then, out of nowhere, a severe heated wind ripped across the surface of the lake. In a blink of an eye, the already hot temperature seemed to jump-up another twenty degrees.

With the furnace-like wind hard against his face, Bennett looked on as the scene above him intensified. The chanting of the birds grew louder as the rapidly moving clouds abruptly transformed into wispy layers of black smoke.

"What in God's name is going on?" Challenging the reality of what he was witnessing.

In no-time, the once clear sky was overrun by an eerie murkiness. As if witnessing a total eclipse, the rays of morning sunlight failed to reach the earth's surface. The usually picturesque vista had become completely devoured in premature darkness. Even the profound blue waters of the lake had turned black as coal. Right before his eyes, the weather and the presence of night and day had become an uncoordinated uncertainty.

In all directions, the vastness of Tahoe's splendor was no longer visible. While attempting to adjust his unbelieving eyes to the sudden darkness, he sat on a large granite rock at the base of the retaining wall.

Glancing at his watch, Bennett pressed the tiny button that lit up the time display. The time was now blinking 4:46am. According to the watch, he had somehow lost an hour of time since he had left the room. There was no logical explanation for what was taking place. And he had grown tired of trying to figure it out.

Staring toward the sky, he no longer acknowledged the bizarre events taking place. All his thoughts were sent adrift in an unwished-for remembrance. Bennett wished he could step back in time and undo what he had done. Underneath the chronic loathing toward himself, there was a dire yearning to be half the man he once was. Somewhere, trapped deep within, a stronger person resided. It was just a matter of finding that prisoner and releasing him.

The necessity to let go of the negativity that enveloped his heart and thoughts was constant. Everything had been taken from him and he was at the bottom of what life had to offer.

While always searching for some sort of salvation, he felt powerless to redeem himself. Lost and alone was not the way he wanted to spend the remainder of his life. More than ready to rise above this dispiriting segment of his existence, Bennett desperately longed to cling to someone or something for help.

Up until a few minutes ago, the possibility for a dramatic change appeared impossible. But now, at a time in his deepest need, Destiny appeared. Was it just grasping at straws, or had his negative, half-empty glass just turned half-full. Bennett was not quite sure, but maybe the mysterious prospect of normalcy had just presented itself.

Sitting in reverence, the woman from his dreams burned in his mind. Bennett could not dismiss the nagging suggestion that she might be able to help save him from himself. Something rare and exciting was happening and he could not let the opportunity slip away. Doing nothing would only enlarge his already darkened heart. Psychologically, there was nowhere to go but up.

Perhaps it was just his present state, but glimpses of a brighter future began to invade his thoughts. At this point in time, anything about his life becoming half-normal was worth a shot.

Just like in his dreams, he was seized with crazed curiosity regarding the woman. Bennett felt himself becoming more attracted to her by the second. It was almost frightening how quickly he became infatuated with her.

While absent from Destiny's presence, an ache of undiscerning hunger had developed in his stomach. Not an ache for food, but rather a craving to know everything about her. In fact, more than a needful desire, it had become a ravenous thirst and he was compelled to quench it.

Somewhat troubled by the unexpected obsession, Bennett tried to get a handle on his new emotions. "Where are these wild thoughts coming from? I don't even know this woman. How could I possibly feel so strongly about her so soon?" Cross-examining himself as he put on his shoes.

There was only one certainty that came close to making any sense. The only undisputable truth was that meeting this mysterious woman was the most uplifting experience of his life. Within a few short moments, all questions and reservations concerning Destiny vanished. In an effort to maintain some kind of dignity, Bennett owed it to himself to seize the opportunity. If he failed to pursue this chance at becoming more complete, there would be no one to blame but himself. Leaving him forever wondering what might have been.

Bennett was not entirely clear on what he hoped to accomplish, but there was no reason to put it off any longer. All at once, nothing could push her image from his mind. Destiny had just obtained the allurement and aura of a goddess. For reasons he could not quit grasp, confronting this intoxicating woman once again was a must. If for no other reason than to verify that she was real - not imagined.

Before he had a chance to change his mind, Bennett decided to abandoned the beach-walk and head toward the park. For his own peace of mind, it was now imperative that he visit the swap meet. Bennett felt very strange as he climbed the concrete staircase. For a man who had never revealed his true feelings to anyone, he was now ready to give it all up.

Swap meet in sight, it was time to kill two birds with one stone. "I can talk to Destiny...And at the same time...Somehow... Convince her to see me again." Quietly preparing himself.

Filled with a sensation of excited anticipation, Bennett ventured directly toward the enclosed area where Destiny had entered. Energized with a renewed confidence, a new bit of excitement took control of his walk.

As luck would have it, once inside the enclosure, it was not business as usual. In fact, there was no business taking place at all. The swap meet was as empty as the rest of the town. Just a bunch of make-shift canopies randomly scattered everywhere.

Walking deeper into the vacant swap meet, Bennett noticed a small, square, cinder-block building. Though hesitant to go any further, somehow he felt drawn to the brick structure. Like a magnet, some kind of strange energy seemed to be pulling at him.

It appeared that there was a single entrance to small structure. Moving closer, there was definitely something written on the door. With increased interest, Bennett stared at the door until he was close enough to read what was written. Large red letters had been hastily panted on the steel door - "SWAPMEET."

The thrill of anticipation cursed through his veins as he lightly tapped on the door. For a few anxious seconds, he awaited a response. When none came, he knocked again. Growing tiresome, Bennett's patience quickly deserted him. It was time to head back to the motel. Just as he turned to leave, a noise caused him to spin around and focus back on the door.

With a sharp metallic click of a latch, the heavy steel door creaked open. While watching the door drift ajar, a fearful knot tightened in his gut. Eyes fixed on the slight opening, Bennett wondered if this were some sort of rude invitation to come inside. It struck him as odd, but then again, everything up until now was beyond odd.

From what was visible through the gap, just a dim sliver of light penetrated the tiny opening. The inside of the building was relatively dark, virtually submerged in gloom.

Eyes peeled open to their widest points; his senses were overrun by a musty, stale, almost dead smell. Not that he was an authority on death; he could not even kill himself. But just the same, it unleashed a creeping allure, like some long forgotten tomb had just been opened.

For some unknown reason, a desperate chill ran up his spin and prickled into his neck. Mystified, Bennett just lingered outside the threshold of the entranceway. When the door finally opened, there was no one there - or so he thought. Attention dropping to the ground, he found himself looking at the smallest man he had ever seen.

As the thick, steel door opened wider, the little man ushered him inside by a quick gesture with his head - and what a head it was. The cranium mounted on this bite-size human, looked like a ninety-year old skull twisted into the neck of a baby's body.

The small man was bare-footed, his fingers and toes were terribly curled as if severe arthritis had turned them into claws. One side of his face was grossly distorted toward his chin. The lines in his face were formed by deep crevices, giving him all the disgusting attributes of an archaic, ill-tempered buzzard.

The grizzled man's vulture-type features included a pot-hooked nose, sun-weathered skin and a sagging, wrinkled neck. Eyes matching his yellow skin, the dwarf's body showed signs that complete jaundice had taken over. Just underneath the discolored flesh, ravenous, protruding veins appeared as if they were ready to explode. Time-warped and disturbing was the only way to explain what he saw before him.

As the sky began to give way to daylight again, he forced his legs to move. Just inside the doorway, an almost paranormal chill swept through him. In ripples of gooseflesh, a strange nervousness began to dominate and engulf his skin.

Once inside, the metal door quickly slammed shut behind him. Listening to the locking mechanism slide home, Bennett turned toward the entrance. But there was nothing there. The door was gone and so was his rude tiny greeter. Bennett's expression became serious as the next several moments were spent looking for the repulsive little man and a way out.

CHAPTER 6

STARING AT THE WALL where the door once existed, Bennett became filled with uncertainty. As he turned around and surveyed the small room, an instant twinge of apprehension gripped him. In the center of the ceiling, dangling by a wire, an exhausted bulb hung in its last glimmers of life. The illumination it possessed was just enough to light the cobwebs that festooned the nearby walls of a staircase. Bennett immediately realized that he had put himself way out on a limb and there may be no retreating.

As if standing in a warming oven, the temperature inside the building increased at a rapid rate. Sweat began snaking down his forehead as the heat became uncomfortable.

While uncertain of just how safe it really was, there was a strange need to explore further. It made no sense, it was as if being urged on by something he could not see or hear. Bennett was hesitant, but at the same time, excited at the chance to see Destiny again.

Mentally praying to himself, Bennett walked to the staircase and descended the first step. Following the stairwell was probably not the smart thing to do. But what other choice did he have. With the flickering bulb now to his back, Bennett followed his elongated, strobe-like shadow down the narrow passage. There was no alternative now - no turning back.

Worked into a state of charged anxiety, Bennett pushed through the heavy cobwebs that were strewn across the stairwell. With each reluctant step, the next landing began to materialize.

Hesitating at the foot of the staircase, his nose crinkled as the air thickened with a fermenting odor of rotten food. Like the room he had just left, the only trace of light radiated from a yellowed bulb that hung from the ceiling. The tainted, sour glow virtually absorbed the background into a musty blur.

One thing Bennett did notice was that there was someone on the landing with him. In the dimness of the shadows, a strange figure was walking back and forth. As his vision adjusted, a man's personage became more distinct.

Sporting a strange lopsided smile, he was a bearded, disgusting, boney man with deep-set eyes. The strange man loudly hummed an unrecognizable, off-tune melody as he glared toward the stairwell.

Watching the decrepit looking man, his mind began to fill with a collection of question marks. Bennett wondered if he was just being paranoid, but his instincts told him otherwise. With each pacing-step the man took, he became more and more ill-at-ease. It was as if sensing an onrushing threat, but not sure where it was coming from. Bennett began to have the same queasy feeling he had experienced the moment he had awakened this morning.

In order to get a better view of the room, he stepped off the staircase. The musty atmosphere finally gave way to other silhouettes. Bennett quickly became captured by the scene developing before his eyes.

Upon closer inspection, Bennett hoped he was not beginning to see things. In momentary fascination, he tried to make some sense of it all. As if lost in a foreign world, he stood there awe-struck by the scope of what he saw.

From his right, an approaching silhouette crept out from the dark background. Stopping a few feet away, a stone-faced old woman stood there holding a small child.

The woman's face was pale and drawn, giving off a death-bed expression. The lines in the old woman's face suddenly deepened into bottomless pits, turning her expression into a toothless snarl.

When the baby's head turned, Bennett could tell it was a little girl. But, after doing a double and triple-take, he saw that the girl's face was terribly deformed. As if it were pressed up against a window, her face was flat, featureless. It almost appeared that her face was developing in reverse - back into her skull.

What kind'a swamp meet is this? This place is like skid-row on steroids! Taking in the surroundings with a scrutinizing stare.

Both of their expressions seemed to possess sinister implications. Maybe he was being totally irrational, but Bennett knew he was in the midst of a very peculiar bunch. It did not take a brain surgeon to figure out that he might have made a terrible mistake. Nerves dicey, his already fragile mind could not afford to lose whatever mental stability it had left.

The rising tension in the room made for an extremely strained atmosphere. The old man was mumbling and carrying-on a heated, one sided conversation with himself. The old geezer seemed to be growling under his breath. Stress induced illusions perhaps? Needless to say, he had seen enough to convince himself to get the hell away from these people.

With the knowledge that Destiny was not there, Bennett turned and headed toward the next stairwell. At the top of the steps, a sudden grip of indecision seized him. Staring down the next narrow passage, he found himself wondering if more unpleasantries just lay-in-wait.

Ignoring his growing uneasiness, Bennett slowly ventured down the steps. It suddenly felt as if someone had unlatched the door to an enormous furnace as he continued to descend. The temperature seemed to increase each step he took. Every time the humid, overheated air burned down into his lungs, Bennett's breathing became more labored.

Descending the stairs, he listened as his footsteps echoed

within the cinder-block walls. The air was so heavy with humidity the walls of the passage were dripping with sweat.

Strange sounds emerged from the lower landing. A million doubts haunted his thoughts as he tried to mentally prepare for what awaited him. Stopping just before the last step, Bennett blinked his eyes in disbelief. Stupefied, he found himself frozen in place. What he now witnessed was far more than he had prepared for.

The entire floor was completely lit by make-shift bonfires. As if the blistering heat was not enough, there were several piles of trash burning in steel barrels. Like the previous landing, this place was not lacking its share of personality. It appeared Bennett had just plunged into the realm of some unknown world. A place he began to fear immensely.

Am I delusional? Am I in the process of a major melt-down. Are my fears actually distorting everything? Or, is all this real? Wondering if he had finally lost his mind.

A steamy rottenness dominated the humid air, a repulsive odor that seemed to ferment from everywhere. The intermingled stench seemed to be a combination of burning garbage and the hideous smell of decay. An odor that even carried the instinctive awareness of death.

The onslaught of unwavering stench began to become overwhelming. The putrid odor of decay was so bad, Bennett's eyes watered against its irritating burn. Wishing to rid his senses from the air-born assault, he covered his nose and mouth with his hands.

While trying to ignore the disgusting smell, Bennett listened to the strange faceless mumblings coming from the darkest shadows. Though the faceless chanters all spoke in unison, it sounded like garbled nonsense. The unrecognizable mutterings did not even seem to be a real language. In fact, it almost sounded as if the chant was a ritual in anticipation of his arrival.

Disregarding the voices that confronted him, he approached

the decadence with a forced calmness. Bennett started toward the next flight of stairs. While focused on the destination, everything around him was monitored from the corner of his eye. Like a hawk, he studied the room for any threatening movement.

More repulsive with each step, the underground habitat wreaked with the presence of demonic dementia. Passing by one atrocity after another, Bennett's peripheral vision was playing like a horror movie. Then, something came into view that stopped him in his tracks. Instantly oblivious to everything else, he became enwrapped by what he was witnessing.

The initial shock was numbing as some kind of small creature crawled through the trash at his feet. Psyche in jeopardy, the vision before him made his mind skip a beat. It was almost too painful to look at.

Like a wounded beast, a small deformed baby crawled and slid itself through the rubbish. Bennett's shocked stare was fixed upon the child's deformed nude body.

While its eyes were sleep-swollen and bloodshot, a nervous mannerism dominated its face. As it rummaged through the insect infested trash, it became obvious that the filthy baby had no legs. Instead, its lower appendages looked more like small, boneless legs with pincher-claws for feet.

Breathing shallow, he watched as it tossed trash from side-to-side, searching for something within the disgusting waste. Just as Bennett felt himself getting sick, he noticed something else in the not-so-distant background.

Nerves sliding along the razor's-edge, his stare became fixated on the nearest fire-barrel. The fire-light illuminated a young woman with a strange bird-like quality. Setting Indian-style, she was perched on what appeared to be a four-foot pile of decomposing, plague-ridden trash. Contently, she sat atop her homemade landfill picking out the maggots and eating them like candy.

No more than twelve years old, she had the half-dead look of a life-long degenerate. Eyes sunken well into their sockets, tears of blood appeared to run down to her mouth. A mouth that was filled by a disgusting tangle of jagged yellow teeth, the likes of which almost he had never seen before.

The girl's dirty, matted mess of hair, combined with her albino skin, gave the impression that she had never seen the light-of-day. Every inch of her exposed white skin was covered with malignant sores. The pus that festered from these endless boils bubbled from the heat of the nearby fire.

Standing upright on her pile of rubbish, her unmotivated, senseless existence suddenly became threatening. Blood and dysentery began running down her bare legs. Once again, his mind was beginning to fray. Sickened with disgust, he turned away from the grotesque sight.

Giving Bennett a sly, mocking smile, she started chanting along with the others. Looking further into the subterranean gloom, Bennett began gasping through an open gawking mouth. As if emerging from beyond-the-crypt, the deplorable habitat came to life. One shiver after another ravaged his flesh as he watched first hand what no one on earth had probably ever seen.

The situation became extremely threatening as several distorted images slowly materialize from the darkest corners of the room. The frightening scene was ready to press in on him.

Neurotic to its very core, this counter balance to nature seemed to be giving birth from its blackest shadows. One after another, the nastiest dregs of humanity revealed themselves. In trance-like states, their chanting intensified as they closed in.

As if being sized up for the kill, the sensation of an awaiting ambush was in motion. Bennett's situation was definitely taking another turn for the worst.

The fact that he was trapped screamed through his thoughts over and over. One thing was for sure, before it was too late, he desperately needed to separate himself from the likes of this nocturnal, psycho-ward. It was time to turn-tail and get out!

Just two levels down into the structure, Bennett was more than ready to retreat. Looking back the way he had come, an instant knot of stress-induced fear consumed him - the stairs were blocked.

Bennett stared at a large man guarding the stairwell. The man glared back from beneath an enormous, tumor-like growth that hung from his forehead. The giant mass of deformed flesh pulsated as a huge protruding vein supplied it with blood.

Turning back toward the assortment of ghoulish degenerates, Bennett froze in terror and indecision. With rustling activity all around, his overwhelming horror intensified as the subterranean inhabitants pressed in.

Bennett felt every stare as the creatures impatiently stalked his movements. Even the mutant baby slid across the floor toward him. Arms stretched in front of them, the multitude of scavengers were now close enough to make out their grotesques features. The lifeless looking souls that confronted him possessed sinister implications.

Drooling at the mouth, they shuffled their rotting bodies through the trash-covered floor. With each step they took, the pungent smell of disease increased. As with their ghoulish faces, all of their bodies showed signs of massive decay.

Faced with a grip of humanity that threatened every fiber of his being, Bennett was on the verge of giving up. Just when he was unable to give himself a reason to continue, Destiny's voice began to softly penetrate his ears. While not quite sure what she said, he could swear her enchanting voice was calling his name.

With Destiny nowhere in the room, there was no doubt she had to be on the next landing. Bennett did not want to take one more step deeper into this lair of decadence, but there were no other options. Avoiding all confrontation or eye contact with the creatures, he quickly maneuvered to the next set of steps. It was time to go further down into the ill-omened maze.

CHAPTER 7

BENNETT'S INNER-FEAR WAS STREWN across his face as he stared down the dark stairwell. At the point of no return, there was only one way to go - down. Weird as everything appeared, unsettling as it was, he readied himself to go deeper into this twisted Hell-hole.

Bennett pushed away all reluctance and descended down toward her voice. There was no hesitation; it was time to distance himself from this decomposing freak-show. Though fighting the urge to be sick, he found himself jumping two steps at-a-time. Just a few panicked strides were all it took to reach the next landing.

Regret churned in his stomach as he found himself staring at more of the same atrocities. The only difference was that these degenerates were already on the move. Judging from what was taking place, they had anticipated his arrival.

As Bennett gawked at his new situation, shuffling noises arose from behind. Unseen for the moment, the terror that followed was close enough to smell. With Hell's dysentery nearly breathing down his neck, the potential for chaos and mayhem now knew no bounds.

Nowhere to be found, it appear that Destiny had pulled a disappearing act. The severity of the situation instantly ballooned in his mind. For until that moment, it was all about finding the girl. Now, it was all about trying to save himself. With no place else to go, Bennett abandoned the stairs.

Arms stretched out in front of them, it was as if they were herding him toward the next set of descending stairs. While fearing imminent doom, everything suddenly became obvious. They were pushing him further down the stairs and he had no choice but to do just that.

With the obscene creatures close enough to make contact, he lunged into the next stairwell. Bennett began skipping steps as he chased his frantic shadow further down into the rabbit-hole. Running deeper into the cavernous corkscrew, he hit the following landing just long enough to witness what no one should see.

Seeing everything in a flash, the depravities and stench were far worse than before. Within a second's time he was already scrambling toward the next landing. Bennett had no doubt that he was just buying a little time, but it might be just enough to find a way out.

Pushing caution aside, his pace quickened and his strides grew longer. The stairs disappeared so fast beneath his feet that his escape turned into a downward vortex. Fighting to stay upright, Bennett's momentum plummeted him down three to four steps at-a-time. As the reek of decay became almost too much to bare, a keener awareness told him that the smell of death was also amidst the air. With each leaping stride, Death's odor inched ever closer.

Resisting the urge to look back, he hurtled further down into the bowls of the demonic habitat. Far beneath the earth's surface, Bennett was sure he had descended at least ten stories. With hundreds of steps left behind, the depth of the passageway seemed to be endless. The more he dared to face the never-ending structure, the more it appeared that he was on a direct path to Hell's front gate.

All at once, life-ending panic forced itself upon him. With pure evil on his heels, Bennett felt himself being absorbed by some strange force. Everything began to slow down. The more he strained to stay one step ahead, the more he was projected into slow motion.

It had become so hot that waves of heat began rippling-up from the steps. Hovering on the edge of immobility, Bennett watched as the stairs and walls started to glow like red-hot coals. The heat was getting so bad, that with each footfall his shoes seemed to melt and stick to the floor.

Refusing to break stride, he fought to stay one step ahead. While anticipating his foot hitting the next wished-for step, noises from the pursuing predators echoed from the stairs behind. With a collection of hidden nocturnal atrocities closing in, time became the enemy and the enemy was fast on his heels. The compulsion to escape was enormous, but the very idea of getting away was now appearing hopeless.

Every flight of stairs drew him closer to complete suspended animation. Fighting deeper into the den of discontent, a bizarre light appeared at the bottom of the stairwell. Desperately lingering in mid-air, he could feel his demise was near as he struggled toward the light.

With one final prolonged lunge, Bennett had reached the last catacomb of the rabbit-hole. The seemingly endless staircase had finally run out of steps. The bottomless dwelling had come to a conclusion.

Standing on the last existing step, he wildly scanned the perimeter of the huge room. Mesmerized in horror, Bennett realized there would be no help, no rescue, no way out.

The whole ordeal was turning out to be a terrible tragedy and there was nothing he could do about it. Bennett let his eyes scan the room one-last time.

With the exiles of humanity nearly upon him, Bennett faced the inevitable dead-end. "I don't believe this...What a perfect ending to my pathetic life." Chastising himself with hysterical urgency.

CHAPTER 8

THE FLOOR OF ROOM was flat, but the walls and ceiling seemed to be carved out of solid granite. The cavernous enclosure was encased by a dull, uninviting reddish glow. The source of the weird light was nowhere to be seen. Not a single bulb burned from above. Like the bricks in the stairwell, it appeared the glow was reaching out from the rocks.

The hollowed out expanse mimicked a long forgotten tomb. Before taking that final step, his eyes scanned the room one last time. While searching for any way to escape, a possible exit caught his eye. On the opposite side of the room, a huge door seemed to appear out of nowhere.

Tormented with the fact that he was trapped, Bennett stared with unyielding interest. Besides going back the way he had come, this definitely presented itself as the only way out. All his wishes turned to prayers as he looked at a possible escape from this lair of human debris.

Once off the stairwell, Bennett was able to move freely. It was as if time and space had finally caught up with each other. Uncertainty mixed with desperation pressed on his spirit as he reached toward the door. Gripping the doorknob, a feeling of morbid dread ravaged through his flesh. A threatening sensation warned him that he was about to put himself out on the thinnest of limbs and there was no coming back.

Fingers strangling the doorknob, Bennett looked back toward the stairs. While trying to will himself to open the door, he began shifting his weight from one foot to the other. All at once, the desperate need to pull open his last remaining hope vanished.

It became immediately clear that the parasites of humanity that were coming down the stairwell were nothing compared to what lay on the opposite side of the door. It was like a hungry tiger was waiting and ready to attack. Bennett suddenly realized that he was standing on Hell's doorstep. Pulse racing in alarm-filled tension, he released the doorknob and took a step back.

True in every respect, he felt like a rat in a cage searching his numb, sluggish mind for a way out. Bennett was ensnared within the secret, decadent confines were the most devious of souls played a never-ending game of damnation

For within this sadistic encampment, resided a barbaric subculture with laws unto itself. For this fiendish population was not governed by the written laws of the land, but by the unwritten laws of Hell itself.

It was a ruthless cesspool, where the capacity for perversion and evil knew no bounds. In this haven of dread, where bedlam and dementia prevailed, aggression and violence were inevitable. For where these types of depraved human elements dwelt, chaos was sure to reign.

There were no openings, no way of escape but the door. Forcing down his fear, he grabbed the doorknob once again. At that moment, the only thought that ruled his mind was the need to free himself. Escaping to the outside where blue sky covered the world and Mother Nature worked her way through another day.

But instead, the evil that possessed this exit made him cringe. Like a serrated knife, defeat sliced through his soul like an animal approaching the meat grinder. Even with no other options, he was not about to go through that threshold. Deep inside, in a place were no light could shine, he understood that this would not lead him to salvation - but total annihilation.

Heart pounding wildly, Bennett slowly backed away once

again. Wanting nothing to do with what was on the other side, he turned back toward the stairs.

With nowhere to go, nowhere to hide, it was as if the final moment of his life had been reached. Bennett had entered a gathering place belonging to a band of humanity where wickedness fed upon itself. An environment that assured itself that death was inevitable. Trapped in this self-contained Hell-hole, he could do nothing but take a couple of steps back. Leaning his back against the door, he closed his eyes and let out one last desperate sigh.

No reasoning or logic could make any sense or explain this crazed, hidden world. Ruled by the evil-doers within, this lowest fabrication of what life had to offer was about to show its ugly face. Only he could find his way into such an awful place, it was his doing and his alone. Bennett had been coaxed into the worst of realities. A malicious nightmare filled with the seemingly never-ending presence of damnation. Because of his attempt at death, maybe it was just his time to rot in Hell.

Of all the ways to die, Bennett could have never imagined going out like this. Maliciously misplaced in this windowless purgatory, he was at a complete loss as what to do next. Bennett opened his eyes just in time to see the shadows of this demon infested habitat approaching along the walls of the stairwell.

Under the circumstances, his odds of survival were none. While trying to make some sense of it all, he realized that he could not become weak or vulnerable. For it would be at that point, if he should lose his motivation to confront his aggressors, he would instantly be devoured. The only chance he had would be to quickly face the enemy and defend himself. There was nothing left to do, but to turn into a crazed dog backed into a hopeless corner.

Weird as everything appeared, unsettling as it was, he readied himself for the worst. It would take a sustained and extraordinary inner strength in order to fight against the atrocities that drew closer. Freedom from the underlying evils that were about to confront him would take nothing less than a miracle.

Bennett's pursuers were not yet in sight, but he could hear their mumblings and distorted voices. In the same strange dialect as before, the unintelligible words and murmurs grew louder as they descended. Quickly, their chorus of whispers swelled into a loud demonic chant. As if casting a wicked spell, the trance-like chant seemed to reach inside him and relentlessly tear at his soul.

Standing statue-still, he could hear them drawing closer to the final set of stairs. Frantic as to what was about to happen, it would not be long before a much more tragic reality would take over. Trying to ready himself, Bennett nervously awaited for what was about to appear. The evil forces that spilled throughout these defiled corridors were about to show their ghastly faces.

Like a swarm of insects they appeared. In complete horror, he watched as the unwanted rejects from nature's mistakes made their way down the steps. The little buzzard-man lead the pack as numerous bodies of endless boils, running sores and festering ulcers followed close behind. Exactly the type of parasites that were also known as "Hell-Spawn".

In rapid succession, they prowled down the stairwell stumbling into each other like drunks. Three silhouettes turned into six, six into twelve, twelve into...

Faces drawn and pale, the gruesome venue grunted and growled as they herded at the base of stairs. Like a band of rabid jackals, the ghoulish images looked like they were ready to go on a feeding frenzy. Things were about to go ballistic.

With an unobstructed view of what he now faced, Bennett's adrenaline became enraged. There was no way past them. The dementia in front of him sent him into a panicky state of anxiety. At that moment, all lingering hope vanished. Confronting a terror so great, made him wish he could die right there on the spot.

Wide-eyed and trapped in indecision, he backed up against the wall preparing for anything. While anticipating a scenario that frightened the hell out of him, demons and assorted depravities of humanity filled the bottom of the stairwell. Then, the terror-filled atmosphere magnified, taking another bizarre turn.

All of a sudden, the chanting stopped. The only other sound was a bubbling, whooshing noise. It took him a moment to figure out where it was coming from, but then he spotted the source. A large drain covered by a two foot square grate occupied the center of the rock floor. Giving the appearance of some sort of toxic gas, the drain began releasing a slow, slithering stream of green mist. The harsh, steamy smell seemed to cut and burn into his nostrils.

As the unknown vapor ascended, it began to swirl around the edges of the grate. Simultaneously, descending the steps, the same creeping mist showed itself, maneuvering its way down between the ankles of the decadence that stood guard.

As soon as the leading edge of the mist trickled off the last step, it was as if it became a living entity. While flowing intelligently along the floor, it broke up into what appeared to be tentacles. All of which were headed directly toward the drain.

Bennett looked back toward the drain, only to see wisps of heavy green fog spewing from the floor. Frantically circling the grate, it looked like a mounting whirlpool was forming. Working its way outward, it began to crawl across the floor.

As soon as the two fogs merged, it was as if it had an agenda all its own, methodically choosing which direction to travel. Continuing to stream down the stairwell and ascend from the drain, the foul fog now ran freely as it devoured the floor.

Bennett was to stunned to move as the advancing fog pooled around the room. Once the entire floor had become tainted by the sour glow of the mist, it began to advance toward him. Within inches of reaching his feet, the mist split apart and circled him. As if taunting him, the green substance acted as if it were going to attack his legs - then back off. Over and over, it threatened to consume his feet but did not.

Scanning his eyes over the threatening haze, he watched as it began to rise and thicken. The cavernous room was possessed in an unearthly quality. It was an ungodly scene as two feet of rolling fog now covered the floor.

Wide-eyed and dumbfounded, he turned his horrified stare down toward his feet. Bennett watched as the threatening mist finally attacked. In a split second, the ocean of eerie green murkiness was just below his knees. The terror-filled atmosphere was magnified as it took another unforeseen turn.

Just as the fog consumed his legs, strange activity erupted within the shallow depths of the thick vapor. Indistinct formations began to materialize and slither along the floor. From out of nowhere, partially hidden beneath the mist, dozens of indistinct creatures swarmed through the fog-shrouded chamber.

Becoming more aggressive, his heart rhythms became erratic as the first of these demon-like beasts passed close by. Bennett stood in breathless awe, mentally waiting for some grotesque ghoul to arise from within this strange membrane of light and escort him into the depths of this hellish murkiness.

Almost touching his right leg, he tried to move away from the threat that stalked him. Enhanced terror filled his eyes as his legs could not move. It was as if his feet had been cemented into the floor itself. But as disturbing as the situation was, it was about to get even worse.

Entering his ears like backward garble, the conglomeration at the base of the stairs began chanting again. Drawing his attention back to the stairwell, his bewildered stare looked on as the band of hell-spawn separated. Presenting a clear path down the center of the stairwell.

Bennett's fear and desperation multiplied by a factor of ten. Gut churning in hideous anticipation, Bennett was sure that something much more forbidding awaited him - something truly evil. Nerves too shot to comprehend what was taking place, his final sinking thought was that he was about to embrace Satan himself.

CHAPTER 9

BENNETT WAS CAUGHT-UP IN, and slipping deeper into the madness of this demented bureaucracy. Besides being unable to move, the numbness of the dilemma was paralyzing.

A sickening wave of vulnerability ran through him as he closed his eyes to this dehumanizing existence. Surrounded by evil, he lowered his head until his chin came to rest on his chest.

In relentless torment, his mind pushed forth a realization that rocked him to his very core. A soul-wrenching conclusion that confirmed that this collection of perversities and atrocities was not a heartless joke or ludicrous misunderstanding. But rather an absolute confirmation of an all new realm of realism. A reality in which fear, hopelessness and desolation were his only companions.

There was nothing to justify such a horrifying scenario. Bennett was being absorbed into a world that threatened every fiber of his being. Somehow, he had to find the strength in his psyche to deal with this unimaginable fate that defied all logic and reason.

With so many questions in which there were no answers, he could not seem to suppress the crushing fears and anxieties that consumed him. In his most fevered imaginations, Bennett could have never conceived how much misfortune could be heaved upon him in such a short amount of time.

Trembling hands covering his face, Bennett squeezed his eyes shut and attempted to negate what was taking place. With what was left of his despondent mind, he stubbornly embraced the possibility that none of this was actually happening.

In a dreamscape state of confusion, he was possessed by the eerie inclination of floating in a realm of some primitive unreality. Caught up and hopelessly entwined in some morbid quirk of fate. Dispelled from the life he once knew, into a merciless altered reality in which there was no escape.

Without warning, he began to feel as if he were suffocating. The air in the windowless encampment was heavy and stench ridden. Giving an essence of creeping decay that seemed to seep from the very filth that clung to its deteriorating walls. As if the putrefied walls which restrained him were closing in to crush the life out of him.

Head shaking in denial, he began to picture himself being hurled into a dark void, within which, there would be no redemption. Throat dry as dust, Bennett refused to give in to the slithering claustrophobic terror that threatened to throttle him.

Slowly retreating from his trance-like state, a myriad of dispiriting thoughts began to play at the corners of his mind. Bennett could not help but wonder if he were not indeed going crazy, looming closer and closer to the brink of madness. As if his sanity were being strangled, it appeared he was holding a fist class ticket on a one-way trip to oblivion.

Withdrawing his clammy hands, he reluctantly raised his head. Eyes at half-mast, everything seemed to be just a green blur. All at once, though she was nowhere to be seen, he could somehow feel Destiny's presence. For some unexplainable reason, an asphyxiating awareness told him that there was nothing coincidental about what was going to transpire.

Like the calm before the storm, the groping bodies that blocked his escape became instantaneously silent. The air of silence was absolute, only interrupted by the soft sound of a voice. Though consumed into the depths of the hellish murkiness,

Bennett's attention became captivated by what he thought he heard. Listening more closely, it was as if the faint sound was saying his name, but he could not be sure.

Seconds seemed to stretch into an eternity as he waited for the final image to appear. In terrified expectancy, a chill of dread ravaged his flesh as his impending suspicions appeared. There was no reason to wonder any longer what had happened to her.

Hands nervously shaking, he was focused intently on the silhouette coming down the stairwell. As if gliding, Destiny seemed to float through the center of her apparent worshipers. Bennett was not sure what disturbed him more, dealing with these deranged derelicts or being face to face with that strange woman again.

CHAPTER 10

AFTER HER DESCENT FROM the staircase, Destiny glided through the green mist. A smug smile tugged at her lips as she stopped in the center of the room.

Trying to ignore the obnoxious creatures in the background, Bennett directed his attention to the vision of loveliness that had lead him here. In the most enchanting voice he had ever heard, Destiny began to speak.

"Hello, Bennett." Even at that very moment, it seemed as if she were somehow seducing him.

In a nervous, hesitant voice, he tried to respond. "Hello... Destiny...I've been looking for you."

Destiny smiled in a way that indicated triumph. "And I've been impatiently waiting for you."

Bennett was not quite sure what she meant. But he knew it was not a good thing. "Do you think we could go back to the park and talk?"

It became quickly apparent there was nothing in her demeanor that hinted at any type of compromise. "I don't think so...You're right where I want you!"

As soon as the words were leaving her lips, something about her began to change. Destiny's behavior had become completely different from that person he had just met.

With a lethal grimace, she lifted her chin and leveled her stare to his. "We are definitely going to talk my dear, Bennett. But, I'll be doing all the talking!" Her voice growing more intense with each word. "You are to do nothing...But listen!"

Something was definitely wrong, the mysterious duality in her demeanor had just been consumed by an untainted animosity. At a total loss, Bennett was completely unaware as to why she was displaying such unwarranted hostilities. Fear now in control, he desperately wanted to do something. But, he realized that fighting back was utterly pointless. There was nothing else to do but listen and pray for the best.

With all her majesty, Destiny presented herself before him. Standing in the center of the granite chamber, a look of unwavering wrath consumed her face. There she stood, but it was not her. Through the forbidding green haze, Bennett could feel the unrelenting weight of her glare. As his vision of impending doom escalated, Destiny's threatening presence was succeeding to make the flesh crawl up the back of his neck.

Like breathing fire, his lungs burned as the sweltering temperature became unbearable. Clothes saturated and sticky with sweat, his hands continued to tremble as drips of perspiration streamed from his forehead.

"Hot enough for ya?" Seemingly unfazed by the tremendous heat, she appeared to be taking total pleasure in his discomfort. "This is nothing compared to what awaits you." Wearing a smirk of anticipation.

"Who are you? What are you? Why are you doing this?" Forgetting to breath as he awaited an answer.

"As far as your questions are concerned...I am Destiny. As of this very moment...The answers you're looking for are ill-relevant." The tone of her words instantly rose to a more elevated level. "My resentment toward you is much heavier than you could ever imagine. And you have pushed me to a point...Where every fabric of my wrath is focused strictly on you." Her comment was accentuated by the unforgiving look on her face.

"I don't understand."

Destiny burst out with a harsh, venomous retort. "You belong to me...And you're not going to slip from my grasp again!" There was a definite air of finality in her voice.

Bennett expected terror to fill his mind, but it did not, he was well beyond that. "I still don't understand what's going on."

"In this realm of existence there are three entities. Good, evil and me. Though good and evil are in a constant battle, everyone must be accompanied by me to thier final destination. Initially, all human souls must come through me. One's soul can then, and only then, be sent to their final destination. There are no exceptions."

While drowning inside himself, Bennett asked the ultimate question. "Am I dead?"

"Let me simplify it for you. Though the three eternal entities are totally separate from each other...We must coexist at the same time. We are equal in the fact that we must play by a certain set of rules. Though your life should have expired, you were given a second chance. But there is only one problem...I do not like to be deprived of what is rightfully mine!" Along with her swift lash of anger, there was a violent twist in her voice. "For whatever reason, you were found worthy, your death was denied - I was denied." Inconvenience and displeasure was very evident in Destiny's expression.

"You must understand that death is not personal, it is a process." A hard-edged voice began to emerge from Destiny's mouth. "When the process is interfered with, our set of rules is compromised. The rules are not blatantly being broken, but they are being severely violated. When one of us is in violation, it opens the others to new options.

You were looked upon favorably and I was deprived from my right to collect you. But like I said, that denial opened other options. After your attempt at death, your subconscious was opened up so I could complete the process. Though I was unable to collect you, your subconscious remained open.

There are no ground rules in the furthest depths of one's mind. Dreams are to be believed or disbelieved depending on the dreamer. I embedded myself within your subconscious where all of your memories and fears were at my disposal. The one place that I could transform your memories into nightmares. I brought about the most unpleasant events of your past to help you believe. Helping you along, enabling your demons to revisit you. A graveyard of memories that you had blocked out from your pathetic existence. Remembrances that could only resurface in your worst of nightmares."

"You manipulated my dreams?" Giving her a look as if he did not believe a word she was saying.

A hard-edged retort emerge from Destiny's mouth. "I not only manipulated them...Except for yourself...I played all the characters...Your sleeping right now. Everything you've experienced – I created.

I was denied the first time, so in your nightmares, I went after you the only way I could." Destiny's voice continued to change pitch, becoming much deeper and stronger. "I gave you several opportunities to flee from your torment...What you had to do was clear and simple. In each nightmare, I presented you with a door, a symbol of free-will. All you had to do was go through the door. The willingness to walk through any of those doors would have symbolized your surrender."

"It was all a mistake...I don't want to die...I'm ready to change." Challenging her motives in horrified disbelief.

Destiny looked at him sharply. "It's too late for that now!"

"It's not too late...I was given a second chance!"

"You chose to leave your world and enter into mine...You can never take that back!" After Destiny had finished forecasting his future, an expression of victory covered her gloating face.

With endless sorrow in his voice, Bennett pleaded. "I can't die...I'm ready to make things right!"

Like bottomless pools of hate, Destiny's raspy, unrelenting

tongue-lashing continued. "Isn't that precious...You know, Bennett...I was there the moment you finally gave up. I watched as you attempted to end your earthly presence."

Nerves strung tight enough to snap, Bennett needed some kind of resolution. "Are you some kind of angel?"

Destiny's expression darkened even further. "You could say that...Some call me the Angel between worlds." She announced in a sudden overpowering male voice.

With a stare of perseverance, she stood like a prize fighter waiting for the bell to ring. The muscles in her jaw began to twitch as her eyes narrowed into an icy stare. All the hidden insanities he had stumbled into were coming to a final conclusion.

All at once, her face drained of all color as she began to howl with laughter. Now, beside his own, every pair of eyes was focused completely on her. The woman that persuaded him with false charm and a sense of hope was now physically changing before his very eyes. Like an erupting volcano, her appearance began to transform.

Bennett was not sure if he was having some weird hallucination or his mind was failing to grasp the true reality.

"What's happening to you?" As his unbelieving mind tried to seize what was taking place.

"The inevitable...You have no idea how much I'm going to enjoy this...It's time to regain what is rightfully mine!"

While Destiny's features became gruesomely distorted, Bennett wondered if his psyche was not in the process of a major meltdown. The lines in her forehead deepened as the muscles in Destiny's jaw expanded. As her facial muscles and tendons began to twist and contort, it was suddenly almost impossible to maintain any further eye contact. Something was happening and Bennett was not sure if he wanted to witness it.

As if an out-of-control eruption were burning within, an inferno began to smolder in Destiny's eyes. A scorching red glow quickly reached out and engulf her stare. Behind those red, flaming eyes, lay an appalling, evil darkness.

Unnervingly spellbound, Bennett looked on as her eyes began to sink deeper into her disfigured face. In the macabre, depressing light, she began to take on darker and more threatening features. Thoroughly seized by the unearthly transformation, he watched as her mutating body amplified. Everything about her was changing.

Without warning, her body began to increase in size. Within seconds, Destiny's perfect body was approaching seven feet tall. At the same time, the atmosphere began to reek of something dead.

As if witnessing the gory decay of a dead body, her skin began to decompose. The only difference was the usually long decaying process was happening at an accelerated rate.

Bennett stood wide-eyed, like a deer in the headlights. Destiny's exposed flesh was transformed to rotted muscle, then, to maggot stripped Bone. The hairs on the back of his neck began to tingle at this unbelievable sight. It did not seem possible, but she slid further into the crazed metamorphosis.

Unable to unlock his stare from the sight, Bennett watched as the process reversed. From flesh to skeleton, and everything in between, she constantly transformed back and forth. It was though she could not decide what side of herself she wanted to reveal. Trapped in front of the unidentifiable adversary, Bennett realized he was up against something obscenely ruthless.

In open-mouthed disbelief, a final image prepared to materialize. The soul-seeker that manipulated everything was about to show its true identity.

CHAPTER 11

JUST WHEN HE THOUGHT it could not get any worse, her once beautiful eyes disappeared into their sockets. After the transformation had concluded, all the demonic stares from the stairwell were turned back upon him. Bennett was faced with a depraved, intimidating presence. The likes of which frightened the hell out of him.

A new type of fear chilled his bones as the image was clear enough to make Bennett shudder inside. Head to toe, the tall dark manifestation wore a black cloak that seemed to flail in a non-existent wind. Its shrouded sagging hood housed bottomless black holes where her eyes once had been. Its skull was a mask of hollowed bone, a grotesque face straight from the grave.

A triumphant and conquering laugh erupted from beneath the hood. A demonic howl that would make a hungry bear turn and run. Bennett cringed inside as unrelenting terror hit him full on.

"Oh...My...God!" Uttering in shocked disbelief.

Bennett's blood ran cold as his imminent anxieties had finally taken form. All unnerving apprehensions instantly hardened into certainty as the image of impending doom stood before him. The one dreaded impediment he could have never planned on coming up against.

Though his faceless stalker hid within the hood, it was instantly recognizable. There was no mistake it was "Death" itself. Where the beautiful woman once stood was now occupied by the Grim Ripper. It was almost impossible for him to believe, that the woman from his dreams was the main ingredient to the Reapers master plan.

Just as before, the seedy, odd-ball scavengers in the background began to chant. While facing this horrific and threatening sight, the "Gatekeeper of Death" unleashed an unearthly roar that sliced right through him.

The words it screamed reverberated and boomed off the surrounding walls. "You belong to me! It's time to get this over with."

While his bottomless, dead eyes burned like fire, a skeletal arm reached out from within the sleeve of the cloak. Unable to breath Bennett stared as the monster regurgitated its final threat. "It's time for you to finally die, Bennett. Everything that you've seen here, will remain here…As will you." Though the Reaper's voice was menacing and wicked, it seemed to be amused by the encounter. Amused in a cynical way as only it could appreciate. "You will now spend eternity with your most feared demons."

Alien and repulsive enough to demand respect, it raised both skeletal arms in triumph. Simultaneously, in a black rage, the Reaper let out another furious and revengeful scream! But, this hideous screech was nothing more than a symbol to the others - a special sign for the final act. A last testament of what would be the end to Bennett's existence.

Bennett now realized the Reaper was no myth, that the last moments of his life was about to be played out. He was standing before the one inescapable presence that everyone must experience once their days on earth have expired.

Bennett began questioning his soul for the truth. *Is there really a God? Does he actually exist? If so, where is he now? The Bible says that even the most evil of demonic forces believed in God. If the demons of the world believe, why is it so hard for me?* In that split second, he came to the understanding that there had to be a Heaven. For he knew without a doubt, there was a Hell.

Eyes watering with dread, he continued to chastise himself. *Does God just hate me? Maybe it's just the price I've got to pay for all the darkness I've put myself through.*

The foundation of this hidden, subterranean society was purely demonic and evil. And the pack of hell-spawn was about to be unleashed.

Bennett's eyes fixated on the figures behind the Reaper. As he stared at the chanting menagerie, "The Concierge of Death" lowered his skeletal arms.

It was obvious that Bennett had worn out his welcome. All at once, they began to emerge from the stairwell. Looking on in stark terror, he watched as their feet and ankles descended into the mist and vanished. The demonic flood-gates had just been opened.

At least a dozen of them were on the move, but they were in no hurry. It was as if they knew he was going nowhere. Bennett's legs were suddenly able to move, he was not entirely ensnared in the evil mist. Looking wildly about the room, he numbly watched as his aggressors approached. Like sharks smelling blood they move in. In what he knew would be a short-lived retreat, he pressed his back against the wall.

Braced against the wall, he slid along the rock until he reached the door. Heart pounding, he put his hand back on the door knob. As if looking through another man's eyes, he watched as the knob vanished from beneath his grasp. Bennett's impending dread grew even deeper with the finality that there was nowhere to go - nowhere to hide. As the door disappeared, all lingering hope vanished with it.

Bennett was too horrified to move as the mass of evil converged. The end was almost upon him. His already terrified expression gave way to one of helpless horror! With the realization of what was about to take place, his body began to noticeably trembled with fear.

Like a gang of blood-sucking zombies, they began frothing

at the mouth as if preparing for the kill. Just predators, zeroing in on their prey, they came toward him with arms extended. Lost in this pit of dementia, his mind was ready to snap as their green-tainted faces inched closer. Screaming inwardly, petrified in terror, he felt as if he were drowning. Unable to breath, he began suffocating in pure panic.

Bennett's sense of urgency was now pure desperation as the demonic inhabitants pressed in. Within a second, the Reaper was no longer visible as they made their way toward him. Bennett was about to be the brunt of a chaotic feeding frenzy. Desperately, he searched the area for anything he could use in self-defense. But with the fog up to his waist, he could find nothing.

Breathless from fear, Bennett watched as their yellow, jagged teeth drew closer. Positioning themselves for an assault, the wall of demons was now close enough to grab and claw at his clothes. Wild with desperation, he tried to jerk away. Shoving at the attacking hands, he tried to fight from their grasp. Eyes consumed in terror, Bennett kicked his legs and swung his arms in violent resistance. But his attempt to get away from the grotesque ghouls was all for not.

Like hungry lions, they tore at his flesh. As their talon claws pierced through his skin and muscles, he ground his teeth and screamed in agony.

While they wailed and clawed at his face and neck, Bennett's screams magnified as a raging tangle of teeth tore into his leg. Though fiercely fighting, his body was being thrashed with flesh-tearing wounds. Every nerve in his body was plagued in agony. It became so painfully overwhelming he finally fell, crumbling into the fog. Back pressed against the ground, everything became just a confused blur. From the depths of the green murkiness, he fought blindly to regain control of his body.

Jaws clinched as he screamed, he struggled for the slightest bit of vision. Instinctively, he raised his arms to shield his face. In the midst of the blind chaos, they continued to tear at his flesh. While unable to visualize his assailants, Bennett fought off whatever he could. Bennett resisted with everything he had, but it was far from good enough.

Bennett's screams of pain were dwarfed by the frenzied screeches and hungry growls of the demon mob. Clothes shredded and soaked with blood, his body began convulsing in pain and shock. As the crazed animals relentlessly ravaged his body, Bennett knew that this was the end.

Bennett screamed in agony as he felt his flesh being torn and ripped from his body. Lying in a pool of his own blood, he could not hang on any longer. The unbelievable trauma he had so quickly sustained was about to take its final toll. Ready to pass out from the pain, his eyes rolled back in his head.

Though Bennett did not have a lot to live for, he did not want to die like this. In a raw surging of hopelessness, Bennett mumbled a prayer that only he and God could hear. He was left with no other choice. It was time to believe that God would answer his prayer. It was a desperate plea for forgiveness and intervention.

A final, agonizing whimper escaped from his lips. "Please God...Help me!"

Unable to resist their grasp, his body went limp in absolute and certain defeat. Too far gone to resist, they quickly grabbed his feet. The demon-seeds drug Bennett's limp body to the center of the room. Bennett eyes were rendered useless as they pulled him through the thick green fog.

Though unable to see, he cried-out in pain as they once again began ripping and taking bites at his flesh. While slipping away, soon to be no longer of this world, everything stopped. No pain, no agony - nothing. It was as if he were in some kind of weird void.

As if being plunged into another man's body, his pain instantly vanished. Then, all at once, Bennett was filled with a strange sense of detachment and unreality. As if rising from the grave, he felt himself being lifted from the grasp of his demonic assailants.

311

CHAPTER 12

NOT SURE OF WHAT had just happened, he was at a total loss. Bennett found himself hovering several feet above his attackers. Besides a fleeting feeling of joy, there was a momentary rush of elation from the fact that he had somehow escaped.

Looking down from above, he could see himself being ravaged to the point of dismemberment. But despite the horrific sight, Bennett felt no pain. In fact, it was just the opposite. He possessed an all-consuming, intoxicating feeling of relief, making him relaxed like never before.

No longer scared, his terror quickly subsided. While watching his corpse being ripped apart, the only thing he could think about was how good he felt. Then, a prevailing fan of brilliant light cut and burned into his very soul.

Bennett stared into the brightest light he had ever seen. To his overwhelming delight, the light was not blinding, but extremely soothing. As if experiencing the sudden calm amidst the eye of a hurricane, he was engulfed with a flood of tranquility. It was the most comforting and beautiful thing he had ever experienced. There was finally an element of relief in his soul.

In this bizarre state of consciousness, he became relieved from all human senses and emotions. All unpleasant aspects of what just happened seemed to fade away. In this comforting numbness, the thought of death entered his thoughts.

Has my soul just escaped from my body? If this is death, I don't want to be anywhere else.

The featureless light seemed to expand forever. Bennett could see or hear nothing. There was no definition to this space in which he now resided. Though unaware if he were standing or sitting, the strange membrane of light seemed to be escorting him somewhere - a final destination.

***

The room was cold and impersonal. No flowers, no get well cards, nothing that recognized that there was a person in the room. Lying motionless, in an ill-fitting hospital gown, the lone patient was propped against the pillows. On closer inspection, she realized he was a younger looking man hidden behind a full beard. Though Diana knew he was a coma patient, an eerie feeling consumed her as she noticed something she never expected. The man's eyes were wide open as if looking right at her.

The man was hooked up to a electrocardiograph and several other monitors. Various plastic fluid bags hung from a metal racks on both sides of the bed. The IV's in both arms were intravenously feeding him with fluids and antibiotics.

Once she looked at the identification band on his wrist, there was no doubt she had found her patient. There was no middle name, no last name, only the name Ziggy. It also verified that he had been admitted six months earlier. Ready to get to work, she located the blood-pressure cuff. Diana could not get over his blank stare as she wrapped the cuff around his arm. While busy pumping the bulb of the blood-pressure gauge, a Doctor entered the room undetected.

As the cuff deflated, the Doctor read the gauge and began writing on Ziggy's medical chart. Once the Doctor finished his notes, he cleared his throat to get the nurse's attention. Unaware that the Doctor was standing right behind her, Diana quickly turned toward the noise.

Slipping the file back into the rack, the Doctor introduced himself. "Hello, I'm Dr. Stevens."

Diana had heard that the Doctor had an easy-going, undemanding demeanor. She just hoped he was like that toward her. "Hi...Dr. Stevens...I'm Diana O'nell. It's a real pleasure to be working with you."

A smile pulled at the corner of the Doctors mouth. "The pleasure's all mine. So how's, Ziggy?"

Unsure what to say, Diana went with what she knew best - the truth. "I'm not sure...I just got here...But I do have one question?" Diana looked back at Ziggy. "Are his eyes always open like that?"

"Pretty crazy, huh?"

While putting away the blood-pressure cuff, Diana responded. "More like creepy."

"It can be a little unsettling. But yes, that's normal for some coma patients. Ziggy just happens to be one of those unfortunate few." Dr. Stevens picked up a dropper prescription next to the bed. "Make sure you give him these eye-drops at least four times during your shift."

Diana sympathetically looked into Ziggy's vacant stare. "I know I just got here, but I can't help but feel so sorry for him."

Slightly concerned, Dr. Stevens turned toward the nurse. "Well, don't get too attached."

Confused, her expression became one of curious concern. "I don't understand,"

"His family is signing him off pretty soon."

"What do you mean, signing him off?"

"The family is signing him off life-support. He's been here for six months with no improvement. The machines are the only thing keeping him alive. The family thinks it's about time to let him expire."

"That's terrible! They can't let him go. What about the possibility of him getting better, showing some improvement."

"If there was any chance of improvement, he would have shown some by now."

"Does he understand anything that's going on around him?"

"No...His brain has no motor function...He has no awareness of anything. He doesn't respond to any outside stimulation. No response to touch or speech. For six straight months, brain activity has been non-existent. Basically, he's been dead since they brought him in."

"It doesn't seem possible that he's physically alive, but mentally dead. You would think he has to be experiencing something."

"For patients like Ziggy that are totally brain-dead, it's impossible for him to experience anything."

"If he's totally brain-dead, does his soul still exist? He has to be somewhere."

"That's the million dollar question. Where is he? Wherever he is...I hope he's having a pleasant experience."

"I can't believe we can't help somehow. I feel so bad for him."

"Everyone in the hospital, especially the ones on this floor grew vary attached to Ziggy. Nobody wants to see him go. It's a shame his time's almost up."

"How do you know that?"

"I heard his paperwork is going through the channels as we speak. It won't be long before we have to shut down the machines."

"I can't believe his family is just giving up on him."

"It's the families call...Not ours. Beside, in the six months since his arrival, he's shown no signs of recovery whatsoever."

Unable to unlock her stare from Ziggy's, Diana continued. "I know this is going to sound crazy, but when I came into the room, I could swear he knew I was here. His stare had a terrified gleam as if he were begging for help."

Standing at the foot of the bed, Dr. Stevens rubbed the back of his neck. "Several times when I gave him the eye drops, I thought he was trying to communicate. But, all the monitors said otherwise. Other times his eyes were just blank, absent of all life. What you probably saw was due to surges in the respirator. A quick overdose of oxygen will cause the pupils to dilate."

"Maybe so," caressing Ziggy's cold hand between hers. "I know what caused the coma." Her eyes began to mist-over. "I just wish I knew more about him. What could have driven him to that point?"

The Doctor cleared his throat preparing to respond to the question. "Well, the paperwork won't be here for a few more minutes. If you want to know more about our patient here, I can give you a pretty accurate heads-up."

"Oh, could you...Please...I really want to know!"

With a reluctant expression, he looked at her with some concern. "I've got to warn you, his story is very hard to listen too."

"You've got my attention...I have to know."

Dr. Stevens crossed his arms and leaned against the bed frame. "Well...Our patient here is a lot more well-known than you think. I've known Ziggy for a couple of years...I take that back...I've known about Ziggy for a couple of years. What we do know about him...And by us...I mean anybody that has lived here in Tahoe for any amount of time. Everyone knows enough to make it clear, that he lead a most peculiar and tragic life." The Doctor paused for a moment. "Especially what happened to his family?"

Unable to contain herself, she immediately confronted the Doctor regarding his last comment. "What happened to his family?"

"Hold on...I'm getting ahead of myself." Dr. Stevens rubbed his chin in recollection. "Where do I start? I guess I have to go back to when they found him in the mountains."

"With teary eyes, she looked at Ziggy and began stroking his hand. "What happened in the mountains?"

Still rubbing his chin, the Doctor began to slowly pace at the foot of the bed. "About fifteen years ago, two forest rangers on horseback found him incoherent wondering around deep in the woods. Once Ziggy saw them, he went wild. Like a scared, untamed animal he began running deeper into the forest.

Once they caught up and subdued him, they realized he was wearing no shirt or shoes. His pants were tattered and his face showed at least a month worth of beard growth. That's when they saw it."

"Saw what?" Her curiosity getting the best of her.

"The perimeter of his back was covered with what appeared to be giant surgical stitches. But, there was no rhyme or reason for the extensity of his scares. It was incomprehensible of what kind of injury would require such a massive, random stitch pattern. They said it was as if he had been sown to something. But there was nothing on his back, there was not any evidence of what it could have been."

"What happened to him? Why was he out there?"

The Doctor gave up half-a-smile at her burst of curiosity. "No one really knows the facts concerning Ziggy. What they did find out was one of the most horrific finds in this area's history... Do you want me to continue?" Having a little fun by teasing the new nurse.

"Yes...Of course...I want to hear everything!"

"Ziggy was mentally spent. The police couldn't find out anything. They said he was lost in some terrifying unreality. Shortly later, he was institutionalized and kept under heavy observation.

For two years psychiatrists tried to pick his brain and unravel what actually happened in the forest. When they asked him about his back, he would instantly go into a terrified psychotic trance. It would take weeks to get him to talk again. When he finally would talk, they considered what he said just a bunch of paranoid gibberish. All he talked about was a madman, dead bodies and all the innocent mutated people. After that, they pretty much just kept him under sedation. They filed Ziggy off as a hopeless case. Until…" Just as the Doctor was about to finish the story, he was called over the loud speaker. "I have to go. I'll be back in a few minutes."

The nurses eyes widened in sudden disappointment. "You can't go! You have to finish!"

Dr. Stevens gave her a quizzical look. "Why do you need to know so much? Like I said before, it's an extremely hard story to listen too."

"I know it's a terrible story. Nobody else seems to care about him… But I do! I want to find out as much as I can before he's gone."

"I'll be back soon….If you still want to hear more, I'll tell you the rest."

Once the Doctor left the room, Diana held his hand once again. "You've got to fight Ziggy. Don't let them get away with this. If you don't pass away once we shut down the machines, then there's nothing else they can do. Stay with us, I'll make sure your taken care of."

CHAPTER 13

WHEN THE DOCTOR RETURNED, he was holding what looked like a legal document. "Is that what I think it is?" Diana nervously asked.

"I'm afraid so."

"So when do we do it?"

With an expression of regret, the Doctor answered. "He's to be taken off life-support at midnight." Simultaneously, they both looked up at the wall-clock. "That's gives us about thirty minutes."

"I can't believe were going to let him die."

"We have to follow the family's wishes and the judge's orders. If it's any consolation, were not killing him, were just shutting down the machines."

"That's just wrong." Turning her stare back to Ziggy. "No matter how small the hopes are, we're still supposed to try and save him. Not stand around and watch his family murder him."

"I'm on your side. I take no pleasure whatsoever in what were about to do."

"Okay, I'm ready." Confronting the Doctor.

"What do you mean...Ready for what?"

"I need to hear the rest of the story before we do this."

After a short period of retrospection, the Doctor continued. "Alright...Like I said before, the institution gave up on Ziggy and kept him under heavy sedation. Then, two years after they originally found him, the Sierra Nevada's had a major forest fire. Tens of thousands of acres were burnt.

While fighting the blaze, fire-fighters came across a huge burnt-down structure. Once the fire was contained, firemen told authorities about what they'd found. To those in charge, it seemed impossible that such a structure could exist in such a treacherous uncharted section of forest.

Authorities went back decades into the building records until they found what they were looking for. Back in the early fifties, some investors began construction of a giant lumber mill. But, the project was so deep in the forest it was costing them a fortune to build. Even though the lumber mill was three-quarters finished, they decided it wasn't cost efficient to continue. The investors decided just to take their losses and abandon the project.

Immediately, a select group of officials decided to go to the sight. Once they arrived, it didn't take long for the arson investigators to come to the conclusion that this site was where the fire originated. As they looked through the rubble, it appeared as if the building had been converted into some kind of massive laboratory. Then, they began coming across skeletons. The more they searched the more human remains they found. All in all, they discovered over ninety bodies. The strangest thing was that all the skeletons featured some kind of physical mutation. Some had three arms or legs. Others had skulls that housed multiple eye sockets. And a few actually had two heads. After this was discovered, the FBI came in and took over. Nothing was ever heard about the lumber mill again.

After a follow-up on the information the specialists gathered, everything he told them was confirmed. With this information at hand, the psychiatrists began to think Ziggy might have been telling the truth.

Once again, the psychiatrists began having therapy sessions with Ziggy. After convincing him that they had found the others that were imprisoned with him, he mentally began to recover.

Within a couple of months of evaluation, it became impossible to disprove that he hadn't actually experienced these events. The institute had no choice but to confirm everything that he had said. Shortly later, they came to the conclusion that Ziggy was stable enough for release."

"That's horrible...All those people."

The strangest thing was that everybody at one point in time had been declared as a missing person. Some of the people had been missing for over ten years."

"So no one ever found out what happened to his back?"

The Doctor could do nothing but shrug his shoulders. "That's the biggest mystery of all. Ziggy's the only one that knows what actually happened. It was probably so horrible and mentally devastating that he blocked it out all these years.

"It's hard to believe that anyone could recover from something like that."

"Don't take a breath of relief yet. That's just the beginning of his story. It gets a lot worse."

"I can't believe what could be worse than that."

Looking at the clock the Doctor continued. "Well, we only have about fifteen minutes left. So I'll try and make this as quick as possible."

"I want to hear it all." Inpatient anticipation etched in her face.

The Doctor let out an uncomfortable sigh. "You're a glutton for punishment, aren't you? Okay...Here goes."

Diana gave the Doctor a quick reminder. "Remember...I want to hear everything."

Dr. Stevens shook his head then stuffed his hands into his coat pockets. "After the institution, Ziggy lived here in town for about five years before he met Julie. She was bad news from the get-go, but he refused to see it. They were together off and on for two years before she got pregnant. After finding out she was expecting, he became ecstatic and ask her to marry him. Julie agreed, then, proceeded to make his life a living hell.

After Sarah was born, he put up with several years of her infidelity and drug abuse. One day, out of the blue, she had him served with divorce papers. The same day, she kicked him out of his own house and moved her new boyfriend in."

Diana shook her head in dismay. "Why in the world would he let her get away with that?"

"Julie threatened to take his little girl and leave town unless he agreed not to object to the divorce. My best guess is that he didn't want to put Sarah through more than he had too. Ziggy loved that little girl.

For months, Julie refused to let him see his daughter. One night he called her hoping that she might reconsider keeping his daughter from him. While on the phone, he heard Steve in the background...Steve was her boyfriend. This guy was a unstable piece of work. Suddenly, Sarah and Julie began screaming and the phone went dead."

Diana covered her mouth in disbelief. "Oh my god...That must have been devastating."

Dr. Stevens nodded his head in agreement. "It was...He immediately went to see if they were okay. When he got to the house, he watched from the woods as police swarmed the neighborhood. That's when he saw the authorities bring out the lifeless body of his daughter. Though Julie wasn't dead, she died shortly later here in the hospital."

"I think I'm going to be sick."

"Near the time of the murders, the police had traced a phone call to Ziggy. At that point, the manhunt was on. For some reason, even with no evidence, the Tahoe police were convinced that Ziggy was their man. Every cop on this side of the lake was after him. It took them around twelve hours before they finally found him in a shed, nearly dead from poisonous spider bites.

For months the police were positive that he had murdered his ex-wife and daughter. But, no matter how confident they thought they were, beside a phone call, there was nothing to connect him to the crime scene.

Even though the D.A. had to release him, he was front page news. The District Attorney did everything in his power to build a case against him. The D.A.'s office even published articles about when he was found in the forest and institutionalized. They portrayed him as mentally unstable and dangerous. But, they always failed to mention what actually took place in the forest. They even had DNA evidence from the murder scene, but it wasn't Ziggy's. That fact was never brought to light either."

Diana's face was laden with disgust as she removed her hands from her mouth. "That's our legal system at work. They couldn't find the real murderer, so instead of eating some humble pie, they found a patsy - Ziggy."

"That's not even the half-of-it. Ziggy became a tabloid regular and everyone wanted him to be found guilty. It took about a year before Julie's boyfriend was arrested in Texas for a traffic violation. Then, low-and-behold, there was a DNA match. A few days later, Steve confessed to the murders.

Finally, Ziggy was off-the-hook, but not in the minds of the locals. With all the previous media bombardment, no one ever looked at Ziggy the same again."

"So do you think that all those years of hardship and pain caused him to get suicidal?"

"I'm really not sure. But, his attempt at suicide is even more bizarre than the rest of his life."

"You can't be serious?"

"I'm very serious. The circumstances leading up to that day, including his suicide attempt are very bizarre."

"You think someone tried to kill him?"

"No. I think he tried to take his life, but certain things just never added up."

"Tell me...We only have five minutes."

Walking around the bed, the Doctor prepared to finish the story. "Well...Even after being proven innocent of the murders, he was still under public scrutiny. The impact of his daughter's death was devastating. Ziggy became totally introverted toward society and everyone in it. After he was cleared of all charges, he moved into a motel room. For months he kept out-of-sight. Except for his early morning walks, he never left that room."

"He went for walks...Where'd he go?"

"Regan Beach...Every morning after daybreak, he walked down Tahoe Boulevard to the park."

Diana gave the Doctor a look of indifference. "So...That's not unusual...Lots of people do that very same thing."

"Yes, that's true. But, nobody else did it quit like Ziggy."

"What did he do that was so different?"

"Supposedly, he would walk down the street like nothing else existed. People would walk past and say hello and he would look right through them like they were invisible. Ziggy would walk across the boulevard during morning rush-hour traffic as if there weren't a car in sight. Several times he nearly caused major accidents. Vehicles would slam on their brakes, honk their horns and drivers would yell at him out their windows. But, without any reaction, he would continue to slowly cross the street like nothing happened. It was as if he were lost in some realm of reality that didn't exist to the rest of the world."

"Maybe he was just preoccupied with painful memories."

"That may be true, but I think it went a lot deeper than that. I think his mind somehow blocked out certain things, anything that might pose as a threat to him. I believe that his mind looked upon all society and everything in it as a threat and refused to acknowledge it."

"Do you think he had regressed back to the same condition when they found him in the forest?"

Dr. Stevens began to rub the nap of his neck. "It's possible... But when they found him in the woods, he was scared of his own shadow. Up until the moment they found him in the car, people say that he never showed any fear of anything."

"What would happen when he got to the park?"

"When he got to the park, that's when things got even stranger. Ziggy would always stand in front of the same park bench overlooking the beach. For hours, observers would see him talking and pointing in the air, carrying on in-depth conversations with someone named...Destiny. The fact was, there was no one there. Ziggy was having an enchanting conversation with thin air.

When onlookers confronted him to find out if he was okay, Ziggy just ignored them, never giving the concerned people the time of day. After he had finished his imaginary conversation, he would always go down to the beach for a few minutes, then, go directly back to his motel room."

The Doctor rubbed his forearms as if on the verge of goose bumps. "Here's the kicker...When they found him in the car, he was setting in the passenger seat. The police report stated that the driver's seat was occupied by a white summer dress. Like someone else drove him there and left the dress behind."

"How do you know that he didn't drive there and then move over to the passenger side?"

"The police report stated that Ziggy's fingerprints were all over the passenger door. But, not one of his prints was found on the steering wheel. They also said that there were so many finger and palm prints on the passenger door and window, it appeared that he was desperate to get out of the car."

"Did the police have any idea where the dress came from?"

"Not a clue."

"Maybe Ziggy put it there."

The Doctor shook his head no. "The dress was sent to forensics lab and they found nothing. If he would have put it there, his fingerprints and DNA would have been on the dress. There was nothing. The forensic scientists said that the dress had never even been washed. If anyone would have worn or touched it, there would have been some sort of trace evidence. It was like it just appeared out of nowhere."

"Someone had to of put it there."

"The police say no. It had rained all night and most the day and the car was parked in the mud. There was not one footprint anywhere around the car. There was nothing, not even an animal track in the entire area. The only tracks they found were the tire tracks that lead to where the car stopped."

Diana's jaw dropped in total disbelief. "That's almost too much to comprehend. Somebody has to know what happened!"

The Doctor looked down at Ziggy. "The only one that knows the truth is lying on this bed. And once we shut down these machines, all the mysteries concerning his life will be lost forever. Well, Ziggy…It's almost time." Dr. Stevens announced reluctantly.

Diana was not quite finished with her questions. "I've been meaning to ask you, why does everyone call him Ziggy. I haven't had a chance to look at the medical chart, but is his name really Ziggy?"

"You won't find that name on the medical charts or anywhere else. It's a name he acquired."

"Ziggy…It's such a strange nickname."

Dr. Stevens let go of a short-lived chuckle. "Yes…It is…But how he got the name is one-of-a-kind."

"What do you mean?"

Picking up the medical chart, the Doctor signed off on the judge's court order. "Well…When he arrived at the emergency room he had no identification. No one knew who he was. Even the police that found him didn't find an ID or anything that could identify him. When the officers arrived at the hospital, one of the patrolmen kept referring to him as Ziggy. When I ask him why he was calling him Ziggy, he just laughed and shrugged his shoulders. The officer told me, they found him unconscious inside a car. They thought he was dead, but they called the paramedics anyway. While they waited for the paramedics, they searched the car trying to find some information on who he was."

Growing anxious, Diana demanded an answer. "How'd he get the name Ziggy?"

"Patients my child," a smile covered his face as he continued. "Anyway...When they found him, the cars stereo was playing. As they searched the car they realized the music was coming from a cassette tape. It was a home-made tape that had just one song playing over and over."

"What was the song?"

"Ziggy Stardust by David Bowie. After the paramedics took him away; the patrolman said that he couldn't get that song out of his head. And since he had no idea what his name was, instead of calling John Doe, they just called him Ziggy."

"If you know his real name, why do you still call him Ziggy?"

"You're just full of questions today." Dr. Stevens continued as he shut down the heart monitor. "Well...As we worked on him in the emergency room, I went along with the patrolman and referred to him as Ziggy. It was almost a week before we found out his true identity. By that time, everyone in the hospital knew him as Ziggy...And it stuck."

Sadness filled her eyes as she asked one final question. "What's his real name?"

"His real name is Jack Nathan Bennett - AKA Ziggy."

CHAPTER 14

PLUNGED INTO A DEEP expanse of emptiness, there was no substance to the space in which he now resided. The silence was absolute as he drifted in this weird and wonderful twilight world. Lost in a tranquil trance, he felt excited, slightly euphoric as everything was perfectly surreal. A suspended realm, a counter balance where all his emotions and sensations had gone astray.

Without warning, the wonderful light, along with his sense of peace and relief began to fade. Bennett quickly became aware that he was no longer floating in a void of nothingness. There was no doubt that something was about to happen.

All at once, he wished he could go back. Back to that tranquil place he was a fraction of a second ago. As his comforting world came to a gradual halt, be began feeling very strange.

Where am I? Confused as what else to think.

Though completely disoriented, he finally began to break through the cloudiness in his mind. While in this dreamscape state of distortion, his new surroundings began to take form. As his confused thoughts drew clearer, he could hear far away voices. While unable to make out what was being spoken, the voices seemed calm and reassuring. Though not sure if he was entirely lucid, he felt as if everything would be alright.

As unknown images began to materialize, Bennett tried to fight through the bewildering blur. As his stinging eyes struggled to focus, odd and disconnected figures began to present themselves.

Drawing nearer to an understanding of his surroundings, he saw a man and woman standing next to him. But they were not paying attention to him; they appeared to be in serious conversation.

Awakening further from his long-term trance, he realized he was lying in a hospital room. To Bennett, it did not matter what was wrong with him or how he got there, only that he was okay.

I'm alive! I escaped from Death's grasp! Rejoicing inside his mind.

Bennett wanted so badly to throw back the sheets and swing his feet to the floor. But, to his dismay, his arms refused to respond. The terrifying fact was, beside his vision, not one part of his body seemed to function. Unable to even move his lips, he tried to force a noise from his throat, but nothing happened. It was as if his body and voice were completely crippled. The only plus in his favor was that his eye sight and hearing were returning. As the nearby voices became clearer, his complete attention was focused on what was being said.

Listening closely, Bennett focused on every word the nurse asked the Doctor. "And you're sure it's not possible for him to dream?"

Mentally, Bennett tried to answer the nurse's question. *I can dream! I just woke up from the worst nightmare!*

"Well, if he can, they'll be the last things he takes to the grave with him."

What do you mean take to the grave? Look at me...I'm alive damn-it!

Once again, the Doctor looked down at the man he was about to let expire. "It's time, shut everything down."

Diana was so frustrated as she began to shut down the machines. It was everything she stood against, but she had her orders.

Though his vision grew stronger, he was unable to move

his eyes. Bennett's peripheral vision was all over the room as he attempted to follow the movements of the strange people. They began working on the machines that surrounded the bed. Judging by their body language, they appeared to be doing something decisive and irreversible.

While staring at the people standing above him, Bennett had the hair-raising realization that he was about to die. All relief from what he had just escaped from quickly disappeared.

Panic-stricken, terrified adrenaline crazily pumped through his veins. The intense expectation of what he might have to face again scared the hell out of him. The only thing that he was sure of was his desire to live.

Alarm shot through him as the Doctor reached for his oxygen mask. No matter how hard he forced himself, Bennett was helpless in manifesting any kind of sound or movement. Over and over he tried to make any kind of a noise - but nothing. Every attempt to get their attention was choked away by a paralyzed larynx. Bennett was the only one that could hear his cries for help.

While Bennett's screams were locked inside, he watched in absolute terror as they shut down the machines. If making any kind of sound was possible, he would let out a cry for help for the entire hospital to hear.

Bennett did not have the strength to fight or resist any longer. A flood of nausea ripped through him at the very idea of what lie ahead. Shortly, he would drift back into the shadows of that terrifying existence from which he had just escaped. Maybe it was just his destiny to descend into an everlasting Hell.

With everything he had, he made one last feeble attempt to communicate. "No...Stop...Help me...I'm not dead!" Like bottomless pools of desperation and fear, the voice in his mind pleaded.

In the smashed landscape of his consciousness, it was as if he were drowning inside himself. Helplessly withdrawing from reality, his semi-comatose condition was on a direct path back toward oblivion. With his demise in progress, Bennett realized he held a one way ticket back into Death's domain. Isolated in hopelessness, his vision dimmed and the room began to vanish.

Now, while just a prisoner of doom, a not-so-distant laugh of anticipation presented itself. Trapped within his own body, grave fear reverberated through him. Bennett's mind twisted into an internal grimace with the horrific realization that he was about to face the "Minion of Death" once again.

**

Dr. Steven's tuned away from the nurse and began to write the last bits of information on Ziggy's medical charts. As Diana prepared to shut down the brain monitor, unanticipated alarm forced her to stand there in shock. With a clutch in her throat, Diana began mumbling incoherently to the doctor.

The Doctor turned toward Diana. "I'm sorry, I couldn't hear you."

"I don't know if something's wrong...Or something's right!"

"I don't understand?"

"Look at the brain monitor...It's off the charts!"

"Impossible," the Doctor mumbled. "It's probably just a power surge."

Diana's hands began to shake as her anxiousness grew. "I don't think so...Look at his brain activity!"

The Doctor quickly stepped toward the monitor. The brain waves from his coma state had dramatically changed. The monitor indicated that he was no longer unconscious. Immersed in disbelief, their amazement deepened as they stared at the monitor. As if they both had just seen a ghost, the realism of what they were witnessing was mind-boggling.

After a moment of total disillusionment, Dr. Stevens responded with shock and surprise. "This can't be possible...There's some kind of mistake. I've never seen anything like this in my life." Shaking his head in disbelief.

"What's going on, Doctor?"

Dr. Steven's thoughts hardened into certainty as he studied the monitor. "He's coming back...He's waking up!"

All at once, the brain monitor changed toward the worse. Gawking at what she saw, Diana called to Dr. Stevens. "Now, his brain activity is decreasing!" Diana turned back to the Doctor. "What's going on?" For a brief second, the Doctor and nurse looked at each other in indecision.

The Doctor spoke in a voice that emanated tremendous concern. "Oh my God...He's going back into a coma!"

With a sense of urgency, Dr. Stevens took control of the situation. "Diana...I need you to stay calm...Or at least try to keep me calm." After giving the nurse a reassuring smile, he continued. "Hook'em up to the EKG and get him back on oxygen before he suffocates! Restart all his IV drips and get some more blankets in case he goes into shock!"

With all the Doctor's requests completed, Diana awaited her next order. The deteriorating patient had the Doctor's undivided attention. Once the machines had re-booted, the EKG monitor suddenly showed a sporadic heartbeat.

The signal on the EKG machine became erratic, indicating a change in the patient's condition. Ziggy's heart rhythm was deteriorating rapidly.

"Get the defibrillator cart!" The Doctor instructed Diana.

Once charged, Dr. Stevens pressed the defibrillator pads against Nathan's chest. "CLEAR!" Squeezing the discharge button, the electrical shock caused Nathan's chest to bounce up from the bed.

Looking up at the EKG monitor, the Doctor realized they were about to lose him. "He's going into cardiac arrest...Start CPR...Apply chest compressions until I get back! Do what you can to keep his heart circulating."

"Where are you going?" Diana received no response as the Doctor ran from the room.

With all of her frantic strength, Diana continued chest compressions. "Stay with me damn-it!" Pushing on Ziggy's chest, she did everything possible to pump more oxygen into his lungs.

Within a few seconds, Dr. Stevens returned. As he approached the bed, he was holding the biggest syringe the nurse had ever seen. Diana wanted to ask what he was about to do, but she could tell the Doctor was in no mood for questions.

With a needle the size of a sixteen-penny nail, Dr. Stevens held the syringe just above his head. "Pull his gown off his chest...I don't care if you have to rip it off."

Responding to the order, she yanked the grown to his waist. Quickly swabbing alcohol on Ziggy's chest with his left hand, the Doctor's right hand came downward with a mighty thrust. The length of the huge syringe tore through the sternum and penetrated his heart.

After retracting the needle, Diana couldn't hold back her question. "What was that? I've never seen that done."

"Pure adrenalin...We have to get his heart stimulated again." As soon as he answered the question, Ziggy's arms began to twitch as he gasp for air. The monitors showed an instant acceleration in heartbeat and brain activity. All vital signs were approaching normal.

Placing his stethoscope on Ziggy's chest and performing a frantic evaluation, Dr. Steven's began to calm. Retrieving a pin-light from his coat pocket, he pointed it directly in Ziggy's eyes. Once his patient's pupils reacted to the light, a smile of victory crossed the Doctor's face.

"I think we did it...He appears to be stabilizing. I think he's going to make it." Looking at the new nurse with a smile of relief.

After successfully resuscitating him from his coma, Diana

still could not believe what she had just witnessed. She grabbed Dr. Stevens and hugged him in excitement, her wish had been granted.

As they both turned their heads and looked at the life they saved, the Doctor gave Diana a quick heads-up. "Ziggy's not out-of-the-woods yet. It's going to be a long recovery...And you're in charge. Take good care of our miracle patient."

"You want me to give him ice-chips instead of water?"

"Yes...He hasn't used a muscle in his body in months. If we try to give him water and he can't swallow...He may choke to death. A couple ice-chips on his lips and under his tongue will melt and absorb in his mouth. That'll have to do until he can get some motor functions back."

While studying the monitors and regulating the IV flows, Dr. Stevens began to speak directly to Ziggy. "Welcome back, buddy. I know you can hear me. You've come along-way to get here... Just be strong...And we'll take care of the rest."

The Doctor stood by the bed for a moment, looking at his long lost patient in astonishment. Dr. Steven's gave Nurse Diana a final order. "I'm going home...Call me if there's any changes in his condition. I don't care how little the changes are...You call me!"

What a wonderful sensation to realize she had actually helped save his life. Diana's had just witnessed a miracle and could not help her eyes from tearing up.

CHAPTER 15

THOUGH DIANA'S NIGHT-SHIFT HAD ended, she refused to leave Ziggy's side. She came to a personal understanding that his recovery was in her hands. Under her constant evaluation, Diana consistently reassured him that he was just fine and everything was alright. After rubbing ice chips on his lips, she placed a digital thermometer under his tongue. While his vital signs remained normal, he still showed no signs of recognition or any type of physical response. After administering his eye drops, for the first time in six months, Ziggy began blinking his eyes. Ecstatic over the fruits of her labor, shivers of excitement rushed through her body.

In what seemed forever, he was back in a reality where he was not afraid. He attempted to lift his heavy head from the pillow - but it was useless. Even the simplest task turned out to be unachievable. Barely able to move his lips, it was almost impossible for him to form words.

Diana's adrenaline from the morning's crisis instantly magnified. Realizing that he was trying to speak, she leaned over and put her ear to his lips.

In a bewildered state, Ziggy's murmurs eventually formed into faint whispers. "Can you hear me? What's wrong with me? Am I okay?" Asking in a strained voice.

"Nothing's wrong...You're back!" Her words were positive and straight to the point. "I've seen all types come through the emergency room, but I've never met anyone like you."

Ziggy's body still refused to function upon his minds demands. "I can't move."

"You just need a little rehab and you'll be just fine." Consoling her patient with all the confidence in the world.

Pressing the intercom button to the nurse's station, Diana spoke in urgency. "Call Dr. Stevens."

The daytime nurse answered with an attitude. "Dr. Stevens went home hours ago."

"I realize he's off duty! Call him at home and tell him Ziggy's awake and talking!" Judging from Diana's reactions, something incredible had just happened.

The nurse yelled into the intercom. "Get a hold of Dr. Stevens." The desk-nurse's tone completely changed. "He's awake...I can't believe it! I'll get a hold of the Doctor right now!"

Returning her attention back to the recovering patient, Diana reassured him everything was okay. "Everything is just fine. The Doctor will be here soon and he'll explain everything. Just try to relax...And let yourself recover."

"I don't remember much...Why can't I move?" Forcing words through his dry throat.

"You've been in a coma"

"For how long?" Ziggy's inability to speak was subsiding.

"Six months...You're recuperating from a six month sleep."

Ziggy's throat and lips were desperately parched. "I want water! I need water!"

"Dr. Stevens will be here shortly and he'll make you hydrate properly. Until then, we have to stick with ice-chips."

✳✳✳

It was already midmorning and with only a few ice-chips left and needing some coffee, Diana reluctantly stepped out of the room.

After a short recuperation from his seemingly eternal sleep, he was beginning to regain some movement in his fingers and hands. Lying on his back, Ziggy stared at the ceiling wondering what was next. Doubts about his life began to seep into his thoughts. After all he had been through; he knew that the need for order in his life was vital. It was time to move in a direction that had meaning and purpose.

Somehow, he had returned from the land of the dead. Ziggy had won the battle against Death. He was finally liberated from the curse of his nightmares.

But no matter what happened to him in the future, he would be forever scared to go to sleep. For in his sleep is where it waited for him. Though he realized no one else would believe him, Ziggy knew for a fact, that if he fell asleep, he would probably never wake up.

Never in his life, had he been so awake as at that moment. The months spent in a coma had opened his eyes to the truth and the sanctity of life. Ziggy had been face to face with death and survived.

Deep inside, he knew it was not all just a bad dream. While the nightmares were temporarily over, he was glad it happened. Seeing things for the very first time, his entire view on life had been altered. Ziggy now understood the balance between life and death and good and evil.

Ziggy's current stress emanated from the fact that he was unable to block-out the tormenting glimpses from his nightmares. Ziggy's body and soul cringed at the very thought of falling back asleep. He could imagine it all too well, if he were to lose consciousness, he may never awaken again. The only way to escape from these nightmarish scenarios was to stay awake. Even with no sleep in the foreseeable future, distinct images of horror continued to race through his head. The terrifying fact was, he knew he could not stay awake forever.

✳✳✳

It had been several minutes since nurse Diana had left his bedside. Ziggy was caught by surprise when a different nurse entered the room. She was a tall blond with a slender build. After seeing her face, he could swear he recognized the woman. Though his recollection was remote at best, there was something about her. The more he focused, the more something seemed terribly familiar.

"Do we know each other? I could swear we've meet before?" Staring at the nurse as if he had never seen a woman before.

"That's the first time I've heard that line used in a hospital." The nurse responded, pulling a loaded syringe from her togs pocket. "Usually, it's a drunk man's pick-up line that never works." Giving him a vindictive, mocking smile as she advanced toward his bedside.

"What are you giving me?" Asking while never releasing his stare from the approaching syringe.

"It's something to help you rest." Without even a hint of a smile, she continued. "You need to go to sleep."

Whatever the syringe was loaded with, Ziggy wanted nothing to do with it. "I've been asleep for six months." Ziggy became unnerved. "I don't want to go to sleep."

Ziggy had no desire whatsoever in sleeping, he had been asleep for six months. Besides, he knew what was waiting for him once his eyes closed.

It was clear in her expression she had no compassion toward his request. The nurse pressed one of the buttons that controlled the beds movement. A motor began to hum and the incline mechanism started its adjustment. Ziggy's bones cracked and snapped in protest as the mattress rose into a sitting position.

There was something unnerving about the nurse's demeanor. Not understanding why this was necessary, droplets of desperate sweat formed on his forehead. "But...I don't want to go to sleep! I don't want to go back!"

The woman said nothing, but her stare instantly fogged over

into a look of impatient irritation. The posture she presented was direct and aggressive as she pulled the cap from the syringe and revealed the needle.

More than wary about falling asleep, Ziggy confronted the nurse about what she was about to give him. Propped up in the hospital bed, Ziggy flexed his hands trying to twist his arms. In dire desperation, he found the strength to squirm and jiggle the IV line.

Unable to insert the needle into the IV port, the nurse became livid. "You're getting it one way or the other!"

Fighting back the annoyance she felt, the woman straddled the bed and pinned his struggling arm against the bed-rail. Twisting his forearm upward, the angry woman finally had his vein exposed. A perplexed expression took over Ziggy's face as he watched in complete vulnerability. All fear and misgivings about falling asleep had just intensified.

There was no hesitation as she swiftly jammed the hypodermic needle into his flesh. Instant pain bit into his vein as a backflow of his blood entered the syringe. Entrenched in horror, Ziggy watched as she quickly depressed the plunger with the unknown substance. After the plunger had discharged its dosage, the strange nurse yanked-out the syringe leaving the puncture wound bleeding and unattended.

As the drug began to invade his bloodstream, she instantly produced a spiteful smile. Putting the empty syringe back into her coat jacket, the woman leaned over the railing. She had the greyest eyes he had ever seen. Within an inch of Ziggy's face, he watched as the pupils of her eyes became elongated - almost lizard-like. The nurse's face was so close he could smell her breath. The air that expelled from her lungs reeked of a dead animal.

"Well, Ziggy...It's time."

"Time for what?"

"Time to go back!"

"Go back where?"

"Back to your rightful owner. You're not going to keep him waiting any longer. Needless to say...This time your fate will finally be dealt with."

As the drug continued to invade his bloodstream, Ziggy began to feel the effects. Whatever had been pumped into his body was beginning to take over. It would only be a matter of seconds before he slipped back and was lost to that hellish world once more.

The nurse stood erect, eyes changing at will. Her pupils disappeared and the whites of the eyes became as black-as-coal. Satisfied, a strange smile of revenge covered her face as she turned and walked away.

"I'm sure I know you!" Ziggy stated in a firm tone.

Stopping at the door, the nurse turned. With an almost lifeless expression, the woman responded. "Only in your wildest dreams...Jack Nathan Bennett."

"Who are you?"

"That's not important."

Consumed in a one-track thought, he searched his memory for an answer. Odd and disconnected images began running through his head. Whatever dose of whatever drug she had administered was surging through his veins. With drowsiness beginning to take hold, Ziggy was assaulted by a fleeting glimpse of how he remembered her.

Then, it hit him like a ton of bricks. A trace of sickened amazement found its way onto Ziggy's face. A perfect remembrance bombarded his thoughts. Like déjà vu, his thoughts flashed back to his nightmares. Playing like a movie in his mind, a rogue memory from his coma began to replay.

Looking on in disillusionment, he recounted that unwanted remembrance. *Destiny! Destiny from my nightmare! The shift-changer from that place of horrors!*

The inconceivable fact that she stood in front of him, scared the hell out-of-him. Now, sporting a snickering, cynical smile, she began to laugh. It was a mocking, conquering howl that reverberated throughout the room. Just as soon as her evil laughter began it stopped. Without any further torment she turned and walked out the open door into the hall.

Wide-eyed, prepared for anything, he laid there in complete silence as he thought about what had just happened. In his own confused, terrified thoughts, everything came to one conclusion. Ziggy was soon to be thrown back into that realm of misunderstanding that threatened his very being. A final destination in which there was no coming back.

Feeling a sudden chill, his hopes shattered into a million pieces as deathly cold air whisked past him. The silence became almost unnatural as a freezing pocket of air seemed to float around the room. Then, all at once, it was gone. But, Ziggy knew it was not gone, it was lingering and waiting somewhere.

CHAPTER 16

INSTANTLY ILL-AT-EASE, BENNETT FELT that something was very wrong. Death was near, lurking somewhere. With an all-consuming sense of unease, a chill of uncertainty shivered through him. It became apparent, that even in an awakened state, he was not safe. The very inclination that it was here sent ravaging spasms of gooseflesh through his skin. "The Grim Foreboding of Doom" had arrived once again.

In terrified anticipation, he wanted so badly to believe that this was not happening. Ziggy shuttered in concern, thinking of what unforeseen consequences lay ahead. But the fact was the evil that had manipulated his dreams had followed his soul into reality. Suddenly, the hospital speaker came to life.

The intercom caught Ziggy's attention as an all-too-familiar voice called to him from overhead. The Reaper's image had not manifested, but it was using the speaker-system to taunt Ziggy about his demise. "Jack Nathan Bennett…It's time to die." Death had once again found his target.

"Leave me alone!" Screaming in terror!

Trying to stifle-out its voice, he pressed his hands against his ears. But it was to no avail, Death's words were just as loud in his mind. Like before, his psyche was being manipulated and stretched to its breaking point. Ziggy had already been to Hell. And he knew, he was about to go back.

Once again, the overhead speaker came to life. "Time to go… I've come to take you back!"

After briefly leaving Ziggy unattended, Diana sipped her coffee as she returned to the room. Penetrating the threshold of the doorway, she instantly stopped in her tracks. Pale white and shaking, Ziggy had a terrified stare of disbelief. Something was defiantly wrong, her miracle patient looked as if he had just seen a ghost. Dropping her coffee, Diana rushed to his bedside.

Ziggy knew that sleep was right around the corner. "I can't go to sleep!" It was a desperate plea, knowing that if he lost consciousness his life would be over.

"You don't have to sleep." Trying to calm Ziggy's desperation.

Ziggy suddenly felt light-headed, his only desire was to stay awake. But, the pharmacologic effects of whatever he was given was taking control. "I can't help it...Whatever she gave me...Is making me so tired." Ziggy knew the closer he drew to unconsciousness, the deadlier things would become.

"Gave you...What who gave you?"

"The other nurse."

"What other nurse?"

"Destiny...The tall blond...She just left."

"Ziggy, there's no other nurse. I'm the only one allowed to give you anything."

"Don't let me go!"

Diana tried to reassure him that everything was alright. But to her dismay, she realized that her patient was drifting away.

With the same fear-provoking words as before, Death continued to taunt him. "This time there will be no misunderstandings whatsoever!" Announcing with extreme prejudice.

The voice became louder as it echoed from above. "I almost had you at the "Swap Meet"...All you had to do was open the door." Then, there was a brief silence. But quickly, its voice returned even louder. "Unfortunately for me, the dream affected you so dramatically, that your only chance to escape was to wake up."

The voice from the speaker was meant only for him. "As soon as I lost you...I brought Destiny back. When she broke the threshold of that door...You were back in my grasp. Some people get second chances...Some people don't. Your second chance is over with...Now, you belong to me!"

Instantly panic-stricken, Ziggy screamed. "He's back! He's taking me back!"

Diana spun around looking for anyone who might be in the room. "Who's here...Where are you going? There's nothing to be afraid of...There's no one here...What's going on, Ziggy?"

The feeling of stark terror crawled through his flesh. "He's here to take me back!"

Giving him a look as if she did not believe a word he was saying. "He's here...Who's here!"

Barely conscious, Ziggy tried to focus on her face. "Death!"

Then in a deep, spiteful tone, the voice seemed to take control of the hospital room. "No one is going to help you now...Your soul belongs to me...And I'm taking it straight to Hell!"

The relentless certainty in his voice sent an electric chill down his spine. Ziggy was a man caught awake in his own private nightmare, in a direct line of communication with the here-after.

With an evil intensity, an onslaught of laughter echoed from the intercom. As the mystery drug continued to attack his bloodstream, everything around him began to become distorted. Diana's voice became thick and distant.

Ziggy's half-hearted attempts at speech were becoming almost useless. The nurse leaned over the bed and put her ear close to his lips. She tried to hear everything he said, but the only thing she could understand through his broken sentences was "HELP ME!"

Diana gripped his wrist and turned his forearm upward.

There was a bruised puncher wound directly into his vein. As drips of blood still seeped from the wound, she looked at Ziggy only to see his eyes roll back in his head. She did not know what to say or think. Diana stood suddenly afraid.

Silent to the nurse's ears, the Reaper continued to laugh and size-up his prey. "Say goodbye...It's time to go."

Whatever the nurse had given him was rapidly carrying him off to an unwanted sleep. Ziggy was being absorbed right back to the last place he wished to be - Dreamland.

Jumping in and out of consciousness, he fought against the drug - but it was hopeless. Somewhere between unconsciousness and a narcotic daze, Ziggy knew he was headed back to that dark borderland between life and death. This time he would most likely never return to the living.

Unable to move, Ziggy suddenly realized that Death's greatest virtue was its patience. Horrified by the aspects of what was happening, he teetered on the edge of his own dream state.

There was no strength left in his body. There was no controlling the inevitable. At first, there was a chiming in his ears. But then, he realized it was the faint sound of laughter. Once again, he was about to become an unwilling participant in the Reaper's everlasting agenda.

About to pass through the entrance to Death's dominion, he was being eaten alive by his own desperate thoughts. Soon to be in the clutches of his most feared nemesis, Ziggy turned to his last remaining hope. *Please God...I know you've helped me all the way through this. I don't want to die! Don't let him take me!*

As his sleepiness deepened, he continued his plea to God. *I know I gave up on you after my daughter died! I know you had your reasons for taking her. Please God don't leave me!*

As Ziggy swam toward unconsciousness, the one thing he tried to hold on to was Diana's voice as he prayed. Each time he drifted deeper toward unconsciousness, he could hear the distant laugh of Death. Beginning to succumb to a narcotic daze, the Reaper's warped sadistic laugh grew louder and closer.

Ziggy was no match for the relentless force of "DEATH". Drowning inside himself, he was lost in an inebriated trance. Past the point of no return, there was no way to stop it. There was no resisting; Ziggy was on his way back. Drifting off to the one place his soul could not afford to go - back to the gates of Hell!

The more the powers of sleep pulled at him, the louder the laugh became. Behind fallen eyelids, a nightmare began to form. Jack Nathan Bennett was about to reenter that unknown province found only "IN A DREAM'S EYE".

"IN A DREAM'S EYE
THE POEM

Once again
It's time to sleep
But the fear of the inevitable
Makes my heart weep
I pray tonight
I can just survive
As I search for answers
That never arrive
In the dark depository
That is my mind
I hope my life
Isn't left behind
It's a desolate place
Where my hidden secrets lie
And the skeletons in my closet
Refuse to die
In a dream's eye
They hide and wait
Hoping that soon
I'll take the bait

Trying to escape
I look for a door
Anywhere to run
Before my soul is no more
I'm trapped at a crossroad
Where evils converge
A spontaneous dominion
Where dirty torn memories merge
Aimlessly wandering
Unable to wake
My fear of death
Is far from fake
In this realm of distortion
Ominous clouds rule the sky
A ruthless encampment
Found only in a dream's eye
It's all I can do
To keep up my resistance
In this graveyard of demons
I fight for existence

ABOUT THE AUTHOR

Houston Cross was born in Michigan. At a very young age, his parents moved the family to California. While attending college he majored in Psychology. Though intrigued by every aspect of the human psyche, Houston studied dream therapy in an attempt to understand the subconscious mind. Once college had come to an end, the next several years were spent traveling trying to find his nitch in life. When all was said and done, it came down to a final inescapable fact. A fact that he had harbored subconsciously his entire life. Houston wanted to be a writer.

With nearly a dozen books in progress, he decided to concentrate on one "IN A DREAM'S EYE". Though never published before, he knew he had something the entire world could enjoy. The first of many exciting experiences Houston Cross wishes to share with everyone.